STRANGER IN THE WOODS

ANNI TAYLOR

FOR MY WONDERFUL FATHER,
WHO ASKED ABOUT MY WRITING
UNTIL THE VERY LAST DAY
THAT HE WAS ABLE TO.

AND FOR MY SISTER KAREN
AND NIECES NAOMI & KYLIE,
WHO LOVE A WILD-HEARTED
SCOTSMAN -
THEIR HUSBAND & FATHER,
MALCOLM

Isla Wilson is thrilled she's landed her dream photography job, but the clients who hired her are getting stranger by the day.

It sounded so perfect - photographing the misty, sprawling Scottish Highlands property of architect Alban McGregor and his wife, Jessica.

But deep in the woods, there is a chilling playhouse. Two years ago, the McGregors' daughter, Elodie, died after being abducted and taken there. Alban refuses to knock the playhouse down and keeps a picture of it on his wall.

Isla senses that both Alban and Jessica are keeping terrible secrets.

The closer Isla comes to getting answers about Elodie, the more the danger mounts. And with a dense cover of snow now blanketing the town, all chance of escape might already be gone.

PROLOGUE

ELODIE MCGREGOR

GREENMIRE, SCOTTISH HIGHLANDS, DECEMBER 2015

THE MORE ELODIE tried to ignore the cold and dark the more it crept in.

Bare branches tapped and scrabbled against the windows. Tall forest stared inside. Chilled air stepped into the rooms like unwanted visitors.

Her fingers fumbled as she set down her game controller and zipped up her jacket.

Be a good girl, Elodie, Mum had told her. *Just play your game 'til I get back.*

Elodie was tall for an eight-year-old. Everyone said so.

But she didn't feel tall right now.

Unable to sit there a minute longer, she tore around the downstairs rooms, switching on every light.

Better. The brightly-lit house looked like a home again.

With her heart pumping hard, she blew white breath into her hands. The air was refrigerator-cold. Running back into the living room, she gazed at the ashen logs in the fireplace. She wasn't allowed to light the fire by herself. But she was allowed to fetch logs from the

1

wood shed. And if she left it any longer, it would turn pitch-dark outside and she'd be too scared to go out there.

Mum had gone into town to fetch a bag of potatoes. *Can't make potato mash for the cottage pie without potatoes*, she'd said.

Mum had been forgetful lately. Forgetful and grouchy and weepy. She said it was the pregnancy. In a month, the baby would be born. Right now, Elodie guiltily thought that Mum's swollen belly was the best and sweetest thing about her. At least once a day, Elodie would steal into the nursery and peek at the empty cot that was waiting for its new arrival.

Maybe Mum would like a toasty warm house to return to. The more Elodie thought about it, the more she was sure Mum would. She could dash out to the wood shed and be back within ten minutes.

The sun winked low and red through the bare trees as she darted from the house. A gust of wind lashed a sprinkling of rain across her face. A gale shrieked over the distant hills, reminding her of a pack of wild dogs.

The wood shed was all the way at the end of the driveway, near the entry to their property. When Mum wanted wood for the fire lately, she drove down to the shed and packed the wood into the car. She'd said that her belly was too big for her to waddle down there and then back again with a load of firewood.

Zipping her jacket higher, Elodie reached the cottage that stood near the woodshed. She briefly slowed her pace to jump on each of the seven stepping stones.

One-two-three-four-five-six-seven

All good children go to heaven

Mum had taught her that rhyme, and now she couldn't walk over the stepping stones without thinking of it.

She remembered to keep her distance from the woody, thorny vines that covered the cottage. Sometimes, Nanna came to stay in the cottage. Elodie wished Nan was there right now.

She hesitated once she reached the shed, the entrance as dark as the inside of a snake's mouth. Adders sometimes hid in the wood pile. They should be hibernating now, but if you disturbed a hibernating snake, it might bite. Once, when she was small, she'd uncovered a pile of what she thought were some kind of worms. But they'd been newly-born snakes, no thicker than her fingers. She'd been lucky—the mother snake had still been busy spilling out her live young.

Snatching up a stick, Elodie poked at the nearest stack of wood. She shuddered, knowing that once adders bite their prey, they go tracking down the ailing animal—sniffing about with their tongues— until they found it. She stuck out her tongue, tasting the bitter air, wondering how it was possible to smell things that way.

No snake uncoiled itself from the stack.

Dropping the stick, she rubbed her arms against the cold, wishing that she'd worn a coat and gloves. She leaned into the shed to gather up two pieces of wood, then two more. She swore—loudly—as a splinter pushed itself in under her nail. Mum would be shocked to hear her say those words, but Mum wasn't here. And the splinter *hurt*.

Balancing the pile of wood against her small chest, she kicked the shed door shut behind her.

She glanced up at the house. It'd take at least twenty minutes to get the living room properly toasty. She had to hurry if she wanted to do it before Mum got back.

Without warning, a figure stepped out from around the side of the cottage.

The surprise almost had her dropping her stack of wood. "Hello?"

The person didn't speak. Just moved closer. At first, she thought it was the person she was expecting. His body shape, his walk and the dark eyes above the scarf that was wound up to the bridge of his nose —they were all familiar. But he wasn't supposed to be here yet. And she didn't recognise the expression in his eyes at all. This was a stranger.

"Mum wants me inside." The words came without thinking. But once spoken, the words seemed to hang in the air, somehow tainting the world darker. Something was wrong and every fibre of her being knew it.

This time, she dropped the wood, preparing to run.

With fast strides, he was straight in front of her. He had her hand now. The cold leather of his glove wrapped around her fingers.

All happening so quick she'd forgotten to breathe.

He began tugging her towards the forest.

An instinct took over before he could tighten his hold. She wrenched her hand away and ran.

He was quicker. Each time she rushed forward, he was there, blocking her path back to the house.

She spun around. Nowhere to go but away. Into the forest.

He followed.

Could she make it to a neighbour's house? There were only three neighbours and they were all so far away. She made a set of frenzied calculations. *No*—she couldn't make it before he caught her.

The bare, wintry trees were doing little to hide her from her pursuer. She couldn't climb one of the trees—the tall, straight trunks provided no lower branches. He'd surely be able to follow her up a tree, anyway.

She could outrun and out-climb most of the boys at school, but her pursuer was no boy. Every time she tried to circle back, he forced her to turn and run deeper into the forest.

The safe world vanished.

Her lungs were starting to burn. Hot. Stinging.

He was faster than her. Too fast. He'd catch her up soon.

She felt her energy flagging.

Wind snatched the wetness in her eyes away.

A stitch in her side swapped from gnawing pain to unbearable.

She cut across to the right, her stomach cramping and leg muscles turning from tight to jelly.

She soon saw her mistake in running this way.

The playhouse was here.

He'd been herding her this way all along. She was certain of that.

As she stopped to gulp a lungful of air, he caught her. The breath of the wind replaced with his.

He made her go into the playhouse.

Walls. Floor. Nothing else. No place to hide. Just an old chair and a scattering of leaves that had blown in through the gaps in the larch.

Elodie whirled around and around in the dark air.

She was a mouse in a trap, with no way out.

1

ISLA

MY HEAD SWAM and sweat oozed in disgusting rivulets down my back. Fierce sun beat down on Sydney Harbour, making the late spring air almost unbearably hot. I needed to complete this photography portfolio before I could get home and kick off my clammy shoes.

Standing at the bow of the client's yacht, I snapped nine or ten quick photos. My client had requested a set of images that captured his sponsorship advertising on a racing yacht that was competing today.

I must have taken a hundred photos so far. But I couldn't quite get the angle I wanted. And angles were everything.

Frustration needled me as I headed down into the cabin for my lunch break. My photography shoots usually went better than this. I set up on the small table with my half dried-out sandwiches.

Flipping open my laptop, I chewed absently on my sandwich and checked my emails. There were the usual social media notifications.

And a few emails from friends and clients. I read them all. That was my routine at lunch each day.

A friend of mine had recently had a new baby. The baby was tiny and squashy and squinty—as newborns tended to be. I commented to say she was beautiful anyway. In a few months, she would be. To me, newborns seemed like the larva before the butterfly.

I scanned the job offers, too, swallowing the last tasteless clump of sandwich. There was a job in Los Angeles, working as a photo editor in entertainment photography. A few European positions, working in the fashion world. And more than a few jobs as social media influencers. All were full-time positions. I wasn't ready for that kind of commitment. I was commitment-phobic in all areas of life.

A job in Scotland caught my eye. The assignment only required a month's work. I lingered on the ad, reading it through twice:

EXPERIENCED *Photographer Wanted*
Nov 18—Dec 18

LOOKING for a photographer to create a perspective on Scottish archi- tect, Alban McGregor, for a major UK architectural magazine.

Mr McGregor is fairly new in his field but is creating a lot of buzz and winning major awards.

You will be staying in private accommodation on his property in the Scottish Highlands, assembling a portfolio of portraits, land- scapes and architecture. The portfolio will include portraits of Alban's family.

We're searching for a photographer with fresh eyes and unique perspectives who can create something very special.

Light snowfall is a possibility towards the last week of the given month.

Offering a very attractive remuneration. All meals included.

If this is of interest to you, please contact Greer Crowley at your earliest convenience. Please include links to recent examples of your work and background.

.   .   .

I'D CERTAINLY HAVE fresh eyes and unique perspectives. I'd never seen snow or been to the UK. And I desperately wanted to see snow. I was experienced, and I'd been seeded in the landscape category in Australia's most prestigious photography awards—the APPA.

But Scotland was on the other side of the world. An instant *no*.

I'd stuck close to my home town for years. Sydney. I lived with my mum and brother in a convenient spot right in the city. Safe in my comfort zone. There was more than enough work here for me, and I didn't want or need to go anywhere else.

Still, I was curious about the job.

The job description had mentioned family portraits. I decided to look up the McGregor family.

On my laptop, I searched for ALBAN MCGREGOR, FAMILY. The first thing that came up was a news item dated two years ago. It featured a picture of a young, dark-haired girl. I clicked on it.

An article loaded in:

GREENMIRE GIRL, *Elodie McGregor, dies in hospital*

EIGHT-YEAR-OLD ELODIE DIED in Greenmire hospital tonight in the arms of her parents, Alban and Jessica McGregor. Five days ago, Elodie was abducted from outside her Greenmire home and taken to a tiny cabin in the middle of the wood – a playhouse made by children.

She was given sleeping medication by the abductor but was otherwise physically unharmed. The high dosage of the medication caused severe effects, putting Elodie into a coma.

Elodie has died without waking up from her coma. Police are still searching for the abductor. Anyone with information should contact Greenmire police as a matter of urgency.

I SHUDDERED. That poor family. I wished now that I hadn't looked them up. Every family had their tragedies, but this one was about as sad as a tragedy could get.

Closing my laptop, I headed back up to the deck.

The sun blasted my face straight away. The wooziness I'd felt before lunch returned, a headache tightening across the base of my skull.

The heat didn't seem to faze my American client, Don Barrington. He and his wife stood a short distance away in their white linen clothing, chatting with the crew.

Moving to the rail, I prepared my camera.

The shots I'd taken so far were good, but I knew I could do better.

As I raised my head, I caught my breath. Right now, the sun was exactly at the right position, a gorgeous translucency coming through the white sails. There was a fluidity in the way the yachts' sails crisscrossed each other that could have music written to it. All against an electric blue sky.

A familiar buzz of excitement threaded itself under my skin. This was the shot I needed.

Put the wooziness in your head on ignore, Isla, and do a job that wows the client. You've got this.

Climbing up to perch on the bow's railing, I leaned out over the water.

I wiped a damp hand on my shirt and gripped the railing, framing up the shot. I snapped a photo that was so perfect it made my heart beat faster.

Immediately, I hit send on my camera's screen. It was a strict habit of mine to send my photos straight to online storage. Not because I was the most organised person in the world, but because I didn't trust myself or my equipment not to screw up somehow. Once a photo screwed up, the record of that moment in time was gone forever.

The heat seemed to suck the oxygen from the air. A short electrical pulse zapped my head.

Without warning, I wet myself.

Confused thoughts swirled in my mind.

How do I hide the wet patch on my khaki-coloured hiking shorts?

How do I get down from here in time to save the camera?

Then I knew exactly what was wrong with me.

A seizure was starting.

I hadn't had a seizure in years. And I hadn't wet myself during a seizure since I was twelve.

Before I could figure anything out, I plunged backwards.

The water engulfed me headfirst.

My body sank through layers of dark green ocean.

Can't breathe.

Panic gripped me.

I couldn't move, couldn't swim, couldn't save myself.

I needed to swim *up*. But my limbs were rigid.

I sank deeper.

Can't breathe.

Darkness so thick.

Lungs exploding.

Can't breathe.

2

ISLA

I BLINKED RAPIDLY in the searing light.

Mr Barrington and a crew member looked down on me, both of them dripping wet. Mrs Barrington was kneeling beside me, her face bright with blue eyes and red lipstick.

I'm alive.

My mind was numbed from the seizure, but underneath that was a sense of shock and relief. I was here on the deck, in the sunshine. I'd just witnessed the whisper-fine line between life and death.

Mrs Barrington grasped my shoulder. "Are you all right, Isla?" The warm, Southern accent of the client's wife filtered through the haze. She wrapped a fluffy, striped towel around me and helped me sit.

Gasping and coughing, I nodded.

I was about to make up an excuse and then stopped myself. I didn't have to make up excuses. I should just tell the truth.

"It was a seizure," I croaked. "I have epilepsy."

"Goodness gracious," Mrs Barrington drawled softly. "A seizure? That explains all the jerking about. You gave us a good old fright. Don and Marco fished you straight out, but you looked pretty peaky before you fell in. I've called you an ambulance."

"Sorry about your camera," Don said, observing me with crinkly blue eyes. "It was around your neck. We hauled it up out of the water with you, but I have a pretty good hunch it's not going to be any good."

I sat up fully, shivering and coughing again. "It's okay about the camera. I'm just so grateful you were able to find me in the water."

"We saw you fall in," he said. "We jumped straight in after you, but you went down pretty deep. Well, you're all safe and sound and that's all that counts. No problem about the pictures."

I detected a note of frustration in his voice as he mentioned the photographs.

"The photos are all saved," I told him, hoping to redeem myself. "I sent them all to the cloud."

His steel-grey eyebrows shot up. "You did?"

"Yes, I've got all of them."

A smile seemed to come out of nowhere and plant itself on his face—large and toothy. "Well, now, that's good news." He turned to his wife. "Isn't that great, Maggie? Isla managed to save all the pictures from today."

"Oh," she scoffed, making a shooing gesture at her husband. "We're not worried about that. We're just glad you're okay."

The arrival of the ambulance at the docks created a stir among the crowds there.

I was raced away to the nearest hospital, the lights flashing and siren loud in my ears.

At the hospital, immediate checks on my lungs and temperature were conducted. The doctor—an older lady of Indian background with hair in a thick plait—asked how long my seizure had lasted for. I didn't know the exact answer to that, but I told her it hadn't been longer than three minutes. Don Barrington and his crew member must have fished me from the water within seconds, because they hadn't needed to try and revive me.

I knew that the length of seizures mattered. A long seizure was trouble.

"Am I able to go home if my results look okay?" I asked her weakly.

She shook her head, pursing her lips so hard she gave herself chipmunk cheeks. "No, I'm afraid not. We'll be keeping you in overnight and keeping you monitored. Have you been taking your medication?"

"Yes."

"Every day?"

"Yes—I only skipped two days in the past three months." I'd actually forgotten to take it on at least two days this month alone, but I wasn't going to admit to that.

"Hmmm, no life jacket? You were on a boat, right, with no life jacket?"

"No one was wearing one."

She tut-tutted. "But it's especially dangerous for you. And your attention was on taking photographs, correct?" She didn't wait for a reply before continuing. "Even just falling into cold water unexpectedly could trigger a seizure. But in this case, your seizure had already begun before you hit the water, is that right? It was the seizure that made you fall?"

I nodded.

"Let me give you an illustration of what was happening to you under the water, okay? You had a tonic seizure and your chest wall was contracting. This contraction resulted in air being expelled from your lungs. When this happens, your body density can become higher than the density of the water—which can cause rapid submersion. Which means you go down deep. And later, when your chest wall muscles ease and relax again, water will enter through your mouth and nose. You'll remain underwater and you won't float to the surface. You'll be hard to see in any body of water and perhaps impossible to find if you're in the ocean. Do you understand?"

I nodded again, this time almost squirming at the picture she'd painted. I knew exactly what happened during a tonic seizure and I knew about the risks when swimming for people with epilepsy, but I hadn't known the specifics before. And today, I'd had a heavy camera with a long-range lens hanging around my neck and dragging me down.

She patted my hand, giving me a kind smile. "But you were fortunate. You're here to tell the tale. Now, who can we contact to let them know what has happened—someone who can keep watch over you for the next few days?"

"Oh, that isn't necessary. I'm fine."

Her expression became stern again. "I'm afraid I'll be keeping you in hospital much longer if you don't name someone. Do you live alone or with others?"

"I live with my mother and younger brother, but…I don't need anyone rushing down to the hospital right now. Especially my mother —she'll freak when she hears what happened."

Her expression didn't change, and I could tell that she wasn't going to budge. I had no choice but to relent.

My mother arrived at the hospital within thirty minutes. She had my nineteen-year-old brother in tow.

"You could have drowned, Isla," were my mother's first words.

A worried look entered Jake's eyes but he hid it quickly, replacing it with a wide grin. "Trust you to fall from the boat."

Jake had the same crop of dark hair as Mum and me, and he wore it almost as long as mine.

"People fall in the water all the time. No big deal." I yawned and stretched to demonstrate that fact, trying not to think of the doctor's description of someone in the middle of a seizure going underwater.

"Have you been forgetting to take your medications?" Mum asked.

"No," I lied again.

Her eyes narrowed. "Well, you must be pushing yourself too hard. You don't have anything to prove. You've already done it all."

"I think it was a combo of tiredness and the heat," I told her, then turned to my brother. "What did you get up to today, Jakey?" He hated it when I called him that.

"A girl called me."

"Really? A bonafide, live girl?" I said playfully.

He nodded nervously. "She's twenty. She watched my band play and asked me for my number. I gave it to her."

I eyed him with interest. My handsome younger brother had strictly avoided girls before—due to his crippling social anxiety.

"What's the girl's name?" I asked Jake.

"Charlotte."

"When are you going on a date?"

"Was I supposed to ask her out on one?"

"Do you like her?"

He shrugged awkwardly. "She's all right. She has nice eyes and was wearing a *Star Wars* T-shirt."

"Then, *yes*. Always date the girl wearing a *Star Wars* T-shirt."

Mum and Jake stayed for another hour. Just before they left, Jake took my laptop computer out of his duffle bag and planted it in my lap. "Here. Thought you could use this as an excuse in case any weird patients try talking to you. It got left behind on the yacht, apparently. Your clients dropped it off at the hospital."

I grinned. I knew why Jake had made a comment about weird patients. Jake hated strangers talking to him unexpectedly—his social anxiety would often make him freeze up.

The only other patient in the ward—a middle-aged woman hooked up to a drip—had been sleeping soundly the whole time.

With my family gone, the room fell quiet and still.

A tremor passed through my body and I rubbed my arms.

I realised that my face was suddenly wet with tears. Shock and exhaustion crawled through my veins. I hadn't admitted it to my mother, but she was right. I could have died. Another few seconds, and I might have sunk so deep that I couldn't be found. The doctor couldn't have stated it in more black and white terms. I was glad Mum hadn't heard her.

More than anything, the sense of a complete lack of control made me feel helpless and hopeless. I'd first been diagnosed with epilepsy at puberty. A doctor had once explained to me that all brains operate by generating electrical impulses—thoughts, emotions and physical movements. During a seizure, the brain got caught up in an electrical storm.

Other people took it for granted that they'd have the control I lacked. The closest thing to losing control of their body that most young people had was a sneeze.

I'd had a severe seizure years ago, one that left me unable to do anything for months. And I'd become afraid to venture out on my own too far in case something like that ever happened again. I hadn't even left Australia, apart from the usual end-of-school odyssey that Australian eighteen-year-olds took to Bali.

And then…today had happened. Today in which I could have died —not really having lived.

The truth was that my life was pretty damned small. No one would guess that from my social media pages. Those were littered with glamour—photographs of exciting people and parties and art galleries and concerts. All of it was from my photography jobs. None of it was from my own personal life.

I documented it all, like a Peeping Tom watching through a keyhole. I had a mental picture of myself as a giant Alice peering through a tiny door she could never enter.

After each job, I'd return home to my quiet room and watch TV and sleep. I barely saw friends anymore.

A depression settled in heavily on my shoulders—an aftereffect of the seizure. I just had to ride it out. I was grateful when a deeper wave of exhaustion pulled me towards sleep.

3

ISLA

TRUE TO HER WORD, the doctor let me out of the hospital the next day.

My test results and scans were good. But tests and scans couldn't see everything, and I needed to rest and watch for signs of anything abnormal. I sat at our kitchen table, composing an email to Mr Barrington, thanking him again for pulling me from the water, and letting him know I'd have his portfolio to him within the week.

My mother had told her boss that she was taking the next three days off, to look after me. She was busying herself sanding some kitchen chairs out in the yard. She always had some project or other going. A week ago, she'd found the chairs on a roadside rubbish pile and she'd brought them all home like they were treasures. She planned to paint them in different colours. My mother had decorated our entire townhouse in 1950s decor and her own eclectic style. She loved old things with history behind them with a passion.

She shooed me when I stepped outside and offered help, saying that I should get out of the heat and go watch TV or something.

But I felt restless. I didn't want to stay indoors.

I continued onto the only private spot in our tiny patch of yard—a place where even the neighbours couldn't see me. Behind the garden shed was a little corner surrounded by bamboo palms and outrageously coloured canna lilies. A swing hung from a low branch on our only tree—an oak. Orange and white floral vines crept up along the trunk of the tree and spilled down from the branches.

The colours of the garden were bright and gaudy, just like the interior of the house. I was used to it. I liked it. Home wouldn't seem like home without the colour palette I'd grown up with.

The door of the shed had been open—Mum had been in there earlier to get sandpaper and tools to fix up the chairs.

Sometimes I tipped-toed past the shed, not wanting to look inside and risk a flash of memory.

The shed was where Jake and I had discovered our dad. Dead.

We'd just been children. Me eleven and Jake four. That day, Jake and I had returned home a week early from a holiday at our aunt's house at the ocean. She'd been meant to have us for two weeks. But she'd gone into hospital with a burst appendix and we'd been ferried back home.

Dad had hanged himself.

I'd plunged into a deep depression that day. I'd gone on like that for months. People describe that kind of depression as being dark and black. It wasn't like that for me. My depression had felt bleached, like coral without colour. Everything a dull white. Nowhere to hide. My mind pried open by child psychologists. Kids at school treating me differently. And police investigating into my father's death, as they did with all cases of suicide. Night had been the only thing that brought refuge, a place to hide away. I guessed that the psychologists had done their best—maybe they'd helped—but it hadn't felt that way at the time. I'd been a private, quiet kind of a child and it'd been painful for me to be in the spotlight. I'd come home from school or from a psych appointment, and just find Jake and hug him, holding him silently for minutes. Jake—then not even old enough to go to school—hadn't understood at all where his daddy had gone.

Today the shed was flooded with sunshine and that seemed to sanitise the lingering memories. Mum had never given a moment's thought to tearing the shed down—she'd said that Dad had loved tinkering away in there and making things for all of us, and that made it rich in love and memory.

Shuffling through the thick floor of disintegrated oak tree leaves, I made my way to a bench seat. Mum never cared about the fallen leaves from autumn building up on the ground.

The world instantly became a little oasis as I settled in under the arch of ivy. I'd long suspected that my mother had created this corner in order to find her sanity after long days of looking after Jake and me when we were younger.

I couldn't stop yawning. I was tired, irritable and feeling flat. Everything was still fringed with a shifting sense of unreality. It always took me days to recover from a seizure and I was still mentally processing this one. There was no getting away from it—I'd almost drowned.

Folding my arms and legs up on the bench, I wriggled down to rest my head. It was hot but shady here, and I could easily let myself drift off to sleep.

I woke with ants biting my bare feet. I'd been dreaming. It was the same dream I'd had multiple times.

In the dream, I stood at the entry of a strange house.

A long hallway stretched before me. Four rooms with three doors hanging open like hungry mouths were situated on either side of the hallway. One door locked. The air dark and a wind blowing dry leaves through the hallway. A picture of a religious cross with a rose in the middle. Legs dangling mid-air in one of the rooms. From the extreme end of the house came the sound of a piano being played, only without any tune. Just chaotic, crashing chords.

And there was me, busybody giant Alice, peering in where I shouldn't be looking.

My psych said the dreams were unresolved issues from my father's death. My neuro said it could be just my overactive epileptic brain or the meds I'd been on, or maybe both. I'd been on so many drugs over the years: *Keppra, Clobazam, Epilim, Trileptol, Zonegran, Tegritol.*

The colour seemed drained from the world as I opened my eyes. The dream always left me feeling wiped out.

My mother carried two tall glasses of drink around the corner. "You had a good sleep out here. A whole hour."

I blinked, rubbing my face. "Seriously? An hour? No wonder the ants were having a field day on my toes. Probably thought I was dead." Taking the drink, I sipped the cool liquid. It was freshly squeezed orange juice.

She frowned. "You don't look so good, Isla. Are you okay?"

"I'm fine. It's just that I woke up having that dream…you know the one."

"Oh, honey. I wish I could make that awful dream go away."

"Why does there have to be so much that's wrong with me?"

She sat on the swing opposite me. "There's nothing wrong with you. Not a thing."

"You know that's not true."

"It *is* true. Seizures. Nightmares. And I'm not doing anything with my life."

"You put yourself under so much pressure. You know, it's okay to just *be*."

"Mum, that's what I *have* been doing. I feel like I've just been treading water forever. I lost so much time when I got sick. I don't even remember—"

"Why do you keep going back to think about that? It was two years ago. Honey, you have to let it go. It's not helping you."

"I know. But it just feels…it feels so bad. Like I'm not a whole person anymore or something."

She moved from the swing to the bench, putting an arm around me. "You're perfect and I've known that from the time you were born." She squeezed my shoulder. "Your dad and I had the nursery all decked out when I was pregnant, but you preferred our room. Your room faced the brick wall of the neighbour's house. But our room faced the garden and was full of yellow sunlight and patterns from swaying palms. And you were right to prefer it, because you were made of sunlight, too. And so that's where you slept for your first year. With us."

"Mum, I'm not five!" I protested. I should have been used to my mother's vaguely hippie-child speeches, but sometimes they hit me unawares.

"In my eyes, you're every age you've ever been. All at the same time. And always perfect." She smiled, shrugging. "Why don't we go to a movie and dinner? That might shift your mood."

"I don't know…."

"Why not? Let's do it."

"I'm kind of tired."

"Getting out of the house might be just what you need."

She was right. I preferred being outdoors and always had. "Sure."

"Oh goodie. I'll pick out an outfit for you, if you like."

She cast me an uncertain look, until I nodded. It made her happy to share some of her vintage rockabilly clothing with me for special occasions. When Dad was alive, she and he used to attend rockabilly dances, and I knew she missed that.

I stepped out with Mum at eight in the night. For me, she'd chosen a little plaid shirt tied at the midriff and a long, spotted skirt. And an elegant retro dress for herself. She'd conned Jake into coming along with us. He wore his usual black jeans and T-shirt, his long hair worn on one side.

The three of us walked along Southern Sails Street to Darling Harbour—an upmarket hive of restaurants, movie theatres and museums. The colour of the sky was starting to deepen, the orange glow of the coming sunset sweeping the harbour.

We settled on eating at a favourite eatery, positioning ourselves in the outdoor section, so we could watch the boats and yachts.

"So, Jake," I said, "when's the hot date happening with—what was her name—Charlotte?"

A blush of red travelled up his throat. "Tomorrow night."

"Oooh. Where are you taking her?"

"You make it sound like I'm going to tackle her and hurl her over my shoulder, caveman style. I'm not taking her anywhere. It's not like that anymore. People just hang out."

He made me feel so ancient sometimes, even though there were only seven years between us. "Okay then, where are you hanging out?"

"Just at Stone Blue."

Stone Blue was one of the nightclubs that Jake played at with his band.

"Good thinking. She'll be eating out of your hand after watching you play guitar."

He exhaled. "I don't know about that. She's got me eating out of *her* hand already."

"You'll be fine, Jake," Mum put in.

"I know, I know…" He grinned. "I'm perfect, just the way I am." Then his mouth turned down. "What my mother thinks of me won't cut it with this girl though. I managed to get this far with her by not opening my stupid mouth. Once I do, it'll all be over."

I laughed at his expression. "Let her do all the talking, then."

"Isla!" Mum admonished, but she was smiling now, too.

It was great, sometimes, just the three of us. Like this.

"So, when are you heading out on a sailing adventure again?" Jake teased me. It was typical of him to try to steer a conversation away from himself.

"No more boats for me for a while." I toyed with the serviette on the table. "I think I need something new."

"I've heard real estate photography and video pays really well," said Mum. "All those mega-rich mansions on the Sydney foreshore. Just imagine how much those people would be willing to fork out?"

"I don't want to do that though," I told her.

Mum didn't understand what I meant. She thought I meant I needed something safer, but I didn't. In all honesty, I didn't know what I needed.

I'd heard that people who'd come close to dying tended to get a shakeup and then wanted to change everything. In my case, it was true. Something had pushed its way under my skin and was trying to peel off the upper layer. It felt almost physically painful.

Two days later, I went back to work. Mum insisted that I call her if I had the tiniest odd sign or symptom.

My first job was for a new client—Pippy Briggs-Hale. This assignment—a set of photos of Pippy for her Instagram profile—should have been a pretty easy and relaxed assignment. A good assignment to start back with. Except it wasn't. Instead, it was an assignment that left my nerves frayed and my feet sore.

Pippy wanted each shot perfect, especially the ones in which she wanted to appear as if the shot had been taken unawares. Getting a shot to look genuinely accidental was harder than it sounded. Pippy was pedantic and demanding, seeming to think I'd love her as much as her Instagram followers. She truly was the shallowest person I'd ever met.

ANNI TAYLOR

I cursed myself for lugging so much camera equipment along because we'd been all over the city now, from Chinatown to the wax museum.

In the middle of a shoot at Darling Harbour, Pippy launched into an extended chat session on her phone. I took the chance to sit and shuffle out of my shoes. The temptation to head across and stick my swollen feet in the kids' waterplay park was almost overwhelming. Instead, I trekked to a nearby cafe and ordered a coffee.

Fifteen minutes later, I watched Pippy tottering around searching for me like a lost child. I knew I should stand and wave at her, but I sat enjoying my coffee for a while longer.

That afternoon, I soaked myself in the bathtub, vowing to choose future clients with more care.

If I was Alice in Wonderland, then Pippy was the insane Queen of Hearts. The queen of Instagram hearts.

Mum rapped on the door. "Everything okay, Isla?"

"Yep. Almost fell asleep."

"Oh, don't do that. Promise me."

"I won't. I'm getting out."

She'd become so much more protective of me since the harbour incident.

Wrapping myself in a towel, I stepped from the bath and towel-dried my hair. I dressed in a tank top and shorts, not able to tell whether I was already sweating or still damp from the bath. Hot air drifted in through the open window as I walked into my bedroom.

I sat at my desk. I'd already worked on the images of Pippy and sent the first batch through to her. She'd been anxious to get them ASAP.

The whole day had felt hollow. *I* felt hollow.

Leaving thoughts of Pippy behind, I binge-watched the rest of a series on Netflix.

But I couldn't focus. The hollowness grew, slowly swallowing me whole, digesting me.

I switched off the TV. I'd finish watching the series another time, when I could relax into it.

Opening my laptop, I browsed my usual sites.

The Scotland photography assignment caught my eye again. The thought of the McGregor family saddened me. But despite my misgivings, the assignment captivated me enough to have me clicking on the link in the ad.

A page opened of images of ultra-modern buildings that had been married to traditional stone cottages. Somehow, they worked—a credit to the architect.

I searched Alban's name on Google image search. There he was— Alban McGregor, the architect. Angular features, dark eyes, messy hair tucked behind his ears—as if he'd been out in the wind the day the photograph was taken. His features were both distinct and irregular, which would make photographing him an easier task than with many other men. Men who had perfectly even features were often harder to make good portraits from, especially if their face shape was round. Alban's was the kind of face that you could draw a statement from. My mind wandered to photographing him against a backdrop of craggy Scottish mountains, the rough edges of him reflected in the scenery.

I had to admit, I was intrigued by him. That was always a good sign when it came to a photography session with someone.

I found his wife next—a pretty blonde woman named Jessica. She looked about thirty years old, her eyes uncertain and a little sad. She held a tiny, fair-haired toddler on her lap—the child's eyes round with innocence. Alban sat beside them. Unlike his wife, the look in his eyes was a little bit fierce.

Photos of another young girl had also popped up in my search— Elodie McGregor. Pictures of her running across a moor. A picture of her standing in between Alban and Jessica at a girls' soccer match, clad in soccer gear. She was dark-eyed and dark-haired like her father, with a slim oval face and a serious, determined set to her chin.

Elodie.

Pieces from the news article that I'd read before shot into my mind.

Abducted from outside her home.

Died in the arms of her parents.

Never woke from her coma.

I was beginning to feel like a voyeur sitting here and peering at them all.

Again, I was Alice. On her knees, bedraggled like a half-drowned rat, sticking her earnest face through that miniature door again. Watching people who she had no business watching.

I returned to the screen where the job was being advertised.

Breathing deeply, I read through it again.

I felt an urge to do something *real*. And this assignment seemed real. These people had been able to move on from their tragedy and keep going. I was fascinated by them.

And the assignment was just a month long. A stepping stone.

With all meals and accommodation provided.

I'd have the space in which to do the kind of portfolio I'd long dreamed of doing. And it would certainly look good on my resume.

My heart began chugging like a steam train on a downward slope when I realised I was actually seriously considering this.

The assignment was nothing like what I normally did.

I swallowed, reading the ad yet again.

A fresh batch of sweat sprung onto my back as I reached for my phone.

Out in the kitchen, Mum had old newspapers spread all over the kitchen table, with two of the old chairs she'd rescued perched on top. She was painting the first one a pretty blue shade.

She turned to me, a smear of bright paint across her cheek, her hair up in a scarf—1950s style. "What do you think?"

"Love the colour," I told her.

"Me too. It's called Tropicana Aqua. I'm doing the others orange, green and pink."

"Nice."

"How was the bath?"

"Great."

She paused her paintbrush on the chair's leg. "Feeling okay, sweetie? You've been pretty quiet since you came in from that job. Hope it didn't tire you out too much."

"Mum, I just called about a photography position."

"Oh?"

"In Scotland."

She seemed to stiffen. "*Scotland?*"

I exhaled tightly. "Yes. All the way over there."

Greer Crowley—Alban McGregor's personal assistant—had been warm and approachable. She'd looked over the portfolio of work I'd emailed her and said yes on the spot.

"*No.*" Mum spoke the word with conviction and without hesitation, surprising me.

"Mum?"

Her rigid pose collapsed, her shoulders sagging inward as she put her paintbrush down and faced me. "You can't go all the way overseas. Don't be crazy." She drew her mouth in. "You think you can do anything...but you can't. I'm sorry as hell that you were born with the condition you've got. But it's all about living the best life you can while managing the risks."

"People with my condition do all kinds of things."

She blinked, eyes opening wide with apprehension. "Oh honey, I didn't mean it in that way. It's just...well, your seizures obviously haven't been under control lately. Imagine that happening to you in a strange country?"

"I need a change. This sounded good. And it's only for a month. You haven't even asked—"

"Is it because of what happened the other day on the yacht? It must be playing on your mind. Because, you know, you could see the psychologist that you used to see for your depression." She nodded as if a decision had officially been made. "We'll make an appointment."

"I don't want to make an appointment."

"Okay, okay. I get it. You don't think you need to see her. But please, think about this some more. It was just a few days ago you were reminding me about that awful time you went through. You'd never want something like that to happen to you again."

"I know. I don't want that. But I've been feeling well for a long time. I'm okay. I feel okay. Really."

"Promise me you'll think about this some more."

"Promise." I shot her a smile that I hoped was reassuring. I was feeling nervous as anything underneath the smile. I couldn't tell her right now that I'd accepted the job.

Taking a step closer to the table, I picked up the paintbrush. "This is going to dry out if you don't keep going." I dipped it into the tin of paint and began filling in a bare spot.

I had the distinct feeling she was going to try every angle to convince me that this wasn't a good idea. And I worried that it wasn't going to take much for her to change my mind.

4

ISLA

I THOUGHT I'd back out of taking on the Scotland job over the next fortnight. At least twice a day, nerves would crackle like live wires beneath my skin and I'd be desperate to pick up the phone and tell Greer Crowley that I'd developed a severe illness and couldn't make it. All apologies.

But I didn't.

I surprised myself by sticking firm.

Jake had been my only supporter.

Mum had grown increasingly despondent. As I'd predicted, she had thrown everything she had at talking me out of going, but even so, I hadn't been prepared for her tenacity. She'd ended up insisting on coming with me, until I'd sat her down and asked why she had so little faith in me.

It'd continued like that until the morning I headed out the door, wearing my most comfortable pair of jeans and my favourite T-shirt. Travelling gear. I wanted to look like a seasoned traveller, even though I wasn't one.

There's still time to back out, I reminded myself as yet another wave of nerves raced through me.

I'd made it as far as Singapore airport. I could turn tail and head back to Sydney if I wanted to. It'd be a terrible thing to do to the people who were expecting me to show up in Scotland. But still, this was my last chance.

I found my way outside, into the hot, humid air. I had two hours to kill while waiting for my connecting flight. I wasn't looking forward to being squashed back into a plane. I hated the sensation of being trapped in a small place in which everything was completely out of my control.

Changi International Airport was enormous, with actual full-size palm trees inside and extensive gardens around the exterior. If I was going to become hopelessly lost—or somehow die of a panic attack— at least this would be a nice place in which to do it.

I ate a noodle lunch in one of the gardens, continually stressing that I had the departure time wrong.

Anxiety central.

All boarding.

An hour later, I was in the sky again, this time with a window seat. I didn't know whether that was a blessing or a curse. The UK was a long way from here, across an endless, terrifying stretch of ocean and countries. I was grateful when night turned the scene outside to black, and I finally felt myself drifting off.

I woke to Heathrow Airport, London, then caught my next flight to Inverness, Scotland. It was already morning. As my plane landed, I looked down on a city surrounded by sea and green space. I didn't know why I'd expected that such a small country would be crowded with buildings, because it was nothing like that.

The plane descended onto the runway at Inverness Airport, my ears painfully popping, despite chewing on a mint.

I couldn't help but feel forlorn as I dragged my suitcase through the streams of people. Everyone seemed to know exactly where they were going, and many of them were being greeted by waiting family.

Greer had arranged a driver to take me all the way to Alban McGregor's property in the Highlands. She'd said to wait in the departure lounge, holding up a piece of paper with my last name on it.

Like an orphan waiting to be claimed, I stood there patiently clutching my crumpled A4 scrap of paper that said WILSON.

A smallish man in his sixties approached me. "Miss Isla Wilson?" he asked.

"Yes, that's me."

"I'm your driver this morning. My name's Craig." He had a heavy Scottish accent and one of the friendliest smiles I'd ever seen.

"I'm so happy you found me, Craig. I'm feeling a bit lost."

"Hey, 'tis natural. A big airport is a bugger of a place. Full of numpties mooing about like cows instead of getting to where they should be. Come on then, I'll show you to the car."

Craig had unwittingly just become my insta-family. Not letting him out of my sight, I doggedly followed him out of the airport.

The drive from Inverness to the country seemed to slide past quickly—helped by Craig's stories about his wife, life and grandchildren, peppered with colourful sayings that I was sure must be the Scottish version of swear words.

We travelled along what looked like a highway to me—Craig called it *the* A9. He turned off to head along another long road, then made another turn at a sign that pointed towards a town named Greenmire. The road twisted around stubborn trees and craggy boulders, as if those landscape features had won sway when the road had first been built.

"Not far now," Craig informed me.

There didn't seem to be anything here. Just long stretches of country landscapes.

A car filled with young people cut in front of us, a blonde guy driving.

Craig threw his hands up in the air. "Ah, you daft flippin' numpty!" He shot a quick glance across at me. "Sorry for that. It's those Chandlish kids—their parents' house is just down the road a bit. Rich idiots, they are."

I grinned. "Don't mind me."

A short distance further along the road, I noticed a tall woman standing by a wide gate, arms waving wildly above her head. She had a thin, hunch-shouldered build, dressed in a long floral skirt, jacket and boots. Her hair—coloured in an unnaturally pink shade of blonde —curved neatly around her ears in a shiny bob. She looked like she'd be in her early thirties.

"There she is," Craig announced. "Greer Crowley. Bold as a thistle."

I wondered if that was a compliment or insult. It was hard to tell with him.

He parked the car. "I'll get your bag, love." He kept talking as he stepped around to the back of the car to fetch the bag, something about the weather and the government.

"You're a marvel, Craig Langley" Greer said, taking the bag from him. "Got her here in one piece and everything, you did."

"Well, I do try my best." He winked at me.

"And Isla! There you are!" She rushed over to me, encasing me in a firm hug before darting back and studying my face. "A breath of fresh air to Braithnoch. It's wonderful to have you here." She spoke with a whooshing sort of warmth, each word pushed out of her lungs with gusto.

It was more of a welcome than I'd been expecting, and I warmed to her immediately. I'd been greeted like lost-long family.

"Craig's a friend of my father's," she told me. "So naturally I knew you'd be in good hands. He drove cabs for decades before he retired. Have you eaten? Of course you haven't. It's a long drive out here. After you've had a chance to freshen up, I'll take you into town for some lunch. Not that you don't look fresh, mind. I'd be fair dead travelling all this way." She took half a breath to add, "Alban and Jessica are away overnight, but they'll be back tomorrow. Anyway, I've got my car just inside the gate. I'll take you up the driveway to the house—it's quite a long one."

Craig blinked his eyes open wide. "You're a windbag, Greer. I couldn't follow the half'o'that. I hope Isla did."

"Oh, you!" Extending an arm, Greer gave him a friendly shove on his shoulder. "Everyone knows I talk ten to the dozen. Och well. Thanks again for looking after Isla. I do appreciate it."

Craig nodded at her. "It's no trouble at all. She was good company."

Their banter had relaxed me.

I thanked Craig warmly for the ride and then left with Greer for the drive to the house. What had she called the property —*Braithnoch*?

My photographer's eye instinctively framed up potential images along the way. We passed a tiny cottage and a woodshed just inside the gate. I guessed that the cottage was where I'd be staying.

A sense of disappointment brushed over me as the house came into view. It wasn't the old stone building I'd been hoping for. A traditional house would have been a delight to photograph. But of course, Alban McGregor was an architect and he'd have wanted to show off what he could do with his design skill. His house was a very modern collection of glass and soaring straight lines. But I had to admit that it was creative, with views straight through the glass roof lines to the mountains and a mossy grass covering other parts of the roof. The vertical wooden cladding on the exterior of the house was a nod to the forest setting. It was stunning, despite lacking old-world charm.

High, wide clumps of white, pink, and rich purple flowers grew everywhere, softening the modern look of the house, giving a dreamy look to the property.

"The flowers—what are they?" I asked Greer.

"It's a variety of heather that blooms in the winter. It's pretty, isn't it?"

"Very."

As the road curved, I caught glimpses of a part of the house I hadn't yet seen. I almost gasped with happiness. The modern part of the building had been joined onto the original—a low, greyish, stone cottage that was almost exactly what I'd been imagining.

Immediately, I felt more positive about the house. "It's lovely," I said.

"Yes, it is, isn't it?" she agreed. "Alban is brilliant with his work."

A set of still figures on a distant hill caught my eye. "Are those scarecrows?"

Greer smiled, hitching a finely arched eyebrow. "They call them *tattie bogles* around here."

"Really?"

"Yep. As far as I know, the tattie part of it is for potatoes, from back in the time when potatoes were the staple food item."

"Do the scarecrows belong to this property? I mean, the bogles?"

"They're right at the intersection of four properties. Imagine a plus sign dividing four lots of land. The spot that they intersect belongs to all of them. You've got Alban McGregor's land here. And next to his is that of the Keenans—they're an older couple. The two properties behind to the left and right belong to the Flanagans and the Chandlishes. The Flanagans have a son—a police officer. The Chandlishes are old money and well known around these parts, and not always for the best reasons." She drew her eyebrows together in a mock frown.

"Let's get you inside," said Greer. "It's getting a wee bit nippy. I'll bet you're feeling it, coming straight from Sydney's weather."

I shook my head firmly. "It's a blessing. I'm not a fan of the heat. And right now, Sydney is an oven."

A wry but relieved laugh twisted from her throat. "Well, you're going to find Braithnoch a treat, then."

The interior of the house had clean lines—lots of white and natural finishes. The ceiling was as high as that of a small cathedral, exposed beams extending from wall to wall. Two mezzanine levels gave glimpses of the upstairs rooms.

Greer took me on a short tour of the downstairs areas. The house was beautiful in every direction.

I walked with Greer down a long corridor. One side of the wall held dozens of framed family pictures, in both colour and grayscale. A few illustrations that had been drawn by a child also adorned the space. The photos and drawings gave a warm feel to an otherwise stark wall.

"And this is the family," Greer told me. "The McGregors." She pointed each of them out. I didn't tell her I already knew their names.

The pictures of Alban commanded attention, the same as they had when I'd looked him up online, his intense eyes staring directly at me.

Alban's wife—Jessica—was the image of the perfect wife and mother, smiling widely in almost every picture.

There were lots of pictures of the dark-haired girl I'd seen on my internet search too—many of them of her running about parks and fields with bright cheeks. The older pictures of her showed a subdued girl who'd acquired a questioning look in her eyes.

The photos of the younger girl were starkly different, and not just because of her very young age and fair colouring. The photos of her all seemed to have been taken by a professional photographer—lots of studio shots and posed family photographs.

Greer lightly touched a portrait of the older girl. In this picture, the girl was staring straight at the camera, her expression unflinchingly serious. "This is Elodie. As I mentioned over the phone, she died in tragic circumstances. She was abducted the night that her sister—Rhiannon—was born. Elodie was just eight years old."

"She was beautiful," I said, shocked to hear that her sister was born that very night. "Did the police ever find out who was responsible?"

Sighing, Greer stepped back from the picture. "A few leads but nothing came of it."

I glanced at a set of photographs of snow. They were good—not professional, but whoever had taken them had a nice talent for bringing out the play of light on the white surface.

"Who did these?" I gestured towards the set of snow images.

"Oh," she said. "That was Jessica. She likes winter best of all the seasons."

"Great shots."

"C'mon, I'll show you the rest of the house." Linking her arm with mine, she escorted me along the remainder of the hallway, into the older section of the house. A doorway led to an office, one wall lined with the same wood as the exterior.

"This is Alban's office," she said. "He had the entire floor of the old cottage converted into office space. He spends a lot of time in here. He's become fairly reclusive. Actually, very reclusive. To be honest, that's part of the reason that Jessica first had the idea to do a media feature—to get his name out there more and put a face to his work. I agreed with her and began approaching magazines."

"Is it okay if I peek inside? Seeing as I'm going to be photographing him, perhaps seeing his office space might help me build a picture of him in my mind."

Greer hesitated. "Maybe just a quick look—Alban's pretty private."

I followed her inside.

A drafting table stood in one corner. Two plush office chairs were parked in front of heavy oak desks—the desks holding a computer and two large-screen monitors. A bar fridge made a low-key hum next to a small table and set of two armchairs.

"He has his office very well set up," I remarked. "It looks very comfortable."

"Yes." A worried look crossed her face then. "I should let you know, he doesn't like to be disturbed when he's in here. I guess it must interrupt his creative flow. But he's not in here now." She winked at me.

The walls of the office, like the rest of the house—apart from the hallway—held no family photographs. Just two pictures decorated one wall, sitting side by side.

One was a modern painting—just a stark black line moving left and right on a white background. It resembled a child's first try on one of those old Etch-A-Sketch toys.

The other picture was an aerial photograph of a winter forest. The photo appeared to be in black and white until I examined it more closely. The lack of colour was solely due to the dark, bare trees contrasting against the snow and wintry sky. Something about the interlocking branches of the forest seemed almost threatening.

I turned to Greer. "Where is this?"

Greer sucked in her mouth as if she were deciding how to answer me. "It's…the section of forest where Elodie was found. The shack that you can see the roof of is where she was taken to the night of the abduction. The shack is just a wee playhouse made decades ago by children."

"And he keeps *this* on his wall?" The words slipped out unchecked and I instantly regretted them.

"Believe me, I've questioned his choice. But it's sentimental, don't you think? I think it helps him feel close to his daughter, keeping a view of the place where the poor girl spent her last conscious moment. She never woke after that."

I didn't know how to respond. It seemed morbid to me, even though I was trying hard to frame it as the gesture of a grieving father.

Greer seemed to pick up on my discomfort. "Let me show you around the rest of this place."

She guided me out of the room. I was glad to leave it.

We stepped through to the other end of the house, out to a wide space. A kitchen looked out to a sunken living room. And then to a stretch of green hills through towering, floor-to-ceiling glass walls.

An enormous stone table dominated the dining space next to the kitchen. I counted the chairs. Twelve. I'd never been in a house that could fit a twelve-chair table in it before.

"Nice, isn't it?" said Greer.

"It's quite a house. Stunning."

"Well, I'll take you back up to the cottage now. You can have a rest and then we'll go grab some lunch. I know you might want to sleep. But, if you can, it's best to keep to regular sleep cycles when you've travelled across time zones. How does that sound?"

"Sounds good to me."

In truth, I was already feeling overwhelmed. I'd arrived at the house of a recluse with a morbid photograph on his office wall.

I hoped that when I met Alban in person my discomfort would dissolve, and things would begin to make more sense.

5

ISLA

"HOP back into the car and we'll drive back up to the cottage," Greer told me. "Normally, you'd walk it, of course, but you'll be more tired than you think. Best to take it easy."

I was happy to let Greer take charge of me. She was right—I was exhausted. Having someone else think for me right now was a relief.

She drove the short distance along the driveway to the cottage. Taking my bag out of the car, she wheeled it to the cottage. I stepped along the mossy garden path.

"Mind the blackberry brambles," she told me as we headed under a garden arch. "Those thorns are quite nasty." She pointed to a small shed that was attached to the cottage. "There's a couple of bicycles in there. That's if you feel like taking one out for a spin at all. I think they're in working order."

The cottage sat at the edge of the woods, covered in vines. It was as cute as I could imagine that a cottage at the edge of a forest could be. Inside though, the cottage wasn't nearly as quaint. It sorely needed fixing up. But it was better than me having to pay for my own accommodation and transport in the town. The job was right here.

I put my bag in the small bedroom. Greer opened the cupboards and fridge, showing me that she'd already fully stocked up. It seemed that I had enough here to eat for the next month, without ever even eating out.

She waited in the cottage until I'd showered and changed my clothing. We sat at the table with cups of tea.

I picked up a tree cone from a bowl on the table. The cones had been half-painted gold. "Who did these?"

Greer plucked a cone herself. "Elodie. As I remember, these were meant to be Christmas decorations."

"Sad." I remembered that Elodie had died a short time before Christmas.

"Well, then," said Greer brightly, replacing the cone. "Do you like pub food or something a bit more refined?"

"Pub food sounds great."

"Excellent."

We drove out of Braithnoch, towards the town of Greenmire.

Trees marched along the side of the road, crowding together against the sharp cold. There was a sadness about them that seemed to enter my soul. Maybe that was because I couldn't help but associate the forest with Elodie now.

Past the stretch of forest, the land cleared again. A white, country style house stood in a field.

"That's the Keenan's house," said Greer. "Lovely people. Salt of the Scottish earth types. They're in their seventies. They've got three kids—all adult of course."

She drove around a corner. The trees thickened again.

Greer suddenly swerved as a group of people ran from the forest and straight out onto the road. She screeched to a stop.

"God Almighty." Exhaling hard, she shook her head.

Two women and two men laughed as they leaned drunkenly on the front of Greer's car. They were the same group who had been in the car that cut across the road in front of me earlier.

The blonde woman waved at us, her smile wide but lazy and her eyes a little glazed. She was extremely pretty, her hair in long waves down her back. She glanced at me with interest for a second before the man pulled her away and off the road. Greer returned a reluctant wave. "That's Aubrey Chandlish," she said to me in a low tone. "And her brother, Diarmid. The red-haired girl is her best friend Bridget.

I'm not sure who the other man is—probably one of Aubrey's boyfriends."

Aubrey looked back at me with curiosity as Greer slowly drove away.

"So, they're also Alban's neighbours? I remember you mentioned the Chandlishes."

"Yes. Their parents—Gus and Deirdre—go away for three months each year. Travelling. And that's when the kiddies come to play. Aubrey and Diarmid are usually in Edinburgh, but they come back home once Mummy and Daddy have gone. The Chandlish home becomes one giant party house at this time of year." She pulled a face. "Lucky, they don't live next door. Well, technically they do, but at least there's quite a bit of distance in between."

A large house came into view. Mansion sized. White and box shaped.

"Do I guess that's the Chandlish house?" I gazed at the multitude of dark windows that were stark against the white brickwork and pale sky.

"Yes, that's it."

"There's a heap of cars parked out the front," I remarked.

"That's what I was afraid of. The more of them there are, the more they rile each other up. There's an older boy, too—named Peyton. He's sensible, at least. Look, Aubrey and Diarmid aren't that bad, really. It's just that they invite too many people around. Then they all get too drunk and things start going wrong." She clucked her tongue. "Oh, listen to me. I sound like an old fuddy-duddy. I know that you're only young once. You know what I mean. You're about the same age as Aubrey. She's in her early twenties."

I gave a laugh that was meant to sound jovial but instead got squeezed in my chest. "I'm twenty-six. And well, I didn't really have any wild years. Too staid for that, I guess."

She sighed. "That's the other extreme. You need to have a bit of fun before it all disappears and you're over thirty. I'm thirty-six, so I speak from experience."

"Just coming here is a bit of an adventure for me," I admitted. "I'm a homebody. But this opportunity just seemed too good to pass up."

Greer shot me a warm grin. "We're very happy to have you here. Your photography is stunning. I can't wait to see what you come up with. I know it will be very special."

I breathed deeply, hoping like hell I could live up to the faith she seemed to have in me. "I'm still pinching myself I got this job."

"Of course you got the job. You were the best choice. And while you're here, you're one of us. I mean that."

I believed her. Her voice had a note of sincerity that few people could muster.

The road into town was lengthy. Somehow, I'd thought the town would be closer. The sense of remoteness and distance here was intimidating.

I breathed easier once I caught sight of the town that had opened up in the valley just beyond the crest of the next hill.

The town was charming with its olde world shops and pubs and the irregular stonework of their facades.

"We're here!" Greer parked the car and jumped out.

She steered me towards a place that didn't look like much on the outside—only a modest sign—but the interior was large. Surprisingly, it was bustling with people. A Lady Gaga song played over a sound system, clusters of young people standing and nodding along to *Poker Face*. Older people sat at the bar and tables alone or in couples.

"It's a lively pub, this one. It's certainly not the usual around this part of Scotland." Greer waved at me to follow as she squeezed through the crowd. "We'll get you fed and watered, my dear."

After ordering lunch and drinks, she found us a little spot near the wood fire. As we sat and chatted over stew and crusty bread, it occurred to me how much I was already enjoying being here. I felt at home, even listening to the accents so different to my own. The Scots drew out their vowel sounds in a delightful way, liberally sprinkled with Scottish cussing. It was a language for sitting and having long chats over a beer or cup of tea.

I'd been missing out on far too much by cocooning myself at home—this reluctant butterfly needed to take flight.

A gaggle of young people burst in through the front door, laughing and talking loudly. It was the same group again—the Chan-

39

dlishes and their friends, except that this time there were more of them.

The heavy melody of the song, *Back to Black* by Amy Winehouse, began playing, Amy's pure, sultry, jazz tones stretching throughout the pub.

Aubrey took the blonde man who she was with onto the dance floor, leading him into a waltzing kind of dance. She kissed him as if there was no one else in the room. Greer had guessed right. He must be her boyfriend. The two of them made a good-looking couple.

When the song ended, a song by the Scottish band, The Proclaimers burst through the loudspeakers: *I'm Gonna Be (500 Miles)*. The entire pub erupted, suddenly singing along. Feet stomping. Hands clapping. People joined Aubrey and her male friend on the dance floor, yelling out the lyrics at the tops of their lungs.

Greer smiled at me. "Hope your poor ears will be okay after this!"

"I'm loving it," I called back over the din.

A man approached. He was one of the men that Aubrey had come in with—light brown hair falling over blue eyes. He appeared to be studying my face, a frown flickering in between his eyebrows.

"Hello," he said, bending down to be heard.

His accent was Australian and his voice a little slurred, beer on his breath. It seemed odd to hear an Australian accent here. But there must be hundreds or thousands of Aussies bouncing around Scotland right now, so I guessed it wasn't that unusual.

"Uh, hello," I replied. "Good to see another Aussie here. Where are you from?"

An awkward silence followed before he said, "What are you doing here?"

I glanced from him to Greer, confused. Greer gave a slight shake of her head.

"I'm just sitting here having lunch?" I told him.

"I mean," he said, enunciating each word, "What are you doing here?"

"Excuse me," said Greer. "That might just be the worst pickup line I've ever heard. Please leave her alone."

The man straightened and decided to walk away as he caught

sight of Aubrey running over, her high-heeled boots clattering on the floor.

"Sorry Greer," Aubrey said. "Didn't mean to run out in front of you earlier. We're all a bit tipsy."

"I noticed." Greer sighed and smiled. "Stay off the roads, okay? Who's driving you guys home?"

"S'okay." Aubrey smiled. "Big bro' Peyton is coming to get us later." She glanced in my direction. "Hey, who's this?"

"This is Isla," Greer told her. "Isla Wilson. She'll be staying in the cottage at Braithnoch for the next month. She's shooting a portfolio of photos for Alban."

"Ooh, that's exciting." Her wide grin seemed genuine as she shook my hand. "Hope you enjoy our wee town, Isla. There's nothing to do here, but don't let that stop you from having fun." Her laugh twisted wryly. "You've just got to bring your fun."

Greer sipped at her beer, her brow crinkling. "Aubrey, who was the man who was here a second ago? He's with you, right?"

Aubrey nodded. "Yeah. That's Trent. We've been friends for a few years. Was he bothering Isla? He's a bit drunk. And high on pot and maybe a few other things."

"It's fine," I said, "He wasn't bothering me."

"I'll bring everyone over to meet Isla." Her eyes opened wide as if that was the best idea ever. "And you can meet my new guy, Greer. His name is Simon. I met him at a concert in Edinburgh. He's a lawyer. Doesn't look like a lawyer though. This time, it's going to last. I really like him."

"That sounds lovely. I'm happy for you, but we've really got to head off. I'm sure we'll get a chance to meet Simon soon." Greer rose from her chair. "I'm going to show Isla around Greenmire a bit and then take her back to Braithnoch to get some rest."

Aubrey inhaled a large breath and released it in a sigh. "Okay, well, see you around, Isla. I'll just be on the other side of the woods from you."

Greer herded me out of the pub. "That lot are all too rowdy at the moment. And you're looking pretty tired, you poor thing."

"I'm really starting to feel it now," I admitted. The encounter with

41

the Australian guy named Trent had especially left me feeling ragged around the edges.

As promised, Greer drove me around Greenmire, pointing out the shops and landmarks.

By the time we returned to Braithnoch, I was feeling heavy as a rock, layers of exhaustion piling on top of me.

When night drew in, I walked down the garden path to spend my first night at the cottage. Greer was staying in the house.

It was only once I was out in the cottage, alone, that I really felt the isolation of its position and sensed the forest all around me.

Despite my weariness, it was hard to get to sleep, and I lay awake for hours, listening for every sound.

6

ELODIE

Greenmire, Scottish Highlands, December 2015

TERROR FLASHED THROUGH HER. There was no way out of the playhouse.

In desperation, Elodie squeezed her eyes shut and made a dash for the only exit. She ran straight into him.

Backing away, she crumpled herself into a corner. His body blocked the door so fully that she could only see the barest glimpses of the forest behind it. Bending low, he moved inside and closed the door behind. She tensed as he reached inside his jacket pocket. Was he getting a knife or something to hurt her? She couldn't see.

A light blinked on.

His phone. A whitish light shone out.

When he yanked the scarf down from his face, a loud gasp sucked from her lungs.

She knew him.

Of course she did.

She'd always known him. And loved him. He'd taught her to love him, instructing her that love comes from respect.

Everything was okay. It was *him*. She'd made a big mistake. Catching her breath, she raised her face to the slivers of sky peeking through the gaps in the ceiling. She'd been running and scared and silly, but now he'd tell her that he was just trying to catch up to her to tell her something. Maybe she'd been about to step on a sleeping adder. Or maybe this was just some kind of test. He'd taught her to expect that he'd test her.

Also, she was afraid of him. He'd taught her that, too. He'd scared her before sometimes, but she hadn't been all alone, like now.

When she moved her gaze back to him, his eyes were different. Steely. Intent. The look in his eyes sent electrical bursts of adrenalin shooting through her veins and made her thoughts of tests and adders scatter into a thousand tiny pieces.

"I'm sorry for running away," she told him. "You scared me. I shouldn't have been outside this late. Mum's making us cottage pie tonight. You'll like it. She's just gone out to get some potatoes."

He breathed deeply, and she could see the white air streaming from his nose and mouth. "This is where I want you right now."

"I'm cold." That wasn't exactly true. She somehow felt cold inside her chest, but she was sweating under her winter clothing. "I need to go light the fire."

"You'll be okay. There's more I have to teach you."

"Please. You know that Mum's feeling poorly. She'll get upset if I don't come straight back."

"But you're with me. Why would she be upset?"

She didn't have an answer for that. She didn't know if there even *was* an answer. She desperately wanted to say something—to talk her way out of here—but her thoughts were all twisted up.

He began speaking about love, like he often did. But here in the playhouse, the words seemed all wrong. Before, they'd sounded like a kind of wisdom only an adult could give. Now, they made shivery waves of pins down her arms and legs. She knew the words well.

He loved her, too. He'd once told her he'd loved her since the moment she was born. Her newborn cry had sounded like a stray kitten to him, he'd said. Like a forlorn, abandoned thing that needed rescuing.

He fixed his gaze on her, shrugging off his jacket and laying it on the floor. "Do you understand?"

She nodded. She was used to saying yes to his words.

He put a hand on her shoulder. "Good."

He'd never touched her before when he was teaching her. She shrank away. In response, he stood, gazing down at her. His body blocked any chance of escape, suddenly seeming as tall and wide and unmovable as a larch tree.

A small branch or twig struck the roof of the shack, scraping like skeletal fingers all the way along until it fell to the ground.

It felt to her as if the entire forest was about to come down.

Every single tree.

7

ISLA

I WOKE IN A GROGGY HAZE, still thinking I was on a plane.

When I realised I was here—Greenmire, Scotland—a slow smile spread across my face. Despite the headache that throbbed at my temples, I had a sense of curiosity about the coming month, and more than a bit of pride that I'd made it.

I changed my clothes three times, not knowing what to wear for the weather. The first two outfits seemed like overkill, too much like a Sydneyite travelling to a cold country for the first time. Settling on a dressed-down thick hoodie, jeans and a knit cap, I headed out of the cottage and up to the main house.

"Come right on in, Isla." Greer's high voice pinged from the interior of the house. When I hesitated to let myself in, she flung the door open and waved me inside, clad in pyjamas and slippers. "No need to knock." With her baggy pyjamas and her hair in a messy ponytail, she resembled a giant child. Even the slippers she wore and coffee cup she held were oversized. "How'd you sleep?"

"Like a log."

"Brilliant. Well, help yourself. There's cereal, croissants, yoghurt, fruit, eggs, whatever you please."

"Oh, that all sounds lovely. But I'll admit I don't tend to do breakfast. I picked up the habit from my mother."

"The air here will change that habit soon enough. You'll wake up starving."

"Mum would be mortified if I came home a few kilos heavier. I won't fit into the clothes she buys me." I rushed my words at the end, wishing I hadn't mentioned the clothing. Yes, at age twenty-six, my mother still occasionally bought me pieces of clothing. It was me who was the giant child, not Greer.

Greer just looked amused. "She buys you clothes? That's cute."

"She's into rockabilly," I mumbled. "So yeah, sometimes we go retro. Actually, she's permanently retro. Everything, even the house."

"I love it. Explains your Instagram."

"You looked at that?"

"Of course. I stick my nose and beady eyes in everywhere. I saw photos of your mother and you."

"Embarrassing."

"Not at all. She looks like fun."

Because Greer had gone to such an effort for breakfast, I sat and ate. And enjoyed it much more than I thought I would. I wasn't used to sitting and savouring breakfast. Mornings had been for getting up and rushing to jobs. But I liked this—this was relaxing. A start to a different me.

An iPhone on the kitchen counter next to Greer burst into chords of *Echo Beach* by Martha and the Muffins. Maybe Greer was a little retro herself. She answered with a short, sharp *Greer Crowley*. During the call, she seemed to grow a little annoyed.

"Ah," she said in an exasperated tone, as she returned the phone to the bench top. "A little drama erupting at the office. Maybe they can sort it themselves—I don't like to leave you here alone. Not very hospitable."

"No, don't be silly. Go! Shoo! I can go check out Braithnoch."

"You're a dear."

Greer rushed away to change out of her pyjamas, returning in a suit, her hair neatly drawn into a bun. "I'll be back in three hours or so. Alban and Jess might arrive before I return, but they know you're here."

"That's fine. I'll just introduce myself."

"Good. Okay well, I'll leave you to have a bit of a poke about and

47

see what you want to capture for your portfolio." She flashed me a smile and half-crossed the floor before she stopped, a frown wrinkling her forehead. "I'll remind you that Alban's just a bit private when it comes to his office and studio."

"I remember. Anyway, I'm dying to get out there on those hills."

She laughed. "You'll need your walking boots on. And a toasty, warm coat. And be careful not to head into the woods—too easy to get lost for days in there."

"Got it. don't worry, I'll be careful." I grinned to emphasise my point.

I heard her drive away as I washed up the cups and plates in the sink. I felt dwarfed by the house as soon as I'd finished. I realised that Greer and her loud, breezy personality had filled up quite a lot of the space while she was here.

I ran my fingers along the gleaming black length of the kitchen bench top. Then, feeling guilty about the finger-marks, hurried to polish the bench with a cloth. I wondered if the McGregors were the types to notice a fingerprint in their house. Probably. The house was just so perfect. As impressed as I was, I doubted I'd ever feel comfortable here. Apart from the photo wall, there was nothing cosy in this house—no little corners with personal touches. Not even any paintings, apart from the minimalist one in the office.

Who are you, Alban McGregor? Your house isn't showing me much. It's all lines and angles and spaces. I'd call it mathematical, but that seemed wrong. Something mathematical should be solving a problem, shouldn't it? This house didn't seem to. It was beautiful, but it had no sense of place. Everything seemed to be just a thoroughfare, a place you drifted through on your way from the front end of the property to the back and out to the forest. How was I going to photo-graph it and make it seem like a home?

A knock came at the door, making me jump. Was it Greer? Maybe she'd forgotten something? Or was it the McGregors?

No, it couldn't be either. Neither Greer nor the McGregors would be knocking—they'd just come straight on in.

I hesitated. This wasn't my house and perhaps I shouldn't be answering the door.

The knock came again.

Okay. Whoever it was, they weren't going away. I backtracked across the stone floors and along the hallway to the foyer.

A figure was visible through the glass sections of the door. A lanky man with tousled hair and a brown, leather satchel in his hand. As I opened the door, I realised I was still holding the dishcloth. I shoved it into a back pocket of my jeans. The man had searching eyes that were set above slightly hollow cheeks. His mouth was straight and serious, framed by deep curved lines like parentheses.

"Hello?" he said with a surprised question in his voice. "I'm Mr Kavanagh—Rory. Who might you be?"

"I'm Isla. A photographer, hired by Alban McGregor."

"A photographer?"

"Yes. I'm doing a portfolio of the house and some other things."

"You're Australian, right?"

"Right. From Sydney. I flew in yesterday. Can I take a message or something?"

He shoved his free hand into his trouser pocket. "No, that's okay. Is anyone else here?"

"Just me." Wondering if I should admit that to this stranger, I added, "But Alban will be here any minute. Maybe you could call back later?"

"Well, I could do that, but—" He glanced down at the satchel.

"Were you dropping that off?" I asked.

He nodded.

I reached for the satchel. "Sure thing. I'll tell Alban you left this. *Rory*, was it?"

He seemed reluctant to hand the satchel over. "I'm not sure it's a good idea just to leave this and go. The contents are a little...sensitive."

"Oh?"

He rubbed his nose, the tip of which was red from the cold. "I don't know if you've had a chance to hear about Alban's daughter? Elodie?"

Sadness pooled inside me as an image of Elodie formed in my mind. "Yes, I've heard."

"I was Elodie's teacher. I've found some of her paintings and I thought Alban might like to have them. They were part of a display in the school hall, selections of the best artwork among our students. The paintings were packed away at some point and forgotten."

"The paintings sound very special."

"Yes." He leaned suddenly against one of the vertical beams of wood that formed the porch. "I'm sorry, I feel a bit dizzy."

I was unsure what to offer him. "Can I get you a drink? Do you need to sit down?"

"I have some medication I might need to take. Could I use the bathroom?"

"Oh, of course."

Stepping back, I showed him inside. He seemed to be heading in a definite direction, as if he knew where to go.

"Have you been here before?" I asked.

He gave a nod, along with a breathy exhale. "My family has been to dinner here. My stepdaughter used to babysit Elodie."

He slid out a folder from the satchel and set it down on a side table, then disappeared down a hall.

I'd just let a strange man into Alban's house. What if he'd come looking for valuables and wasn't a teacher at all?

I sidestepped over to the table where he'd left the folder and peeked inside. At least he was telling the truth about what was inside the folder. There were indeed children's paintings in there. I closed it again, waiting for him to return.

He seemed to be taking much longer than he should. How long did it take to swallow some medication and splash your face with water, or whatever he was doing in there? What if he'd been sick enough to faint? If he'd somehow fallen, he could be lying on the floor with a bleeding head. I guessed I should go and check.

Walking down the hall, I peered into each room, trying to find the bathroom that Rory had ventured into. I found a bathroom, but it was empty. Where on earth had he disappeared to?

I spotted his shoes at the bottom of the staircase. Okay, so he'd bypassed a bathroom and gone upstairs.

Why?

Feeling responsible for this random man that I'd allowed in, I made my way up to the first floor. It didn't take long to find him. He was standing in a bedroom, his back to me. It was a girl's bedroom by the look of the furnishings.

Rory was going through the drawers of a desk, pulling out a bundle of drawings.

The drawings weren't something that a toddler could produce, so these had to be Elodie's. And this had to be Elodie's room. I gazed around at the furnishings. A bed with the covers turned down. Stuffed toys and plastic collectibles on the shelves. A child-size guitar in the corner. A framed birthday photo of Elodie and friends.

The school teacher studied each picture thoughtfully, tilting them to each side before replacing each one in the pile.

I began feeling protective of Elodie's things. She wasn't here to give permission for this intrusion, and so it was up to me to stop him.

"Mr Kavanagh?" I queried.

His back flinched, and he pivoted around. "She was very talented, wasn't she?"

"I'm not sure you should be in here."

"Ah, yes, I understand. I shouldn't be. You're right. It's just that Elodie told me that she had a big stack of artwork at home. I always encouraged her, you know, to practice her art. She was very good. Some students are just special, you know? They're the ones that are going to stick in your mind."

He rubbed his forehead as if remembering that he was supposed to be feeling a little ill. "Well, thank you. It was nice to meet you. I'll be going now."

He gave me a smile as he exited the room, a smile that seemed not to be tethered to anything, barely there before it was gone.

Relieved I didn't actually have to ask him to leave, I followed him out and down the stairs.

"I'll be sure to let Mr McGregor know about the paintings," I told him as he walked ahead of me in the hall.

He turned. "Could I ask that you not mention it to the McGregors that I had a wee look at Elodie's paintings here? I was forgetting myself. I think the dizzy spell must have affected my judgement."

"I—certainly." I kicked myself as soon as I'd agreed to that. But his expression had seemed so earnest.

He gave me an appreciative nod and strode to the foyer.

Poking my head out the front door, I watched him leave.

8

ISLA

GREER RETURNED JUST before the McGregors were due to arrive and we had a quick lunch together. I'd spent the morning taking a walk about the bottom floor of the house and the exterior, looking for the best aspects. I hadn't taken any pictures. It had been a dull, heavy sort of day so far and I wanted to wait until the light and sun were at their best.

I'd changed out of my jeans and hoodie into a pantsuit and scarf about an hour ago, worried that I didn't look professional enough. Plus, I could hear my mother's voice at the back of my head, telling me I needed to *pull my look together*—something she was fond of saying. She liked very fitted clothing and hated the sloppy clothing I often wore.

I was relieved that Greer was with me right now and I didn't have to meet the McGregors alone. I felt the same way I had as a teenager going for an interview for my first job, a nervous bubble rising in my stomach. I told myself to calm down. I already had the job. I'd won it over a list of worthy contenders and there was nothing for me to be nervous about.

The car that pulled up in the driveway was a silver, very expensive-looking Volvo. The people who emerged from the car looked just like the kind of family who would travel in such a car. Well dressed and beautiful—a tall man with dark hair pulled back in a fashionable knot and his pretty wife, thick blonde waves of hair touching her shoulders. The toddler resembled one of those children in celebrity paparazzi shots: winter edition.

Alban and Jessica McGregor turned their heads in my direction in unison. Their expressions were half-hidden behind chic sunglasses, but they seemed a little stiff or something.

Greer seemed oblivious, taking my arm and walking me down the steps, parading me to my new clients. "Welcome home. This is—"

"What's going on?" Jessica demanded. Up close, I could see that her face was blotchy, as if she'd been crying. Her eyes seemed swollen beneath the sunglasses.

I flinched. This was worse than any introduction I could have pictured.

Alban simply stared at me, in a way that seemed both curious and scrutinising. The child gave me a shy glance while half burying herself in her mother's long tweed skirt.

"This is Isla Wilson," said Greer, undeterred. "The wonderful photographer from Sydney who'll be making Braithnoch look like something out of a dream."

"I hope I can do it justice," I said, forcing myself to speak. "Great to meet the three of you." I held out a hand in greeting to Jessica, hoping my voice didn't sound as shaken as I felt inside.

Jessica's shoulders crumpled. "I'm sorry, I—It's been a long trip. I have a shocking headache and I need to go lie down." Clutching the child's hand, she hurried away.

"Seems I've arrived at a bad time." Dropping my arm to my side, I glanced awkwardly from Greer to Alban.

"Please forgive my wife." Alban shook my hand, flashing a brief smile. "She's not her normal self at all—she's feeling quite ill. She'll be fine once she's had a rest. So, you're the photographer that Greer hired? An Australian, no less. You've come a long way to this little part of the world."

"Yes, a very long way," I said. "But Greer was very convincing that this job would be the right fit for me."

He nodded. "Our Greer could convince Eskimos to buy ice blocks."

"You'll be blown away by her work," said Greer. "I couldn't believe my luck in getting her. I'm excited to see what she'll produce."

"It's my understanding that you'll be here a couple of weeks—is that right?" he asked me.

"A month." Then I rushed to add, "But we can make it shorter. A week, if that suits better. And—"

"None of that," said Greer briskly. "I'm not taking shortcuts with this portfolio. It's taken a lot to arrange this."

"Of course," I told her apologetically. "I wasn't thinking." Somehow, in the space of a minute, this job had all gone wrong.

Greer slid an arm around my shoulders. "Oh, I just meant that you'll need that much time to do your thing. We don't want to go short-changing you. How about you go get some rest, now, and I'll meet you back at the house for dinner." She looked at Alban. "Seven 'o'clock?"

"Seven's fine." His gaze flicked over me. "We'll see you then, Isla."

I wanted nothing more than to run away and escape to the cottage, but I needed to tell Alban about Rory Kavanagh. At least, I'd tell him that Rory came to the house. My scalp prickled at the thought of holding back the information that Rory had been in Elodie's room. But I'd agreed not to tell. And considering the way things had gone so far with the McGregors, part of me was glad I didn't have to.

"I almost forgot," I said. "Someone came to the house a bit earlier. One of your daughter's teachers. Mr Kavanagh."

"What did he want?" Alban's reply came fast and sharp.

"He just wanted to leave some paintings of hers that he found. From school."

A deep crease indented Alban's forehead, a sudden hurt apparent in his eyes.

"I was so sorry to hear about her…about Elodie," I added.

"Thanks for letting me know about the paintings," he responded, not acknowledging my condolences for the loss of his daughter.

I gave him a tight smile of acknowledgment.

"Come on, then." Greer squeezed my shoulder. "I'll walk you to the cottage."

I went with Greer over the line of seven overgrown stepping stones, sensing that Alban was still standing there and watching us walk away.

"I'll be honest," I said, when we were out of earshot, "that was all pretty uncomfortable."

She sighed. "I know. They both knew and agreed to this, but it seems that they got too caught up in their affairs today to remember. Well, I'm assuming that Alban remembered, but Jessica...." She sighed again, this time long and heavily. "Her head is in the clouds most of the time."

"She seemed really upset," I said.

Greer turned to me as she unlocked the cottage door. "I'll admit that there is never really a good time with the McGregors. They have a lot of...issues."

"They do?"

"Unfortunately, yes. For years now. The loss of their daughter affected them both in very deep ways. So, please don't think that it's anything to do with you. I'm used to it. From my side of things, I'm simply doing my job and helping Alban along in his career. That's what he pays me to do. And you're here doing your job. That's all there is to it."

I stepped inside the cottage with Greer.

She went straight over to switch the heater on and then she filled the jug in the kitchen with water. "You look like you need a nice cup of tea."

"Thanks." I smiled. "I could use some tea right about now."

"How's the jet lag going?"

"I'm still really feeling it."

"Thought so. You look a little pale. Be sure to take it easy. There's no rush to get anything done."

I seated myself at the table. "Greer, I have a thought. I could still stay for the month, but I could go get some accommodation in town. I think that might work out best."

She clucked her tongue. "Then you'll risk missing the sunrises and sunsets at Braithnoch."

"But if my being here causes upset—?"

"Like I said, it's not you. Look, we're both professionals. I'm sure you've had your share of difficult clients?"

I nodded, exhaling. "You bet." Wryly, the thought came to me that she hadn't made any mention of difficult clients back when we were first discussing the job.

"It's the way it goes." She fetched two cups from the cupboard. "I'll be here many of the days, and you can call me if you need anything. I'm only just in town, so I can zip down here lickety-split."

Greer stayed and had tea with me and chatted some more. I was grateful for that. It helped me feel better after the tense meeting with the McGregors.

She rose from her seat after half an hour had gone by. "I'll be back for dinner. In the meantime, why not find a book to read—there's a shelf of them in there—or watch some TV. Or go for a walk if you feel up to it. And then you can have a proper talk with Jess and Alban later on at dinner and get to know them a little better. It's best if you don't sleep until your normal bedtime. Keep the body clock going."

"Thanks, Greer, for everything today."

She smiled warmly as she left. "I'm excited that you're here."

With Greer gone, the cottage fell quiet. I washed up the tea cups in the sink. From the tiny window in the kitchen, I saw a curtain brush back in the main house. Someone—possibly Mrs McGregor—was looking out in the direction of the cottage. I guessed the McGregors had a right to be curious about the stranger who was staying here on their property.

Taking up Greer's advice to do some reading, I went to inspect the book shelf. Alongside a slew of fiction titles were a couple of touristy books about the Highlands. I decided on those and nestled into bed with them. The first book I opened was a little dry—filled with facts and tiny, indistinct photos. I realised how sleepy I was as soon as I started reading. Greer was right though—I shouldn't let myself sleep.

I decided to write an email to Mum. I knew that most of all, what she'd want to know was how I was feeling. Was I well? Was I happy?

I tried my best to allay her fears, making everything sound rosy. Later, I'd snap a picture of the cottage and send it to her. She'd love that.

As I finished the email, I glanced at the view of the forest through the bedroom window. The sun had finally made an appearance, late afternoon rays sparking gold and red through the forest. The trees were so close that I could see a small bird hopping on a branch. Maybe I could go take some photos today, after all.

I sat up straight. Something else was in the forest.

Not something—*someone.*

I rose and padded over to the window.

The jacket. The hair. The lanky build. It was Rory Kavanagh.

Why had he returned?

As he moved from my line of sight, I walked out to the living room to keep my eye on him from the window there. Again, he disappeared from view, then he re-emerged out on the road. I caught a brief glimpse of him cycling away. I made a bet with myself that he'd been here the whole time.

He'd been wearing green and brown—good colours to choose if you wanted to be hard to spot in a forest, even if the trees were bare.

For all I knew, he had a perfectly good reason for being in the forest, but I couldn't think of one. If I saw Rory in the forest again, I'd tell the McGregors.

Changing back into jeans and a hoodie, I pulled on boots and a big coat. Then I grabbed my camera and headed out. The afternoon sun splintering through the trees really did look pretty.

I made my way up the hills. It quickly became obvious to me that I was seriously unfit.

To the far left, the sun rays were glinting on a line of craggy, rocky hills. The bottom boulders were drenched in green, mossed over and claimed by the earth, seeming as if the earth were pulling them down into itself. I snapped a few photos.

Squinting, I could just make out the remains of a crumbling stone cottage up there in the hills.

I decided not to head any closer to the rocky ranges. They were already mostly in shadow. I wanted to walk up to the group of scarecrows, but they were still a long distance from here. I liked the look of the sun in the forest. That meant walking across the moor to my right, but at least the moor was flat.

As I started across the moor, I felt the chill beginning to bite through every layer of clothing I wore. I made a mental note to wear a thicker jacket next time. Best to keep moving. I was wearing good walking boots—that was one thing I'd gotten right. I stopped to take a few pictures of the forest across the moor. Then, turning to get the sun behind me, I snapped a selfie. I checked the picture on my viewfinder. My cheeks were pink, and my hair blew freely under my knitted cap. I looked cold but alive. That was something that had been missing from the pictures of me over the past years. I was often smiling but there was no excitement in my eyes.

Braithnoch, for better or worse, was going to be the start of me challenging myself.

As I switched the camera off, I realised I'd have to be quick to get closer to the tree line before the sun dropped too low. Huffing, I ran in a bee line across the moors. The ground had seemed a lot flatter from up in the hills. But underfoot, it undulated in low peaks and troughs.

I'd never run a distance as long as this. I had a whole month here —I didn't have to rush like I did in my normal job to catch a scene before it vanished. Things were different in Braithnoch. There would be more sunsets over the forest.

I slowed to a steady pace.

By the time I'd made it, the sun had dropped lower than I would have liked. I wasn't going to get the shots I wanted. But at least now I knew the landscapes and time of sunset here better, I reasoned. I stepped towards the tree line. Stopping suddenly, I inhaled a heavy breath. It was actually the perfect time to take photos. The sun's rays ringed the tree tops, giving the impression of tall kings wearing dark gold crowns. I needed the right angle to capture what I was seeing in my mind's eye.

Taking a minute to catch my breath, I got my camera's settings right, and then began framing up shots. I hoped the pictures would look as powerful as they did in the moment, with the contrast between the stark, bare branches and the golden crowns of sunshine.

Satisfied that I'd achieved something good today, I packed the camera back into its bag. It'd be quicker to head along the tree line, all the way back.

The cold and fatigue made my head feel raw and sluggish as I stepped back inside the cottage. I uploaded the photos to online storage and curled up on the sofa. I made a half-hearted plan to listen to some music. But the room was warm now, lulling me into closing my eyes. The more I tried to stay awake, the more I could feel myself drifting towards sleep.

9

ISLA

I WOKE IN THE DARK. I'd been sleeping crunched into the tiny sofa. My limbs protested as I unfolded them.

Rubbing my neck, I glanced at the clock on the wall. 6.45pm. I was meant to be at dinner at seven. Hell. That didn't give me long to get ready.

My hand slicked from the back of my neck. Ugh, sweat. The heater had been running the whole time and the cottage was cooking.

After a two-minute shower, I felt a lot fresher. I dressed in a pair of my nicest jeans and a slimline jacket. With a minute to spare, I reapplied a light layer of makeup and brushed my hair out from its ponytail. I was as ready as I was going to get. I wasn't looking forward to dinner, but there was no avoiding it.

I turned the heater down to its lowest setting and stepped out.

Greer drove in just as I reached the front porch.

I waited for her. "I can't tell you how glad I am that you're coming to dinner tonight."

She shot me a smile and a wink. "I said I'd be here for you during your stay, and I meant it. I'm not going to abandon a poor wee lass to the wilds of Scotland—*and the McGregors*—on your first couple of days here."

The house was surprisingly warm inside, considering the huge expanses. It must have very good insulation and double glazing. I made a mental note to mention that to Alban later. It might win me a point or two with him. I had to attempt to win over my clients some-how. A month was a long time when you were practically living in someone's home.

Alban was in the kitchen. Jessica wasn't around. Their little girl was sitting at a child-sized table setting, scribbling with crayons.

"Hope you're cooking up a feast, Alban," called Greer. "I'm right starved."

He grinned. "One of your favourites."

"Well, thank goodness," she told him. "This is no time to be trying out one of your fancy gourmet meals. Too many of them have gone wrong."

"Ingrate." Alban washed a couple of tomatoes under the sink. He wore his hair back in the same style as he had earlier in the day, a chef's apron over his clothes.

I was relieved to hear the chatter between Greer and Alban. It made him seem a lot more approachable.

"Can I help with anything?" I asked, crossing the room to the kitchen with Greer.

He glanced at me. "I think I've got things under control. Hope you're well-rested, Isla."

"I am, thank you," I answered, wondering if he'd seen me madly running across the moor earlier.

Greer took a couple of steps over to Rhiannon and crouched down —somewhat awkwardly. She was one of those tall people who seemed not to be in total control of their gangly limbs. Her knees and elbows stuck out at odd angles. "Well, what are we drawing, hmmm? Is that a tree?"

Rhiannon shook her head. A ponytail on top of her fair head was half falling out. She wore a grey skirt, pink top and matching pink boots that seemed a little too formal for dinner at home.

"I know...is it Daddy?" asked Greer. "Daddy's got a big head."

"Aye, right." From the kitchen, Alban gave a short, protesting laugh.

Rhiannon giggled and shook her head again, then eyed me nervously.

Greer raised her eyes to me. "Wait, I don't think you two met properly earlier. Rhiannon, this is Isla. She's going to be staying in the cottage here. And she's going to be taking lots of pictures with her camera. Isla, this little moppet is Rhiannon. She likes to draw and paint and cook pumpkin scones with her Auntie Greer."

"Hello, Rhiannon." I walked across and knelt beside her. I knew from my photography work that getting down on the same level as small children made you seem a little less scary.

But in response, Rhiannon shrank back slightly.

"Oh, you two'll get used to each other in no time." Greer met my eyes, shrugging with a smile. "Okay now, Rhiannon, you're going to have to tell me what your drawing is. I'm all out of guesses."

In response, Rhiannon drew four spindly legs on her figure. She pointed at the picture with a tiny finger. "Ruff."

"Eh?" said Greer, angling her head around at Alban. "I need a baby translator. What is a ruff?"

A voice came from across the room. Jessica's. "Giraffe. That's her word for her toy giraffe."

Jessica stood in a stiff pose, wearing a grey pencil skirt and pale pink long-sleeved top. Her outfit looked a lot like Rhiannon's, apart from Rhiannon's little pink boots and tights. She came and fixed Rhiannon's ponytail.

"Well, that's a mighty fine giraffe, Rhiannon," said Greer. "Of course I knew it was a giraffe. What else could it be?"

Rhiannon looked pleased.

Greer shot me a lopsided *saved-by-the-bell* grin.

Jessica gave me a very different sort of grin—all tight and tense. "I have to apologise for not greeting you properly earlier. My stomach was upside-down and so was my head. I haven't been well lately."

I shook the limp hand that she proffered. "I'm sorry you've been ill."

"Time for dinner now. Please join us at the table, Isla." Jessica gathered her daughter up and sat her in the special child seat at the table. She began bringing bowls of food and items across from the kitchen.

I stood, my legs still feeling a little stiff from the long walk and the sleep on the sofa. "Let me help you with those."

"No," Jessica answered quickly, then took a breath. "Just relax. You're our guest. Come sit at the table. You too, Greer."

Greer and I seated ourselves directly across from the McGregors. The table was already set with plates and cutlery.

Dinner was lasagne and salad, served with crusty bread. It looked and smelled amazing.

"Did you make the bread, Alban?" asked Greer as Jessica served her a portion.

"No, I cheated and bought some." He smiled.

Jessica finished serving out the meals and started making up a small plate of food for Rhiannon.

"This is wonderful," I told Alban. "Really tasty."

I was actually relieved to know that he hadn't made the bread himself. It was a thing that made him seem more human. I was already feeling a slowly grinding unease in my stomach. How was I going to photograph him if I couldn't get some real sense of who he was?

Alban poured me a glass of red wine. "How did you go today, Isla? Did you have a good look around Braithnoch?"

Okay, so you did see me wandering off this afternoon. I nodded. "Yes. Well, not all of it. I had a wander around the moor and the edges of the forest."

"Careful of the peat marsh. At the far end," said Alban.

"Oh, yes, the marsh. I'd forgotten about that," Greer mumbled through a mouthful of crunchy salad. "But I'm sure you wouldn't go heading into a load of sticky mud just for a photograph." She laughed. "Wouldn't be nice to have wee Isla stuck out there in the middle of a bog."

"Well, I've done some crazy things for a photograph before," I admitted. "In one of my last assignments before I came here, I was on a yacht in Sydney Harbour, taking pictures of another yacht that was racing that day. The weather was stinking hot and I'd already gotten too much heat. I was trying to get a special shot, sitting on the railing on the bow and leaning way over. And then I fainted, falling backwards, straight into the harbour."

Greer's eyes opened wide and she gasped. *"No."*

I grinned at her. "Pretty stupid of me, right?"

"You could have drowned," said Jessica in a serious tone. She dabbed at the sauce on Rhiannon's chin with a napkin.

"That's what my mother said," I quipped.

My words fell flat with Jessica. Alban was also staring at me strangely. What I'd considered a funny story obviously made me seem less than professional in their eyes.

I sipped my wine, feeling distinctly uncomfortable. Maybe they were wondering if I'd been drinking too much that day on the yacht. I hadn't been drinking at all. Alcohol and I didn't mix. Toying with the stem of my glass, I debated whether I should mention my seizures. Then I made a firm decision not to. The subject hadn't really come up.

"Anyway, the client fished me out, so no harm done," I added, trying to fill in the awkward space that had opened up.

"Sounds like your work takes you on some big adventures," said Greer brightly.

"Not really," I admitted. "I generally accept work close to home. Lucky that I live in a big city."

Greer nodded. "Oh yes, you did tell me that the first time we spoke over the phone. Well, we're very glad you're here with us now."

With a clatter, Jessica dropped the plate that she was feeding Rhiannon from, its contents splattering over the table and the little girl's clothes.

"God, I'm such a butterfingers," Jessica exclaimed.

"It's okay, Jess," said Alban. "We'll get her cleaned up and I'll grab her another plate."

"It's not okay," Jessica stressed. "These fabrics will stain. Anyway, she was finished and just playing with her food."

"You've barely touched your own," Greer told her. "I can go change Rhiannon while you eat."

"I'm fine." Rising, Jessica took Rhiannon from her chair. The next minute, I heard Jessica's shoes heading up the wooden staircase.

Alban sighed, taking a gulp of his wine. Greer carried the conversation for the next few minutes, which I was grateful for. I didn't seem to be able to say the right thing around these people.

But then a phone call took Greer away, and it was just Alban and me sitting at the dinner table. I glanced across at him with a quick close-lipped smile, finishing up my last mouthfuls of lasagne.

Okay, relax, I told myself. This is your chance to find out more about him.

"Braithnoch is beautiful," I began.

"I'm glad you think so," he replied. "Greer tells me that you've never been to Scotland before?"

"No. It's actually my first time in the UK."

"Hmmm." He studied me for a second. "So, tell me what life is like for you in Sydney?"

"Well, to be honest most of my time is taken up with my photography. I seem to be always either at a job or editing images."

"No hobbies?"

"Nothing too dramatic. I go out cycling sometimes, around the harbour. I like old movies. I read." Shrugging, I gulped a mouthful of wine.

"Boyfriend?"

"Not at the moment." I kicked myself for answering that. It was too personal. I'd had clients ask me that question before and it was always intrusive, whatever their reason. Some of my male clients made it their mission to try to flirt with every woman who crossed their path. Alban hadn't seemed like the flirting type. But I might have been wrong about that. Maybe Jessica had good reason to be arguing with him.

Alban turned his head slightly and glanced in the direction that Jessica had gone. Was he checking to see if she'd walked back into the room and heard his last question?

I decided to steer the conversation away from myself, maybe even attempt to rescue his opinion of me. "I'm impressed with the design of your home. It's so modern, yet it just fits so well into the landscape."

A small smile flitted on his lips. Was that because he knew why I'd changed the topic?

"That's what I aimed for," he told me. "The house was made from the land. Centuries ago, the first house built on this land was made of wood from the forest. Eventually, that was torn down to build a cottage of stone, up in the hills. After that, it was decided that a house on the flat, closer to the entry would be best, and a second stone house was built. The stone of the old part of the house was cut right here in Braithnoch. The new addition is clad in wood from the forest. So, you could say it has come full circle."

"I think I spotted the old house in the hills a bit earlier."

He nodded. "Yes, you would have seen it from where you were. I've long had delusions of restoring it, but so far I haven't made a start."

I wondered how long he'd been watching me for from the house. "Well, it's wonderful that you've kept the connection strong to the land's history on the new extension. I love the look of the wood on the exterior."

"Thank you. It's scorched larch. From the forest here."

"Is larch a traditional Scottish building material?"

"It's Japanese larch. But my ancestors planted it hundreds of years ago. Many properties in Scotland were planted with different species of larch."

"So, Japanese larch has become part of the identity of Braithnoch?"

"Yes, very much so. It was planted sometime in the 1800s."

I finished my wine without realising it. I hadn't meant to drink it all. "The name, Braithnoch, where did that come from?"

Alban sat back in his chair. "Quite a bit of history in that, too. In 1672, a small battle happened here. Really you could call it a bit of a skirmish. But three of my people—all brothers—spilled their blood on the land. The only brother who survived—Griogair—decided that he should buy the land in honour of their deaths. The brothers' last name was Braithnoch."

"Wow, what a story."

"Aye." A wistful smile spread across his face.

He was really very handsome when he smiled, I decided.

"Are there any descendants of Griogair's that bear the name, Braithnoch?" I asked.

"Unfortunately, no," he replied. "But I am Griogair's closest blood descendant. He had three daughters, and when they married, he divided his land into four. It was called Braithnoch square. This lot of land was where Griogair lived, and the other lots are where the Chandlishes, the Flanagans and the Keenans live today. Those families are distant blood descendants of Griogair. Only this lot of land retained the name, Braithnoch."

"Well, knowing the history of Braithnoch helps me," I told him. "And I'll be sure to play up the look and texture of the house's stone walls and larch cladding in my photographs. I'll emphasise that as much as the modern lines."

"It's a funny thing about designs that seem modern," Alban mused. "Because in time, that will pass, and they'll no longer be modern. I think the challenge is to design something that's timeless. Something that merges with nature."

I nodded. "Do you think it's true that, in the past, buildings weren't designed with that function in mind. I mean, people seemed to want to separate themselves from nature quite a bit."

He looked at me closely. "Yes. I believe so."

I exhaled silently. Finally, I'd said something right. "What would you say is your concept of a home, Alban?"

He stroked his chin. "Hmmm. Most homes are like closets—a place to lock ourselves away from the world. People are all caught up with bringing obscenely edited snippets of the natural world indoors —potted plants and floral wallpaper and the like. Myself, I prefer to be confronted by nature, in all its moods. And I like the exterior to be a living, breathing skin rather than resembling a dead shell."

Alban would hate the house where I lived, with all its potted palm trees. I liked them as much as my mother did, but I wasn't about to admit to that now. The way his gaze was fixed on me, I worried that my expression would reveal the awful truth—my house was filled with palm trees and palm-tree wallpaper.

"Can I offer you another glass of wine?" he asked.

"No, thank you. I'm not a big wine drinker. Just that glass alone has made me sleepy, I'll admit."

"You do look tired. Perhaps you should go and have a good, solid sleep. I'd best go check on Jess." A vaguely distracted look came over his face.

I stood. "Thank you so much for dinner. I'll clean up the dinner things before I go."

"Greer and I will do the clean-up. You're obviously still recovering from jet lag. Goodnight." He left the room before I could object.

Unsure whether to feel pleased or dismissed, I wandered out into the hallway to find Greer and tell her goodnight. I caught sight of her through the door of a small sitting room. She stood by a window, facing away from me, one ear to her phone. She was crying, saying in a subdued voice, "No, I didn't want this. You know I didn't...."

I backstepped quickly and headed back through the dining area, feeling like I'd eavesdropped on a highly personal conversation. It seemed odd to find the bright and capable Greer in such deep distress.

A single, dim light illuminated the path from the house back to the cottage. I felt almost spooked walking it alone at night. The glass of wine made my head a little woozy and I stumbled here and there on the uneven stepping stones.

Stepping inside the cottage, I shut and locked the door. During the day, I'd wished the cottage was further away from the house, for added privacy. But at night it seemed isolated and vulnerable.

I put the kettle on to boil and went to change into pyjamas. Tonight had gone a little better than my first meeting with the McGregors. But I still hadn't been able to connect with Jessica. My phone rang—it was Greer.

"Isla, gosh, sorry. I lost track of time. Did you make it back to the cottage okay?"

"Of course," I told her. "Alban sent me off. He wouldn't let me help with clearing anything away."

"He's...used to that. Jessica is unwell quite often."

I stirred my tea. "That's not good—about Jessica. Does she have some kind of condition?"

"Nothing with a name as far as I know. Just a lot of headaches and tummy upsets. Well, I won't see you most of tomorrow. I have some things to attend to. But I'll be back for dinner. At seven, like tonight."

"I'll see you then. And thanks so much again for everything."

I sat nursing my tea in the dim kitchen. I checked my phone and found five messages from Mum—all asking how I was. Typing out a quick text, I let her know that I'd just had dinner with the McGregors and then said goodnight.

Crawling into bed, I pulled the covers up high. I felt myself quickly drifting into a heavy sleep.

I woke with a start hours later.

A twig snapped somewhere outside my bedroom window.

Is that what woke me? Is someone walking about out there?

Immediately, I thought of the school teacher, Rory.

10

ISLA

MY EYES FLEW OPEN.

A shadow moved in the mirrored wardrobe directly across from me. The mirror reflected the bedroom window.

Remaining perfectly still, I eyed the mirror. A gasp caught silently in my throat. Moonlight cast a feeble light across a man's face.

Alban.

As soon as I'd seen him in the mirror, he was gone. I could hear him walking away into the forest, twigs crunching underfoot. I listened until the sound of his footsteps faded away.

What was he doing there? Spying on me? Trying to see if I slept naked? I checked the time. Half past one in the morning. Why was he even outside at this time of night?

He wouldn't know that I'd seen him. I hadn't turned to face the window.

I stayed awake for the next hour, in an alert mood, until fatigue pulled me into sleep again.

In the morning, I roused with a shiver. Fog completely obscured the view outside the window.

An image of Alban's reflection in the mirror jumped into my head.

I wanted to march right up to the house and ask him what he was doing there. I knew that if I did that, this job would be over. It would be too awkward to continue. I'd faced creepy behaviour before in a job and put up with it. I'd been a lot younger then—seventeen.

I sat on the side of the bed, deliberating. I was twenty-six years old. Not seventeen. As soon as I came across Alban alone, I'd ask him straight out. I guessed I'd be on a plane soon afterwards.

Right now, I'd carry on as if nothing had happened.

I decided to head out and grab some shots—Braithnoch would look gorgeous through a veil of fog. I prepared my equipment, choosing just one lens and fitted it to the camera. I didn't want to go changing lenses out in misty weather and risk getting moisture inside the camera.

After dressing in warm clothing, I headed to the kitchen to make myself a quick breakfast of porridge. Then stepped out into a world of swirling white.

I allowed myself to feel a small hum of excitement. Heading into the Scottish fog felt like an adventure. This was what I'd travelled all this way for. To extend my range of photography and extend myself. Maybe the adventure would all be over once I'd confronted Alban, but for now, I was going to enjoy this.

The fog seemed theatrical, sets of heavy white curtains showing me exactly what it wanted me to see and no more. The bare larch trees were hauntingly beautiful—tall and thin, with fragile branches that spanned to give each tree the shape of a feather.

What are you showing me, Braithnoch? What do you want me to know?

I braved the thick fog, wandering along the path that led to the hills. I hoped that going higher would get me out of the thickest area of fog. But the mist stayed unrelenting, shielding almost everything from me. The distant mountains were just shadows that floated in the sky.

It was a hopeless mission. I stumbled about, losing and finding my way again. With my luck, I'd end up blundering into the peat bogs that Alban and Greer had warned me about.

A warm cup of tea and a book in front of the heater was about as brave as I was going to get until the fog thinned.

Retracing my steps, I returned to the cottage. I switched on the heater, watching the fake, flickering flames. It was soothing. The cottage quickly warmed.

The thought came to me that I could get used to this kind of life, once I got used to the slow, subtle rhythm. Braithnoch revealed what it wanted at its own pace.

My phone's ringtone shook me from my thoughts. It was Mum, again asking if I was okay and if I liked the people I was staying with. I wasn't sure how to answer her second question. Alban was proving to be strange in a number of ways. As a couple, Alban and Jessica had deep problems. I felt tension buzzing underneath everything they said to each other and about each other.

I just told Mum I was doing great and that the McGregors were very hospitable. As an afterthought, I added that they dressed like celebrities—the classier ones. She was fond of details about what people were wearing.

"I'm glad the people are nice," she said, "What about your meds? How are you going with them? You've been remembering to take them? You haven't been out nightclubbing or anything, have you?"

"Of course. I mean, of course I've been remembering to take them. No, I haven't been nightclubbing. I'm out here in the sticks, not in the city. So, stop worrying." I said the last bit with a smile in my voice to reassure her.

As I replaced the phone in my pocket, I realised I'd told her an unwitting fib. I'd run out of the cottage this morning without a thought to my medications. I couldn't remember if I'd taken them last night either—the wine at dinner had fuzzed my mind.

The best thing to do was just to take my morning dose as usual. Then settle in and read until the fog lifted.

After selecting a book from the shelves, I stepped across to the tiny kitchen bench where I'd left my seizure medicines.

They weren't there.

My handbag was lying open and my passport was on the bench. I hadn't gotten my passport out, had I? Had someone been in here, looking through my stuff? I checked for my wallet. It was there, with the money still inside.

Perhaps, in my exhausted haze last night, I'd been looking for something. Forgetting about the bag and the passport, I kept looking for my medication. In a flurry, I checked my suitcase, and the bathroom and bedroom drawers in the cottage. I even checked cupboards I was sure I hadn't opened yet.

My medications were missing, and I couldn't think where they'd be. Unless, instead of putting them on the bench, I'd put them in my bag and they'd somehow dropped out on the hills. I couldn't think why I would have taken the whole lot with me, but I'd been a little shaken after seeing Alban at my window last night. I might have done it without thinking.

I'd have to retrace my steps and try to find them. Pulling my boots on again and a knitted cap, I headed out. As a last thought, I threw the camera bag over my shoulder before I shut the door. It was a habit for me to take my camera everywhere.

The mist was eroding.

A thwack thwack sound came from just over the rise, between the cottage and the road.

Curious, I turned and went in the direction of the noise.

I didn't recognise Alban at first. Through the mist, I could just make out the back of a man in a loose, chequered shirt and faded jeans. He lifted the axe high and brought it down hard on the wedge, sending wood chips splintering. There were defined angles in the strikes he took at the wood, precise and clean.

It was a perfect rustic scene. Putting everything else but my job out of my mind for a moment, I took my camera from my bag, I carefully framed up the picture and then snapped a couple of images. Stepping closer, I took a couple more.

I must have been too noisy, because his back twisted, and he pivoted, pushing up his safety goggles. "Did you just photograph me?"

"Yes, I did. Hope you don't mind."

He stood observing me for a moment, his brow crinkling.

"I just thought it could be good to put those kinds of shots into the mix," I said, defending myself against his silence. "Y'know, down-to-earth photos, that kind of thing."

He shrugged in an easy, good-natured way. "Show the man behind the public image, eh?"

"Yes. That's what I'm here to do."

"Go ahead. But it's all fake. Those pictures you see of people living their lives. All they show is a heavily edited version of their real lives."

"Greer told me you weren't exactly impressed by the idea of doing the shoot for the magazine."

"Well, you've got that right. Everyone but me knows what's good for my career, apparently." He paused. "If you don't mind, I have a mountain of blasted wood to chop."

"If you prefer I didn't take photos of you unawares, then I won't." I drew in a quick breath of damp, misty air. "And I'd prefer that you didn't look in on me through my window at night."

He stared at me for a moment with a surprised expression, then exhaled noisily. "I'm sorry, Isla. I go for a walk every night. It's a habit of mine. I don't sleep well, so I go out and do a round of the grounds, checking on everything. Then, if I'm lucky, I can go to sleep."

"So, I'm now included on the list of things that you check on each night?"

"No. I wasn't checking on you, I was checking that all was all right. Ever since the events that happened with my daughter, I can't rest. I don't trust that someone isn't out there, you know? But I won't check the cottage again. I'm dead sorry that I startled you. I didn't mean for that to happen."

I felt the stiffness in my back and shoulders relax. It was an explanation I hadn't thought of. I hoped he was genuine. "That sounds awful. I mean, never to be able to rest at night."

"Sometimes I feel like a ghost knocking about Braithnoch. There was my life before and my life now."

"I'm sorry."

"Eh, you don't need to be sorry. It's my lot." He shrugged and brushed back his hair with the palm of one hand. "I'd better get back to this."

Turning, he struck the log with his axe.

As I strode away, I could hear the blunt blows of the axe echoing through the forest.

I could either accept his explanation or reject it. I decided to accept it. The exchange with Alban had been awkward but I was glad I hadn't held back.

I retraced my earlier steps along the path towards the hills as far as I could. Until I was certain I'd ventured further than I had the first time. I could see the ground now. No plastic package of medicines turned up anywhere.

I couldn't go without the pills. It was a bother, but I'd have to go see a doctor in town. I wasn't about to ask Alban or Jessica for a ride, so the only option was to call a taxi or go for a bicycle ride. I didn't even know if they had taxis in Greenmire. Everything seemed so remote here.

I opted for a bicycle. I just hoped they were road worthy.

Heading into the tiny shed that Greer had said the bikes were kept, I selected the women's bicycle. I guessed it was Jessica's. I hoped she wouldn't mind. Donning the helmet, I wheeled down the driveway and then headed out. The bike was a little rusty but not too terrible.

The hilly road dipped down into a section where the fog was still like pea-soup. The first time a small truck passed me, I nearly jumped off my seat. It seemed to come out of nowhere. I regretted not calling a taxi—a misty day was not the kind of weather in which to go out cycling down a country road. I'd get toppled like a bowling pin if a vehicle just happened to swerve in my direction.

Both relief and dread came at the start of the incline of a hill. The fog was thinner at the crest of a hill, but the inclines were more extreme than I realised. When Greer had driven me into town, I'd been too focused on the scenery and Greer's gossip about the neighbours to notice.

Puffing hard, I finally made it into Greenmire. The trip had taken a good hour.

The streets of the town were busier than I expected—*where did all these people come from?* I chained the bike on a street pole.

I located a medical surgery and asked if I could be seen by a doctor. At first, the pointy-nosed receptionist said the books were full, but when I explained my situation, she'd said she could give me a five-minute slot with a Dr. Fiona McKendrick—but only if I was prepared to wait a couple of hours. She made it sound as if there were an alternative clinic I could attend if I wanted an earlier appointment, but it ended up being that this was the only clinic in town.

I told her I'd wait.

The clinic was filled with retirees and mothers with small children. Lots of coughing and sneezing. I wondered if the pointy-nosed receptionist caught one bug after the other working here. I took a seat as close to the door as possible, braving the chill for a chance that the greater air flow here would help thin out the bugs in the air.

The two hour-wait turned into almost three before my name was called. I hadn't had lunch and my stomach was protesting.

I stood, gathering up my coat and handbag, feeling awkward as all eyes tracked my movements. I knew exactly why everyone was doing that—the boredom of waiting got to you and you started wondering what the other people had wrong with them. Plus, I was a stranger in their town.

"I'm grateful you could squeeze me in," I told the doctor as I sat myself down inside her room.

She was thin and red-haired, with serious pale eyes. "That's fine. I couldn't see you go without your medication. So, are you from New Zealand? Australia?"

"Australia. Sydney."

"Ah. I wasn't quite certain of the accent. Here for a holiday?"

"No, unfortunately. I'm working. I arrived two days ago."

She smiled. "Oh, well, hopefully you can take a break now and again and go sightseeing. Now, did you bring any scripts with you?"

"Yes, I have them here." I produced the scripts from my handbag.

"Okay, these medications shouldn't be a problem. Might be a day or so ordering one of them in."

"That's okay."

"How did you manage to lose what you had?"

"I'm not sure, to be honest. I've dropped them somewhere. Careless, I guess."

"Well, as long as you're here, I might as well check on your health. Have you been feeling well?"

"Just a bit of jet lag."

"Any seizures lately?"

"I've been pretty good. I had one seizure though a fortnight before I came here."

She raised her eyebrows. "Okay, that's very recent. Were you doing anything out of routine prior to that instance?"

"I'd just been pushing myself too hard at work. Putting too much stress on myself."

"Yes. That'll do it. Stress is a big no-no. What kind of work are you doing here in Scotland?"

"Just my usual. I'm a professional photographer."

"Oh, nice. I love photography. With me it's just a hobby though, of course." She bent her head as she wrote out a script. "Do make sure you don't go pushing yourself to extremes again. Do you have a full work schedule at the moment?"

"Nothing too busy. I have a whole month to put a portfolio together, and most of the photography will be happening right where I'm staying. It's at a place called Braithnoch, just down the road."

Her eyes flicked up to me in surprise, pen pausing mid-air.

"Braithnoch?"

"Yes. My client is Alban McGregor. He's an architect—"

"Oh, I know who *Alban* is." Her voice was almost harsh as she spoke his name.

"Of course," I replied. "I should have realised you'd know the McGregors, this being a small town."

She returned to writing out the script. "What's he like to work for?" Her tone seemed casual now, but I immediately understood that it wasn't casual at all. It was the same tone I'd heard people use when they had a keen interest in procuring some information, but they didn't want you to know that.

"He's, uh, very professional," I answered. "A little aloof. He's not going to be an easy subject when it comes to the portraiture. I'm leaving that to last. But to be fair, I've only just met him. I had dinner with him and his wife, Jessica, last night."

"Jessica—oh, she's lovely. I've known her since she was a teenager." After a moment, she added, "I've known Alban that long, too," but without any kind of recommendation.

"I'm sorry, I might have this wrong, but you don't sound fond of Alban?"

She straightened, smoothing strands of hair back from around her face. "I'm sorry I gave you that impression." After a moment, she took out a small card from a drawer behind her desk and handed it to me. "Do call me if you need anything or if you have any concerns."

Thanking her, I stood and tucked the card into my jacket pocket.

I decided to stay in town and browse the shops, stopping for a tea, pie and a doughnut. Before leaving, I grabbed a loaf of freshly baked bread from the bakery and some light foods to snack on. It was just after 2pm by the time I began cycling back to Braithnoch.

My thoughts jumped back to the business card in my pocket. Did doctors here normally hand you their cards and tell you that you could call them anytime? In Sydney, you'd have fat chance of that. If you had even a small concern, you'd have to make an appointment through one of their front desk receptionists. And then pay for the visit. But this was a small country town and maybe things were different here.

Still, did Dr McKendrick give me the card because she was worried about something? Her tone seemed to change as soon as I'd mentioned Alban. Her view of Alban and Jessica seemed almost opposite to Greer's. Greer, from what I could tell, thought a lot of Alban but was frustrated with Jessica. I guessed I'd be making up my own mind about the pair of them soon enough.

11

ISLA

THE CALVES of my legs were tight and burning by the time I made it back from the town. The mist was still clinging to Braithnoch in the outer reaches of its forest, bleaching it to a pale palette of greys and whites.

Exhausted, I wheeled the bike into the shed.

I was startled to see Jessica standing at the entrance when I turned to leave.

She looked extremely pretty, with straightened hair and perfect makeup. Except for her vaguely tense expression, she could be a magazine model. She wore the same pastel hues I'd seen her in on the previous days, her fingers laced together over her abdomen. Her pose reminded me of a client I had in the early days—a Sydney socialite who'd just recovered from uterine cancer, her hands always protecting her stomach.

She eyed me from head to foot. I was keenly aware that my hair, already damp from the mist, had become hopelessly sweaty underneath the bike helmet, and my face was heated from the exercise.

"Alban and I will be away for the weekend," she told me. "Rhiannon is turning two in a few days, and we'll be seeing some of my family in Edinburgh for an early birthday thing. Hopefully Greer will be around to have dinner with you. I've made sure we've lots of fresh food in the fridge and pantry." A nervous tone ran through her voice.

"Happy birthday to Rhiannon," I replied. "I'll be fine. I probably have enough right here in the cottage. Besides what I bought in town just now." I held up my bags. "I've actually just been to the bakery."

"The bakery?" She glanced over at the bicycle. "You rode all the way into town? Goodness, that's a hike. I would have given you a lift in."

"Oh, I like going for long rides." That wasn't quite true, but it was true enough. I'd enjoyed the independence of being able to get away from Braithnoch on my own.

"Well, be careful on these foggy days. The visibility can be quite poor."

I smiled ruefully. "So I discovered."

A frown stippled her forehead. "I should have warned you about the fogs. They can be extreme, here. Never mind, you're back again safely. Hope you've been okay staying out in the cottage. I imagine it can feel a wee bit scary out there on your own."

"I'm liking the quiet, to be honest. A refreshing change from Sydney."

"Good." She twisted her fingers around her wedding ring, her eyes hesitant. "I feel that I didn't get a chance to chat with you last night. What made you decide on this particular job, Isla?"

"Just looking for a change, I guess."

"So, you just found our little ad in the magazine?"

"It was also posted online."

"Oh, okay. Greer arranged all that. She's a lot savvier with that kind of thing than me. How's everything going so far?"

"Things are good. I have lots of ideas. Alban's probably not going to be the easiest subject to capture, but I'll manage it."

"Oh? Yes, Alban can be a bit difficult. Look, I think Greer's given you too much to do. I know a local photographer who can handle the portrait side of things. This photographer is a bit of a gruff old billy-goat—he'll be able to wrangle my Alban."

"Oh gosh, no, I didn't mean to complain or anything. I have clients like this all the time. I just need to learn to be firmer." I grinned. "Like a billygoat."

She returned a smile that didn't reach into her eyes. "Well, I'd best let you get on with things."

Stepping back, she allowed me space to move out of the shed.

"I meant to tell you," I said, "your photography is lovely. I saw your images of the snow in the hallway. Have you thought of taking it up professionally?"

She batted that idea away with a slim hand. "Alban wouldn't be happy with that. He'd prefer I be here with Rhiannon. He's very traditional. I used to do nursing, but not since Rhiannon was born."

"What about *you*?" I said carefully. "What do you want to do?" It was a risk being so personal with her, but I hoped she wouldn't take it the wrong way. Maybe I could find a way of making friends with her, after all. Photography could be a common ground.

She shook her head. "Alban's work takes up all the space in this family. That's how it is sometimes in marriages. I guess I knew it when I married him—he was always ambitious."

I inhaled a short breath. "Why don't you come out with me later today? We can take photos of Braithnoch together."

"That sounds lovely. I haven't really thought to take pictures of the scenery here. I guess I've always been caught up taking pictures of my girls." A sadness gathered in the corners of her lips and eyes.

Two cars drove in, straight past the cottage. The first was Alban's. He turned his head, noticing Jessica and I standing there together, a frown causing a deep crease in his forehead. The second car was Greer's. She smiled and waved.

"Isla," Jessica said, "I'll have to say no to the photography. It was a nice thought, but I really just don't have the time or the energy. And it's really too difficult with Rhiannon to take care of."

I didn't have a young child and didn't know what it took to look after one, but it seemed to me that there was something that was not quite right with Jessica, but I didn't know what it was.

Greer stopped her car and jumped out, running back up the driveway towards us. Alban continued driving up to the house.

"Is Rhiannon still having her nap?" called Greer, as she made her way over. "I told her we'd make some drop scones for afternoon tea." She looked across at me. "How about you? Fancy some nice hot drop scones?"

I gave her a confused smile. "What's a drop scone?"

"Oh," Greer said, "you're in for a treat. They're like pancakes...or flapjacks—not sure what you call them in Australia—but they're decidedly yummier."

"Sounds good to me," I said. The rest I'd wanted to take would have to wait.

"Yes, Rhiannon's still sleeping," Jessica told Greer. "I shouldn't wake her. She gets terribly grumpy."

A grin dimpled Greer's cheek. "I can wait for her to wake. I haven't any work this afternoon."

I sensed that Jessica wasn't happy about Greer's intrusion into her house, but she said nothing more.

I put my bags away in the cottage and the three of us walked up the driveway together. I wished Jessica had agreed to the photography. It might have been nice to have some girl company out on the moor.

I perched on a stool in the kitchen while Greer started pulling things out from the cupboards. Jessica seemed a bit disconcerted by the mess.

Alban walked down the stairs with a very sleepy Rhiannon.

"You didn't go waking her, did you?" Jessica rushed to take her from him.

"I went to check on her and she was awake." He shrugged. "If you'll all excuse me, I'll be in the office."

"Yes, go away Daddy." Greer shooed him away. "We're making some very yummy drop scones and you'll just eat them all up!"

"I'll be back for the scones." Alban grinned as he walked away in the hallway.

Rhiannon suddenly perked up, clapping her hands.

"Not too much sugar and jam, Greer," Jessica warned.

"Of course not." Greer winked at Rhiannon, making her giggle.

Jessica lifted Rhiannon into her highchair and switched on a small TV nearby, putting it onto a children's show.

Jessica seemed a little more relaxed now, helping Greer with the pancake mixture. Greer was a whizz with the pancakes, making a high stack and then dividing them up on plates. She presented Jessica and me with a plate of three fluffy pancakes with strawberry jam, and a plate for Rhiannon.

"Oh dear, I forgot to tell Alban the scones were ready," Greer said, wiping her hands.

Jessica rose quickly. "I'll take him a plate." She hurried away with the stack of five pancakes that Greer gave her.

Greer caught my eye. "I think she's a wee bit tense at the moment. It's coming up to the anniversary of when Elodie…."

I understood immediately. "Oh no. How sad."

She nodded. "But what can you do? Life goes on. How's the scones?"

"Delicious," I told her. "If I ate like this every day, I soon wouldn't fit into my clothes."

"Nonsense," she replied. "It's good cold-weather fare. And nothing wrong with some meat on your bones."

I was about to point out that there was very little meat on Greer's bones, then stopped myself. She might be one of those people who were unable to put on weight even if they wanted to.

Jessica returned to the dining room, heading straight across to her daughter. "No, sweetheart. Don't play with the food. You'll just get sticky fingers."

Rhiannon rubbed her hands together, seemingly to investigate the degree of stickiness.

Her mother sighed. "I think your little tummy must be full." Grabbing a damp cloth, she began cleaning the toddler's hands.

The children's show on the TV abruptly changed to a news broadcast:

Next week will mark the two-year anniversary of the death of Greenmire schoolgirl, Elodie McGregor, who was abducted outside her Greenmire home. Eight-year-old Elodie died five days after the abduction due to the effects of the sleeping medication she'd been forced to take. She was found in a playhouse in the woods surrounding her home. Authorities are no closer to discovering who is responsible for this shocking crime—

Greer practically flew across the room to switch the TV off.

Just before the TV screen went blank, an aerial image flashed up of the forest, pinpointing the location of the playhouse. The trees were bare, as they were now. The aerial picture had shown a thick line showing the route the abductor had taken out of the forest.

I frowned. Had I seen the exact line of that route somewhere before? The route was very distinctive, consisting of oddly straight lines instead of curving around the trees. Like a soldier marching. Who would walk—or run—through a forest like that?

A cry choked from Jessica's throat and every part of her seemed to crumple, her hands shaking as she wiped Rhiannon's face. Rhiannon, oblivious that it was her sister's face that had just flashed up on the screen, clapped her hands, still fascinated by the sticky jam.

"Jess?" Greer whirled around to her. "If you need to take some time out, we can watch Rhiannon."

Nodding, Jessica stood. With her head bent low, she headed upstairs. Greer and I exchanged sad glances.

Greer lifted Rhiannon out from the highchair. "C'mon, Rhi, where's that lovely tea set of yours? I'll pour you out a nice, warm tea."

Rhiannon lit up, taking several trips to fetch an exquisite, ceramic set of teacups and saucers. They looked way too fragile to be children's toys. By the way that Rhiannon was cradling them in her arms, I guessed that her mother had instructed her to be careful with them.

Greer set a cup and saucer down on Rhiannon's child-sized table and poured some tea. Then she let Rhiannon put the milk and sugar in and stir it.

"Could I have a tea, too, please, Greer?" I said, playing along.

"Of course you may, Isla," said Greer, winking at me.

We set up the whole tea set on the table. I cut miniature round shapes out of a leftover pancake and arranged two of them on each plate. The little girl almost fainted with delight.

Half an hour passed before Jessica returned. She'd redone her hair and makeup and announced that she was taking Rhiannon to the park.

Greer walked me out to the cottage. "I'll be back for dinner a bit later on."

"Oh, good. It'll just be you and me. The McGregors will be out."

She raised an eyebrow. "They are? They're normally such homebodies."

"Jessica told me they'll be going away for the weekend. For Rhiannon's second birthday."

"Oh, of course. Of course that's coming up." She sighed. "Rhiannon's birthday and Elodie's abduction—those two events will always be linked, sadly. I'm glad they're taking Rhiannon away and making her day special. There was no party on her birthday last year."

"She seemed to love playing tea parties."

Greer's thin eyebrows knitted into a frown. "Just between you and me, I don't think she gets to play nearly enough. Jessica is focused on protecting her—understandably enough—but Rhiannon rarely even gets to play with other kiddies. Well, I'll see you later on. Best toddle off to the office and get some work done."

As soon as I was inside the cottage, I found myself curling up on the sofa with a blanket. I felt guilty that I hadn't achieved anything today. I hadn't taken a single photograph. But I was aching and exhausted from the lengthy bike ride today and desperately needed to rest. Putting ear phones in, I listened to my favourite music on my phone.

Outside the window, the light was still drab. The mist had disappeared, and a wind had blown in, shaking the branches like a madman. I had to admit that the cold was starting to get to me.

Already, I longed for a warm Sydney day.

You're just tired, I reminded myself.

I was glad the McGregors wouldn't be here for dinner. The constant tension between them set my teeth on edge.

Glancing back at the trees, I was reminded of the news segment on the TV, and the aerial image that had been shown. I remembered the precise path that the abductor had taken when they exited the forest on the night that Elodie went missing. Where had I seen it before? Had I come across it in town today?

It was going to bug me until I remembered. I always noticed lines. With my photography, I paid close attention to the invisible lines that connected and dissected a scene. Such as a horizon sitting on the two-thirds line. Or a subject positioned to the middle or off-centre of a grid. Or a child's kite flying high on a diagonal, drawing attention to the rising sun.

There were invisible clues in lines.

12

ELODIE

Greenmire, Scottish Highlands, December 2015

ELODIE TRIED TO WAKE. Boots crunched the ground all around her, somewhere out there in the darkness.

Urgent voices called her name.

Elodie! Elodie! Elodie!

Who were they? Did she do something wrong? She remembered nothing. Her head felt somehow squashy and heavy.

She could hear the forest. The rustling wind. The sound of boots on old, dry leaves. Why was she in the forest? And where was Mum? She'd gone to get potatoes. Was she back yet?

A woman cried out, *there's something here! A kiddies' playhouse of some sort.*

A playhouse? The only playhouse Elodie knew of was an old thing made of greyed wood, somewhere in the forest. Daddy had taken her to see it a couple of times. He'd told her that he and his friends made it when they were about as old as she was now. She could see the top of it from her bedroom window. It had always seemed like something from a fairy tale, from a faraway place that wasn't real.

Others came running.

Voices of adults grew louder. Men and women.

She heard them calling out:

I can't see in. How do we get this thing open?

There's a latch. Look.

She can't have latched it from the outside.

Yes, but someone else could have. Right?

What if—?

She was scared. Couldn't breathe right. Couldn't move.

All she could see was a flashing light. But no people. No faces. The people were just invisible figures in a dark world. She wanted to protect herself, but her body felt wooden. Like a doll, lying discarded on the floor.

Why couldn't she see?

The voices came again, this time surrounding her:

For the love of—

There she is!

Don't frighten her!

Is she alive?

We're not supposed to touch her. Better call—

She's a child. I'm not waiting for instructions—

Their words and questions made panic spiral in her stomach.

One of the women was close by her now. "She's sleeping. Just sleeping. Thank God."

Elodie knew she wasn't sleeping—because she could hear them. She couldn't hear people when she was asleep. The people didn't seem scary now. They were going to help her.

She could hear volleys of shouts in the forest.

There weren't normally all these people in the forest.

She was being taken away.

Carried.

For a moment, the people fell quiet. She tried to take her chance to speak, but, somehow, she couldn't make herself form the words inside her head.

All she heard was the wind picking its way through the bare

branches, until the crackling sounds of a radio came. She heard her name again—her full name this time.

Elodie McGregor has been found. Repeat. Elodie McGregor has been found. Condition not yet known. Currently unconscious.

Suddenly a roar. A deep voice. Someone crashing forward, scooping her up. *My girl, my girl, my girl....* Daddy. It was Daddy. She'd barely recognised his voice at first.

His voice struck terror in her. Was that because he sounded so different? She didn't know.

"Sir," someone said. "Mr McGregor. I'm afraid you can't take her away. Evidence, and all. The less people who handle her, the better."

"Who did this? Who?" His voice cracked in a way Elodie had never heard before, filled with a barely controlled rage.

"I can't answer that, sir. She was alone when she was found."

"Where was she found?"

"I can't answer that either, sir. We need to race her off to hospital. Please give her to the officer and stand back." The motors of vehicles whirred and rumbled.

They were taking her to the hospital. That was what the policeman said. They'd make her better, and then she could see again, and she'd be able to figure out what was happening to her.

All the way along the dark road, she could hear the wind and the sound of an engine and the occasional lorry as it passed.

She battled to stay awake, to move through the strange squashiness in her head and find her way out.

13

ISLA

DINNER LAST NIGHT with Greer had been fun. We'd sat with plates of pasta in front of the fireplace in the house, watching a movie, talking and laughing. I'd been quietly disappointed when Greer had said she couldn't be here the next night. With the McGregors away for the weekend, I'd be winging it here at Braithnoch all alone. She offered to cancel, but I told her not to worry. I'd be fine. I couldn't expect to have my hand held every day.

I peeked outside a window of the cottage. This morning had dawned much brighter than it had the day before.

Slinging my camera over my shoulder, I set out. I'd made sure to dress for the weather this time, bundling myself into a thick jacket and scarf. I felt like a scout, prepared for anything nature had to throw at me.

The world was beautiful in every direction. I almost decided on going up into the hills again, then changed my mind. I wanted spectacular light for when I photographed the hills and mountains. Instead, I walked to the end of the driveway and took some long shots of the house with the mountains behind.

I spotted a path leading between the forest and the fence. A path would be easy to follow, and I wouldn't be risking getting lost, as I could just follow it back again. I headed in that direction. It was a long walk before the forest thinned and the scenery changed to grassy fields. The fields were a lot prettier than the tussocky moor I'd walked the other day.

As I turned a corner on the path, a long fence came into view. I realised I'd wandered off Braithnoch onto the neighbouring property. The land on the other side of the fence must belong to the Keenans.

A girl perched on the fence while an elderly man hammered away at the wooden posts. Puffing on a cigarette, the girl eyed me suspiciously. She had a young face, with dark blonde hair and long gangly arms and legs. Although she'd easily be taller than me, I guessed she was thirteen or fourteen.

"Hello," I called, waving.

The girl threw her cigarette down and stalked away.

Hello to you, too, I thought.

The old man either didn't hear me or was ignoring me.

The path continued along the Keenan's fence line. I decided to follow it. The forest belonging to the McGregors ran alongside it. I might find something pretty to photograph—a bird or a squirrel or something. I'd read in the guide book back in the cottage that there was a red squirrel population here.

A voice called out—that of an older lady. I scanned the fields, unable to see anyone.

The voice rang out again. "Hello there, love."

I spotted her now, not far from the man. She was tiny, with silvery-white hair in curls and wearing a house dress that didn't seem anywhere near warm enough for the weather.

"Oh, hi. Sorry. I didn't see you."

She stepped up to the fence. "Are you lost?"

"No. Just taking a walk."

"You'll be taking a long road if you keep going, love. Goes forever, it does."

"I wasn't planning on going much further. Hi, I'm Isla. I'm staying at the McGregor's. Well, not at the house, exactly—"

"I know who you are. Greer told me. She's a chatterbox, that one."

I smiled, relaxing a little when she mentioned Greer's name. "That she is."

"I'm Nora Keenan. Come over and meet my husband. Then you can come in and have a cup 'o'tea with us."

"Happy to meet you, Nora. But I don't want to impose."

"Och, he'd be glad of a bit of company, especially a pretty young girl. You'll brighten his day, you will. He hurt his hip in a fall. Isn't getting out much. But I can't stop him from doing things about the place. He'll do himself another injury soon enough."

I climbed the fence and she took me over to her husband, Charlie. He seemed happy enough to stop fixing the fence and come inside for a cup of tea. He ambled along silently beside Nora and me while she chatted on.

Their cottage was everything I was starting to love about old Scottish houses. The simple, white-painted walls holding up a slate, gable roof. And always a chimney. A green garden surrounded the house, with holly trees and some sort of red-leaf hedge with red berries.

"Your gardens are lovely," I commented.

"We spend a lot of time on them," she said. "And we like growing things that feed the birds. Like our cotoneaster over there." She pointed at the hedge. "Shame the lot will be buried soon."

"Buried?"

"Under the snow, love. It's coming on quick. I can feel it in my knuckle bones—I always can."

"Snow, goodness. I thought I was going to miss out on seeing it. I looked up the weather before I left home and there was no snow forecast."

"Oh, you can't go by what they tell you. Different parts will call the winter in early. I shouldn't complain. We could pick up and leave if we wanted to. Move to Spain or whatnot. But we choose to stay, year after year."

She ushered me inside the house. The interior furnishings were old but comfortable, the air warm from a crackling fire.

"Sit down, Charlie," she told her husband, "and I'll get the tea and some butterscotch pie."

"She makes the best butterscotch pie," Charlie said, his blue eyes crinkled and wistful. "What's your name, lassie?"

"My name is—" I started.

"She already told you her name," scolded Nora. "It's Isla." She turned her head back to me as she assembled tea cups on the kitchen bench. "He's got a touch of dementia, poor Charlie. He might ask you who you are a few times over."

"I don't mind at all." I sat next to Charlie at the table. "I'm Isla. A photographer. I'm here to take photos of Alban and his work for an architectural magazine."

"Well now," Charlie said. "You'll have your work cut out for you, with Alban."

I raised my eyebrows. "Oh? Do you think he'll be a difficult subject?"

"Let's just say that Alban wouldn't win a Miss Congeniality contest." He winked.

His statement pulled a laugh from me. Charlie might have dementia, but his wit was still sharp.

"I've noticed that about Alban," I said.

Nora began cutting up a pie. The sweet smell of butterscotch joined the scents of smoky woodfire. "I'm not sure how Greer talked him into having photos taken."

I smiled. "She must have been pretty persuasive."

"Can't persuade Alban of nothing," Charlie remarked. "Known him since he was a boy. Stubborn as they come. I've been telling him for years about the larch, but he'll not listen."

"What have you been telling Alban about the larch?" I asked curiously.

"Been telling him the disease is coming." Charlie shook his head. "Damned larch is infected with a fungus. It's just over the mountain, and it will come here, too. Alban doesn't want to know. I told him, we need to chop it all down and start again. Plant a different tree. The larch never belonged here."

Nora muttered under her breath as she brought the tea and cups over. "Don't go banging on about the larch again. And your hairy bum's out the window if you think you can get out there chopping down trees. Those days are long gone. Silly old bugger."

I grinned at Nora's colourful turns of phrase, her accent so thick that I only just caught the words. "Must be hard on Alban. He seems to love the forest. He told me a story about his ancestors and how they planted the trees."

She sighed. "Aye, he loves the trees. But they'll all be gone soon enough and Braithnoch Square is goin' to look like a wasteland."

I had a sudden moment of clarity. "That's why he agreed to the photos, isn't it? Because he wants a record of his land, as it looks now. Because he knows the forest will be gone one day."

Her eyes widened, and she nodded. "I think you're right, love."

A man lumbered into the kitchen, wearing pyjama bottoms and an ACDC T-shirt, his hair crumpled. He glanced at me in surprise, rubbing the stubble on his face.

"This is our Hamish." Nora served out four portions of pie and poured everyone out some tea. "We only have the one son."

There'd been a tinge of regret in her voice. I wasn't sure if it was regret because she wished she had more than one son or if it was regret that Hamish was the one that she had.

"Hi, I'm Isla."

"I see my mother roped you in for a tea and chat. There's no escape. You'll be here until the cows come home." Pulling out a chair with his foot, Hamish sat heavily. He looked like his father—same blue eyes and ruddy complexion. I guessed he was about thirty years old.

"Bah," said Nora, playfully swiping her son's head with a tea towel. She turned to me. "He gives me hell, he does. But then so do my daughters. Headstrong as they come. Kelly and Camille. Kelly lives over at Aviemore and Camille lives here in town. Kelly's my baby. Just twenty-three. She was a surprise pregnancy when I was forty-seven. I nearly died of shock, I did. I'll show you pictures of them all later."

"I'd like that," I said, cringing internally.

"Don't lie," joked Hamish, winking at me. "There's easier ways of getting Mum's butterscotch pie than sitting through her family albums."

I laughed. "The pie is really delicious."

Nora beamed. "Oh, I'm so happy you like it. It's one of our favourites."

"How're you liking staying in the cottage there at Braithnoch?" Hamish asked me.

It seemed that every member of the Keenan family already knew all about me.

"It's not bad," I replied. "Nice to be able to stay right where I'm working."

"Aye," he said. "Just don't let the tattie bogles bother you. They tend to walk around by themselves at night 'round these parts. They mostly don't cause trouble. But if you should hear 'em knocking on your door late at night, whatever you do, don't let them in."

"Hamish!" his mother scolded. "Don't rabbit on with those old myths. You'll scare poor Isla out of her wits."

"A myth, eh?" Hamish leaned back in his chair, folding his hands across his stomach. "Try taking a look at how the expressions on their crafty faces change each day. You have to sneak up on 'em to catch 'em out, and then you'll see what I mean. When they look mean, that's when you need to start worrying."

"Och, you!" exclaimed Nora. "Shut your piehole, Hamish. You and your silly stories." Her forehead creased in a sudden frown. "Speaking of pie, where did Stella get to? She's a big fan of my butterscotch pie."

Hamish yawned. "Don't know. Don't care. I've been asleep."

"Is Stella the girl I saw sitting on the fence earlier?" I asked. "She walked off along the path."

Sighing, Nora sat at the table. "She's a handful, that one."

"Send her back to Kelly," said Hamish.

"I'll not do that," Nora said scornfully. "If she wants to come and stay at her grandparents' house, she's always welcome."

"Stella's your granddaughter?" I asked.

"Aye," Nora told me. "She's fourteen. Camille's daughter. Stella's got a lot of problems, poor wee lass. She ran away from home when she was just twelve. Plain refused to come back to Camille. We offered to take her in, but she didn't want that. Ended up moving in with my other daughter, Kelly, in Aviemore."

"Maybe Stella just didn't like Rory?" Hamish said, stirring his tea noisily. "You have to admit he looks and acts like a bit of a weirdo. Always tinkering in his garage with his wee science experiments."

"It's his thing." Nora cut a chunk of pie with her fork. "Better that he be passionate about what he teaches than just going through the motions."

Hamish shrugged. "Maybe. But he still looks like Einstein crossed with a hipster."

She clucked her tongue at Hamish but then tried and failed to suppress a hooting laugh. "Och, I'll give ye that. He's got that mad professor look about him."

"Wait," I said, "I think I might have met Rory. Is his full name Rory Kavanagh?"

"That's him." Nora nodded. "He's my daughter Camille's partner. Moved in with her and Stella about three years ago. Camille's ex-boyfriend—the father of Stella—was a no-good petty criminal. Rory is head and shoulders above him."

Hamish ran a hand through his hair, ruffling it and making it even messier. "Rory's just perfect in your eyes, isn't he?"

Nora pursed her lips. "What's happened between you and Rory, anyway? You two used to be such good friends. You, Rory, Kirk, Alban and the Chandlish kids—Peyton, Aubrey and Diarmid—you were all thick as thieves."

"Rory got damned boring." Hamish shovelled the rest of his pie into his mouth in one gulp. "He was odd back when we were teenagers. He's gotten even odder since. Kirk became a cop—do I need to say any more? The Chandlishes are bearable, except they act exactly like the rich toffs they are. As for Alban—he just distanced himself from everyone."

"Well, it's a damned shame," Nora said. "To be such good friends and now you all barely speak to each other."

"It's not a shame, Mum. It's life."

Nora exhaled loudly, shaking her head. "Well, at least they all have a life. Unlike you, Hamish Keenan. You still behave like you're eighteen. Getting drunk all the time and not bothering about getting a job. That's probably why you've grown apart from them."

"I don't have to listen to this again." Standing, Hamish shoved his chair away and strode out of the house, banging the door behind him.

The room fell silent. Hamish's father sat slurping his tea, barely seeming to notice the altercation between Hamish and Nora.

"Sorry about that." Nora twisted her thin lips into a grimace. "I try to stop myself from saying anything, but it's like I'm a kettle just on the edge of boiling."

The exchange had been uncomfortable. I wanted to get up and leave, but before I could say anything, Nora jumped up and told me she was going to get the family photos. I'd wished I'd been quicker to exit the house.

Gritting my teeth, I looked through the pictures of various groups of people that Nora showed me. I noticed pictures of Elodie a few times and younger photos of Alban and Jessica.

Nora was patient with me as I kept mixing people up.

"I'll draw you up a family tree, you poor love," she told me. "So that you can keep everyone in Braithnoch Square straight." She'd hurried away to fetch a notepad before I could lodge a protest.

Her pen moved across the page in black strokes and then she handed me the piece of paper:

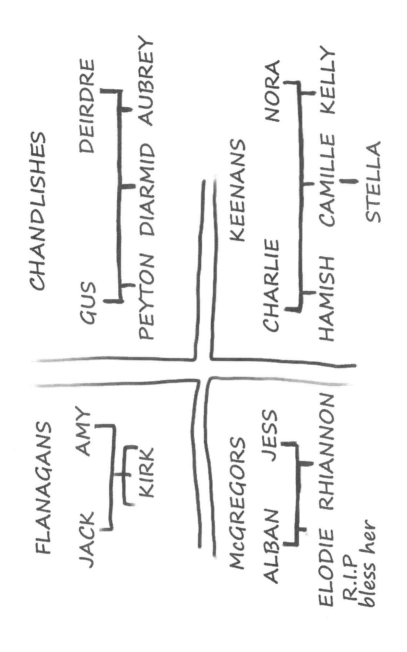

"This is too kind of you, Nora." Folding the paper, I slipped it inside the pocket of my jeans, hoping she wasn't about to go crazy and write out a family tree that included everyone back to the time of Griogair, or whoever that ancestor was who Alban had told me about.

"Oh, don't mention it," she said, pulling out another teetering stack from her box of photos. "You'll note I didn't put the name of Stella's father in there. That's because he's an *eejit* and doesn't deserve to be there. Camille's with Rory now, anyway."

"Rory came to the house the other day," I told her. "He wanted to give the McGregors some of their daughter's artwork, from school."

"Ah, poor wee Elodie," she said. "Breaks my heart thinking about her. She's fair two years gone now." She scowled. "That damned playhouse is still standing there in the wood. I told Alban he should pull it down, but he won't hear of it."

I sipped the last of my tea. "I saw it in the news—the playhouse. I didn't know it was still there."

Nora pulled her mouth so far down it made her chin dimple. "It distresses me, it does. I hate the fact that it's still standing. Like an omen. I feel like if we leave it there, something else bad is going to happen."

Charlie was studying his wife's face. "Now, Nora. We can't go worrying about things that might or might not happen in the future. All that does is make your pie go sour in your guts."

"I sense things that you don't, you old coot," she scolded.

I sat looking at a few more pictures with Nora, before excusing myself and telling her that I really did need to get back to work.

Bracing myself for the cold again, I stepped out of the warm cottage.

Hamish was sitting on a high pile of logs, still in his pyjama pants. I kept a brisk pace, across the field and over the fence.

Crossing my arms close to my chest, I wished there was a bit more heat coming from the sun.

As I walked back along the path, I stared up at the trees and was reminded of the playhouse. Why didn't Alban want to dismantle it?

I rounded a corner and almost bumped into a dark-haired woman who was rushing along, her head down and chatting into her phone.

"You could meet me out in the wood. Why not? I'm walking up that way anyway—"

She broke off suddenly, plunging the phone into her pocket without even saying goodbye to whoever she was talking to.

"Who are you?" she asked brusquely.

When I told her, her sharp expression didn't change. "Have you seen my daughter—Stella? I was coming here to see her, but Mum said she ran off."

Although she didn't tell me her own name, I guessed that she had to be Camille, Nora and Charlie's daughter. Nora had told me she was the mother of Stella and I'd seen her in the photographs Nora had shown me. Her face seemed thinner and somehow pinched in real life, a slash of red lipstick vivid against pale skin.

"I saw her sitting on the fence earlier," I said, swinging around to point in the general direction.

In the arc of my gaze, I spotted Stella perched high on the branch of a tree. Stella stared at me coldly, probably expecting me to tell Camille where she was. I remembered Nora telling me that Stella wanted nothing to do with her mother these days. I made a swift decision that it wasn't my business. *Not my circus and not my monkeys*, as the saying went.

I turned back to Camille. "Sorry, I don't know where she went."

"Okay then." Camille kept walking, without even so much as a goodbye.

Not wanting to give Stella's location away, I didn't look up at her again, but resumed walking towards Braithnoch. I wondered who Camille had been talking to on the phone. Who had she wanted to meet up with so desperately? It hadn't been Stella—Stella had been holding onto the branch with both hands.

Nora had invited me to pop in again on another day, but there was no way I was going to do that. They were nice people, but there was enough tension at the McGregors' house without listening to the Keenans bicker as well.

14

ISLA

I HAD dinner alone in the cottage—melted cheese and tomato on sourdough bread—while I watched an episode of the Scottish TV comedy, *Still Game*. Munching on my dinner, I giggled all the way through the show.

A night here alone was actually quite nice.

With dinner done, I stretched and took my plate to the kitchen. My limbs were sore from all the walking and activity of the past few days. Even my toes felt sore. I'd have a shower and then head off to bed. It was already ten at night.

I trudged to the shower and stood under the warm water, letting my back and shoulders relax.

A sharp knocking at the door had every one of my muscles jumping.

No one was supposed to be here. The McGregors were in Edinburgh and Greer was away.

My heart racing, I wrenched the water off.

The battering knock came again.

Grabbing a towel, I dried off quickly and then threw a track suit on. I felt a tiny bit less vulnerable now that I wasn't naked. For a moment, that stupid story that Hamish had told me about the scarecrows coming knocking raced through my head. It was crazy how the dark and isolation made things like that seem like they could almost be real.

I made the decision not to answer. I'd stay here, in the bathroom, until the person left.

Another insistent knock had my teeth on edge.

They weren't going to go away. What if it was the police? The knock had been loud, the same way police tended to knock on doors.

"Isla? Isla? Are you in there?" A woman's voice rang out. A young woman. It couldn't be Nora Keenan.

Whoever was out there, she knew who I was. Still, I was wary as I headed to the door.

I cracked the door open. A girl stood there, cold and shivering, pale hair tangled around her shoulders. I didn't recognise her at first. But then I realised she was Aubrey Chandlish.

"Hope you don't mind. I just needed some company," she said.

"Oh. Oh, of course." I drew a long, silent breath. "Are you alone?"

"Yes. All alone. I was with Simon, out walking in the woods, but I'm not now."

I waved her inside. "Come in and get warm."

Giving me a faltering smile, she entered the cottage, planting herself next to the heater and rubbing her hands against the warmth. She glanced back at me as I closed the door. Even with a blotchy face, she was beautiful. She had porcelain skin and huge eyes and perfectly arched eyebrows. The glow of the nearby lamp highlighted tear stains on her upper cheeks.

"Something's wrong, isn't it?" I went to put the kettle on.

She threw up her arms. "Simon. He's what's wrong."

"That's your boyfriend, right?"

"Yeah. Well, he was. Maybe not after tonight. I've had a gutful of him. He's such a nice guy but then he starts drinking and he says the meanest things to me."

"Hope this isn't rude, but why are you still with him?" I had my mother's habit of being blunt.

"Oh, after each time he always says he's going through a rough patch and he's sorry. Trouble is, his life seems to be one never-ending bad patch."

"Will he be out there looking for you right now?"

She shrugged. "I think he's too drunk to care."

"Feel like a cup of tea?"

"I'd go for a coffee, if you have it."

"Yep, there's coffee here." With the water boiled, I made the hot drinks and sat down on the sofa with her. "Sounds like you need to make some decisions."

A wrinkle appeared between her eyebrows and she eyed me steadily. "See, this is what I need. A voice of reason. My girlfriends tell me that's just what men are like. I keep telling Simon that he's hurting my feelings, but he just keeps on."

I shook my head. "My mum always tells me that if you have to draw a line because of someone's bad behaviour, then draw the line around *them*, not yourself. That means that it's up to the other person to improve and you shouldn't restrict yourself because of their behaviour."

"My mum says just to pick a man before I'm thirty and stick with him. As long as he fits a list of certain criteria. She says they've all got problems and us women just have to see it through." She shrugged glumly. "What about you, Isla? Are you seeing anyone?"

"No, no time for that." It seemed that almost everyone I'd met so far had asked me that same question. It must be a small-town thing.

"Sounds like you have a super-busy life."

As soon as she spoke the words, I knew that it wasn't true. I didn't have to work as much as I did. I did have time for someone special. But I just...hadn't bothered. It'd been years since I'd dated anyone.

"Would you like a piece of banana cake?" I asked her, changing the subject. "It's from the bakery."

"Thanks, but I should be getting back." She puffed up her cheeks and exhaled. "Hey, would you walk with me? I'd rather not go alone."

She caught me unprepared with that question.

"I don't—" I started saying.

"I'll drive you back here," she pleaded. "Please come with me. I have a stupid fear of the dark. I've had it since I was a kid. I hate the tattie bogles, and I have to pass them to get to my house. It's way too long a walk if I go around the road."

"They do look kind of freaky."

"They're *so* freaky. So, you'll come with me?"

The last thing I wanted was to go marching through the Scottish countryside at night, especially with someone I didn't know. But she hadn't left me with any room to say no. "Oh, sure," I told her, trying not to sound as reluctant as I felt.

She broke into a grin. "Yay. You're a superstar. You'd best dry your hair first. You'll catch your death like that out on the moors."

I ran my hands through the wet ends of my hair. "I was in the shower when you knocked."

"I must have given you a fright." She inclined her head, shooting me a quizzical look. "You'll stay for a while, won't you? Everyone's there."

"Who's everyone?"

"My brothers—Peyton and Diarmid. And a couple of friends. Simon, too, if he's made his way back there by now, that is."

"Really, no, I won't stay."

"C'mon," she pleaded. "You can't spend all your time here stuck in the cottage. Or hanging out with a boring old married couple. And I need you with me so I can feel a bit bolder when I have to talk to Simon again. You're the only one with any sense. Anyway, if you're walking all the way over there, you might as well stay for a wee bit."

I bit my lip, giving her a nod. "Just for a few minutes."

Dashing to the bathroom, I towel-dried my hair and blow dried it. I applied a small amount of makeup—enough not to look washed out —and changed into jeans, boots and a thick jacket.

Aubrey grinned at me. "Let's go!"

The air had a savage bite to it as we stepped out into the dark and started walking along the tree line.

"You know the way in the dark?" I asked her nervously.

"Of course. Don't worry, you goose."

This was probably the first time in my life anyone had called me a goose. I'd thought that it was something only grandmothers called their husbands. *Come on in out of the rain before you catch your death, you silly goose!* But here I was, with the glamorous Aubrey, in a deep, dark Scottish forest, being called a goose.

"You should come out with us one night while you're here," said Aubrey. "There's some great nightclubs in Inverness."

"I didn't bring any clothes with me for that kind of thing."

"Oh, I can loan you some clothes. Hey, you can be like my sister or something while you're here. I don't have any sisters, just brothers. Well, I have Bridget—I've known her forever so she's like a sister—but she's a drunk. That's both the best and worst thing about her."

She started telling me about Bridget's drunken escapades. I was grateful she seemed to have forgotten about the nightclubs of Inverness. I was also grateful for her prattling. It filled in some of the empty, pitch-dark space.

But Aubrey fell silent after a while. I grew increasingly anxious. I didn't walk around the dark spaces at night back in Sydney—I stayed well away from alleys and behind buildings and kept to the busy, brightly-lit areas.

The forest seemed too high and too absent of light. I worried that Aubrey would change her mind about driving me back to the cottage, and I'd have to walk back alone. But I'd said that I'd do this and now there was no turning back. I tried to keep my mind blank and just keep walking.

Up ahead, a set of inhumanly tall people stood motionless on a hill. The scarecrows.

Aubrey linked her arm with mine. "I don't know why we have to keep these things here. None of us grow crops anymore."

"They're scary in the dark."

"I know, right? Ugh."

We turned a ninety-degree angle from the scarecrows onto a wide path through the forest.

Finally, after twenty minutes or more on the path, the Chandlish house came into view. I would have liked it to be lit up like Christmas, but just the odd window here and there displayed a yellowish glow.

"They'll all be in the cellar," Aubrey said. "That's where the booze is."

Into the cellar with a set of strangers, I thought, cold threads of uncertainty running down my spine. No, I reminded myself, they are only strange to *me*. The McGregors and Keenans and Chandlishes had known each other for generations. The families were distantly related. They were safe. I was safe.

I followed Aubrey into the house, instant warmth closing around me. The walls were covered in a velvety, misty-green wallpaper, the doorways and staircase framed with chunky white-painted wood. Lots of family photographs, paintings and sculptures. Comfortable furniture. A lot more homely than Alban's house.

"C'mon," Aubrey said, unwrapping her thick woollen scarf. She took me through to a hallway, which ended in a set of steep, narrow stairs that led down. Music with a deep bass beat punched the air, growing in intensity as we reached the bottom.

Four people—three men and a woman—lounged in the plush armchairs, drinking wine and beer. The cellar was a large open space with a dark patterned wallpaper and grey carpet. A bar stood at one end, fully decked out with glass shelves of spirits.

Two enormous dogs lay at the feet of the people—greyish, shaggy animals with the longest legs I'd ever seen on a dog.

"The doggies are Mitzy and Boomer," Aubrey told me. "They're Scottish deerhounds. Big babies, they are."

"Simon's looking for you!" the redhaired woman announced to Aubrey.

Aubrey scowled. "He's being a right jerk. Anyway, I swapped him for someone much better. This is Isla Wilson. You've already seen her about, but you didn't meet properly. She's a photographer who's staying at Braithnoch." She gestured towards the woman. "This is Bridget. She's a travel agent. When she can be bothered to work, that is. It's her mother's agency."

Bridget gave me a slow, cheesy smile. "That's not true—about me not working. I go and check out holiday locations a lot. All damned year 'round." She had a bored tone to her voice, as if she'd seen every possible holiday location the world had to offer, a few times over.

"And this funny little person in the leather vest over there is my big brother, Diarmid," said Aubrey. "He sings bad karaoke at pubs and was working as a ski instructor in Val Thorens, France—until two of his students broke their legs in the same week."

Diarmid raised his glass to me, then rolled his eyes at Aubrey. "You seemed to have missed the last decade of my life in that summary, dear sister."

"Did I?" she said playfully. "Oh well. Those were the standout items from your life. And this," she turned to gesture at a tall guy sprawled in an armchair, "is my other big brother, Peyton. He does something or other at one of the companies our parents own. What is it you do, again, Pey?"

Jumping up and coming to shake my hand, he gave a laugh. "I'm the general manager at Chandlish Industries. Basically, I'm a gopher for the CEOs—which are our parents." He had engaging eyes and much darker hair than his siblings.

I returned the laugh. "Happy to meet you, Peyton."

Aubrey pointed to the man standing against the bar. "And that shady-looking character is a friend of mine, Trent. He's Australian, like you."

My heart sinking, I realised he was the odd guy from the pub that Greer had taken me to.

Trent lifted his glass in the air. "We meet again."

Aubrey frowned. "Oh, that's right. You already intro'd yourself to Isla."

"Hello," I said to Trent.

I couldn't help but notice that his eyes weren't smiling, despite the grin he wore.

Bridget sighed loudly, dropping her head back over the side of her armchair as if the introduction exchanges were boring her. "Anyhoo. Have a drink and put your feet up, Isla. Good to see another girl around here. All this testosterone is getting a bit...smelly."

"It's good old-fashioned sweat, woman," said Diarmid. "Not that you'd know anything about that. I didn't see you out there getting the wood ready for the fire."

Bridget held up a hand and brushed Diarmid's words away. "I spent four years at university because I have the brains to do more than chop wood."

Diarmid made an exaggerated yawn. "What's the point of the degree? It's all for show. The men you went to uni with will end up working for their Daddy's company. And the women will fan about competing at equestrian events and doing busywork in vanity business ventures, before they marry a rich clod and produce an heir and a spare."

Bridget put down her beer and clapped slowly. "That's harsh."

"And you're drunk," said Diarmid.

Nodding, Bridget took another slurp of her beer. "You call a spade a spade. And a drunk a drunk. I like that."

Walking across the room, Aubrey gave Diarmid a playful shove. "Had to have a dig about show jumping, didn't you, Diarmid?"

"To be fair, Diarmid had a dig at himself first," Trent remarked, still standing at the bar. "He knows he'll end up working for Daddy, too."

Peyton held up his drink to Diarmid. "But he's avoided that duty so far. A toast to you, brother, you magnificent bastard."

"A toast to Diarmid," Aubrey said, raising an imaginary glass.

Peyton glanced across at me. "Look at wee Isla over there. We've got her thinking we're a bunch of toffy brats."

"I'm not. Really," I protested.

"You're just too polite to tell the truth," said Diarmid. "We actually *are* toffy brats."

"I was never any good at show jumping," said Bridget in a sad voice.

"That was random," commented Diarmid.

"No, it wasn't." Bridget shrugged. "I just can't keep up with your conversation. I'm lagging."

Diarmid raised his eyebrows. "Never mind, how about you practice your show jumping on me later?"

Bridget shot Diarmid an icy glance. "You've been asking me that for the last ten years. The answer's still no."

"Anyway," said Aubrey, "will someone throw Isla and me some beers or something?"

"I'm not drinking," I said quickly.

"Okay," said Aubrey in a disappointed tone. "Something non-alcoholic for Isla."

Peyton put a small glass bottle of cola in my hand and handed Aubrey a beer.

A blonde man lumbered into the room. He was obviously drunk or on drugs, his eyes heavy and roaming. I recognised him as being Aubrey's boyfriend, Simon.

"Why'd you run off on me, Aubrey?" he said.

Aubrey looked immediately defensive, her shoulders drawing

inward, fingers clutching her beer. "Because I have better things to do than listen to you put me down. I've had enough."

Peyton stood. "Touch my sister and you'll have me to deal with. And Diarmid."

"You've always had my back, Pey." She eyed her boyfriend from beneath a deep frown. "We'll go talk in Daddy's office. No one else wants to hear our blather."

"Let me know if you need me, Aubbie." Peyton cast a glare in Simon's direction.

Bridget seemed oblivious to Aubrey's distress. Humming, she poured herself another drink. The next minute, she began reminiscing about her string of failed love affairs.

Now that Aubrey had gone, I had no way of getting home. Unless I walked through the forest on my own. I didn't know any of these people well enough to ask them for a lift. And they all seemed pretty inebriated. Worse, Trent hadn't stopped staring in my direction.

Anxiously, I looked about for something to distract myself with. I rose and stepped across to the various paintings and photographs on the walls.

The paintings looked expensive, yet here they were adorning the walls of a basement. There was one of a sunset over somewhere called the Cairngorms. It was gorgeous.

"How are you liking Scotland, Isla?" came a male voice behind me. "Hope it hasn't been all work and no play for you."

I wheeled around to find Trent directly behind me. I hadn't even heard him walking up to me. His voice sounded almost mocking.

What did this person have against me? I decided to answer as if I hadn't noticed the tone in his voice. "It's been fun. So far. A bit hard to come straight from an Australian summer to these temperatures though."

"I'll bet."

"What part of Australia are you from?"

"Darwin. Crocodile country."

"Oh, you're at the opposite end of the country to me. I'm a Sydneysider. I've been meaning to visit the top end, but I keep putting it off. I guess I'm not much of a traveller."

"Yet, you're *here*," he said. "You'd have to be pretty determined to travel to the Scottish Highlands in winter."

"Had to shake the cobwebs loose sooner or later."

He smiled, his gaze brushing over me. "I like your hair like that."

I gave a confused laugh. "It's exactly the same as it was last time you saw me—in the pub."

"Is that so?" Touching my hair, he leaned in. About to *kiss* me. Startled, I shrank back.

His expression darkened. "You can drop the act, you know."

I stared back, searching his face. "What act?"

"Are you honestly going to say you don't know me?"

"You really think I know you? Sorry, if I've ever come across you somewhere, I don't remember."

"What is it with girls like you? You think it's fine to just ghost a guy and act like you never knew him."

"This is getting weird real fast, Trent. Think I'll go find Aubrey and see if she can take me home."

Did I really want to go back to the cottage now? Trent was actually a bit scary and the thought of being alone in the cottage now made a chill creep along the back of my legs.

Peyton approached, a questioning expression on his face. "What's going on here?"

"Nothing," Trent told him tersely, then strode out of the room.

Peyton watched him walk away. "Okay, that was odd," he said to me. "Do you two know each other from before?"

"No. He's a bit strange. Actually, a *lot* strange."

"Well, you shouldn't have to put up with any nonsense. I'll take you home, if you like. My sister's busy with that excuse for a human being she calls her boyfriend. And everyone else is too wasted."

I exhaled a tight, relieved breath. "That would be great, thanks."

"You sure you don't want to stay for a while, though? We don't bite."

"I'm just tired. I only came because Aubrey didn't want to walk back here alone."

He laughed. "That's my sister for you. She always was a scaredy-cat."

Two minutes later, I was sitting on the leather seats of Peyton's

Audi coupe. I almost expected him to tear down the driveway, like most young men would who owned a sports car like this. But he didn't. He drove smoothly, putting me at ease.

"I'm dead sorry about Trent," he said. "I won't abide men being rude to women. You were just there minding your own business."

"He's one of Aubrey's friends, right?"

"Unfortunately, yes. She's always picking up strays. He's been coming to the house for a few years. As far as I know, his father is in mining—iron ore I think—and Trent runs a division of that. He and Bridget had a thing going there for a while. It didn't last. Bridget doesn't last long with anyone."

"Trent seems like he has a screw loose."

"I wouldn't argue with that." He rounded the corner. "So, is this your first time coming to Scotland in winter? I thought I heard Trent mention something about that."

"Oh, he was just questioning my decision to come here, for some strange reason. It's actually my first time coming to Scotland. And the UK, for that matter."

"Seriously? Your first time?"

"Yes."

"Well, I hope you don't run into any more nutters. It'll give you a bad view of your time here. I'm just glad Trent's not one of ours. He's one of *your* nutters, from Australia."

I laughed.

"How's your photography gig going so far?" he asked.

"It's been a bit of a rough start," I told him. "But I'll get there."

Peyton pulled into the McGregors' driveway and drove up to the cottage. As he turned to me, I noticed that he had the same full mouth that Aubrey had and the same classic good looks.

"I'll have to look up your work, Miss Wilson. You must be good for Greer to think it was worth getting you here all the way from Sydney."

I felt almost shy. "I hope I'm worth the trouble."

"I'm sure you are." He sighed. "I think I'll tell that Trent character to get lost. He and Simon can pack up and go together. As far as I'm concerned they're not welcome if they're going to cause trouble."

"Well, don't do anything on my account. I'll be okay. Tell Aubrey goodbye from me. And tell her...tell her to draw a line around Simon."

He grinned. "Draw a line around him, huh? I like the sound of that."

"Thanks for the ride." After jumping out of the car I bent low to wave him goodbye.

A wind sprang up as I walked to the cottage. I completed my usual bedtime routine once I got inside—getting into my pyjamas, brushing my teeth and taking my medication. But I still felt unsettled. I wished that Trent guy hadn't been at the Chandlish house.

I put myself to bed, and I couldn't help but listen out for every tiny noise outside.

By midnight, I still hadn't managed to drift off to sleep. Lack of sleep was bad for me, and the worry of that added to the ball of anxiety already rolling about in my head.

My thoughts stopped as an unexpected sound floated on the wind.

My name.

Someone was calling my name.

Trent's voice.

Isla... Isla....

He sounded drunk. *Isla....*

Pebbles rained on the glass of my bedroom window.

I held my breath.

15

ISLA

TRENT STOMPED around the outside of the cottage for the next fifteen minutes. Finally, he gave up and seemed to leave.

As I roused from a heavy sleep in the morning, Trent's face was the first thing to flash into my mind.

Despite what I'd told Peyton last night, I really did hope he ordered Trent to leave. I was tired, irritable and more than a bit worried.

I stepped out to the kitchen for a morning coffee, opening the shutters to flood light into the little dark cottage. I'd been closing all the shutters tight during the night hours.

But only a weak, gun-metal coloured light limped in. A mist almost obscured my view of the McGregors' house. I could see that they were back—Alban's car was parked outside the house again. They must have returned very early morning while I was still sleeping.

I wished I'd slept longer, until the mist had all vanished. I needed to see sunshine. But it was already late morning. I probably hadn't dropped off to sleep until well after midnight.

I had to stop hoping to see sun. There might be nonstop days of fog and dull weather ahead. I was here to work and to make the best of whatever the weather threw at me. And the fog wasn't as anywhere near as thick as it had been the other day. Whatever I found out there this morning, I had to take my inspiration from it. Perhaps I could go up into the hills and take pictures of the mossy, rocky ranges that would be half hidden by the mist. The more I thought about how that could look, the more excited I became.

Returning to the bedroom, I dressed myself in warm, comfortable clothing. Then, packing up the camera, I left the cottage, locking it securely.

I stepped around the cottage to the forest. A chill sped down my back.

A dark figure hung high in the trees, slightly swinging in the breeze.

Too large to be human.

Grotesquely long arms and legs.

A scarecrow. One of the scarecrows from the hill.

Someone must have dragged it all the way from the hills and hoisted it up in the tree last night. Right across from my bedroom window. I hadn't heard anything.

I marched up to the hanging scarecrow, anger boiling blood-red in my mind.

Who did this?

Was it Trent? Surely, he wasn't so resentful that he'd go to this extreme for revenge? But maybe he would if he really thought I knew him and was blowing him off.

Digging my hands deep into my jacket pockets, I headed into the woods, searching for clues. Too angry to think straight. Maybe the culprit had dropped something.

I'd been wandering and searching the ground for barely five minutes when two hands clamped onto my arms from behind.

"Trent, what do you think you're—" I spun around.

But it wasn't Trent behind me. It was Alban.

He eyed me quizzically. Dropping his arms, he stepped back. "Trent, eh?"

"Forget it," I said quickly. "You startled me."

"You shouldn't go off into the woods in fog. You'll lose your way in no time. I didn't think you'd be quite so daft."

Before I could answer, he said, "You look a wee bit upset. Is something the matter?"

"You could say that," I answered. "Someone has strung a damned scarecrow up in a tree outside the cottage."

"Say what?"

"A tattie bogle or whatever it is you call them."

"I know what a scarecrow is, Isla. You mean to say there's one of those things hanging up there in a tree?"

"Yes. That's exactly what I mean."

He swore loudly, apologised, then sprinted away.

I ran behind, giving up on finding anything useful in the forest.

Alban stopped in front of the figure in the tree. "Who in the blasted hell would want to go pulling a prank like this?"

Two figures stepped through the fog. One adult and one small child. Jessica and Rhiannon.

Both Jessica and Rhiannon wore long, cream-coloured winter dresses—Rhiannon's with a thick ribbon around the bodice. The misty air made their hair colour look even paler than usual. Rhiannon pointed at the scarecrow, looking puzzled.

Jessica stared from Alban to me, gasping. "What in the name of —?" She gathered her daughter in her arms, nestling her protectively against her shoulder. "Is this some kind of stunt?"

"A stunt?" I eyed her blankly.

"I don't know," she said, "something that you think will look artsy in the photographs?"

Shocked, I glanced up at the slightly-swaying figure in the tree, then back to Jessica again. "You're saying *I* did this? Of course I didn't. How would I even manage to get him up there?"

She squeezed her eyes shut for a moment. "I'm sorry. I read this all wrong. I came looking for Alban and I saw that thing up there, and I jumped to conclusions." She stopped for a breath. "This is just crazy. Please, let's all get away from here. I don't want Rhiannon getting distressed."

"Aye, get Rhiannon away." Alban stepped over to Jessica, shielding Rhiannon from the sight in the trees. I joined them as they walked around to the other side of the cottage.

I noticed that Jessica had been crying again, her eyes swollen and her lips pressed together tightly. I guessed that the trip away hadn't gone well for the McGregors.

"Did you hear anything out there in the wood last night?" Jessica asked me.

"There were some people. One of the Chandlishes and a friend of theirs."

"Oh?" she said. "Whatever were they doing?"

"Aubrey was out walking with her boyfriend. She ended up knocking on my door and inviting me over."

Jessica's eyebrows shot up. "You went across to the Chandlish house?"

I nodded. "Just for an hour or so. One of Aubrey's friends—Trent —was about in the forest later on. I heard him talking." I neglected to mention that Trent was calling my name. I didn't want to have to explain that.

"They're troublemakers," Jessica told me. "Aubrey's the worst of the lot. She's the ringleader." She sighed, smoothing Rhiannon's hair and turning to Alban. "Should we call the police?"

He sighed heavily. "Ach, I don't know. If it was just the Chandlishes larking about, then maybe it's not such a big deal."

"Not a big deal?" said Jessica. "It's scared the daylights out of poor wee Rhiannon. And probably Isla, too. They get away with too much."

"I'll go take a look about in the woods," he told her. "And then maybe go pay the Chandlishes a visit."

"I had a look to see if I could find something," I said. "But I didn't spot anything."

"You will come up for a tea, won't you?" said Jessica. "I feel terrible about what I said. Let Alban deal with this. You don't want to be out there. Whoever did this might still be roaming around."

I wanted to say no but instead bit my lip and gave her a nod. Tea with Jessica wasn't something I had on my agenda this morning. I wasn't even sure which I preferred—being thought of as the scarecrow culprit or being thought of as so delicate I had to bustle myself inside and have tea.

Up at the house, Jessica began making me eggs and toast as well as a cup of tea.

Rhiannon played at my feet with her giraffe, repeating her word for giraffe over and over—*ruff, ruff, ruff.* She sounded like a puppy. When Jessica noticed, she came and sat Rhiannon at the table.

"Sorry," Jessica told me apologetically, "you don't need a toddler under your feet."

"I don't mind at all." I truly didn't. Rhiannon was a quiet presence. I'd even enjoyed having her play near me.

"Oh, you're just being polite. Children are so frustrating. Never a minute to yourself." She gave a high, thin laugh. "I do love her like crazy though, despite all that."

She seemed nervous and jittery—even more than usual. When she pushed her sleeves up to wash a bowl in the sink, I noticed small purplish bruises on her lower arms. As if someone had grabbed her. She seemed to realise the bruises were showing, shoving her sleeves down again quickly.

What had she and Alban been fighting about? I thought of the domestic violence posters I'd seen back when I was at university. The poster had asked people to speak up if they saw something. It was a fine line between sticking your nose in and trying to help.

I ate breakfast while Jessica dashed about, feeding Rhiannon, clearing things away in the kitchen and wiping down surfaces that already seemed clean. She refused all my offers of help, claiming to enjoy cleaning. I seriously doubted that, because she displayed no sign of enjoying a single second of it.

It was now or never. I was going to tell her that I'd noticed her puffy eyes and then I'd ask if she was okay. Picking up my cup and plates, I headed over to the sink.

"I'll do them," Jessica told me.

"No," I said firmly. "I'd feel bad if I didn't clean up after myself." As I washed the plates in the sink, I swallowed hard, finding the courage to speak. "Jessica?"

She turned, cleaning cloth in hand, a smile that seemed forced and frozen on her face. "Yes?"

"I wanted to ask you—" I began.

The front door crashed open just then, and Alban raced in, a tense expression on his face. "Call an ambulance."

Jessica dropped the cloth on the floor as she ran to grab the house phone. "Oh my God. What's wrong? What—?"

He raked damp hair back from his eyes, catching his breath. "Should have taken a phone with me. Someone's overdosed out there in the woods. Just tell the ambulance that."

"Who is it?" Jessica whispered as she dialled the number.

"It's one of those people that Aubrey and Diarmid have hanging around. I've seen him before, but I don't know his name," he answered.

Jessica spoke into the phone. "Uh, yes, hello, someone—a man—overdosed in the wood on our property. No, we don't know him." She gave the address, then looked across at her husband. "What's the exact location, Alban?"

Alban's tone deadened. "He's in the playhouse."

Jessica stared at him, speechless for a moment before she gasped, "The playhouse?"

Alban nodded.

"I'm sorry," Jessica said into the phone, "the man is located in a child's playhouse in the wood. It's quite near to the road. My husband will meet you out there when you arrive."

Her face was white as she ended the call. "He's got no right being anywhere near there. None at all. They all know what happened there. They *know*."

"He's a drug addict, Jess. If he did know, he was probably out of his head. I was introduced to him years ago, but I can't remember his name now."

"Is the name *Trent*?" I took a shallow breath.

"Yes, I believe that's it." He looked at me curiously. "How did you guess? Wait, wasn't that the name you said earlier? You thought I was him at first."

"He was acting strange last night."

Alban frowned. "Was he? Well, he's got himself in a wee bit of trouble now. I'm going to head back, to see what I can do for him. He's breathing, but that's all."

Alban dashed back to the entry and out the front door.

Jessica was clutching the edge of the kitchen bench, her head bent. "I can't deal with this right now. It's bad enough that the bloody playhouse is still standing, but to have someone just come in and desecrate it, it's too much. Just too much."

The look of raw grief in her eyes made me look away. "Can I do anything?"

"No, there's nothing. Wait, no, there is something you can do. I'm not in any state to talk to anyone. I'm taking Rhi upstairs to get her cleaned up. You can stay here and answer the phone if it rings. Take messages. An important client of Alban's called early this morning—that's why I went looking for him. He'll probably call back. And—"

"I'll take care of that," I assured her. "Don't worry. And I'll clean Rhiannon up and watch her, too, if you like."

She shot me a glance that was almost hostile, then clenched her eyes shut and shook her head. "She's very clingy. She just wants to be with me, I'm afraid."

Jessica scooped Rhiannon up and then the two of them headed upstairs.

With everyone gone, the entire downstairs area fell into a jarring silence. I felt at odds, not knowing what to do with myself. I even felt somehow responsible for all this. If I hadn't gone with Aubrey last night, I wouldn't have met Trent—and all that followed might not have happened. The whole thing was all the worse for the fact that the McGregors were obviously not fond of the Chandlishes and their friends.

My phone buzzed in my pocket, breaking the silence.

It was Greer. "Oh, gosh, Isla, Alban just called to tell me what's happening down there. He's waiting for the police and ambulance to arrive. Unbelievable. Are you okay?"

"Yes, I'm fine. All pretty crazy."

"Well, I'm not letting you work today. I'm taking you out."

"No, that's not necessary, Greer. It's just a scarecrow. And while I'm sad that a man overdosed in the forest, I don't know him. Jessica's not taking it well, though."

"I thought she wouldn't. But I lied a bit about you not doing any work today. I'm taking you to Inverness. Some of Alban's best work is there and we need some photographs as part of the portfolio. I was planning on taking you there at some point anyway."

"In that case, yes, I'll go."

"I'll pick you up at ten thirty, okay?"

The sharp rings of a landline phone echoed suddenly through the house. It wasn't the house phone—it was coming from Alban's office. Jessica had instructed me to take calls for Alban's business, but I remembered that Greer had said that he didn't like anyone being in his office. I guessed that seeing as I'd agreed to Jessica's request, I should just go answer it.

"Sounds fantastic, Greer," I said. "See you soon."

I sped through the hallway and into the office.

The call was from one of Alban's clients. He sounded impatient, saying that Alban wasn't answering his mobile phone. I didn't want to explain the whole drama that was unfolding here at Braithnoch and didn't know whether I should, either. So, I just scribbled down his message.

Placing the pen on the desk, I raised my head and took a breath.

The last hour had been awful.

I was about to step out of the room when something caught my eye. The painting on the wall.

Unable to tear my gaze away, I stood there frozen to the spot.

The painting hadn't changed, but something else had. What had changed was that I'd seen something else that looked exactly like it. The day before yesterday, just after Greer had made the pancakes, I'd seen the news broadcast about Elodie McGregor. They'd shown an aerial display of the forest, with the strange path the abductor had taken out of the forest clearly marked.

The line of the painting matched the path the abductor had taken through the forest.

No, that was crazy. Surely, I had to be wrong.

The painting was just a white square with a single black line that stretched through the middle of it, from top to bottom. The line moved at straight angles, left and right, like a soldier marching.

It was so much like the line shown on the aerial photograph—of the path Elodie's abductor had taken out of the forest—from the play-house to the road.

And I was someone who paid a lot of attention to lines.

Grabbing my phone, I browsed the internet, seeing if I could find the same aerial map shown on that news broadcast.

I found it.

This map showed both the path the abductor had taken when he chased Elodie to the playhouse and when he left the forest. His path to the playhouse was ragged, as you'd expect—he'd been chasing a little girl who was desperately trying to get away from him. But his path out again was very exact—all straight lines. Quickly, I read through the accompanying information. Apparently, it had been lightly raining the night of the abduction, making the ground slightly muddy. People who'd been looking for Elodie that night had entered the forest from close to the cottage where I was staying. They'd trampled on the abductor's footprints leading up to the playhouse, but the search party had stopped there and returned the way they'd come, as she'd been found. The abductor's exit path had been discovered by police the next morning, untrampled by the search party.

Squeezing a breath tight in my chest, I raised my eyes to the painting again.

I wasn't imagining it. The two lines were a match—the line in the painting and the abductor's exit path.

My gaze moved to the aerial photograph of the spot where Elodie was found.

Cold needles charged down to the small of my back.

It was no coincidence.

The only question now was why was Alban keeping a replica of the abductor's exit path on his office wall?

What possible reason would he have? He'd be looking at this every single day.

"Lost in thought?" came a voice behind me.

I jumped, dropping my iPhone as Alban's voice punctuated the air behind me. Scrambling to the floor, I collected my phone and switched it off. I hoped he hadn't seen the picture I'd had up on the screen.

"Alban," I breathed. "I didn't hear you come in. I was just... taking a message for you." I jabbed my finger at the piece of notepaper on his desk. "Jessica asked me to take any phone calls. She's upstairs."

A frown snaked across his forehead. "You seem really anxious, Isla."

"Me? Yes, I guess I am. It's not every day that things like this happen."

"One would hope. Look, if this morning has rattled you too much, I'll understand if you want to cut this assignment short and go back home."

"I—I'll let you know. How is the guy? Was it Trent?"

"Yes, it was Trent Dorrington. He's in a critical condition, but they think he'll be okay, if that helps any. Well, I'm back now, so you can go and have a rest in the cottage for a while. I understand that Greer is taking you to Inverness soon. That might take your mind off a bit."

I nodded. "Thanks. Yes, I'm sure it will."

My throat felt closed and tight as I walked out from the office. I felt his gaze sharp in my back.

He'd have to have seen me staring at the two pictures he had on the wall.

Did he guess I'd made a connection?

16

ISLA

LEAVING Alban behind in his office, I ran down to the cottage through the mist, my lungs tight.

All the way, I saw the two pictures in my head. The aerial photo of the forest and the painting.

The scarecrow that had hung in the tree was gone—cut down by Alban, I guessed. A ladder stood poised against the trunk of the tree.

As I stepped inside the cottage, my head swam and I had to grab the door frame.

If I was going to leave, now was the time. Stress was bad for anyone, but for me it could lead to seizures. Alban had offered it to me to finish up and return home. If I stayed, I'd have to stay to the end.

God, there'd been no mistaking it. Alban was keeping a replica of the abductor's exit route on his wall.

It made no sense. Why would he keep such a thing?

I plonked myself down at the tiny kitchen table, trying to think. I picked up one of the gold-tipped larch cones Elodie had painted, twirling it slowly between my fingers.

The reason Greer gave for Alban having that painting on his office wall might be right. I had no idea of the depth of the anguish and trauma that he and Jessica had undergone. Perhaps the drawing was

Alban's way of trying to gain control in the aftermath of his daughter's death, in some way I couldn't grasp.

But what if the unthinkable was true, and it was Alban who harmed his daughter? And the painting was some kind of sick trophy?

I became aware of my heart drumming against my ribs.

Surely not. Surely, a father wouldn't harm his own daughter in that way?

But there were stories all the time in the news. Stories of parents who had done just that. The unthinkable.

The breakfast that Jessica had given me sat heavily in my stomach. Could this be the source of the friction between Alban and Jessica? Did Jessica suspect her husband of hurting their daughter? If so, was she in torment, confused and wondering? Or, worse, did she know for sure that he hurt Elodie and she was covering up for him?

My mind jumped from scenario to scenario.

Opening my laptop, I conducted a search on Elodie and her abduction. I found a news item in which the reporter had laid out the whereabouts of all the neighbours on the night that Elodie had been abducted. This might help answer some questions for me.

The article said that Jessica had been in Greenmire hospital, having just given birth to Rhiannon. Alban had been returning home from a job in Edinburgh—but there was a window of time in which he could have been the abductor. The Keenans had been at home, including Hamish. The Chandlishes had been at home, too, apart from Peyton and Aubrey—Peyton had been at a bar in Inverness and Aubrey had been in London. The Flanagans had been away overseas, apart from Kirk, the police officer, who'd been at work.

According to the alibis in the article, the abductor could have been Alban.

I could go to the police and tell them what I'd discovered about Alban's office painting and leave it with them—safely on my way to the airport. There was no way I could remain here after speaking to the police. They'd probably want to visit Alban's house and see the picture and he'd know that I had told them.

Replacing the larch cone in the bowl, I dropped my head into my hands. I hadn't come here for this. I'd come to do a job and that was all. I shouldn't get involved in things that were not my business.

But a life had been taken away from a young girl—a girl whose face I saw every time I passed through the hallway of her house. I couldn't stop that face from haunting me. The last photos of her were particularly sad and evocative. I saw secrets in her eyes.

Elodie, was it someone random who chased you that night? Or was it someone you knew? And who was it that was making you keep secrets?

My gaze came to rest on the card that Dr McKendrick had given me. Days ago, I'd tossed it into the bowl with the larch cones. Could I call her specifically to talk about Alban? I knew that doctors weren't legally able to share information about their patients, but perhaps she'd be willing to share some information on a personal basis. She obviously didn't like him, so maybe that would prompt her to share what it was that had caused her to feel that way.

An image of Rory Kavanagh's thin face jumped into my mind then. He seemed to have some kind of problem with Alban, too—and Alban had acted strangely when I'd told him that Rory had come to the house. So perhaps there was friction between them.

The whole episode with Rory looking through Elodie's paintings had been odd, but perhaps he'd taken his chance because Alban was away at the time. I'd been a stranger alone in the house and Rory might well have known that. Greer had told the Keenans everything it seemed, and Rory was part of that family. He could easily have heard that the McGregors were away. And what exactly was Rory's interest in Elodie's paintings anyway? I was now certain that there was more to it than a teacher wanting to see more of the work of his favourite student. Maybe I could find out why Rory still had such an intense interest in Elodie—after all, two years had passed.

Picking up my phone from the table, I browsed an internet residential directory, looking for Rory's address and phone number. It wasn't there. I tried looking up schools next. I took a breath and held it while I dialled Greenmire primary school. I stopped the call before it even answered. What was I going to say? It was too awkward.

Greer's car pulled up outside the cottage. I hadn't even gotten myself ready for a day out yet. Dashing to the bathroom, I brushed my hair and applied some quick lipstick and mascara. I studied myself in the mirror. I looked like I'd seen a ghost.

I was pulling on a nicer jacket by the time Greer tapped at the door.

She wore a thick plaid skirt and brown boots, her pink-blonde hair in a glossy bun.

"You're a bit pale, Isla." She frowned in concern.

"It's been quite a morning."

"It's insane. I can't believe all that happened. Well, I'm glad I'm getting you out of here for a few hours. Leave old Braithnoch behind for a while and get some different air. You'll love Inverness. We can take a walk around the Ness Islands—so pretty. We'll go see a few of the buildings Alban has designed. His theatre is just beautiful—he won a huge award for that design. Oh, and I'll take you to see Loch Ness. It's a magical place."

Greer's enthusiasm was infectious. "Sounds amazing," I said.

The drive, along a couple of long roads, took over an hour. After seeing almost nothing but country views and small towns, suddenly we were in a city on the edge of the water. A wide river separated the city centre, up to an inlet that flowed into the North Sea. The smell of salt in the air made me a little homesick for Sydney.

Greer took me on a boat ride along the River Ness, stopping for lunch at a little cafe inside the Inverness Botanic Gardens. Walkways through the gardens led through an astonishing variety of plants within a set of glasshouses—from tropical oases with waterfalls to desert cacti.

After lunch, we walked to the Ness Islands that Greer had told me about. They were a set of tiny islands in the middle of the River Ness. We stepped across the bridge onto the islands.

I snapped picture after picture of the gorgeous scenery—autumn-yellow leaves contrasting with a natural floor of red, dried leaves.

"You got here to Scotland a bit too late to see the Halloween show on the islands," Greer told me. "That was on the last night of October. But it's a lot of fun. Well, we'll take a boat ride now back to the car and I'll take you to see the sights around the city."

Greer was right. I loved Inverness. All of the historic buildings and cathedrals. Clouds had formed a thick, sombre blanket in the sky, but they seemed somehow to add to the charm. I was kicking myself for sticking so long with my home city and not doing things like this sooner. Putting the events of the morning aside, I allowed myself to enjoy the day.

Alban's award-winning theatre took my breath away—its sweeping curves and glass majestic in scale and design. I asked myself, not for the first time, just who was Alban McGregor?

The next port of call after Inverness was the mythical Loch Ness. The temperature seemed to have dropped a few degrees by the time we got out of the car. I pulled my knitted hat down over my ears and wound my scarf up over my mouth and nose. The sight of mountains and ruined castles and the intensely green surrounds of the lake were beautiful, but the icy wind made my eyes water. I did the best I could to take photos but felt defeated. I decided to pack the camera away and just enjoy walking around a lake I'd heard about ever since I was a child. It felt surreal to be here.

I looked around for Greer and found her nearby, talking into her phone with a hand cupped over it.

"I just don't think this can work. Please understand," Greer said into the phone, in an almost begging tone. "I didn't want this. Trust me, I didn't."

I stepped away again, not wanting to intrude. She sounded so different to how she'd been earlier.

She walked up behind me. "Isla, get any photos?"

"Yes. Not many. My eyes are stinging a bit."

"The weather's turned. Shame." She dabbed at her eyes with a tissue. I was certain her watery eyes were mostly due to the phone call and not the wind. "I'll try bringing you back on a nicer day."

"Don't even think of it." I shook my head firmly. "I appreciate it like crazy that you brought me here today. It's lovely in any weather."

She smiled, her mascara running slightly beneath her lower eyelids, her nose and cheeks reddened.

We jumped back into the car and Greer turned the heater on. I was soon cooking beneath my layers of clothing. That had been a common theme since I'd arrived in Scotland—I'd either been too hot or too cold. I hadn't had time to acclimatise yet. I unwrapped my scarf and pulled my hat and gloves off.

Greer wasn't her usual chatty self on the road. She kept apologising for the weather until I had to remind her that she wasn't God and the weather wasn't in her job description. At least that got a laugh out of her.

From my passenger side window, I noticed a small, stone church off a small dirt road. It was almost obscured by brambles.

"How cute," I remarked. "That little church down there. Like something out of a children's picture book."

She peered across. "I didn't see it." Slowing the car to a stop, she backed the car up.

"Oh, I didn't mean for you to stop," I protested.

She shrugged. "I've stopped now, so we might as well take a look. I've never noticed it before." She drove off the road and down the side street.

"Probably because it's nothing to see," I said. "It just reminded me of something. I think maybe it looks like a page from a Sleeping Beauty book I had when I was a kid. Brambles and thorns grew all over the town and castle while Beauty slept."

"I remember that story." Greer parked the car. "It fair freaked me out when I was a little girl."

The air was cold outside the car, but at least it was a little bit protected from the wind.

The brambles obscured the arched, leadlight windows and doors of the church. There was no way in. I stepped around taking photographs. "These pictures are going to look lovely in black and white." I smiled at Greer. "Thanks for stopping."

"Oh, that's all right. I know you're here to work on the portfolio, but you don't want to go missing any photo opportunities. I have a friend who's a photographer and I know what's she's like. She'd go to any lengths to get the perfect shot."

Immediately, I wondered why Greer's friend hadn't been given the magazine job that I was doing.

Greer seemed to read my mind. "She's a pet photographer. That's all she does."

"Sounds like a lot of fun. I'm sure it's better than having to deal with people a lot of the time."

She laughed. "You're not wrong. Hey, I forgot to tell you. We're having dinner tonight with the Chandlishes."

"Aubrey and her brothers?"

"Yes, they'll be there, but I meant the parents. Gus and Deirdre."

"I thought they were away?"

"They came back yesterday morning, apparently. Alban and Jess will be there, too."

I took a couple more photographs of the church, but I was glad to get back into the car and out of that wind. I didn't feel like having dinner with a set of strangers, but there was nothing I could do about it, except plead an illness or headache.

But Greer had gone to so much effort today that I didn't feel that I could turn this down.

17

ISLA

IT WAS dark by the time we got back to Braithnoch. Greer and I freshened up in the cottage and then she drove us around to the Chandlishes' house.

We stepped past the formal lounge room. With its mossy-green wallpaper. A fire danced in the fireplace. I wished I could just sit by the fireplace, alone, with a book. Today had been cold and tiring. In the kitchen, food was cooking in big pots and in the oven. A woman that I didn't know was there doing the cooking. She introduced herself as a chef that the Chandlishes sometimes used.

Greer and I kept walking. We found the Chandlishes out in the family room, drinking red wine near the second downstairs fireplace —Peyton and an older couple who had to be his parents. An inky night stood beyond tall, arched window panes.

Greer introduced me to Gus and Deirdre Chandlish.

Deirdre was thinner than her daughter Aubrey—still very attractive but in a stiff, over-done sort of way. Her bobbed hair was perfect, her eyebrows sculpted into high sweeps.

Gus cut a fit-looking figure in his suit, but his deeply hooded eyes had dark shadows beneath them. I imagined him in an office all day making million-dollar deals and then working out in a gym until dark. The two of them didn't resemble people who had just been travelling for a month on holiday. They didn't have that *exhausted-but-happy* look that people tended to have when they returned from an overseas trip. The Chandlishes must have already seen it all—several times— and nothing entranced them anymore.

"Can I get you a red wine, Isla?" Peyton asked. "It's quite a good one." He looked handsome in a casual suit.

"No, I'm fine," I told him.

"I hope you're enjoying our part of the world," said Mrs Chandlish.

"It's beautiful," I replied. "All so green. I hope to see snow before I leave. I've never seen snow."

In response, her lips tightened into a small, pursed smile. "You won't be so fond of it when it smothers us."

Mr Chandlish rolled his shoulders in a half-shrug. "It's my favourite time of year. The snow. Like a blank canvas, from which we all start again anew."

She gave a wan smile. "You read too many philosophy books, Gus."

He winked at me. "Watch the sun glistening on the snow when there's a full cover, Isla. Or the soft glow of the moon. You won't believe how light it is at night when it snows. Magical. But don't stare too long or you might just start to think there isn't a better sight in this world."

Greer wrinkled her brow. "Where's Jess and Alban?"

"They were here a minute ago," said Mrs Chandlish. "I think they might have gone upstairs to settle their little one off to sleep. We have a guest room up there with a cot for little ones."

"If so, they've got an escapee on their hands." Peyton waggled his finger at a pyjama-clad Rhiannon, who was running along the distant corridor. She had her giraffe tucked under one arm and a blanket under the other.

"There's an open fireplace up that way. I'll go get her." I was glad of an excuse to leave the room. I could already tell that the Chandlishes weren't going to be my favourite people to have dinner with.

I caught up with the escapee toddler. "Hey, are you supposed to be in bed?"

She stopped, shaking her head.

I grinned. "Are you sure?"

Guiltily, she chewed her lip and then nodded. Spinning around, she ran in the opposite direction and headed for the stairs.

She'd dropped her giraffe. I stepped down the hallway and stooped to pick it up. Voices carried in the air. I looked around, not seeing anyone, then realised that Alban and Jessica were close by.

I took a few steps and found them in a luxurious-looking powder room. All the lights were off.

Jessica was standing at the window looking out, her arms tightly crossed. Alban was standing a short distance behind her.

They were speaking in quiet, tense voices. I knew that I should leave. But I stood fixedly, unable to make myself move. After seeing the bruises on Jessica's arms and finding out what the painting on the wall represented, I was morbidly curious to know more about who Alban and Jessica were.

"I don't know if I can do this," Jessica was saying. "The pretence. Having to act like everything's okay. Why'd we have to come here tonight?"

"They invited us, Jess. I went to speak to them about the tattie bogle thing. Gus said he might want a design done on an investment property of his in London. Anyway, it's just a dinner and a bit of a chat." He shrugged.

"I'm tired of the chat," she snapped. "I'm tired of pretending like everything's all right when it isn't. And I'm tired of having a bloody photographer living under our noses. I'm falling apart, and you don't care."

"Of course I care."

"No, you don't. If you did, you wouldn't put me through this. I'm just trying to do the best thing for Rhiannon. We need to get away from here. Move to Edinburgh and start to live again. This house, Braith-noch—it's like it all exists on an island away from the world. And we're trapped on it. How do you think I feel knowing that the play-house is still standing there in the woods? Like some kind of macabre memorial. Every time I look at the woods, all I can think of is her."

"I'm not leaving the place where our daughter spent her years here on this earth." Alban's voice was wracked dry with emotion.

"We have another daughter to think of," Jessica cried. "Have you forgotten her? You're obsessed with Elodie. It's not healthy, Alban. She's gone. And obsessing about her isn't going to bring her back, no matter how much we wish it would."

Drawing in a deep, silent breath I backed away. I hurried along the hallway and back to the kitchen. I felt stung by Jessica's words. I was that *bloody photographer* staying in the cottage on her land. I knew I shouldn't take it personally—it was obvious she was feeling trapped and angry and she was lashing out. But it was impossible not to feel bad. I wished I'd never come here. It'd been a stupid idea from the start.

I found Rhiannon sitting on the bottom stair and picked her up.

The Chandlishes and Greer turned around to me as I re-entered the living room.

"I'm not sure where the McGregors are, but I managed to catch this little imp." I grinned, trying to cover up my discomfort.

Alban and Jessica walked in a minute after I did.

Jessica took Rhiannon from me. "What's she doing here?"

Peyton smiled widely, winking at me. "She escaped from Alcatraz. She heard people downstairs and came to party."

Jessica sighed. "She must have climbed out of the cot."

"Goodnight, Rhiannon." I waved at the toddler as Jessica took her away.

Aubrey and Diarmid came in just as the chef was serving out dinner.

"Oh my God, Isla," said Aubrey as she seated herself at the table. "I'd have absolutely freaked if I'd seen that bogle up in the tree. You'd have heard me scream clear to Inverness."

"Lucky for our collective ears that you weren't there, then," remarked Diarmid dryly.

"It's okay," I murmured, sitting down next to her. "I wasn't scared. I hope Trent is all right."

She nodded, squeezing my arm assuredly. "He's recovering. Don't worry, we'll find out who strung up the bogle. And they'll have hell to pay."

"Such an absurd thing to happen." Deirdre Chandlish had a

distasteful expression as she flicked her gaze over me. "Completely absurd."

"We certainly don't want people like that hanging about." Jessica toyed with a spoon, her chin tense beneath tight lips. "I find it frightening. I mean, I have to live here. And when Alban is away, I worry for Rhiannon."

"Of course." Deirdre shook her well-coiffed head. "You of all people don't need rubbish like this happening. Aubrey, you really need to be more careful about who you bring to the house."

Diarmid munched a bread roll. "Told her that Trent guy was a dick."

"Language, please." Gus Chandlish's voice boomed out. "Leave that talk for when you're away from the dinner table."

"We don't know for sure that it was Trent," Aubrey mumbled, drawing her fingers through hair that was messed from the wind.

"Aye, right." Peyton rolled his eyes tiredly. "Well, that leaves your boyfriend, Simon."

"Come to think of it," added Diarmid, "both Trent and Simon were roaming about in the woods that night. Deduce from that what you will, people. One of them—or both—is the bogle rustler. Now, what reasons did they have to accost a poor bogle and string him up in a tree? How did they even manage to ascend said tree with said bogle? These are the questions that must be asked." Diarmid smirked, apparently feeling pleased with himself.

"That's enough," called his father. "Just drop it."

In response to her brothers, Aubrey let her head drop, staying silent. I guessed that things hadn't gone well in her relationship with Simon.

Greer smiled around at everyone. "Isla and I had a lovely day today in Inverness. The weather was good to us. Isla certainly gave her camera a workout. The Ness Islands and the Botanic Gardens. Even Loch Ness, though the wind had gotten a tad bitey by then."

I blew out a breath, glad that Greer had saved the strained mood at the table.

"Oh, how marvellous," said Deirdre, seeming as glad I was that Greer had changed the subject. "I'm glad you two enjoyed your day."

"We did indeed," said Greer. "We even stopped at a little abandoned church on the way back. Isla thought it would be a good photo opportunity. These creative types notice things the rest of us don't."

"Don't write the rest of us off," Peyton joked. "I've got a fondness for old places myself. Lots of history. Will you be uploading today's pictures on your website, Isla? I'd be interested in seeing your church. I had a peek at your other work earlier today. It's bloody brilliant."

I broke into a grin. "Thank you."

The chef served out dinner—fish and vegetables. All beautifully cooked.

During dinner, the conversation flowed naturally. I was content to sit quietly, answering questions when I was asked.

Deirdre took a delicate dab at her mouth with a napkin. "So, Jessica, what have you been up to lately? Gus and I have been away for quite a while. We need to catch up with you both."

Jessica waved a hand. "Oh, nothing much. I can't speak for Alban, but you know me. I'm just there at home with Rhiannon. Can't do much else when they're that age. We went to look at some houses on the weekend. There's some lovely ones at Corstorphine. And of course, it's right near Edinburgh Zoo, and Rhiannon would love that. She adores animals."

"Do tell?" Deirdre opened her eyes inquisitively. "Are you thinking of buying there in Edinburgh? Are you moving?"

"Just an investment," said Alban quickly.

"Oh, who knows," said Jessica. "We might just fall in love with one of the streets there and decide to move."

"Move away from Braithnoch?" Gus Chandlish looked startled. "That would be a big change." He settled back in his chair. "But, you know, it could be a positive one. Lots more there for a wee bairn to do. There's not any other children around this part of Greenmire now."

Alban's back grew rigid, his mouth twisting a little. "I'll not leave Braithnoch, not even when I'm cold and dead in the ground."

No one spoke. It seemed that nothing was going to bring the conversation back from *that*.

"I'm sorry," said Jessica, placing a hand on her stomach. "I'm feeling a wee bit ill. Please, everyone, carry on. I think I need to have a lie down."

"You poor thing," said Mrs Chandlish. "I'll walk you upstairs. You can have a rest on the bed next to Rhiannon."

The chef brought dessert out, but the mood at the table was definitely stilted. I was relieved when Peyton suggested going to sit out in the lounge room. At least, everyone wouldn't be sitting so formally and staring at each other then.

The night lasted barely an hour longer.

Greer drove me back to the cottage. "I'm sorry that tonight got a bit difficult in a few spots," she told me apologetically.

"I'll survive." I stifled a yawn.

"Poor thing. It's been a long day for you. Tuck yourself up into bed and have a good sleep."

As soon as Greer was gone, I crawled into bed, feeling like a child who'd had a confusing day. I was Alice in the *underland*, trying to make sense of people and things that made no sense at all. Somehow, I'd stopped looking in through the door and found my way into that strange world.

When I dreamed that night, I dreamed of the old house with the long corridor.

The dream left me gasping and reeling as I woke in the middle of the night.

This time, feet dangled mid-air in a room of the house, same as last time. I stepped inside, not wanting to enter but compelled to anyway.

I looked inside the dark room.

It wasn't my father hanging from the rafters of that room, but a scarecrow.

18

ELODIE

Greenmire, Scottish Highlands, December 2015

EVERYTHING WAS QUIET, but for the steady *beep, beep, beep* of a machine.

Elodie knew she was in a hospital because everyone kept reminding her, from the nurses to the doctors to Daddy.

She was in a hospital and in a coma. That much she knew. Only, no one would tell her why or what happened to her.

You're in hospital, Elodie. My name is Nurse Lucy. You're going to be all right. You just need to rest here for a while. Good girl.

That was all she was told, over and over again. But she still couldn't wake or open her eyes or see.

"We need to keep grounding her," Nurse Lucy told Daddy. "People in comas easily get confused."

"Can she hear us?" Elodie heard Daddy's voice clearly.

"It's best to assume that she can. Just keep holding her hand and talking to her."

Daddy was holding her hand? She couldn't feel it.

"Please, is she better than she was last night?" Daddy's voice cracked on the word *night*.

Elodie listened hard for the answer. Nurse Lucy took her time before she said, "You'll have to wait for the doctor. I can't give you an answer to that. She'll be here soon."

"What's keeping her?" Daddy snapped. "I don't want to wait for the damned doctor while she takes her sweet time. I'll go find her myself and drag her in here."

"Mr McGregor—"

"I'll be back in a few minutes, Elodie," Daddy told her. "I won't be long."

But she didn't know what long—or short—meant anymore. She'd vanished into a darkness that seemed like forever.

She heard Daddy's footsteps grow fainter.

With Daddy gone, a mist entered her mind. Thick, swirling. Frightening.

Wheels softly squeaked from across the room. The squeaking came closer.

"Elodie," came a voice, "it's Mummy."

Mum. She'd gone out to get the potatoes. Elodie recalled the cold, quiet house—the air inside growing dim. She'd run about switching the lights on one by one. What happened after that? How did she end up in the playhouse? Maybe Mum would tell her.

"I'm in a silly wheelchair," Mum said. "Can you believe it? A wheelchair. So, I can't come up there and hug you like I'm dying to."

Mum was in a wheelchair? Too many things were happening that she didn't understand.

"My sweet girl, I love you so dearly. I need you to get better. Can you do that for me, Elly?"

Silence followed. A response pushed sluggishly through Elodie's mind, like a current in a mud-choked creek, the way the creek that flowed through the back of Braithnoch sometimes looked in summer. But she couldn't speak. Her lips were unable to form sounds.

"I have some news for you," Mum said. "A surprise. Your wee baby sister was born last night. You have a sister, Elodie."

Elodie attempted to process the words. The baby wasn't supposed to be born yet. Mum had said it'd be a Christmas baby.

"That's why I couldn't come back straight away," Mum told her. "Your sister was in a big hurry to come out and meet you. I wish it had happened differently and that you could see her. How I wish."

Mum hadn't come back with the potatoes because the baby had to be born. Elodie understood now.

She's beautiful, just like you," Mum continued. "I'm going to call her Rhiannon. You always said if Daddy and I had another little girl, we should call her Rhiannon. And so that will be her name. She's a wee bit ill at the moment—she's in intensive care. But she's going to be okay. And so are you, sweet girl."

Mum's voice kept fading to a hoarse whisper and she said the last part through tears, but Elodie understood it all. She was used to Mum crying.

"You have to wake up and see her," Mum whispered, still crying. "She's got blonde hair and blue eyes, and a cheeky little dimple like Daddy. Oh, she's so tiny, Elodie. Little fingers and toes. I've told her all about you and she can't wait to meet you."

Elodie pictured a tiny, wriggling baby. The picture in her mind made her want to cry. She'd been waiting to see the baby for so long. And now she couldn't see anything at all. Would Mum let the baby share a room with her? The baby was a girl, so maybe Mum would. Elodie wouldn't mind if Rhiannon cried in the nights.

"I have to go now, Elly Belly, the baby will need feeding again soon. I'll come back as soon as I can. Just rest and get better. And when you're ready, you can see Rhiannon. Okay? Promise me you'll wake up soon. Bye for now, baby girl."

The wheelchair squeaked from the room.

Mum hadn't called her *Elly Belly* since she was small.

She held what her mother had just told her tight and protected deep inside her. She had a baby sister. And her name was Rhiannon. And she had dimples.

Elodie heard shuffling noises and realised that someone else was in the room.

"A baby sister, Elodie. How lovely." It was Nurse Lucy. She'd never left. It felt comforting to know she wasn't alone. She didn't want to be alone.

Another nurse entered the room—at least, she guessed she was a nurse because she and Nurse Lucy seemed to be checking things and talking briefly about scans and readings.

When she next heard them speak, they were quieter. They'd moved across the room and they were using voices that were just above whispers. Elodie knew they thought she couldn't hear them. But she could hear every word.

"Was that Jessica McGregor—the girl's mother?" said the nurse who was helping Nurse Lucy.

"Yes," replied Nurse Lucy. "The wheelchair is only temporary. She's on strong medication and she's not okay to walk about yet. She went into shock apparently when she heard about her daughter."

"The poor thing. It's totally understandable."

"She'd only just given birth, too. Last night."

"What? Oh, Lucy, my goodness, that's harsh."

"She apparently popped out to grab something for dinner and then lost control of the car. The car crash put her into labour. She came in by ambulance. She was quite confused, apparently."

"How terrible. That explains the nasty bump on her head."

"Yes, it does."

"Oh God. So, this means, when the mother was in labour—after the crash—that's when Elodie was abducted?"

"As far as I know."

Elodie strained to hear more. What did *abducted* mean? Mum hadn't said she was in a car crash. All of it explained why she hadn't come back to make dinner. Elodie remembered how she'd wanted to get the house warm for Mum before she returned. To make Mum happy. She remembered going out to the wood shed—

"Is the baby okay?" was the next thing Elodie heard the other nurse say.

"Yes, thank goodness," said Nurse Lucy. "She's four weeks early, but she's doing well."

"That's a big relief. Does Elodie have anyone to sit with her? I mean, the mother is going to be kept busy with a new baby to care for."

"The father was just here, but he stormed off to look for a doctor, all angry and cursing."

"I hate it when they do that."

Nurse Lucy sighed. "Yep. I told him the doctor wouldn't be long. Och, but I can't blame him being anxious, considering the circumstances. I'd be out of my mind with worry, too. I'll give him a pass."

"You're a good nurse, Lucy."

"I try my best. Just like you, Ally."

They moved closer again to Elodie, continuing to check on her, touching things and moving them about. They spoke louder now, and they spoke *to* her, telling her what they were doing and that she was going to be okay.

For a moment, Elodie could see shadows flickering through her eyelids and she thought she could almost see the nurses' faces. But then her world went completely dark again.

19

ISLA

WHEN I WOKE at first light, Elodie was on my mind.

The ghost of Elodie had been silently threading through my time here at Braithnoch from the moment I'd first arrived. She was everywhere, in the McGregor's house, in the wood, on the moor and even inside this cottage. I couldn't stop myself from thinking about the little girl who once lived here.

I made my mind up. I was going to go to Elodie's school and talk to Rory about her. I'd do a full morning of work on the portfolio and then head to the school.

A nervous feeling uncoiled in my stomach. I had no business doing this. But something not entirely rational had taken over me. The path the abductor had taken from the forest kept drawing and redrawing itself in my head. I had to know more about what happened to Elodie and why Alban was keeping that painting on his wall.

I ate a bowl of warm porridge, trying to relax and settle my nerves.

Through the kitchen window, the sky behind the McGregor house looked clear and unusually bright. It'd be a great morning to do a photo shoot in the house's interior, as it would be filled with light. The last thing I wanted to do was to deal with Jessica today, after what I'd overheard her telling Alban about me last night. But I had a job to do.

Gulping the remainder of my porridge, I packed up my camera and lenses and then headed along the seven stepping stones to the driveway, and then onto the house.

Jessica was bleary-eyed and still in her pyjamas as she answered the door to me. "Isla, so sorry, I was upstairs."

I patted my camera bag. "The light is great for an interior shoot this morning. Would it be all right if I—?"

She shook her head before I'd had a chance to finish my sentence. "It's not a good time. Rhiannon had a bad night. Nightmares about tattie bogles."

"Oh no. Poor little girl."

"She's quite delicate. It was a shit of a thing to happen." She eyed me coolly.

Was she partly blaming me for the scarecrow hanging?

"Yes, it was a terrible thing," I replied. "Have the police found out anything more?"

"Nope. Here's hoping that Trent will be well enough to talk to the police soon and he can tell them what exactly went on that night."

"Definitely. Are you sure I can't take just a few photos? I'm starting to realise that sunny days are not the usual here. And even the sun on sunny days doesn't seem to last."

"The house is upside-down. I haven't had a chance to clean up properly after going away. I'm afraid I'm very tired and so is Rhiannon. Neither of us got a good night's sleep."

I'd never seen the house anywhere near approaching upside-down and I doubted it was in that state now. Jessica was obsessive about cleaning.

"Oh, no problem. Hope you both manage to take a nap."

She flashed a quick, exhausted smile. "That would be lovely. Rhi's not good with napping—she's hit the terrible two's and has decided that she's too big for naps."

I was about to step away when my gaze fell to a fresh bruise on Jessica's wrist, easy to see due to the loose sleeve of her top.

Noticing where I was looking, she tugged her pyjama sleeve down to cover it.

"Did you hurt yourself?" I couldn't just walk away and say nothing. Not now that I'd seen the bruise.

She puffed up her cheeks and exhaled in a short laugh. "Yes, stupid me. I don't even know how I did that one."

"That one?" I said, startled. She'd just admitted to having more. Taking a breath, I told her what was on my mind. "Forgive me for saying this, but if someone's hurting you, you don't have to put up with it."

Shock registered on her face. "What? Oh, it's nothing like that," she gasped. "Gosh, no. Really. I'm a klutz. Always knocking myself about."

"Well, take good care, okay?" With a warm smile, I left without giving her a chance to protest further. I knew that a wall had been put up and it was pointless trying to press any harder. I didn't believe what she'd said for a second. At least I'd said what I wanted to say. Maybe sometime, even months from now, she'd remember that someone told her she shouldn't stay silent about this.

She closed the door quickly as I stepped away.

I wandered about the property, finding the best angles to take pictures of the house. The glass and smoked larch cladding looked incredible under the morning sun, a crystalline sheen on the windows. I was almost glad Jessica had sent me away. These pictures were going to be stunning. It was only when I checked the viewfinder that I noticed Rhiannon at her upstairs bedroom window, fingers against the glass. It wasn't my intention to have a child in these photographs, but I guessed a homely touch suited this particular portfolio.

A short distance away from Rhiannon's bedroom was a room where the blinds were permanently halfway between open and closed —Elodie's bedroom. She must have looked out on Braithnoch from up there just like Rhiannon, except her view was of the forest.

I noticed another figure up there at one of the windows then. Jessica. She resented me being here. Maybe I understood why. If she hated Braithnoch, then she'd hate the person who was photographing it and trying to show it at its best.

Happy with my pictures of the house, I uploaded them to my online storage and then started the walk up to the hills. I could take sweeping shots of the property from up there.

I ended up spending a couple of hours in the hills. Venturing across to the rocky side of the hills to the left, I walked up close to the ruins of the stone house I'd seen before. This must be what Alban had been talking about—the original stone cottage that his ancestors had built.

I began snapping some photos.

An hour later I was done. The photos I'd taken this morning were going to look incredibly beautiful, sunrise glowing on the house and lush green land.

I tidied myself up back at the cottage and then set out on the bike. I'd have lunch in town before picking up the rest of my prescription medicine—it should be ready by now. It worried me being without my full round of medication. After that, I'd head to the school.

During my ride into town, I found myself stopping repeatedly to take photos. It really was a pretty day.

Sitting in a café in Greenmire, I watched the residents pass by, while I indulged in a long and leisurely lunch. I had lots of time to kill before the day at the local school was done. At two-thirty, I picked up my prescription from the chemist and hopped back on my bike.

The school was located next to a wide river that was fringed by willows and nestled between rolling green hills. I headed along the path that led to the school gates, trying to still my nerves and rehearsing in my head what I'd say to Rory.

The bell rang at a quarter past three. It was an actual school bell, not a loud buzzer or a snatch of music. I didn't think I'd even heard one of those before, except in a church.

Streams of kids emerged from the school gates. Threading through the crowd, I stepped inside the school, stopping to ask an older child where Mr Kavanagh's classroom was. The boy pointed to the right, telling me it was the second-last room, right next to a willow tree.

Be bold, I told myself. The worst that can happen is that you sound like a bit of an idiot.

I poked my head inside the classroom and immediately spotted Rory. Windblown hair framed his long face, thick glasses perched on his nose. He wore skinny jeans and orange shoes. I was reminded of Hamish's description of him—like Einstein crossed with a hipster. It was fairly accurate. A chatty mother had Rory's attention, holding tight to her chubby toddler-son's hand. A bored looking boy of about eight sat on a chair, swinging his legs. I slunk back a little, intending to wait my turn, but Rory noticed me.

A frown flickered between his eyebrows. "Just a moment," he told the mother. "Isla, isn't it? Are you here to see me?"

"Yes. It's not anything urgent." I smiled self-consciously as the woman turned and inspected me with curious eyes.

"Oh, I'm done here," said the woman. "I'm glad to hear my Lyall is doing better with his literacy. He's a lot like his father. I don't think that man has so much as read a set of Ikea instructions in his life, let alone a book." She nodded at the teacher as she laughed, as if prompting him to laugh along with her.

Rory did laugh, and to his credit it sounded natural. "It would be a boring old world if everyone was the same."

He ended their conversation with a promise to push Lyall a little harder to get his work done. The boy on the chair—Lyall, I assumed —didn't seem pleased with that. The woman hung around in the classroom as Rory motioned for me to come and sit on a chair near his desk.

"Was there anything, else, Flora?" Rory asked the woman.

She gave a small, sheepish smile. "No, I guess not. Come on then, Lyall, we'd better go, or Mr Kavanagh will set you some work to do."

A confused Lyall jumped up and fled the classroom, his mother following.

"It's a small town," Rory told me once they were out of earshot. "There'll always be a few who are looking for morsels of gossip. Flora Penwright is unfortunately one of them. Nice lady, but you have to be careful what you tell her. I've learned that the hard way." He puffed up his cheeks and exhaled. "Now, what can I do for you?"

I noticed that the Scottish had a way of ending a sentence on an upward inflection that sounded honest and casual, while their eyes might tell a different story. I guessed that he knew I wasn't here to chat about the weather.

"It's really nothing important," I started. "I'm just…curious. I just wanted to ask you a couple of things. About Elodie."

His expression barely changed, but his fingers curled around the pen that he held. "Oh yes?"

I'd already decided not to ask about Alban first up. That was going to be a difficult subject to broach. I stuck to the script I'd rehearsed in my head.

"I'm meant to be doing a perspective on the McGregor family," I started, "for the photography portfolio. And that naturally includes Elodie. I'd like to put something of her in the portfolio. To that end, I'd like to know more about her. Who she was and all of that."

"I think the best source for that might be her parents," he said carefully.

"I did try asking Alban, but the subject of Elodie seems just too raw for him. And Jessica hasn't been well, so I don't want to bother her with this."

"Jessica's unwell?"

"She's not sick, exactly. I guess it's stress. Which is understandable, after all she's been through."

"Yes, of course. Okay, well, Elodie was a lovely girl. A great sense of humour. Very serious at times, but deep thinkers tend to be. She'd argue a point if she thought she was right. She wasn't at the top of her class, academically, but she was one of the most curious and eager to learn students I've ever had the pleasure to teach." He paused. "She wasn't perfect. There was an incident in which she pushed another child. We never did get to the bottom of that one, as Elodie unfortunately died the week after."

"You have no idea why she pushed the other child?"

"These things happen all the time amongst kids. It was a good friend of hers, actually, so it was probably just some wee tiff between pals. I was just trying to give you a well-rounded view. People tend to put the dead on a pedestal and I think it does them a disservice. Elodie was a living, breathing little girl. She was real. Anyway, it was also true of Elodie that she'd be the first to stand up for the kids who were getting picked on."

"Oh. Of course, kids do fight. But I wonder, did Elodie seem unhappy at all in those last weeks?"

His fingers uncurled and curled again on the pen. "You're asking some very specific questions, if you don't mind me saying."

I felt my chest tighten. "It's just that, after you left the other day, I started wondering if there wasn't something more to you wanting to see Elodie's paintings."

"What do you mean?"

I steeled myself. "Rory, you don't go to all that trouble of going up to a former student's bedroom to check their paintings *just because*. You had a strong reason."

He exhaled, considering my words. "If you think I had some kind of bad intent, let me assure you that I didn't."

"No, I don't think that. I'm just curious, that's all."

"Well, I'm afraid I can't tell you too much. I did notice something a little odd about Elodie's drawings at school, and it made me wonder if she drew the same way at home. I knew she was pretty prolific with her art."

"What was unusual about her pictures?"

"Nothing extreme. And I'm no children's art expert. But I've noticed that kids tend to draw themselves larger than life. Which stands to reason—they do play the starring role in their own lives, after all. But in Elodie's pictures, she tended to draw herself smaller than everyone else, even smaller than much younger children. And she was not really ever doing anything. She'd draw other people having fun—playing, throwing balls, swimming—but not Elodie herself. She drew herself with her arms by her side."

"Okay. And the pictures in her room were the same?"

"Yes, they were. At least, the ones that had her in them at all. She often left herself out. Which is another unusual thing. If kids are drawing a group of their friends or family, they usually draw them-selves front and centre."

"So, it was like she was invisible?"

"Exactly."

"Did you draw any conclusions—from her drawings?"

"As I mentioned, I don't pretend to be an expert. I'm just a teacher. It did seem to me though that she was trying to erase herself. She'd become increasingly quieter in class and things like that as well."

"That sounds really sad."

He nodded, exhaling.

I drew my mouth in, nibbling on my gum and trying to figure out how to say what I wanted to ask him next. I'd been surprised by how open he'd been so far, and I didn't want to say anything to make him close up. "You still have an interest in finding out about Elodie... don't you? I mean, even though she's gone now?"

He hesitated. In the silence, I felt as if I were falling down a rabbit hole.

"Yes, I admit that the whole thing has haunted me," he said finally. "I still want answers."

Taking a breath, I clasped my hands together firmly. "Can I ask if you think Elodie's pictures have any connection to her abduction?"

His fist closed on the pen. "I'm not putting together those kinds of conclusions."

"Okay, but is it true that you have put some thoughts together on the abduction?"

He blinked at me, then sighed under his breath and glanced away. "Okay, yes, a part of me has wondered if her art has anything to do with what happened to her. I mean, the jury is still out as to whether the guy was passing by the town or whether he's a local. If he's a local, would she have had an interaction or two with this person before—something that had a terrible effect on her? That's what plays on my mind."

"I appreciate your honesty, Rory. Did you ever talk to the McGregors or go to the police with your concerns?"

"As a matter of fact, yes. The police took an interest at first. They were looking for any possible leads, any clues, as you can imagine. And I told them my thoughts on her paintings. They came here to the school to talk with me and see her work, and as far as I understand, they did go to the McGregor house to take a look at her work there. But nothing came of it." Letting the pen drop, he rubbed his eyes tiredly. "Alban was angry with me after that. Told me to stay away from his family."

"Wow, that's odd," I said, even though I'd already guessed as much. "Did you know what made Alban so mad?"

He shrugged. "Eh, I don't know. Perhaps because I spoke to the police rather than Alban himself. He's very protective of his family."

He eyed me with a direct gaze. "Perhaps we're better to leave this discussion here. It's starting to veer off track."

"Please, something's been on my mind. I need to know, is that the real reason you came to the McGregor house that day—because you wanted to see Elodie's work, and you knew that the McGregors were away at the time? I haven't told the McGregors you came into the house, if you're wondering."

Rory looked distinctly unsettled, his palms pressed flat against the desk. "Look, Isla, this all involves things that happened a long time before you arrived here. What I'm saying is that there's a lot of history. If all you're wanting is to know about Elodie, I hope I've provided you with some information."

"I...there's something else. Something that I discovered. It concerns Elodie. I don't know who to talk to about it."

A subtle gleam of interest entered his eyes. He seemed to have suddenly forgotten about ending the discussion. "Perhaps you could tell me."

"I could, but before I do that, I want to be sure you'll handle this in the strictest of confidences. In return, I'll keep your visit to Elodie's room in confidence." I drew a breath. "Also, I'll keep it secret that you were still there, on the McGregor's land, an hour or so after I thought you'd left."

His shoulders sank. "You saw me? I went looking for the play-house. Do you know about the—?"

"Yes, I know about the playhouse. Why did you want to see it?"

"I heard by chance that it was still there, that it hadn't been taken down. I guess I wanted to see for myself."

"Someone overdosed in the playhouse the other night."

"Seriously? Who?"

"A friend of Aubrey Chandlish. Trent. He'd been staying at her house."

"Ah, that lot, eh?"

"Do you know the Chandlishes well?"

"We used to be friends when we were younger. Now, there was something you were going to tell me?" He settled back in his chair, waiting.

"Yes. It's the oddest thing. I guess you might have seen a map of the path Elodie's abductor took in and out of the forest that night?"

"Indeed, I have."

"And you would have seen that his path in—when he was chasing Elodie—was very random. But his path out was very strange."

"Yes. A lot was made of that at the time. People came up with all kinds of wild theories." His eyes seemed to harden. "What have you found out?"

"There's a painting on the wall in…a room, in a house here in Greenmire. All it consists of is a single black line in the middle of a white canvas. The line exactly matches the path the abductor took out of the forest."

Rory's mouth dropped, and he pushed himself away from the desk, silent for a moment as he processed what I'd just said.

"Are you certain?" he said, his voice tight.

I nodded. "Unmistakeable. I checked the lines side-by-side."

"Well, I don't know what to think about that. I seriously don't. Is there anything else that you discovered?"

"No, just that."

"Whose house is this, if I may ask?"

"I don't wish to say at this point."

"You can't have been to many houses in Greenmire so far."

"No, I haven't."

His eyes flicked over me. "Well, perhaps they are trying to figure it out. Maybe that's why the person has that picture on the wall."

"That's what I thought. I'm relieved that was your first thought, too. I'll be honest—I've had all kinds of thoughts running through my head."

"It's best not to speculate. That way lies madness. I should know." He pulled his chair back in towards the desk.

"I know. I shouldn't."

He gave me a concerned smile. "How's the job going—the one you're doing for Alban?"

I cleared my throat, wondering if this was a good time to talk about Alban. The conversation so far had been a little tense, but it probably had gone as well as it could have. Rory hadn't ordered me off the school grounds—yet—so that was something. By the way I was stalling, I was certain that he could already tell that things with the job weren't going well.

"Braithnoch is lovely and I'm enjoying myself," I started. "Greer took me to Inverness yesterday and I loved every minute."

"Great stuff. What are the McGregors like to work for?" He was leading me to say something. I could tell.

Still, I found it difficult to say. "They're nice people. They've had a lot to deal with and I'm sure they're doing the best they can." I shook my head, my eyes jamming shut for a moment. "But...there's a lot of tension there at the McGregor house. Tell me what you know about Alban—you two used to be friends?"

"Yes, we were friends years ago. But Alban's notoriously moody. I used to think he was just cultivating a kind of creative genius persona, you know? But I've begun thinking that maybe he really is a wee bit unstable."

"The whole thing with his daughter would make anyone unstable, right?"

"True enough. But this has been going on for five years or more. And since Elodie died, he seems to turn on people who are just trying to help."

"Like you requesting to see Elodie's paintings...."

"Exactly. I've even started seeing him as a bit big-headed." He drummed his fingers on the desk. "I shouldn't say that. Listen to me, running off at the mouth. I shouldn't be saying any of it. But I feel comfortable with you, and you're not from this town or even from Scotland. In this town, people are very proud of Alban McGregor. He's a success story."

"I'm glad you're comfortable with me. I find you easy to talk with, too. I didn't know who to speak to about this whole thing with Elodie, or even if I should."

"Well, I'm glad you did. I'm finding that no one wants to speak about her. It took a stranger to this town to start up that conversation again."

"This question's bit bold. But have you had any suspicions about anyone in particular—in regard to Elodie?"

"No one definite. I have some thoughts, but that's it. And I know it's been two years and all, but I feel that I keep getting thwarted in my attempts."

"By Alban?"

"Yes, but not just Alban. Jessica, too. And others. Like I said, I almost feel like there's a conspiracy of silence. It's as if no one in this town wants the culprit to be a local. They'd rather the whole mess just blow over and for the media to stop taking an interest in Greenmire." He sighed heavily. "Ah, I didn't mean to tell you that. It's just born of frustration, I think. Sometimes I almost feel like an outsider in this town. Which is crazy, seeing as I grew up here."

I smiled sympathetically. "I guess I can understand why they don't like the thought of it being someone from Greenmire. Because if it is, then it's going to be someone's relative, someone's friend, someone's neighbour. No one wants that kind of connection."

"That's right. And no one wants it to be someone ordinary, either. Because that's disturbing."

"Do you have any thoughts on the abductor himself? Any clues?"

"There isn't much to go on. Just the path he took from the forest and the fact that he medicated her. It doesn't seem that his intention was to kill her."

"Giving a little girl sleeping pills is fraught with danger."

"Indeed, it is. But if he wanted to ensure her death, he could have done so."

"It's so odd. He took her there, medicated her but did nothing else, and then left. Maybe he's someone who is mentally impaired."

"It's a possibility."

"Maybe something spooked him, and that's why he left the playhouse?" I ventured.

"I think that's likely," he agreed. "But if he was running away, he did it in a very strange way. He took his time to leave, as if he wasn't in any hurry."

"There has to be an answer in all of this somewhere."

He studied my face with his intense blue eyes. "Yes, indeed there does."

"Well, I should let you get home now. Thank you for talking with me. I feel a bit lighter."

He leaned forward in his chair. "I'm glad. If you have any more questions or concerns, don't hesitate to call me, okay? I really mean that." He wrote down his name and number. "And could I get your number, too—just in case I get an idea about something and we want to do some sleuthing."

I scribbled down my number and handed it to him, then tucked the notepaper he'd given me away in my handbag. "You have the neatest handwriting I've ever seen. I think most of us are losing the art of writing—we're all so used to computers."

"Och," he said with a grin, "Neat writing is an occupational hazard for teachers trying to teach first graders how to form letters."

A grey light had overtaken the sunshine by the time I walked out of the school. I did feel lighter. At least I'd told someone about the painting—someone who was interested in finding out who Elodie's abductor was.

20

ISLA

SNATCHES OF SHOUTED words reached my ears. Crossing to the kitchen window, I peered out.

Despite the morning sun, a mist rolled around the grounds. Alban and Jessica stood in the mist just outside the house. I could only see the top halves of them, making the scene seem surreal. She was flinging her arms up in the air. He was ordering her back into the house, roaring at her. Dropping her arms, she turned and headed inside, her head down. The sunrise was splintering on the rooftop and I could only just make out that a little girl was standing at the window of her upstairs bedroom—Rhiannon. I wondered how often the McGregors argued and how much Rhiannon heard. It was sad.

I'd planned on trying to do the interior shoot of the house this morning. But now it was out of the question. Again.

I knew what Greer would say—you're here to do a job and it's never a good time with the McGregors. Still, I couldn't just barge in there in the middle of them having an argument. If I'd known what I was walking into on this assignment, I'd have done the interior shoot before the McGregors returned home from their trip.

I sat down to breakfast. Yesterday, before heading over to talk to Rory, I'd bought some lovely pasties to have for breakfast. Greer was right about the weather making me hungry. Luckily, I'd found that I could stuff quite a lot into the front basket of the bicycle.

Last night, I'd dined by myself in the cottage. Greer had been in Inverness and I'd turned down Alban's invitation to dinner. I'd enjoyed the peace and quiet of being by myself, watching some Scottish shows on the little television. The conversation I'd had with Rory had also been constantly replaying through my mind and I'd needed some space.

I gazed past the house, into the hills and mountains. Perhaps I could photograph the odd collection of scarecrows on the hill. The more I thought about it, the more I liked the idea. It would be my way of claiming back power over the scarecrows, after finding one of the damned things hanging in the tree.

After breakfast, I packed up my gear and headed out. Jessica was driving away from the house. She stared across at me as I walked down the steps of the cottage. I waved at her, but I didn't expect her to wave back. She didn't.

It seemed to me that the fog that I was walking through smelled of the forest. Of lichen and leaves and damp ground.

My talk with Rory still tumbled in my mind. Before I'd come on this trip, I couldn't have imagined myself sitting down with one of Greenmire's teachers to discuss a terrible crime committed against a young girl. I felt as if there was an undertow in this town, tugging me.

Puffing as I walked up and down endless hills, I eventually reached what I called *scarecrow hill*. The scarecrows would now number one less than when I'd arrived in Braithnoch.

Tired from the walk, I sat on a rock. From this angle, the scarecrows loomed like ancient sentinels on the hill, half silhouetted by the sun, mist swirling at their footings. It was actually a great perspective.

I pulled out the camera and took a set of photographs. Rising, I stepped around the pack of odd figures, snapping a picture here and there. The photos were going to look eerily good. If I couldn't use any of them in the portfolio, at least the followers of my Instagram page would love them.

The muscles in my back flinched as one of the figures moved.

Someone was standing in front of one of the scarecrows, arms and legs outstretched and head hanging down. A teenage girl. I hadn't seen her due to the sun being in my eyes. Her faded overalls and floppy hat blended well with the scarecrows, too.

When she jerked her head up, I recognised her as the girl who'd been sitting on the neighbour's fence the other day. What had Nora Keenan said her name was? *Stella.* Yes, that was it.

The girl laughed. "Saw you coming a right mile away. Thought I'd give ya a bit of a scare." Her particular brand of Scottish accent sounded a lot like her grandmother's.

"Well, you got me good, Stella. Almost dropped my camera!"

"How'd you know my name?" Eyeing me suspiciously, she flounced away from the scarecrow and marched up to me.

"Your grandparents told me about you. Come here often?"

"Yeah. When I want someone sensible to talk to."

That pulled a grin from me. "Do the scarecrows give out any good advice?"

"No, but I sure do give them an ear bashing. Well, I would, if they had any ears."

She sounded so young. She *was* so young. Despite her height and angular cheekbones, she was just a child. Fourteen, I remembered Nora saying.

"If you try'an'take my picture again," she added, "I'll moon the lens."

"I didn't even know you were there, to be honest."

"People who say they're being honest are never being honest."

I smiled ruefully at that. She was being deliberately antagonistic, but I knew better than to play that game. I'd played it when I was a teenager and I knew better than anyone it was a game an adult couldn't win. "Try not to hide that you're hanging out with scarecrows, Stella, and I'll try to avoid taking your picture."

"I hate the scarecrows. I'd make 'em all burn if I had my way. And don't call me by my name when I don't even know you. Haven't you heard about stranger danger?"

"I was just being neighbourly. Even though I'll only be a neighbour for a short while."

"I'm not very neighbourly. Haven't you heard?"

"I haven't heard much at all," I lied. I wasn't going to tell her that Nora had told me quite a bit about her.

"What are you doin' up this way? You make a habit of heading into other people's property, don't ya?"

"I'm just looking around, that's all. I don't have a car and I'm kind of stuck here most of the time."

"You don't sound very professional, for a photographer. My nan told me what you do for a living—photography."

I stretched my shoulders, looking away and casually snapping a picture of the forest. "That's right. That's what I do." I ignored her first comment.

"Do you have a boyfriend?"

"No. I did, but he dumped me. Years ago. Now, I don't bother. You?"

"None of your business."

"You don't like to talk about yourself, do you?"

She shrugged. "Better that way. I don't want things about me getting back to my mum."

"Well, I've got no interest in telling anyone anything. Like I said, I'll be heading back home, soon." Stepping away from her, I followed the path of a bird with my camera lens and took a photo of it in flight.

"Do you make a lot of money, doing what you do?" she asked.

"I'm doing okay. Hope you don't think it's bigheaded if I say I'm good at what I do."

"You do sound like you have tickets on yourself." After a brief pause, she said, "You should do celebrity photos. Online magazines would pay a lot of money for those. You know, like, what are the Kardashians doing today? And, what did Harry Styles have for break-fast? That sort of thing."

I spun around to her. "I can't see myself as one of the paparazzi. I don't like to invade people's private moments."

"They're gettin' paid big money to be famous. They expect people want photos of 'em."

"I guess. But not every minute of the day."

"I'd be sticking up my rude finger at the paparazzi big-time if I was famous. Every single photo of me would be like that. They wouldn't be able to print them in most places."

I laughed.

"Sometimes I'd moon them just for a change," she added.

"Now *that* they would print," I said.

She sobered. "You're probably right. Scumbags. Can't go giving them what they want. People just take pieces of you without a second thought, if they think they can get away with it."

"You sound pretty wise for your age."

"Yeah, well, I've had to wise up quick."

I snapped another picture of the forest. "I did hear one thing, about you. That you left home two years ago."

For a moment she looked taken aback, then nodded cautiously. "That's true. I did and all."

"You must have had a good reason."

"I left because I'm a giant brat."

"I don't know if I believe that."

"Why not? Everybody else does."

"You wouldn't come back to visit your grandparents if you were such a brat."

"They're sweethearts. How could I not come and visit them once in a while?"

"See? You're so not a brat. You must have had a reason for leaving that made sense to you."

Her cheeks were flushed. "I don't wanna talk about it anymore."

"Sure. I'm sorry. What's it like over where you live? I've only seen Greenmire and Inverness so far."

"Aviemore's okay, I guess. More interesting than here. I'm not doin' too well at school. Gonna leave soon as I get a good enough job. I'm working at a burger shop after school three days a week."

"Oh, good on you. It's not always easy for kids to get a job."

"Grandma says I could be a model if I wanted. I'm not pretty enough though."

"Are you kidding me? You're *so* pretty."

"You don't have to say that. Even my own mum says I look a bit goofy. Big teeth and all."

"What? No. She was probably just teasing. You have the height and the looks if you wanted to do modelling. It's not an easy path though. I've done a bit of photography for a model studio. The girls cop a lot of disappointment—they don't get most of the jobs they turn up for. It's not for the faint-hearted by any means."

"I'm not faint-hearted. I want to make money. Then I can go wherever I want and no one can make me do what I don't want to do." She indicated towards my camera. "If you like takin' picture of birds, I know where's there some ducks and grouse. The females aren't much to look at, but the males are real colourful. Up near the creek, where the berries grow."

"Show me the way."

"Okay, but you have to keep up."

She broke into a run. I knew straight away that I wasn't going to be able to keep up. She was probably hoping I'd try to run and then fall flat on my face on the moor. I wasn't going to give her the satisfaction. I kept to my own pace. If I lost sight of her, then so be it.

My phone rang. Plucking it from my pocket, I saw that the call was coming from a number I didn't recognise.

"Hello? Isla Wilson speaking," I said gingerly.

"Isla, it's Rory."

"Oh, hi. What's up?"

"It's just...I was wondering if you're planning on talking to anyone else? About the line painting that you saw?"

"No, I mean, it's not like I can go to the police with that. It's probably nothing, as you said. And who else could I tell?"

"Okay, good. It's better that you don't, at this point. Because, if the culprit is someone from this town, they could be tipped off that we're on their trail. It's better we fly under the radar, you know?"

"I agree. I'd better go, Rory. I'm trying to follow a teenage girl across a bumpy moor, and she's fast."

"A teenage girl?"

"Oh wait...she's your stepdaughter. Stella. She's taking me to see the creek here at Braithnoch." I'd forgotten that Rory was married to Stella's mother, Camille.

A clipped laugh came through the phone line. "Well, I'd better let you go then."

Stella had stopped, waiting for me to catch up. I sped up my pace.

The ground was growing stickier. With alarm, I realised where we must be headed.

"Stella," I called. "We can't go this way. The McGregors told me there's a peat marsh here. It's not safe."

Breathing hard with the exertion, I caught up with her quickly. At least I knew that the ground was solid enough up to where Stella was standing, as she hadn't disappeared into a pool of mud or anything.

She crossed her thin arms. "I used to go through here all the time. Or don't you trust me because I'm a kid?"

"Of course I trust you."

Without replying to that, she kept walking, picking her way through. Maybe I trusted her, but I didn't trust the ground not to fall away beneath my feet. Actually, no, I didn't trust her. She was just a kid and I should be ordering her back to her grandparents' house.

But she was already too far in. And there was no way a head-strong girl like her was going to obey a stranger. A thought came to me. Maybe this was some kind of test. To see if I trusted her enough to follow her.

Gritting my teeth, I followed, walking where she did, tracking her path. I didn't watch my feet—I just watched her.

The ground felt firmer and firmer underfoot.

We were on the other side of the bog. Already, I could hear gurgling water. We must not be far from the creek.

She turned to me, unable to stop a small smile from flitting across her face. "Your boots are muddy."

I shrugged.

Her smile grew wider.

"Hey," I said. "If you like, I can take some photos of you and show you just how pretty you are. I'd need your mother's permission first though."

She had a hopeful glint in her eye, then turned away shaking her head. She started walking fast. "No. I don't want to. Okay?"

I caught up. She was my only ticket out of here and I didn't want to lose her. I wouldn't be able to find my way back out of that bog. "Of course. Of course that's okay."

We walked in silence for another few minutes. Then we rounded a stand of trees and the creek came into view. A small wooden bridge spanned the width. After the muddy expanse of peat marsh, it was unexpectedly picturesque.

As we approached the creek, she stooped to pick up a handful of rocks and tossed them one by one into the water. I was reminded again of how young she was. Immediately, I felt bad for being annoyed with her earlier.

"When I was little, I thought a troll lived under that bridge," she said.

"It looks exactly like the kind of bridge a troll would live under." Taking my camera out, I took a few photos. There were no ducks or birds here at the moment, but I wished there were.

She picked a flower, twirling it between her fingers. The way the sun framed her, I ached to capture her in a photograph. To show her how lovely she was. But she'd asked me not to, and I had to respect that.

She let the flower drop in the creek. The water carried its newfound cargo downstream, spinning and dancing with it.

"Now I remember," I said.

"What?" She squinted at me.

"I saw a picture of you and Elodie on the McGregors' photo wall. I didn't realise it was you until now. You were younger. Maybe nine or ten. Elodie was little."

"I used to go over there sometimes when Mum brought me to visit my grandparents."

"And you were Elodie's babysitter for a while, right?"

"Yes. When she was eight. I was only twelve, but I'd done a bit of babysittin' already that year. And the McGregors knew me, so I think they felt okay with me."

I turned back to watch the trickling water. The flower had disappeared from view. "What did you think of them—the McGregors?"

"Why?"

"Just curious, I guess. They've been a little hard to get to know. Especially Mr McGregor."

She was silent as I glanced at her. There was a sudden hint of tears in her eyes.

"Stella? I'm sorry, what is it? Is it Mr McGregor?"

She nodded. "He scares me."

"Why does he scare you?"

"Because he'd make Jess cry. I'd hear them arguing upstairs."

You and me both, I thought darkly. I've seen and heard quite a bit of that even though I've only been here a few days.

162

"Do you think he scared Elodie, too?"

She bit her lip. "I don't know. She said some strange things sometimes."

"What kind of strange things?"

"She said—" Stella raised her head abruptly, looking past me.

I turned to see Rory Kavanagh stepping up to the bridge, his long legs making fast strides. "Stella. Hoo boy, you went a long way. Didn't think I'd ever find you."

"What do you want?" she said in a guarded voice.

Rory ignored her tone. "Your mum knows that you're staying at your grandparents' house. She'd love to have you over for dinner. I mean it. She really, really wants you to come—"

"No," Stella said.

"Just like that...no?" Rory lifted his eyebrows.

"You heard me, Rory," she answered.

"What about if dinner was at your grandparents'?" he countered. "You know, I'm sure your mum would agree to that, if you'd—"

"I said, *no*. If you or her come anywhere near Grandma's house, I swear I'll run off and hitchhike back to Aviemore."

Rory's shoulders slumped. "You're hurting her a lot."

"Get knotted." The teenager stalked away, then broke into a run.

"Will she be all right?" I asked. "Going through the peat marsh?"

"She took you *that* way?" Rory shook his head. "You don't have to go through the bog. The dirt road that goes past the Keenans and Chandlish properties goes all the way here. If you start at the hill with the scarecrows and take the path through the forest, and then go left, you end up here. Or if you keep going straight, you'll end up at the Chandlish house."

I sighed in response. "She tricked me." I remembered the straight path that led from the scarecrow hill to the Chandlish house, because I'd walked it with Aubrey. But it had been too dark to see that the path also went upward.

Rory was right—Stella was heading a different way than the direction we'd come in.

He watched as Stella disappeared from view, then swung his head back around to me. "I can't manage to say a thing right to her."

"She certainly seems to have a few issues."

"What were you two talking about?"

"Photography, mostly. I also asked her about Elodie."

"Drives me nuts how she won't talk to me." He eyed me curiously. "What did she say about Elodie?"

"She was about to say something. About strange things that Elodie had been saying. But then you walked up to us."

"Really? Damn. If there's one talent I have, it's that I have the best timing."

I stretched my mouth into a wry grin.

"Well, I've achieved nothing today except to make a mess of everything," he said mournfully.

"You didn't know," I told him.

I walked with Rory to the path and we started along it.

If Stella caught sight of me walking with Rory—and I was sure she would—she probably wouldn't open up to me again.

Life was a series of missed chances. You thought your life consisted of options, but it didn't. There were only ever chances, and you had to grab them while they lasted.

With Stella, I'd probably missed my chance.

21

ISLA

I STIRRED myself a hot chocolate back at the cottage, suddenly realising I was stirring so hard the cup was at risk of shattering.

What had Stella been on the edge of saying about Elodie?

I gazed out the kitchen window. Jessica's car was still gone. That meant it was just Alban at the house. Should I just march up there and ask him if I could photograph him and the house interior today?

I had to complete this portfolio, one way or another.

Making myself a quick lunch, I mentally prepared myself.

Just as I was washing up my plates, I saw Jessica drive back in.

Okay, that's a flat-out *no*. I knew what she'd say.

But I felt restless. I couldn't just stay inside the cottage all day.

I made myself a second hot chocolate, dropping three marshmallows in this time—rationalising that running about in freezing cold weather required chocolate and marshmallows.

I took my cup over to the table and sat glumly. Plucking one of Elodie's gold-tipped larch cones from the bowl once again, I fixed my gaze on it.

Who was it, Elodie? Who hurt you?

The one place in Braithnoch that I hadn't yet seen was the last place she'd ever stepped foot in. The playhouse. The thought came to me that my time here wouldn't be complete if I didn't see it for myself. The idea solidified in my mind. The playhouse wasn't far into the forest from the road. If I walked out to the road first, the McGregors couldn't see where I was headed.

But I could also get lost.

Taking out my phone, I brought up the image of the abductor's exit path that I'd copied. I could try to follow this, just in reverse.

I swallowed the last mouthful of hot liquid and then got myself ready in warmer clothing, stretching a knitted cap over my head. The afternoons often turned colder. I locked the cottage door behind me and set out.

On second thought, I grabbed the bicycle from the shed and rode it down the driveway and around the corner. If the McGregors spotted me, they'd think I was going into town or something.

A truck carrying hens rattled passed me on the road, heading into town. Nerves fizzed like electric wires under my skin. I told myself to settle. I was just going for a walk. No one knew what I was really doing. And it wasn't as if I were doing something dangerous.

I stashed the bike behind a tree.

Checking my phone, I found the spot where the abductor had emerged from the woods—just behind the speed sign, next to the spruce tree. The spruce tree was easy to spot. It still had its needles. Even in summer it'd be easy to spot, due to the blue colour of those.

Okay, just left of the sign and spruce—the entry point. Together, the sign and the spruce completely hid me from the road. It was a good place to be if you didn't want to be seen.

The news article had estimated the number of steps the abductor had taken. The interest in every tiny detail must have been intense in the weeks after Elodie was abducted and drugged. To follow the path, I just had to take extra-big man-sized steps. Maybe I'd get it wrong, but the playhouse wasn't too far in.

I couldn't get totally lost, as in *days-out-in-the-wild* lost, could I?

I remembered my brother telling me once that people thought they could walk in a straight line through a forest, but they couldn't. Without any reference points, people tended to walk in circles. Something about the brain constantly recalibrating the direction. I had to be extra-careful.

I counted my steps from the spruce into the forest. Then I stepped to the left, passing a tree blackened by lightning strike, trying to memorise everything for the path back. Straight ahead then until I came up against a wide tree that wasn't a larch—it was a tree that didn't fit the forest. I didn't know what it was, but I reached out and touched its smooth bark. You and me, tree. I don't fit here either.

There shouldn't have been a tree blocking my path. That meant I'd gotten the steps wrong. Already.

Should I go back and start again? Frustrated with myself, I tugged the elastic from my ponytail and used it to wind my hair up into a knot. I decided to keep going. It was when I came face to face with yet another tree that I kicked the ground and my gaze dropped to the forest floor. There was a thin path underneath the dry leaves. I hadn't needed to count my steps at all. Someone walked this way often.

Walking the path, I noted that it was the same kind of path the abductor had taken—All straight lines and ninety-degree angles. Whoever was walking to the playhouse and back was keeping to a strictly regimented route. If it was Alban, why would he do that? Was it the abductor, revisiting the playhouse over and over again?

I shivered. It was an awful thought that the abductor was returning to the forest all the time.

Did I just hear a shuffling noise? I stopped, listening hard.

Nothing.

A tall figure appeared in my side vision. Until I pivoted and saw nothing but forest.

Get it together, Isla. This isn't helping.

I had the abductor on my mind, that was all.

Steeling myself, I kept walking.

In the middle of a small clearing, there it was.

The playhouse.

It wasn't anything much. Just a shack made of bits of cut larch and twigs, roughly hammered together. It looked as if it had been repaired numerous times—mismatched and buckled lengths of wood turning the exterior into a patchwork.

I drew the latch back and let the door swing open. A flurry of leaves blew inside. It was barely big enough for six adults to stand. The ceiling so low I had to bend my head. How terrifying this would have been for a little girl, to be locked in here with someone who wanted to hurt her. The horror of an eight-year-old child having their life effectively snatched away in the playhouse made my head swim. It seemed so raw and real now that I was here.

Papers littered the floor—wrappers, crinkled and balled up in the corners. Old, empty men's razor packets and a few mint and chocolate wrappers. A couple of cigarette butts. One old condom wrapper. People must sometimes still come here—probably Aubrey's friends stumbling around drunk and on drugs in the middle of the night. It seemed wrong. This was the place Elodie had been taken.

Stepping back outside, I framed up the playhouse in the viewfinder of my camera and took several photographs. I wouldn't be using these for the portfolio, of course. But somehow my photos of Braithnoch would seem unfinished without these.

An odd electrical sensation zipped through my head, as if a swarm of bees had just passed.

Blundering for a few steps, I leaned against a tree trunk for support. Black spots swum in front of my eyes.

I knew what this was.

Impending seizure. Incoming.

The days without my full round of medication had caught up with me.

I barely had time to sit before my world went dark.

When I came back to consciousness, it felt like I'd been away for a long time. I was lying on the forest floor, among the leaves.

I checked my watch, panicking. Less than a minute had passed. I exhaled slowly, ordering myself to breathe. I was okay.

A cloud of depression swiftly followed. Along with muscle aches and a deep tiredness.

Seizures were like that.

You thought you could do this, Isla. Come all the way to a foreign country and work all alone. Well, there's your reminder that you can't, and you shouldn't be here. Mum is right.

Pulling myself to my feet, I rubbed my arms. That was my anxiety talking and it was the worst thing about my condition. That black cloud that would settle on me.

I just wanted to get back to the cottage now. Crawl into bed for a while and try to unpeel the sadness and despair from my skin.

At least I didn't have to try and calculate my steps and direction on the way out. The worn path was a Godsend. I straightened my clothing and picked leaves and twigs from my hair and scarf.

Rewrapping the scarf around my neck, I hurried along the path.

No one saw me exit the woods.

I was rushing now along the grassy edge of the road. My feet tangled in the roots of the spruce tree and I came down hard. I rolled onto my side. My hip bone hurt, and my hands and knees were covered in mud.

A large hand reached down. "Flap about like a headless chicken and you're bound to come a'cropper."

I looked up to see Diarmid Chandlish's wry face.

Without waiting for any kind of reply, he bent to grab my hand and he pulled me up. "Least you're the right way up now. People can tell which end is your head and which end is your bum."

I gave an embarrassed laugh. "Thank you. I wasn't looking where I was going at all."

"Aye."

"What were you doing out here?" I hoped I didn't sound suspicious, but I spoke before I'd stopped to think.

He shrugged. "Jus' walkin'. Drives me fair mad being around Aubrey all day."

"My brother feels the same about me."

"You women don't know what you do to us men. You've got too many words in you just busting to get out."

"Not me. I'm the church mouse type. My brother just doesn't like any chatter that's not about music."

"Ach, I don't believe ya. I can practically hear those thoughts clattering about in your pretty head right now." He winked.

Diarmid Chandlish spoke like a much older, politically incorrect man who liked to tease young women. But he was probably the same age as me. Yet, something about him was endearing, because I could tell that nothing he said was serious.

"You should come back to our house," he said. "You can help dilute the effect of having Aubrey and Bridget there in the one space."

"Thanks for the offer. I'll keep it in mind." I smiled. "Well, see you, I'd better get back to work."

As I stepped towards the gate that led to the McGregors' property, he called after me, "Isla."

I whirled back around. "Yes?"

"I hope you weren't too rattled. With that business about the tattie bogle and all. I know I spoke about it like it was a joke at dinner the other night, but it wasn't a nice thing, really."

"I *was* rattled. But I'll get past it. You don't happen to know anything about it, do you?"

"Me? No. I haven't had the chance to talk with that Trent fellow yet."

"So, you think it was Trent?"

"Well, if we can't blame the unconscious fellow, who *can* we blame?" he said with a playful lilt in his voice. "Besides, who else would do something so daft? He's Australian, after all."

Diarmid Chandlish went on his way, whistling.

I headed on through the open gates.

As soon as I was inside the cottage, I uploaded the photos from my camera—to both my computer and online storage. I studied the pictures of the playhouse. Of all the photographs I'd ever taken in my life, these would be among the ones I'd never forget.

I swiped through them.

My back froze suddenly.

Near the playhouse, in the shadow of the trees, a figure stood. Just a sliver of a person was all that was visible, a tree obscuring most of their body.

There had been someone in the forest with me.

22

ISLA

GROGGILY, I answered my phone.

I hadn't slept well again last night—thoughts and questions running through my head about who was in the forest yesterday, and what Stella might have been about to tell me about Alban. Added to all that had been the feeling of being both wired and weary—a typical aftermath of my seizures.

"Hello—Isla Wilson speaking," I croaked into the phone.

"Isla, it's me, Greer. I'm calling to see if you want to come up to the house for breakfast. It'll just be Rhiannon and me. Jessica has an appointment this morning and she asked if I could babysit. Alban's in Inverness, working on-site on a new design. I'd love your company, if you're up to it. But if you're not well, that's okay."

"That would be nice." I frowned. "Is there a reason you think I haven't been well?"

"Oh…I'm a big mouth. I didn't mean anything by it. Someone told me you'd been to see the doctor. And you sound a bit hoarse this morning. I wondered if you'd picked up a flu or something."

"No, I'm just a bit tired. And I saw the doctor days ago for something minor."

"Good, good. Sorry, small town. Everyone knows everyone else's business. Terrible, really. Well, I'll be down there in half an hour."

"See you then."

Jessica going out would be a welcome reprieve. With her out of the way, maybe I could finally get the interior house shots that I needed.

Someone tapped on the cottage door. A soft, delicate tap—definitely not Aubrey. When Aubrey had knocked on my door, it'd sounded like Scotland Yard was out there.

A slender figure stood on the step.

Stella. Rubbing her arms and teeth chattering. She wasn't dressed properly for the brisk morning.

"Stella, you look cold."

"I'm not."

She very obviously was, but I let it go. My gaze dropped to the cigarette butts on the ground. "Wait, have you been out there for a while?"

"Yeah. Didn't want to wake ya up too early. It's not polite."

She was the oddest mix of brash teenager and anxious child. But there was no sign of the angry girl who'd told her stepfather to *get knotted* just yesterday.

"Do you want to come in? Or is this about something else?"

"Just thought I'd drop 'round. For a chat."

"Lovely. Well, come in then."

She stepped inside, looking around curiously. "I haven't been in here for yonks."

Her breath smelled of mints. I guessed she'd popped one in her mouth to cover up the odour of the cigarettes she'd just smoked.

"Would you like a cup of tea?"

She nodded. "Coffee, if you have it."

"Hot chocolate?" I poured water into the kettle and put it on to boil. "I've got marshmallows."

She chewed on her lip for a second, then broke into a small smile. "Okay, hot chocolate, it is."

"So, you're still staying with your grandparents?"

"If you're asking why I'm not back at school, well, I don't wanna go back yet. It's almost Christmas anyway. We're not doin' much stuff at school."

I shrugged. "How many marshmallows?"

"Two. Three."

"Okay, three."

"Whatcha doin' today?"

"Just getting on with the portfolio I'm doing. I'm heading over to the house for breakfast in a minute. Alban and Jessica won't be there. Just Greer—she's Alban's assistant. She's babysitting Rhiannon this morning."

"I know who Greer is. Known her for years. She used to be a friend of Kelly's too."

I tried to place the name, Kelly, then remembered that Nora Keenan had two daughters—Camille and Kelly. Camille was Stella's mother, but Stella had run away from home two years ago, and she'd lived with her Aunt Kelly since then. I wondered what had happened that such a young girl hadn't returned home in all that time. Hamish had blamed Rory—Camille's husband. But Rory seemed so mild. Surely he wasn't behind Stella running away?

"Would you like to come to breakfast?" I offered.

Stella seemed hesitant, then said, "I haven't been back to the McGregors since Elodie died. I haven't even met the baby."

"You haven't met Rhiannon?"

She shook her head. "I miss Elodie. I'd like to meet her sister." She picked up one of the gold larch cones. "I helped Elodie paint these."

"The cones are lovely. Why not come along to breakfast? Have you eaten yet?"

"No, I've not had breakfast. Hamish is making up a big batch of porridge, but I don't like porridge. Tastes like sludge. The way he makes it, anyway."

"Okay, then it's settled."

We waited together for Greer to arrive and Jessica to leave.

Greer looked up from her newspaper as we walked in. "Stella!" Putting her newspaper and glasses down, she rushed across to hug the girl. "It's been an age, it has."

Stella remained stiff, not returning the hug. "I won't stay long."

"I'll make you some toast and eggs," Greer said as if she hadn't heard. "Isla, toast and eggs for you, too?"

"That would be great," I answered. "I'll come and help."

Rhiannon, sitting on the rug, wearing tiny white boots and a white jacket, looked from me to Stella. I waved to her. She smiled shyly.

Stella stole across to Rhiannon while I was getting the bread out on the kitchen bench. Rhiannon inched away from the unfamiliar face.

"You look a lot like your sister," Stella said wistfully. Sitting cross-legged beside the toddler, she gathered up her toys and gave her an impromptu puppet show.

Rhiannon giggled and clapped.

"You have the magic touch, Stella," I remarked.

"Yes, you're a real natural with kids," Greer told her, cracking eggs on the sizzling pan.

"I like kids," said Stella. "They're honest. If they like ya, they like ya. If they don't, you'll soon know it."

With the food made, Stella carried Rhiannon to her seat at the table.

"How's it all going over there in Aviemore, Stella?" Greer asked, as she spooned some food onto a plate for Rhiannon.

Stella pulled her mouth down. "Oh, y'know. Okay I guess. But school is school wherever you go." She chewed on a piece of bread. "I see you in town quite a bit."

Greer looked startled. "Me? No, I don't have any business in Aviemore."

Unperturbed, Stella nodded. "I'm sure it's you."

I could have sworn that Greer seemed a bit guilty, gazing down at her food.

"Well, come to think of it, I've been there a couple of times this year," Greer said. "Anyway, would anyone like more scrambled egg?"

Rhiannon gave an unexpected shout, putting her hand up.

"Oh, you'd like some more, would you, missy?" Greer served out another portion to her.

I'd noticed that Rhiannon seemed to barely finish her food when sitting with her mother, but right now, she seemed excited to sit and eat with us. I could guess why. Jessica was always hovering with a cloth to wipe at Rhiannon's hands and face, whereas this morning's meal was a lot more relaxed.

The three of us waited patiently for Rhiannon to finish, then cleaned the plates and kitchen, putting it all back into the exacting order that Jessica liked.

"Guess I'd better go." Stella was awkward as she rewrapped her scarf around her neck. It was obvious she'd enjoyed her morning here and wished she could stay—but I knew she'd never admit to that.

"Hey," I said. "I'm planning on taking some photos of the house today. And maybe some portraits of Rhiannon. Would you like to help out? You could keep Rhiannon entertained."

A smile slipped onto her face. "Like an assistant?"

"Yes, just like that."

"Would you pay me?"

The girl was nothing if not focused on money. It wasn't a bad thing, but it certainly gave her a harder edge. "Sure, but we'd better ask your guardian first. That's Kelly, isn't it?"

"I'll call her," Greer offered. She made the call to Kelly, then smiled and nodded at me. She then stepped away to continue her phone conversation.

"So, how much will I owe you?" I asked Stella.

She shrugged. "Just a wee bit. Should we get started?"

"Yep. Would be a shame to miss this light."

I began with the interior. I didn't want to risk Jessica returning early and telling me that it wasn't a good time. Stella took Rhiannon to another room, to ensure my shots weren't randomly photobombed with a runaway toddler. The house was beautiful even though it wasn't homely. The photos were going to look awesome. I took far more shots than I'd originally intended, but I didn't know if I was going to get the chance again.

With the architectural shoot done, I called Stella to bring Rhiannon back into the living area.

Slinging my camera strap over my head, I knelt to the toddler. "Rhiannon, I'm going to take a few pictures of you." I held up the camera. "With this. Is that okay?"

She tilted her head, frowning as if this was a deep question that needed careful consideration.

"The pictures of you will go on the wall inside your house," I told her.

She nodded, but her eyes remained cautious.

Like father, like daughter, I thought. She might look just like her mother, but her personality and intense expression were her father's.

I took some photos of Rhiannon standing by the fireplace with her giraffe and playing her child-sized grand piano. For once I was glad that Jessica had dressed her daughter up—the white clothing was going to look lovely.

We all headed outside then so that I could start the portraits of Rhiannon. These were mostly going to be closeup shots, and I wanted the gorgeous heather as a soft background.

"Stella," I called, "could you put the blanket down near the front of the heather, and sit Rhiannon down there? Actually, could you also give Rhiannon a stem of heather?"

Rhiannon studied the flower that Stella had picked and handed to her, as if this one must be more special than the others just because it had been given to her.

With the little girl in position, I moved about until I found an angle in which a halo of light appeared around her shoulders and blonde head, sunlight glowing on the pillowy mounds of heather in the background. The scene took my breath away. It perfectly showed Rhiannon's quiet, reflective nature. I almost forgot to take the photographs.

"You're a wee princess, Rhiannon," came Stella's voice behind me.

I angled myself around to her. "Could I get a photo of the two of you together?"

Stella shook her head. "I'd ruin the pictures. I'm not wearin' any makeup and my hair's a right mess."

I knew I wouldn't be able to convince her that she looked great just the way she was. Somehow, over the span of her short life, she'd become convinced that the way she looked wasn't good enough.

"Just a photo for you to keep." I shrugged. "That's all."

"Okay," she said with a doubting tone. "What do you want me to do?"

"Let's just try you being on the blanket with Rhiannon. The light looks lovely there," I said.

Stella stepped across and jumped onto the blanket, tickling Rhiannon, making the toddler squeal and roll around. Stella glanced over at me suddenly, looking guilty. "I'm messin' up her hair, aren't I?"

"No, messy is good. Trust me." I had Stella and Rhiannon lie on their stomachs, both looking at the flower stalk that Rhiannon held. Then the two of them facing each other while Rhiannon held out a bunch of heather to Stella.

I checked the photos on my screen. I was right. Stella was incredibly photogenic. More than that, the photos had a kind of purity about them. The two children had a silent communication between them, their hair dotted with flower petals. Stella looked like the fourteen-year-old that she was, on the cusp between childhood and becoming a young woman.

Greer returned, dropping her phone back into her pocket. "Beautiful," she gushed.

To complete the portraits of Rhiannon, I took a few more of her around the front of the property, with Stella assisting.

"Okay," I announced, "we're all done."

"This was fun," said Stella in a completely open manner, surprising me. "Let's get one of all of us. Y'know, to remember this day. You too, Greer."

"Eek, I'd break the camera," Greer protested.

I laughed. "You so would not."

We bunched together, Rhiannon in Stella's arms, while Greer—who had the longest arms—held out my iPhone to snap a couple of pictures of the four of us.

"How will I see the photos?" Stella asked me anxiously. "I mean, once I go back to Aviemore and you go back to Sydney?"

"I'll make sure you get them," I assured her. "I'll get Kelly's email address and send them on."

While I was talking with Stella, Rhiannon stepped up to a clump of heather and closed her dimply fist around a stem and tore it loose. She handed me the mangled stem. I understood that she was giving me a gift.

"Thank you," I told her. "This is just beautiful."

I won the first smile that I'd had from her in the whole time I'd been here. I threaded the flower in through the top button-hole of my jacket. She seemed to like that.

Gazing about at the heather ruffling in the light breeze, I felt a peace and rhythm that had been missing from my life. Here at Braithnoch, despite the wintry Scottish weather and despite the strangeness of the McGregors, I was finding enchantment in the smallest of things. I made a vow that when I returned to Sydney, I'd take time out to just smell the roses, as the saying went.

Even Stella looked content, lying on her back on the ground now, twirling a flower between her thumb and forefinger. She caught me looking and the old self-conscious expression slipped back onto her face. She shrugged. "Easiest money I ever made."

A car's wheels crunched the gravel in the driveway. Jessica drove in, her expression pinched. She parked and stepped out, raising her head high as she looked from Greer to Stella to me. "What's going on?"

Greer smiled at her. "We've been helping Isla get her portfolio done. I can't wait to see the photos. Oh, they'll be lovely."

"Jessica, I'd love to get some photos of you and Rhiannon," I ventured. "Out here near the heather."

She removed her sunglasses, blinking in the sun. "I'm not feeling the best, I'm afraid." She called Rhiannon to her. "Oh dear, look at you. Run inside now."

Rhiannon immediately obeyed.

Jessica's forehead wrinkled as she watched Rhiannon enter the house. "I hope you didn't take photographs of my daughter in that condition, Isla? I didn't realise you were planning a photo session with her this morning."

"I wasn't, but the light was perfect. Alban did say I could take photos of her whenever I had the chance. I think you'll like the portraits I got of her."

"I'm sorry, I'm sure I'll love them," she said. "I was just surprised to see her so untidy. Thank you all for minding her while I was away." She shot Stella a thin-lipped smile. "It's been quite a while since you've been around."

Stella folded her arms defensively. "I should of come before, to see the baby. I meant to."

"Well, you've seen her now," said Jessica. "Shouldn't you be at school?"

"Yeah," Stella answered. "I guess I should."

I noticed that Stella didn't respond to Jessica with any of her usual smart-talk.

Jessica walked off to the house. Rhiannon had already shot upstairs and she was gazing out at us from her bedroom.

I waved at her.

"Well, I have some work to attend to this afternoon," Greer told me. "I'll come back tonight. I'll bring soup. How about just you and me tonight, Isla? In the cottage. If Jessica is feeling poorly, we'll give them some breathing space."

"Sounds good to me," I said.

"I better go, too. But I'll get my *twenty* first," Stella said unflinchingly.

"Twenty?" Greer chirped. "I hope you know that's thirty-five Australian dollars, Isla. I know because I've been busily converting currencies in order to pay you."

Stella gave a small smile. I guessed that she'd held back on discussing money for a reason. I was lucky she hadn't asked for a *fifty*.

I walked back to the cottage with Stella. Without an invitation, she stepped inside and sat at the table. "I used to play in here with Elodie. Back when I was a kid."

Like, two years ago, I thought. She obviously didn't consider herself a child any longer. Either that, or she didn't want me to see her as a child.

I went to fetch my wallet from my handbag, then hesitated. She'd brought up Elodie's name. This could be the perfect time to ask what she'd been going to tell me about Elodie before. I didn't expect to get another chance, but now that I had it, I should make the most of it. If I handed her the money, she might grab it and run. In fact, I was sure she would.

I took my wallet to the table but then stalled. "Stella, there was something you were going to tell me yesterday? About Elodie. Just before Rory walked up to us."

She picked up the pine cone she'd left on the table earlier, spinning it like a top. "I don't remember."

"It was about something that Elodie told you. Something strange."

I realised I sounded too intense. I exhaled, giving a small shrug. "You just got me a little curious."

"Oh, that. I don't know if I should say it. Because I don't want you to go telling people. Because then people will wonder why I didn't say something sooner."

"I don't know anyone here very well. Who would I tell?" The first part of that was true, but the second part wasn't exactly true. Some things had to be told.

"You seem to know Rory," she said. "I saw you walking back on the path with him."

"Oh, he came to the house the other day. Just because he'd found some paintings of Elodie's that'd been stored away in the school hall. That's all."

"They weren't stored away at school."

"What do you mean?"

"The paintings. I bet I know which ones they were. He kept a bunch of her work at home. And newspaper clippings about Elodie."

"How do you know that?"

"Because I saw the paintings and stuff at home, in the garage."

"Okay. Well, I didn't know that."

"Yeah."

I'd think on the puzzle of Rory and the paintings later. Right now, I wanted to know about Elodie. I closed my fingers over my wallet. Was this even ethical? Sitting here and keeping back the money I'd promised Stella was starting to seem a bit like bribery. Still, I felt desperate to know.

"Would you mind telling me what Elodie said?" I asked her gently.

Stella looked uncomfortable, pulling her sleeves over her hands. "Weird stuff, I guess. She said stuff like...love comes from respect. Being scared of someone just means you respect them. And you have to prove that you love someone, or it isn't love. Sometimes you have to be tested."

The skin on the back of my neck and shoulders felt like it was crawling. "Tested how?"

"Anything the other person wants. If they don't test you, they don't love you."

I shook my head. "That's not right."

"You don't think so?"

"No, of course not."

"That's what I thought. But I wasn't sure."

"Do you know what kind of tests she was talking about, specifically?"

"I don't know. She said that the tests are supposed to make you feel bad, but if you're brave, you'll get through them."

"Can you remember anything else that she said about all this?"

She eyed me suspiciously. "You're going to tell the police, aren't you?"

"What if this helped find the person who hurt Elodie?"

"The police say it was a stranger."

"But what if it wasn't? I mean, they don't know for sure. Look, if I do tell, the police might want to talk with you. Are you going to be okay with that?"

"Go ahead. I'll just say that you've lost your mind. Can I have my money now?"

"Of course you can." Quickly, I took the money out. "Here. Twenty pounds. Maybe you can be my assistant again on another day."

"I might be going back home tomorrow." She stuffed the money into her jeans pocket.

My gaze was drawn to her wrist, as her sleeve rode up. I noticed scars—thin, crisscrossing lines.

"Stella, what's that?" I gestured towards her wrist.

She dug her hands into her jacket pockets. "Cat. Kelly's got a wee bitch of a cat. Scratches you if you try to pat it."

"Better stay away from it."

"Yeah."

"Well, if I don't see you again, I just want to say I'm glad I met you. And thank you for helping out today."

She stood just looking at me for a moment as if she had more to say, then turned around and left.

23

ISLA

THE NEXT MORNING, I worked on sorting out my photographs I wanted to put into the portfolio. A hum of excitement buzzed in my chest as I saw the best of the images together as a package. The portfolio was really starting to come together.

What I was missing was photos of Alban. And photos of the family together. I also wanted a few more landscapes, especially pictures of Braithnoch under a covering of snow. I hoped it would snow before my time here was up.

Sipping on my hot tea, I paused on the photographs of Stella and Rhiannon together. There should be photographs of Elodie and Rhiannon like this—together as sisters. But Elodie had never even had the chance to hold her sibling before she died.

I was glad though that Stella had finally met Rhiannon. I could tell that spending time with Rhiannon had meant a lot to her.

A thought struck me.

Stella had run away soon after Elodie died. Could there be a connection between Stella and Elodie that everyone had missed? Stella wasn't giving any clear reasons why she'd run away.

The more I thought about it, the more it seemed to make sense. *A connection.* Those strange things that Elodie had said to Stella—did Stella know or guess who had put those ideas into Elodie's head?

I needed to talk to Rory.

Digging in my handbag I found his number and called him.

"Yo. Rory speaking." I hadn't picked him for the type of guy who'd respond with a *yo*.

"It's Isla. Could I talk with you for a minute?"

"Ah, yes, just a tick. I'm driving. Call you back in ten."

I waited patiently until my phone rang.

"I'm out with Camille," he told me. "Just getting a few groceries and things."

"Oh. We'll talk later, then?"

"It's okay. I'm sitting here waiting in the car. Camille wanted to browse a couple of clothing shops first. So, what's this about?"

"It's a bit personal, so please tell me if I'm treading too far in. It's about Stella."

"Yes?"

"You remember how Stella had told me about odd things Elodie had said? Well, yesterday, Stella related a little of those things."

"She did?" He sounded surprised.

"Yes. She didn't want me telling anyone. But you're a teacher and her step-father. And, also, I feel like this shouldn't stay hidden."

"You've got my interest, Isla."

"Okay, apparently Elodie said things like…love comes from respect. Being scared of someone just means that you respect them. And…you have to prove that you love someone or it isn't love. Sometimes you have to be tested."

A dead silence stretched, making me wonder what reaction Rory was having.

"That does sound odd," he said finally.

"Yes, it does. It's not something an eight-year-old would say."

"Perhaps she got it from a movie or something?"

"According to Stella, Elodie was being directly told this stuff by someone."

"Have you considered that Stella might be telling you what she thinks you want to hear?"

"No, why would she?"

"Because she's a wee bit lonely and you're giving her attention?"

I chewed my lip, thinking that he might be right. She *had* sought me out yesterday. Perhaps she *was* lonely.

"There's something else," I said. "Something that I've been thinking about. It's about the reason why Stella left town."

"We don't know exactly why Stella left."

"Yes, that's what I was wondering about. She ran away soon after Elodie died, right? And she won't tell anyone why? What if there's a connection between what happened to Elodie and something that only Stella knows? I mean, she told me about the odd things that Elodie was saying, but I also get the sense that she's holding something else back."

"What do you think she's holding back?"

"I don't know. I could be wrong. But when I talk to her, it feels like there's something else she wants to tell me. I can't really explain it any other way than that."

A heavy sigh came through the phone line. "Isla, you weren't around in the months before Stella decided to up and leave home. She was rude and belligerent. She's a difficult girl. She made life very hard for Camille."

"I was a teenage girl once, and I went through a very messy phase."

"Then you know exactly what I'm talking about. Stella left because she thought she knew better than her mother."

"Running away is a pretty major step though. And refusing to come back. Is it...I mean, is it at all possible that she knows some-thing? About Elodie? Just something small?"

"Look, I really don't think the two things are connected. I can't see Stella holding back that kind of information. She was really fond of Elodie. I don't honestly know what got into her head to make her run off like she did. Teenage hormones running crazy maybe. There were a couple of boys she liked at school. Big, stupid types with *fight me* written all over them. Petty criminals. She left here with one of them, but he dumped her after a few days."

"You think that's all there is to it? Teen hormones?"

"Well, I don't have a better explanation. I tried going to see her on my own and convince her to return. No dice."

A deflated silence followed. My theory had gone nowhere. I imagined that Rory wasn't feeling too good either after I'd dragged all of this stuff up.

"Okay, Rory. Thanks for talking with me. I might try to talk with her again—see if I can get her to tell me anything more."

"I'd rather you didn't," came the swift reply.

"I'm sorry. I didn't mean to step on any toes. I—"

"It's just that Stella rarely comes back here. This is the longest she's stayed at her grandparents' house. Camille and I were hoping that she's starting to want to return home."

"I understand. But, I might have to tell someone about this—about the things Elodie told Stella, I mean. It might be all made up, but on the other hand, it might not be."

"I didn't want to say this, but I have a good reason to think she might have made it up. Look, do you want to meet me later? I have something to show you. In Brigg's cafe in town, at two?"

"Briggs? Okay. I'll be there." I tried to sound like I wasn't disappointed. I'd thought that maybe I'd discovered something that might lead somewhere. But Rory knew Stella a lot better than I did. I'd have to wait until this afternoon until I'd find out what it was he wanted me to see.

The more that I found out, the more it seemed that walls went up —even with Rory.

With the call ended, I went back to sorting out the photographs for the portfolio. Once I had the portfolio together, I'd start editing it, making each photograph magazine-worthy.

I kept the pictures of the playhouse and mysterious person in a separate folder. Would I ever find out who that was? I doubted it. No one was going to admit to following me in the forest that day.

For the next few hours, I took some more landscape shots from aspects I hadn't taken photos from previously. The changing light and mood of each day brought new perspectives and inspiration and I found myself enjoying the morning. The wind today was intense, bending the trees to its will.

As the time grew close to one in the afternoon, I dressed myself for brisk weather and set out on the bicycle.

Choosing a window seat in the cafe, I ordered stew and a couple of bread rolls. They called the rolls *baps*.

I was stirring my tea when I noticed a tall man jogging down the street, head down against the wind, clutching his jacket lapels. Rory.

He looked gaunt and tired as he sat opposite me in the cafe.

It occurred to me that the cafe wasn't the most private of places to hold a conversation of this nature. But at least it had an old-fashioned booth-style layout. If we kept our voices down, it was highly unlikely anyone would hear us.

Rory ordered himself a tea, his face pinched with cold.

He blew out a sighing breath. "Thanks for coming. You were good enough to relay to me what my stepdaughter has been telling you. And I felt that I needed to get you clear on something."

"Certainly," I said.

It seemed that was how Rory and I operated. We exchanged pieces of information—a piece for a piece. It was a little ridiculous, when I let myself think on it. Neither of us were police officers. We were just an Australian photographer and a Scottish school teacher. But at the same time, it felt as if we were working on this thing together, the mystery of what happened to Elodie.

"So, Stella just started talking about this stuff out of the blue?" he asked me.

I nodded, not wanting to admit that I'd practically bribed it out of her.

He rubbed his eyes blearily and blinked before speaking again. "Well, that's something. Hard to get Stella to talk at all." He took his tea from the waiter and then gulped a mouthful. "I'll show you what I brought here today."

Setting the cup down he drew out a small pile of school books from his satchel.

The books had doodles scrawled all over them—the work of a bored child. Flowers and monstrous faces and winged love hearts. At first, I thought they must be Elodie's. But when he turned them over and set them down on the table, the name on them was clear. Stella Keenan.

Rory flipped through the first one—an English grammar book—until he found a certain page. Rotating it around to me, he raised his eyebrows. "Take a look at this."

I quickly read it: *Everybody tests you. The one who loves you most will test you the most.*

He flipped forward another few pages. I read: *Stephanie Dougall is a big-nosed slut face. I'll make her show me some respect.*

Rory drew out another book and opened it up on a page. Stella had drawn a page of tattoos she apparently planned to get when she was older. Most of them were love hearts designs, with the name of one particular boy in them—Eddie Dougall. I guessed that he was Stephanie Dougall's brother. The capital letters underneath the hearts said, *LOVE IS RESPECT.*

"Do you see what I mean?" said Rory quietly. "There's more, but I think you might have the picture. Lots of talk about love and respect and tests. These were her books from when she was twelve."

I exhaled a tightly held breath. "It does sound a lot like the thing that Stella told me."

"Yes, that's what I thought."

"How did you know she wrote these things in her books?" I asked curiously.

"When she ran away, Camille and I were looking for clues as to where she'd gone. Understandably, Camille was hysterical. This was a very young girl we're talking about. Camille tried calling all her friends, but none of them knew anything. The only thing I could think of was to look through her school books for clues. Something I'd noticed as a school teacher is that kids often scribble angry messages to the world in their books. They don't feel they can talk to anyone for whatever reason, so they put it down in the margins of their work or right at the back of the book." He sighed wryly. "Of course, the other thing they scribble in their books are dick drawings."

I shot him a cringing smile in response to the last thing he said. I remembered the boys at school drawing penises over everything. "So, did looking through her books help find her?"

"Yes. Pretty quickly, too. You can see the name of a boy there in those love hearts. Camille and I went to see his parents—the Dougalls—and they discovered that he hadn't gone to school that day. They were terrified then that their son had run off with Stella because he was fifteen and she was only twelve. They were pretty scared he'd get charged by the police. We told them we wouldn't press charges if they got him to tell us where he and Stella were. Anyway, you know the rest of the story. They contacted Eddie and he broke it off with Stella and left her behind. We went and picked Stella up. But she refused to come back home, and she ended up going to live with Camille's sister, Kelly."

"Goodness, a fifteen-year-old boy. Did he and Stella—?"

"Have sex? Yes, unfortunately. Once we found that out, I thought we should go to the police. But neither Camille nor Stella wanted to. I couldn't convince Camille, and well, Stella is *her* daughter. She thought that it was enough that Eddie had ended the relationship and told us where to find Stella."

"Does Stella still see him?"

"I don't think so. She doesn't come back to Greenmire very often."

"Okay," I said, "if the stuff about *love being respect* is all coming from Stella, where did she get that kind of talk from? She was just a young kid herself. From Eddie, maybe?"

"Maybe. Certainly not from her mother or grandparents." Rory threaded his long fingers together and rested his elbows on the table. He observed me with a worried expression. When he spoke, he kept his voice to just above a whisper. "Did you manage to find out any more—about the painting you said you saw?"

"Nothing more."

"Hmmm. Last time, you weren't willing to tell me whose house you saw this painting at. But it might help if you do."

"It's at Alban's house. In his office," I said in a low tone, then shook my head. "I probably shouldn't have told you that."

He pressed his lips together tightly. "Don't feel bad. Thank you for telling me. It *is* interesting that he has that on his wall."

Two young women walked past the coffee shop window. Aubrey and her friend Bridget.

Noticing me, Aubrey tapped hello on the plate glass. I smiled and waved, but hoped she'd keep on walking. No such luck. I heard the bell on the entrance door tinkle and then Aubrey and Bridget were standing at our table.

"Mind if we park our bums here a while?" Aubrey wriggled in beside me without waiting for a reply. "We were going to grab a coffee before heading to see a friend's new baby. Over at the hospital. I don't like the coffee there."

Bridget nudged Rory over and sat beside him. "Miss fussy boots dragged me all over Paris once just to find a specific coffee shop." She rolled her eyes at Aubrey.

Aubrey laughed. "That coffee shop was nowhere near where I remembered it being. I'm such a doofus with directions." She eyed the schoolbooks on the table. "What's all this?"

Rory snatched up the books and stuffed them back into his satchel. "Just some of the kids' work. Isla here was asking about the local school. I actually need to get moving. Nice to see you again, Aubrey." He nodded at me. "Isla, I hope I've been helpful."

"Yes," I said. "Very helpful, thank you."

Watching him leave, Bridget pulled her mouth down. "Hope I don't smell or something. He left in a right hurry." She sniffed her underarms.

I laughed and then told a lie. "He was actually about to leave before you girls walked in."

Aubrey and Bridget accepted that without question, ordering themselves coffee and cake.

"How are things going with Simon?" I asked Aubrey, half-wincing, as I'd already guessed things weren't going well.

She scowled. "Och, he's out on his ear. Good riddance to him."

"I'm glad to hear it," I told her.

"Shame," Bridget mused. "He was damned hot."

"He was and all." Aubrey looked sad for a moment, then she turned to me. "Hey, did you know that Trent has been asking to see you? I did tell Jessica, but she might have forgotten to pass it on."

"Trent? The guy who overdosed in the forest?" I answered, shocked. "I don't even know him."

"I think he wants to apologise," Aubrey said. "Peyton told me that Trent made a pass at you, is that right?"

I nodded. "Yes. But please tell him that I'm okay about it. He doesn't need to apologise in person."

Aubrey wrinkled her nose. "He's insisting on seeing you. Says there's something important he needs to tell you."

"Ooh," Bridget exclaimed. "He's the one who supposedly strung the scarecrow up in the tree, right? I wish I'd seen it. Frrreaky. Maybe he wants to admit to it."

"He told the police he didn't do it, right?" I asked.

Bridget nodded, a gleam of interest in her eyes. "Maybe he'd had a change of heart. But if he didn't do it, who did? We should get everyone together who was there that night and play Murder in the Dark. And find out who did string up the poor scarecrow. Sorry, *tattie bogle*, I should say. I just can't get used to calling them that like you lot do 'round here."

"Ignore her," Aubrey told me. "She watches too much CSI." She shot a derisive glance at her friend. "You're as bad as Diarmid. It's not a murder investigation, you right twit. The victim is a bit of wood and straw."

Bridget shrugged. "Most exciting thing that's happened in Greenmire for yonks."

"Trent sounded awfully sincere," Aubrey told me. "If you don't see him, I'm afraid you might not get another chance. Peyton banned him from our house forever. We're heading over to the hospital in a minute. I can drop you there and then take you home again."

"Thank you, but I—" I started.

"Oh, you can't say no," Bridget said. "How are we ever going to know if he's the scarecrow culprit or not? Seems there's something he's only willing to tell you and I bet that's it."

I had to admit to myself that I was curious. It would be reassuring to know for sure that he was the culprit, so that I didn't have to wonder anymore.

I glanced out the window. "But I have a bike outside."

"Then we'll drop you back in town after the hospital." Aubrey waggled her eyebrows at me in a mock stern expression, as if I were a stubborn child.

"Okay." I exhaled, trying to gather myself. "I'll come along with you."

24

ELODIE

Greenmire, Scottish Highlands, December 2015

ELODIE HAD VISITORS. Nurse Lucy told her so.

Above the steady beeps and shuffling noises of the hospital, she heard Aubrey's voice.

"Everyone knows I hate hospitals," Aubrey told her. "Takes a really special person to get me to one. So...here I am, Lo." She was the only one who'd ever called her Lo. She was sometimes called Elly or Lodie but never Lo.

Aubrey sighed. "I flew back from London just to see you, you little punk. So, you'd better make my trip worthwhile and wake up. I bought a sparkly dress when I was there and it's so pretty you *have* to see it. And if you like, I'll have one made up for you. A pint-sized one. Because you're a pint-sized squirt. And we can wear them together and have a karaoke singing contest. And—"

"Ach, stop flapping your gums," Diarmid broke in. "You're going to burn poor wee Elodie's ears before long. It's not like she can get up and run away and get some peace from ya."

But Aubrey didn't stop flapping her gums. She talked on and on and on. She was always like this. She'd take a thousand words to tell you what would take other people just ten. Elodie loved Aubrey but thought that she often made her ears tired.

Right now, Elodie felt like Grandma McGregor, demanding that her grandchildren shush because she was vexed. Elodie and her family would visit Grandma in her little house where she lived all alone—the house with all the windowsills filled with tiny statues of cats and dogs. She didn't have any real pets. Sooner or later, the noise of all the children would start to annoy her.

Just like Grandma, Elodie was vexed. She imagined the nurses putting up a sign on the wall over her bed that said, *Shush, Elodie is vexed.*

Grandma would like that.

Elodie giggled inside.

Had Grandma come to see her in the hospital yet? She didn't know. Sometimes she entered long, twisting black tunnels and she could barely hear anyone. Maybe Grandma came when she was in a tunnel. She desperately wanted to hear Grandma's voice.

Other people entered the room. Aubrey and Diarmid's parents and older brother, Peyton. Elodie was suddenly anxious and wanted them all to go away. She heard moaning and she only realised that it was herself when Nurse Lucy stated, Elodie's had enough for today.

At least Nurse Lucy knew. She couldn't speak for herself, but Nurse Lucy said the words she often wanted to say.

Diarmid sounded smug when he said, "See, Aubrey? You fair made her sick with all your blathering. Takes a blabbermouth like you to pull someone out of a coma enough to start groaning."

"Not at all," said Nurse Lucy, clucking her tongue. "It's a common myth that people in comas are always silent. They're usually not. They go in and out of dreamlike states, and they can almost completely wake and become quite confused before heading back into a deep coma."

Her voice seemed faint and loud at the same time, like it was rushing in and out of the room in waves.

"Thank you for explaining, nurse," said Aubrey. She said something to Diarmid, but Elodie couldn't catch it. The wind inside her head had caught Aubrey's words and tossed them skyward.

Elodie felt terrible and sick and she wanted to vomit.

She actually must have vomited because Nurse Lucy told her that she was cleaning her up and she could feel the pressure of her hand on her face.

"There you are, sweetheart, all beautiful again," she said. "Just relax. You're safe. You're with people who care about you."

Despite her sore stomach, she liked it that she could feel hands on her face and that she'd heard her own voice, even if it was just herself groaning.

But the next minute, a strange feeling took her, like she was pulling away from the room. She held fast to Nurse Lucy's voice. It was the only thing anchoring her.

"You're doing well, sweetheart," Nurse Lucy said. "I think we'll let you get some sleep. Your mum and dad are close by. They'll be back to watch you sleep any minute now. But I'll still be here. You won't be alone."

The room went still.

No voices or sounds.

Elodie was still in another place.

She could see Aubrey and Diarmid in her mind. It was the morning of her sixth birthday. Mum told her to go play so that she could get the house ready for her birthday party. She played in the field until she got bored. Then she decided to go to the Chandlish house and play with their deerhounds. It was a long way, but it was okay. Mum let her go to the houses of the Chandlishes and Keenans all the time, so that Elodie could *get out of her hair.*

Sneaking back to the house, she snatched her new straw hat from her bedroom. She wanted to wear it over to the Chandlish house. If Aubrey saw it, she'd want one, too.

Tying the hat's red ribbon under her chin, she sped from the house and along the edge of the forest, all the way to the tattie bogles on the hill.

She clamped a hand tightly over her eyes as she passed the tattie bogles. She didn't used to be frightened of them until Diarmid told her scary stories about them.

When she reached the Chandlish house, the dogs weren't in their enclosure.

Diarmid was sitting on the front steps of his house when she got there, his head in his hands. He looked like he was sick.

"Lookie here, it's Red Riding Hood," he laughed. "And I'm Grandma. Where's my scones and jam?" His words slurred, like they were sliding from his tongue.

"Where's Mitzy and Boomer?" she asked.

"Aubrey took 'em out for a walk. Now, where's my scones?"

"It's my birthday, Diarmid. You have to be nice to me."

"I don't have to be nice when I'm drunk." He smiled, showing all his teeth. "You know what happens to little girls in the woods?"

She shook her head.

He threw back his head and made a growling sound. "The tattie bogles. They're right mad you got away from them. They're coming now and they'll eat you if they find you!"

He jumped up, growling again and she squealed.

"Aubrey! Aubrey! Save me!" Elodie giggled, running up the stairs and into the house. She was scared of the tattie bogles, but this was just Diarmid, and Diarmid wasn't scary.

She ran and hid, but Diarmid found her straight away.

There was nowhere to go now except the basement. She ran down the stairs and crawled under the pool table.

"Rah! The tattie bogle's coming!" Diarmid jumped the last few steps and landed hard on the floor, crashing into a cabinet filled with trophies. The trophies swayed and clattered.

Aubrey came charging down the stairs.

Elodie clapped her hands over her mouth, suppressing a giggle.

She knew Aubrey would join in the fun, now.

Except, she didn't.

Aubrey forced Diarmid back against the wall, both elbows and arms hard against his chest. "What. Did. You. Say?"

"I said the tattie bogle's coming," he screamed in her face. "It's coming and there's nothing you can do about it."

She slapped him across his cheek and temple.

He stared at her like he hated her. "Up the stairs, Auuuubreyyy. Quick, he's coming. Thump, thump, thump on the stairs. Watch you don't trip or he'll get you. You remember, don't you? You remember the straw under your pillow? That's how you knew the tattie bogle had been in your room."

She breathed furiously through her nose, nostrils flaring. "Don't...."

His cheek grew red where she'd slapped him. "It's coming for you, Aubrey."

"What's wrong with you? What in the hell is wrong with you? Why have you always been like this?"

Elodie curled herself into a ball. She knew the story well, because Diarmid had told her. The tattie bogles on the hill weren't like other scarecrows. These ones could tear away from their moorings, and plod towards your house. Then they'd climb in through a window and up to your bedroom. You knew if the tattie bogle had tried to come for you if there was straw under your pillow in the morning.

It was just a story, but Diarmid had told her it as if it were real.

With a final shove, Aubrey backed away from her brother. "Where's Elodie? I heard you chasing her. Probably scared her out of her wits, you have."

"I don't know," he answered. "Thought she went this way, but, yeah, looks like she doubled back."

"Well, someone better go find her." Aubrey stormed away. The room felt like it had kept some of her rage, even after she'd gone.

Diarmid stood there for a moment, as though he didn't know what to do. Then started laughing. He reached towards some of Aubrey's show jumping trophies and made them tip from the shelf. Seeming satisfied, he left then.

Elodie wasn't sure if she'd made Diarmid do something wrong. She'd never seen Aubrey so angry before.

Two sets of legs came down the stairs. At first, she thought it was Diarmid and Aubrey and that they'd realised she was in the basement, after all. She crawled out, but it wasn't Diarmid or Aubrey.

Peyton and Hamish stood at the foot of the stairs, peering down at her in surprise.

"What were you doing under there, kid?" Peyton rubbed his chin and looked vaguely annoyed.

She sniffled. "Just playing a game."

"Were you crying?" he said.

"No." She wiped her eyes to show that she wasn't, but her eyelashes wet the backs of her hands.

Peyton softened his voice. "Maybe you should go home, huh? We're going to play a game of pool and you'll get a big headache if you stay under there." He gave her an exasperated grin. "Did I hear my brother yelling some blasted thing about tattie bogles?"

She nodded.

"Did he scare you? C'mon kid, we'll walk you back to your place." Peyton glanced at Hamish. Hamish sighed loudly.

Diarmid was passed out on the sofa when they walked through the living room.

Aubrey came running in. "There you are, Lo."

"She's all right," said Peyton. "Our numpty of a brother scared her. We're walking her home."

Aubrey cast a glance at Diarmid then nodded. "Good. I'll be glad when he's back at college."

Outside, the dogs were back in their enclosure, sticking their noses through the gate. Elodie went to pat them, then ran behind Peyton and Hamish as they headed for the forest.

Leaves blew ahead of her new party shoes. She wanted to chase the leaves, but she held back, daunted by these tall men walking beside her. But they barely seemed to notice her, chatting to each other about things she didn't understand.

When the tattie bogles came into view, she turned her head away and covered her face, as she always did. She knocked into Peyton by accident.

"Hey now," Peyton said, "don't you go being scared of those old things." He took her by the hand, right up to the tattie bogles. Grabbing the nearest one, he shook it. "See? They can't come after you. They're fixed into the ground. They've got no proper hands, no teeth. They can't eat you. Just sticks and wood and hay is all they are."

Hamish jumped in front of a tattie bogle and pretended that it pulled him towards it. "Help! It's got me!" He held the arms of the tattie bogle, jerking about as if he really couldn't get away.

"Och, we're surrounded by numpties, Elodie." Peyton sighed. "I think the tattie bogles have got more brains than Hamish and Diarmid put together."

That made a giggle rise inside Elodie's throat, but she didn't let it out.

Hamish dropped the tattie bogle's arms. "Ah, don't mind me. Just having a wee bit of fun."

"She's just a kid, Ham. Save it for Diarmid. He'd appreciate that kind of carry on."

Elodie didn't understand grownups at all today. Not even Aubrey. Aubrey had recently turned eighteen, so that made her a grownup, too.

They kept walking, until her house was in view.

Peyton squinted. "Is that balloons I see down there?"

She nodded, a small thrill of excitement seeding itself in her chest. "I'm six today."

"Well, a big happy sixth birthday to ya," Peyton said.

"Don't drink too much," Hamish added.

"Och!" Peyton elbowed Hamish.

Saying goodbye, she tore home across the moor and up and down the hills. Only when she was almost home did she remember that she'd left her new straw hat at the Chandlishes' house. The hat was meant to be for a special photo session later. Mum had a special hat just like it, too.

She couldn't go back to the Chandlish house now. Peyton and Hamish just took all that time to walk her through the wood and they might be cranky if she returned.

Maybe she could tell Mum that one of their dogs got the hat and chewed it or something. But the deerhounds were so well-behaved they'd probably never chewed hats and shoes, not even when they were puppies.

She stepped closer, rounding the side of the house. Tables and bright tablecloths had been set up outside. A piñata hung from the tree —a piñata of a tattie bogle.

Disappointment pushed down in her stomach like a stone. She'd asked Mum for a pony piñata.

Mum always forgot stuff like that. Often, it felt like Mum barely listened to her. She was always busy, always telling Elodie to go and play.

There was only one good thing about it being a tattie bogle. She could hit it over and over again with a stick and no one was going to stop her.

25

ISLA

I WALKED past the white walls of the children's ward, with their brightly-coloured motifs of balloons and cartoon animals, I shivered, thinking that this must be where Elodie spent her last days.

I found Trent's ward on the second floor. He was asleep as I peered in from the doorway of his hospital room, a meal lying half-eaten on the swing table beside his bed.

"Let's go." Aubrey prodded Bridget. "He probably won't talk if we stay here."

Reluctantly, Bridget allowed Aubrey to pull her down the corridor. Aubrey waved a silent goodbye to me.

Trent woke, his eyes tracking me as I entered the room, measures of surprise and wariness on his face. There was no hint of an apology or regret in that expression. Was Aubrey mistaken? It must be someone else that he so desperately wanted to see. Not me.

"I didn't think you'd come," he said, pushing himself up on the pillows.

Okay. Aubrey wasn't mistaken.

"How are you?" I asked.

"Feeling like I got churned through a cement truck."

I moved closer, not knowing where to put myself. It seemed too intimate to be here alone with this man—he lying there in a loose hospital gown and attached to a hospital drip. Hospitals were for family and close friends.

"Pull up a chair." He gestured towards two plush, plastic armchairs. "You've got the best seat in the house."

I pressed my mouth into a rigid smile as I perched gingerly on the chair. "I'm glad you're recovering."

A silence unravelled between us, until he stopped it by saying, "If you don't mind, I'd like to have a talk with you."

I didn't know whether to be relieved or worried at his directness. There was something in his eyes that was making me distinctly uneasy. "Go ahead."

"First of all, I'm sorry—about going in for the kiss. I shouldn't have done it."

"It's okay. I'm guessing you weren't yourself."

"No, that's the problem. I *was* being myself. It's about time I quit being myself and showed some manners."

I wasn't sure what to answer to that, so I changed the subject. "They seem a very high-spirited bunch, the Chandlishes—and Bridget. How do you know them?"

"I met Aubrey at an art school in Inverness. We were both doing commercial art. She invited me to her house for a party, just as friends. I got on well with her and her brothers. I've been back a few times. There's often a lot more people than were there the other night. It gets pretty rowdy."

"I can imagine. So, you're both artists, you and Aubrey?"

"Yeah. She's better than me. Have you seen her handiwork on the scarecrows?"

"What do you mean?"

"She did the faces. Hand sculpted them when she was a teenager. Each one different. That's Aubrey in all of her many moods."

Why would Aubrey—who had professed to be terrified of the scarecrows—have crafted faces for them? Was Trent lying?

"Hamish told me that the scarecrows had always been like that. He said they changed by themselves. Like it was folklore or something."

Trent shrugged. "He's just pissed because Aubrey broke up with him when they were teenagers."

"I can't picture them two together. They must have changed a lot."

"Why can't you picture them? Is Hamish not good enough for Aubrey in your mind?"

His voice remained friendly but there was still that undercurrent in his eyes. I wasn't sure how the conversation had taken this turn, but I wished it hadn't.

"No, it's nothing like that," I said. "Their personalities just seem very different. That's all."

"Well, maybe he did get a bit quiet after she strung him along for six months and then dumped him when she got bored."

"That was a long time ago, right? He must be over it by now."

"Maybe I just find that kind of story a bit hard because the same thing happened to *me*."

"I'm sorry," I told him.

I wasn't actually sorry at all. He had a hard, bitter edge to his voice. I'd been dumped by a boyfriend in the past. But I didn't go around trying to make strangers feel bad because of it. When Trent had mentioned the scarecrows, I'd thought that was going to lead up to a confession or something. But instead, it had developed into an odd rant about men being wronged by women. I started to worry that he was unhinged. Maybe I should just make an excuse and get myself out of here. I stared down at my hands, twisting my fingers together. No, I'd come all the way here. I wasn't going to leave without at least talking about the scarecrow.

I raised my head, drawing more air in than I needed. "Trent, did you hang the scarecrow in the tree?"

He laughed, shaking his head. "You think I did that? You do, don't you?"

"I heard you, near my window that night. After I returned from Aubrey's house. You were calling my name."

"My apologies."

"So, you admit to that."

"Yeah. I do."

"And you dragged a scarecrow down from the hill and hung it up on a branch," I continued boldly.

"I was in no condition to do any such thing."

This was pointless. He was playing with me.

I rose from the chair.

He held up a hand. "Just wait. Can I tell you a story?"

"I don't think so. I have to go."

"It won't take long. Then I'll tell you the truth about the scarecrow."

My shoulders hunched as I considered my options. Walking out now seemed more satisfying than staying. But he somehow sounded genuine.

"Make it short." I sat back in the seat.

"Oh, it's short. There's not much to tell. It's more about the emotion of the story than what actually happened. That's what I want you to picture. It was a little over two years ago. I met a girl. Straight red hair that fell to her shoulders. With a bit of a—what do you girls call it—a fringe? Bangs? She had a pretty smile. Fun to be around. We went out for about a month. Guess you might say that's not long, but I fell hard for her anyway. I connected with her in a way I've never connected with a girl before. I guess I fell in love. But one day, she ghosted me. Do you know what that feels like?"

"Of course. I had a guy do that to me once. We'd been on three dates. I thought he liked me. But I never heard from him again. That's what dating these days is like. People ghost you."

"Yeah, and it hurts. She hurt me a lot. The girl. Well, that's it. That's my story."

"Okay," I told him, glad that he was done but confused that he'd told it to me.

"Wait," he said. "I've got a picture of her. A photographer at a nightclub took it—one of those dudes that come around and take a snap and then try to sell it to you for an inflated price. And you're drunk and happy and so you buy it. Or maybe, in my case, I just wanted a picture of me and her. Because I couldn't believe my luck that a girl like her was going out with me." Leaning over, he took his phone from the bedside table.

"I've got the photo in here. I'll find it for you."

Silently, I waited.

He turned the phone around and I glanced at the screen. It was the name of a website: *Trent Jay Dorrington.*

"Is that your blog?" I asked.

"It's everything. A bit of my adventures. A bit of a personal journal. And my art portfolio. Anyway, I just wanted to prove that the photo I'm about to show you is mine and I didn't just pull it randomly off the interwebs." He swiped through a few screens and then handed me the phone.

A picture of two young people filled the screen. As he'd said, it was taken at a nightclub.

The man in the photo was Trent—his hair longer but it was definitely him—looking a little younger and a lot happier. The redhaired girl was resting fondly against his shoulder. He had his arms wrapped around her. It was clear that the two of them were a couple.

I was about to hand the phone back to Trent when something made me hesitate and inspect the picture more closely.

My stomach lurched.

"What is this?" I asked coldly.

"It's two people who wanted nothing else but to be together, at the time," he responded.

"You're crazy." I jerked my head up to face him, feeling queasy. "Why did you do this?"

"Do what?"

"Photoshop my face onto this girl. That face is mine."

"You have a habit of accusing me of things I didn't do."

"I was never there in this nightclub and certainly not with you."

"Are you sure?"

"Why are you doing this to me?"

His face creased into a scowl. "Doing this to you? Try to see it from my point of view. A girl I was once very fond of crosses my path. I didn't think I'd ever see her again. I'm still hurt but maybe a little hopeful that she'll want to rekindle the romance. But—she sees me and then acts like I'm a complete stranger."

"You *are* a stranger to me." I flung the phone onto his bed.

"So, you're really going to keep this up, huh? You're really going to keep pretending."

"If it's true, why don't I remember you?"

He sighed, staring at the picture. "Maybe you don't want to. Dump 'em and burn the memory."

I turned suddenly at the sight of two figures entering the room.

Aubrey and Bridget. They gaped at Trent and then at me.

Bridget's eyes opened wide. "Hoo baby, these two are at it again."

"Is everything okay, you two?" asked Aubrey, a note of concern in her voice. "Isla?"

"I have to go," I crossed the room, not looking at Trent again.

"Isla," Trent called.

I paused at the door, still not turning around.

"I didn't put the scarecrow in the tree," he said, enunciating each word slowly.

I felt Aubrey's hand on my arm. "Isla, would you mind waiting at the hospital cafe for me? I want to talk to Trent for a minute. He's my friend—but not for much longer if he's going to behave like this. Okay?"

I nodded, just wanting to get away from him.

With legs of jelly, I blundered along the corridor.

I didn't even know where the hospital cafe was. My lips felt almost too numb to talk as I asked a nurse where it was. I made my way to the ground floor.

Inside the cafe, the antiseptic smells of the wards and corridors gave way to smells of hot baked foods and coffee. Whoever had decorated the cafe had made an effort to make it cheery—yellow chairs and rows of plastic potted plants hanging above the tables. A small outdoor section lay through double glass doors, but no one was heading out there. Too cold and windy, leaves eddying around in listless circles.

After grabbing a tea at the counter, I sat myself down in a corner, away from the clusters of people.

Drawing out my phone from my handbag, I called my mother.

She answered sleepily, stifling a yawn. "Yes, Lana Wilson speaking?"

"Mum, it's me."

She sounded a lot more alert when she spoke next. "Oh, Isla. Sorry, I didn't even look at my phone before answering. I just woke up. It's a quarter past six in the morning."

"Sorry I woke you."

"Don't be silly. Call anytime. Time for me to get up soon anyway."

"I just need to know something. It's about something that happened two years ago—you know, that time I got really sick."

"Yes?"

"Did I have a boyfriend back then? I'm having trouble remembering."

"Isn't that all best left in the past, Isla? You're having an adventure right now. Why are you thinking about that old stuff?"

"It's important. Because when I think back to those months, it's like one big tumbleweed blowing around in my head. I lost a chunk of my life. I need to know—did I have a boyfriend then? I mean, before I got sick?"

"Oh...you'd been on a couple of dates. Nothing serious."

"With who? Did his name happen to be *Trent*?"

My question was met with silence. Then she said in a careful tone, "I didn't meet him."

"Okay. But was his name Trent?"

"It might have been, yes."

"My God. Why can't I remember him?"

"Honey, why don't we talk about this when you get home? No point upsetting yourself when—"

"He's *here*, Mum. Trent. I'm at a hospital in Greenmire, where he's a patient. Trent had a drug overdose days ago. He just showed me a photograph of him and myself. I was shocked. I accused him of altering the picture to put me in it. But then I remembered how sick I was back then, and I wondered—"

"Oh, I can't believe this. He turned up there, in *Greenmire*? How does something like that even happen?"

"I don't know. I don't know anything. I can't believe that I went out with this person and I don't even remember him."

"How did you find out? And how did you know he was in the hospital?"

I didn't want to explain the scarecrow incident to her. "It's a bit complicated. I'll tell you another time."

"Look, honey, you need to stay away from him. He's bad news. He must have been stalking you to turn up there."

"What happened? Please tell me."

"I wish I didn't have to tell you any of this. But he left you in a terrible state. Bruises on your arms and face. You hadn't showered or brushed your hair for days. You were in a state of confusion, barely able to talk to me."

"Oh my God. So, it wasn't just a seizure? This man hurt me?"

"Yes. I'm sorry honey."

"Why didn't you tell me?"

"It was a terrible time. You were in such a state. You began having awful dreams. And you were having seizures every day. You had to spend weeks in the hospital and then you were completely zoned out for months afterwards. When you came out of it, your memory of all of it was gone. I thought it was better to let it go."

"I know how sick I was. But you should have told me about Trent. Who is he? How did I—?"

"Isla, listen to me. He's dangerous. You need to get on the first plane home."

"He's in a hospital ward. He's no danger to me."

"But he'll get better and get out. Whatever he did to you, it took you months to recover. Do you understand me? He's a bad person. You don't need to stay there. Your safety comes first." Her voice rasped and she sounded terrified.

"I'll be careful, Mum. I—"

I caught sight of Aubrey and Bridget entering the cafe.

"Mum," I said into the phone, "I have to go. I've got some more questions, but I'll call you later, okay?"

I thrust the phone back into my pocket, my heart hammering.

26

ISLA

THE AIR WAS CHILLIER than usual when I woke and climbed out of bed, as if the weather had suddenly dropped ten degrees.

I'd called Mum back last night, but she didn't have any more information for me. She didn't know anything about who Trent was or what he'd done. All she knew was that I'd called her one day and she'd come to get me from my apartment, and she'd been shocked by the condition she'd found me in. Next, I'd tried the two friends who I used to see the most two years ago. Only one of them remembered me mentioning a guy named Trent and only vaguely.

I opened the bedroom shutters.

A gasp flew from my throat.

The world had turned white while I slept. The trees looked as if icing sugar had been sifted over them.

I noticed then that it was still snowing. Just barely. Individual snowflakes spiralled past my window.

Distracted and entranced, I stood there watching for minutes.

Photos. I should grab photos. What if the sun came out and the snow melted, and it didn't snow again for weeks?

Dressing in a thick layer of clothing, I headed out.

My boots crunched the icy ground. I caught a snow flake in my hand. Then, crouching, I trailed my gloved fingers through the snow and packed some snow into a tight ball. I pelted the snowball at a tree, hoping I wouldn't lose my footing and send my butt skidding across the ground. I'd been waiting a lifetime to throw a snowball.

Only, now that I'd seen snow for the first time, I had no one to throw snowballs with.

A curtain moved aside upstairs in the McGregors' house. It had to be Jessica. Alban's car was gone and the figure at the window was an adult. Well, I didn't care if she was watching.

Maybe Jessica would decide to go out and leave Rhiannon with Greer again. If Stella was still in town, the four of us could build a group of snow people in the front yard.

I guessed I should start taking photos.

The figure at the window vanished as I took out my camera and aimed it at the house. The snow-encrusted roof line and whiter-than-white surrounds gave the house an entirely different look. There were no puffy mounds of heather to soften and make the architectural lines prettier. But somehow, the starkness made the house design come into its own. Again, I could see why Alban had won awards.

Stomping about in the soft snow, I climbed the hills and captured pictures of the snow-covered mountains and ghostly trees. Then I trekked back down along the tree-line, snapping small details. A bird alone on a bare, snowy branch. A snow-jewelled larch cone.

I was spellbound by the wintry-white world, but a continual stream of thoughts ran rampant in my mind. *Who was Trent? What had he done to me? What was he trying to do to me now?*

My phone's ringtone jingled in the crisp air.

Taking out my phone, I glanced at my screen. It was Rory.

I'd thought our conversations had come to an end. I'd pushed too hard when I'd tried to find out why Stella had left town and I'd stepped on Rory's toes. At least, it felt that way. But maybe he'd remembered something.

"Rory, hi," I said. "I can't believe it's actually snow—"

"Isla!" he jumped in. "Have you seen Stella today?"

"No? I've only been awake about an hour. I've been out on a shoot here at Braithnoch. Why? Anything wrong?"

"The Keenans say she didn't sleep in her bed last night. They don't know where she is."

"Oh, Rory, that's awful."

"Camille is beside herself. Trouble is, I don't know where to start looking."

"Could she have gone back home? To Aviemore I mean?"

"Aye, she could have. But we called her aunt Kelly and she said she hasn't seen her."

"What about her friends here? Does she keep in contact with them?"

"No. I mean to say, she did have friends, but she didn't keep in contact. It's like she threw everything about this town away when she left it. Apart from her grandparents, that is. But Camille's calling them all anyway, just to check."

"What can I do to help?"

He sighed. "You don't have to do anything. This is *our* problem."

"She's just a young girl. It's everyone's problem. I'll head around to the Keenans to see if there's something I can help with."

Ending the call quickly, I hurried down to the snow-buried driveway and along the pathway through the forest that led to the Keenans. I kept sinking into unseen ditches and pitching forward. I wasn't at all used to running in snow.

I climbed the Keenan's fence and crossed the field. Their lovely flowers and trees were now hidden under a white cover.

Nora Keenan threw open the door quickly, her face pale and anxious. "I have to tell you I was hoping you'd be Stella."

I touched her arm. "I know. Rory told me. I can help look for her if you have any idea where I should start."

She clamped her eyes shut for a moment. "I just don't know, that's the trouble. Come in, anyway—we can all put our heads together and sort this out."

Charlie Keenan was sitting at the table, calmly drinking tea, seeming oblivious to his wife's distress.

Hamish stomped in through the door, shaking powdery snow from his hair and jacket. "I tried calling out to her all over the woods. *Nothing*. She's not out there."

"She's a fighter," said Charlie.

"What?" Nora sounded clearly annoyed.

"She's fighting her battles, wherever she is," he said. "It's in the blood. It goes way back. There was a battle here in the Middle Ages. Griogair Braithnoch got cut fair in with a sword. Bleeding out, he was. He weren't gonna make it far. He fell into the peat marsh. When he crawled out, he was covered in the thick, sticky mud. It sealed up his wounds. And he made it back to his wife and bairns alive."

"Charlie! Not now with your old war stories," she chastened.

"Could Stella have fallen into the peat marsh?" I said in alarm.

"No, our girl Stella knows where the marshes are," Nora said. "Charlie just has a habit of drifting off into his own world. Hamish, go take a run over to Aviemore and see if you can find Stella. And while you're there, why not stop in at Kelly's place to see if she's got any suggestions?"

"It'll be a dark day before I go to Kelly's house," he responded.

"Why would you say such a thing?" said Nora.

Hamish raised his dark eyebrows. "Maybe because Kelly's always a rude bitch to me?"

"Ach." Nora waved a hand dismissively. "You three kids should try to get along. I don't know what's up with you lot, I swear."

"I'm not going," Hamish told her. "Hell can freeze over for all I care." He sounded more annoyed than deathly serious.

Nora pressed her lips together with so much pressure they turned white and her neck strained. "Well, I'll have no rest until I know where my little Stella is."

"Bloody hell," Hamish huffed. "All right, I'll go to Aviemore. But I'll not go to Kelly's."

Incensed, Nora turned her head to me. "Isla, you wanted to do something? Could you perhaps go with Hamish? He'll have to quit his silly carry on if he's got you with him. I'd go, but someone needs to stay here with Charlie. If he wanders off in that snow, he won't last long. And he does wander off at times."

"Of course." I glanced at Hamish hesitantly.

Hamish muttered under his breath. "I don't need a chaperone."

"Please," his mother begged him. "This cold war between you and Kelly and Camille has been going on way too long. But if you can't end it, then at least take Isla with you so that you stay civil. Between Stella missing and your father bleating on with his old war stories, I can't take much more."

Drawing his mouth into a firm line, he gave his mother a single nod.

Moments later, I was sitting in Hamish's beat-up car, freezing on the cold seat and wondering how I was going to survive a trip to Aviemore with him. He wasn't a happy person and I guessed it would be easy to say the wrong thing.

He drove away, through the town of Greenmire.

We chatted in awkward fits and starts but mostly stayed silent. His car heater didn't work very well, and I remained cold all the way, listening to his selection of heavy metal music. I wished now that it hadn't snowed. Everything was carpeted in white and I couldn't see much of the scenery. Worse, the snow might make finding Stella harder.

Mountains rose higher and higher in the distance and the roads climbed higher, too. Hamish drove a bit erratically and I was starting to worry about coming along with him on this trip. Rory was right. These people weren't family—I barely knew them. If Stella was in Aviemore, she was probably safe and with a friend.

The main street of Aviemore was lined with low sets of buildings, the snow cleared to either side.

"We're here," he announced, even though I'd seen the Aviemore welcome sign quite a distance back. "Guess we'll just drive about and see if we can spot her."

In their winter clothing, the Aviemore townspeople all seemed to look similar. Everyone in thick dark coats and knitted hats. Trying to pick Stella out would prove difficult. We tried to peel our eyes for groups of teenagers, especially young girls on their own.

Hamish ringed around a couple of the town's resorts and then along a river.

"That's the River Spey," Hamish remarked, breaking the silence. "Goes all the way through the Cairngorms and out to sea."

I stared out of the car window. Some of the trees that lined the riverbanks were still holding onto their fiery red and orange autumn colours. The effect was stunning—white snow topping autumn trees, along the bank of the fast-flowing river, with the snow-encrusted mountains in the distance. The photographer in me wanted to take some shots, but this wasn't the right time.

Hamish kept driving. At one point, we were driving through a housing estate and ended up at the site of a small, ancient stone circle, the stones half-buried under snow. So casual and yet so Scottish. It seemed that the Scots were used to remnants of their ancient structures everywhere in their towns.

"Well, nothing left to do but show our faces at my sister's place," he said morosely. "Keep my mum happy, if nothing else."

He drove for a short distance further, then parked outside a line of townhouses not far from the stone circle.

Kelly Keenan cracked her door open and peeked out after Hamish banged on her door. She had the same dark hair that Camille and Hamish had, with quick brown eyes. Her mother had said she was twenty-three, but she looked even younger than that, like a teenager.

She gazed at me openly. "Don't tell me you've got a girlfriend, Hamish."

"As if I'd tell you *anything*," he retorted.

I held out my hand. "Hi, I'm Isla. I'm not his girlfriend. I've been staying at Braithnoch with the McGregors."

Kelly shrugged as she shook my hand. "Oh, you're the one Greer told me about." She cast a scrutinising eye over her brother. "I didn't think you'd actually have an adult for a girlfriend. How old was your last one again? Oh, I remember now. *Fifteen*."

He shoved his hands deep into his coat pockets. "Stop, Kelly. I didn't come here for any of this."

"Well, then you can leave," she said pointedly. "I already told Mum that Stella didn't come back here. Why she had to send you over here is a mystery."

"She wanted me to take a look around the streets," he muttered, his bravado of a minute ago crumbling. "Something you're not able to do because for some unknown reason, you don't drive. Anyway, you don't want me here any more than I want to be here. So, now that I can tell Mum I talked to you in good faith, I'll be on my way."

She sighed. "Look, you're here now. May as well come in and have a hot drink. I've made scones, too. Do you like scones, Isla?"

"I...don't think we'll be here long," I replied.

"You'll be here long enough," she said firmly. "Hamish can stomp around looking for ten minutes and satisfy everyone that I'm not stowing Stella away somewhere."

She waved us in.

I followed the grudging Hamish into the house and sat myself down on a stool in Kelly's tiny kitchen. Everything was painted in yellow and blue, looking a lot cheerier than the grey exterior of the building. The underfloor heating warmed my chilled body.

Hamish went into another room to call his mother to see if there was any news on Stella.

"Your place is cute," I told Kelly. I smiled at a teenage picture of her standing with her mother—a fluffy black puppy in her arms. "Is the pup yours?"

"Yes, he was mine. He died last year. I wasn't able to bring him here—they don't allow pets at this rental."

"That's a shame."

"He was a lovely little dog." She sighed heavily. "Gosh, I feel so helpless with Stella missing. Especially seeing as I don't drive or have a car, as Hamish was so rude to point out."

"How's she been doing?" I asked her.

The way she sighed and shook her head reminded me of her mother. "She's a handful. As I see it, I deserve a medal for taking her on. But I'm treated like I'm leading her astray. She was going to run away from my sister, no matter what. If I didn't convince her to stay with me, she would have headed for either Inverness or Edinburgh. And just what was going to happen to a wee girl of twelve on the streets of a city? Nothing good, that's what."

"Do you have any idea why she wanted to leave so badly?"

She chewed her lip as she poured me out a tea. "She won't tell me. What can I do? You know, sometimes I wonder if there's something rotten there in Greenmire?"

I studied her pinched expression curiously. "What do you mean?"

"Things have been going on for a while. I don't know if Stella got caught up in any of it. But there's been a few odd things happen. It seems to me that someone must know something. But nothing ever comes out into the open. Sometimes, bad things happen in families and everyone rushes to cover it up. You know how it is. They just keep patching up the broken bucket, so it can keep carrying water."

I smiled briefly as she pushed a cup of tea and a plate of scones towards me. "I'd be interested in knowing what those odd things are. Stella's been hanging out with me for the last couple of days. She seems like a young girl who needs help, but I don't know where to start." I ate one of Kelly's scones. They were dry and lumpy, but I chewed as if I were enjoying it.

"Well, none of this is about Stella," said Kelly. "It happened a long time ago. But if the same person is still around, then who knows?" She stirred her tea. I noticed she put lots of sugar in, just like Hamish. "When I was ten—thirteen years ago—I used to do ballet classes with Aubrey. One day, when we were getting ready for a recital, we noticed a couple of tiny holes had been put into the wall. This was in the girls' changing room. Someone had been watching little girls get changed."

I shivered. "That's awful."

"Yeah. A year later, the photographs were found. Not just of us, but other girls, too. All from the ballet hall. The pictures had been stuffed into a hidey hole in a playhouse—between the McGregors' and my parents' house."

"The playhouse?" I said, startled. "Where Elodie McGregor was found that night?"

She nodded.

"What happened about the photos?"

She exhaled, staring fixedly into her tea. "Nothing. Nothing happened. There was a bit of a fuss for a while, but it died down quickly. My mum told me I was overreacting. *You girls' chests are flat as pancakes*, she said. *You've got nothing to show*. Well, true enough. None of us had breasts. But those photos made me aware of my body for the first time. That might sound strange, but what I mean is that I was suddenly aware that others might see me differently to the way I saw myself. That was a big revelation for a ten-year-old. Up until then, my body had been something that could do things. I could make it spin and jump high. But now it had become something to leer at."

"I get it," I told her. "I went through the same thing at that age. Not in the same way you did. For me it was just noticing men staring at me in the street sometimes."

Kelly talking about the photos reminded me of Stella having been hesitant of photographs being taken of herself. Had anyone ever taken bad photos of her, like the ones Kelly was describing?

We both looked up suddenly as Hamish entered the kitchen. "Stella still hasn't turned up. Just called Mum."

"Have some tea and scones, Hamish," Kelly offered.

"No thanks. Your scones are shite."

"Thanks, brother." She rolled her eyes at me.

"You haven't changed and neither have your scones," he stated. "Let's head out, Isla."

I nodded reluctantly. There was nothing to do but say goodbye to Kelly and get back into Hamish's chilly car.

Hamish drove back through Aviemore in silence. Faint sunlight glistened on the snow on the rooftops and put a sheen on spots of thin ice on the road.

I was disappointed I hadn't been able to stay longer and keep talking with Kelly. She knew things about Greenmire that I wanted to know more about. I wondered if Rory knew any of those things? The person who'd taken the photographs of the little girls was certainly creepy. That had only happened thirteen years ago. That person could certainly still be living in Greenmire.

Stella had reacted strangely the first time I'd asked her if I could take photographs of her. Was it possible that there was a connection?

Thoughts came and went through my head, like the flurries of snowfall outside. The countryside flattened out. We were nearing Greenmire again.

"I didn't know," Hamish stated, staring straight ahead at the road.

Confused, I glanced at him. "What didn't you know?"

"I didn't know that the girl was fifteen. The last girl I dated. She worked next door to my shop. I thought she was nineteen or so. She wore a hell of a lot of makeup. She was the one who persuaded me that we should go out together. Catch a movie or something. So, we went out a few times. But I ended it when I found out just how young she was."

"It's none of my business, Hamish. You don't have to explain."

"My ever-delightful sister made it your business. She doesn't think much of me, but she doesn't have to spread stuff around that isn't true."

Hamish hit the wheel several times with the heel of his hand. "You think I'm a total loser, now, don't you?"

"Of course not. I'm sorry, it didn't help much to bring me along, did it?" I shot him a nervous smile, trying to lighten his mood. In truth, I wasn't sure if I believed him or not. Guys who spent their time chasing after the youngest girls they could legally—or illegally—get were creeps in my eyes. I could especially understand Kelly having an adverse reaction to men who were attracted to very young girls, after what had happened to her with the dance practice photographs. I didn't know Hamish well enough to know whether or not he was telling the truth.

Hamish hit the wheel one more time.

The car swerved and slid.

"Shit. Ice!" He grappled with the wheel, but the car spun us completely around, slamming into an oncoming car.

The impact threw my body back into the seat, a grinding noise filling the air.

Dizzily, I watched the dim sky through snowflakes, while searing hot pain shot up my leg.

27

ISLA

I WOKE GASPING, shielding my face from an oncoming car that was no longer there.

"You're all right, Isla," came a woman's voice that I didn't recognise. "You're in the hospital."

I snapped my eyes open. A young woman with deep olive skin and a black braid gave me a reassuring smile.

"I'm in hospital?" I rasped.

"Yes, in Greenmire. A doctor will be here soon to check on you again."

"What happened to me? Am I hurt? I remember my leg—"

She pulled back the sheet on my lower body and let me see the bandages that wrapped my leg from lower calf to ankle. "You sustained a cut to your leg that needed twelve stitches and you also have some bruising. Nothing major, fortunately. You were given anaesthesia and a sedative. You've been asleep for two hours."

"There was a man in the car with me. His name is—"

"Hamish Keenan. He's got a head injury and a few cuts, but he'll be okay. He's in another room. You can see each other later on, but for now you both need to rest. Maybe they'll be able to arrange for you both to share a room."

"No, I don't know him."

She shot me an odd look. "Okay, no problem."

"I mean, I don't know him well enough to share a room. We went looking for his niece—a young teenager. Have you heard if she's been found?"

"I'm afraid I don't know anything about that. Just have a little rest, all right? If you need us, don't hesitate to press the big red button, okay then?" She turned her head as a woman walked in through the door. "Well, looks like you have a visitor. The doctor will be in to see you soon, too."

Greer bustled in carrying a basket of fruit, a small collection of mints, and a large bag, her eyes round. "Oh, you poor thing. I can't believe this has happened. What a time you've had since you've been here!" Placing the fruit and mints on the small table beside me, she sat herself down. "How awful you were in an accident. How's your poor leg?"

"To be honest I'm happy it was just my leg. Hamish got pretty scary in the car."

"Oh dear. That's not good. I heard that you two went looking for Stella. He does have a bit of a temper, from what I've seen. You should report him if he was driving dangerously."

"He wasn't driving dangerously, exactly. He was just angry about something his sister said. Thumping the steering wheel. Then we hit a patch of ice. I think I'd rather just let it go. That family has enough problems at the moment. Have they found her—Stella?"

"No, she's not been found. I hope they get to her quickly. That poor girl seems very troubled. The police are out looking for her now." Her brow wrinkled deeply. "What was said between Hamish and Kelly that made him so mad?"

"She said he'd dated a girl who was just fifteen."

"Oh, I remember that debacle. Kelly should let it go. She and Hamish have been feuding since they were kids."

"Did you grow up in Greenmire, Greer?"

"Until I was about seventeen. But then my family moved to Inverness. To be honest I love the city. I find small towns too quiet, too sort of eerie."

"You'd like Sydney."

"I'm sure I would. I'll have to come and visit, and you can show me around."

"That would be fun. There's so much to do there—I don't appreciate it as much as I should." I stifled a yawn, stretching. The anaesthetic had made me sleepy.

"Oh, you look like you just need to curl up and have a nap," Greer told me. "I'm told you might be allowed out in a little while. I'll go grab a coffee, but I'll be sticking around to see what the doctor's verdict is. If you can go, I'll be taking you back to the cottage." She put the bag that she'd been holding onto the bed. "Apparently, the paramedics cut your jeans off when they had to assess where the bleeding was coming from. So, I went and grabbed some of your clothes from the cottage. Hope you don't mind."

"Oh gosh, thank you. I was wondering where my clothes were."

She gave my arm a squeeze and then left.

I drifted back into sleep.

It was an hour later that a doctor gently shook me awake and told me that my leg was fine, and I could leave. I had to keep the leg dry for at least two days and I couldn't do any kind of exercise that might cause the cut to reopen. The stitches would need to come out in a week or so.

After he left, I dressed in the clothing that Greer had brought for me. She'd picked out a tracksuit. I was grateful she'd chosen something loose and stretchy.

I picked up my phone to call Greer. The battery was dead. Was she still here at the hospital?

Slipping my shoes on, I stepped across to the doorway and peered out. I assumed Greer would be at the café.

I walked along the corridor, following directory signs.

Too late, I recognised the ward. This was the ward that Trent was in. His room was the very next one.

I felt my palms grow sweaty.

What would I say if I saw him?

Confront him? Ask him what the hell he put me through?

Part of me wanted to barge in there and confront him. I wanted him to fill in some of the blank spots from those months of my life.

But he wasn't going to admit to hurting me, right? Of course he wouldn't.

Anger twisted inside me.

Holding my breath, I strode forward and turned into the room.

It was empty.

The bed made and the floor smelling strongly of antiseptic.

He was gone.

I whirled around, feeling stupid. He was probably already a long way away from here. Aubrey had told me he was banned from their house, so he wouldn't be going back there. I guessed I wouldn't ever have that confrontation with him. I had to let it go.

Letting myself breathe, I continued down the corridor.

Walking to the end, I spotted two women just around the corner.

Kelly and Greer.

Kelly was bending to fetch a bottle of water from a vending machine, her dark hair cascading down. Greer—a sleek blonde in a business suit—stood beside her.

I was about to approach when I noticed the two of them had begun arguing.

Greer seemed upset, using the same tone of voice that she had the times that I'd heard her talking on the phone.

"You don't understand," Greer was saying. "How can I make you understand?"

"I'm not a child," Kelly replied angrily. "Don't you dare treat me like one."

I ducked back. I guessed that Kelly was here to see Hamish. But what was she arguing about with Greer? Could it be about Hamish and his erratic driving?

Finding my way back to my room, I perched on the side of the bed and decided to wait for Greer to come to me. I unwrapped a mint and ate it.

Unbidden, Stella's face flashed in my mind.

I know where she is.

28

ISLA

I DIDN'T WAIT, racing back to the hospital corridor where Greer and Kelly were still standing, locked in a dispute.

Greer eyed me in alarm. "Isla, what—?"

"It's Stella. We need to go."

"You heard from her?" Greer exchanged confused, worried glances with Kelly.

"No, but I think I know where she is. If my hunch is right."

Kelly plucked out her phone from her pocket. "Tell me where. I'm calling the police and then we'll head there in Greer's car."

By the time we reached the car, rain had broken free from the dark clouds. All traces of snow were swiftly vanishing from the landscape. We made it just in time to avoid getting soaked.

I sat in the front seat of the car—Kelly in the back. My mind kept flashing back to the sight of the SUV coming straight towards me when I was on the road with Hamish.

Drawing deep breaths, I attempted to steady myself.

"Are you okay, Isla?" Greer's voice was taut with concern.

"I'm fine. I'll be fine." I crisscrossed my arms across my chest, rubbing my shoulders, even though the temperature inside the car was warm—far too warm. "The police are definitely on their way?"

"They're meeting us there," Kelly told me. "God, I hope she's—"

"Stella'll be all right," Greer broke in. "She will. She has to be."

As we neared Braithnoch, I caught sight of red and blue lights flashing on the mounds of snow on the roadside. The police had just pulled up. A female officer jumped out as Greer parked her car, introducing herself as Officer Tash Bradley.

Greer held up her hand to me as I stepped from the car. "Stay here. You're in no state to go stomping through the wood."

I shook my head. "I want to. The playhouse isn't far in."

Picking up a stout stick to ensure I didn't fall, I followed the police woman, Greer and Kelly. My leg was sore but not broken. Walking on it wasn't going to hurt it any worse.

Night was swiftly coming in.

The rain was light, but there was no shelter from it—it came directly through the bare branches. I was relieved when the drizzle stopped a minute later—I wasn't meant to get my stitches wet. But either way, my stitches could be fixed. Stella might not be able to be fixed, if she was in the playhouse doing what I suspected she was doing.

In the hospital, when I'd unwrapped one of the mints that Greer had brought me, it'd reminded me of Stella. The last day I'd seen her, she'd been eating mints, trying to cover up the odour of the cigarettes she'd smoked. I'd seen mint wrappers and cigarette butts in the playhouse. I'd also seen empty razor blade packets in there. I'd put all that together with the fact that Stella had said that Kelly's cat scratched her, but Kelly had told me that she wasn't allowed to have pets at her rental house.

We'd checked with Hamish to see if he'd looked in the playhouse. He hadn't—because it'd been locked and bolted. But someone who didn't want to be found could find a way to lock it from the inside. The playhouse was roughly made and had been repaired in patches— it would be easy to put a hand through and bolt it from the inside if you were determined. And I suspected that Stella was very, very determined.

The police officer was fast. She reached the playhouse first. I heard her call, "It's bolted."

Breathless, I cried out. "Just get it open."

Greer and Kelly, already way ahead of me, relayed what I'd said to the officer.

I reached the clearing, panting.

"Stella! Are you in there, lass?" Officer Bradley rattled the locked door.

No answer came that I could hear.

"Well, this bolt is on firmly," said the officer to Greer and Kelly, who had just run up behind her. "We have to force our way in." The officer gave two hard kicks at the door. The old wood snapped and gave way.

The three women pulled at the splintered door together.

The door fell from its hinges.

Taking a pen light from her pocket, Officer Bradley shone it around the interior of the playhouse. "Oh, Jesus...."

In between the figures of the police officer, Greer and Kelly, I caught a view of the floor. My heart thudded upward into my throat.

Stella lay in pools of blood.

Blood thinly covered the razor blade on the floor beside her.

A bag and blanket were also splattered with spots of blood.

Kelly's hand flew to her mouth and she cried out. "No. *No, no, no*...."

Crawling in, the officer picked up Stella's wrist. "There's a heartbeat. We have to be quick."

Twisting her head around, the officer looked back at us. "I need two credit cards. Hurry."

Greer was the fastest to act, tearing her wallet out and producing two cards.

The officer instructed Greer and Kelly to each hold a card against the cuts on Stella's wrists. Using the razor blade, the officer cut strips from the blanket and wrapped them around Stella's wrists, holding the credit cards tight against her skin.

I held my breath, silently pleading with Stella to hold on.

The three women and I exhaled in relief as the sound of an ambulance wailed in the cold air.

It seemed an age before the paramedics made their way in-Kelly showing them the route—but it was just minutes.

Precious minutes.

Greer made a few hurried calls, informing Stella's mother and grandparents that Stella had been found.

Rory and Camille turned up just as the ambulance drove away.

Running out of the car, Camille stormed up to Kelly. "How'd you know where she'd be?"

"It wasn't me, Cam. It was Isla," said Kelly. "And if I were you, I'd be following that ambulance right now. Your daughter is in there and she's in a very bad way."

Ignoring the last thing that Kelly said, Camille turned her head to me. "How did you know?"

I cringed under her glare. "I just put a few things together."

"What's going wrong with this family?" Camille cried. "My brother gets into an accident and now this happens to my own daughter. She was in your care, Kelly. And look how that's working out."

"She wasn't in my care at the time," Kelly pointed out. "She was staying with Mum and Dad. But you can't blame *them* either."

Camille crossed her arms tightly. "All I know is that my child is being rushed to hospital right now. And who saved her? A complete stranger. A stranger knows more about my daughter than anyone else it seems."

"That's not fair," Kelly said.

"Listen, that's enough," Greer told Camille. "Kelly did her best."

"It's all right." Kelly turned her head to Greer. "If Camille wants to have this conversation instead of being with her daughter, so be it." Greer sighed heavily, stepping away to stand beside me.

Camille's mouth twisted, her eyes fixed on her sister. "We wouldn't have to have this conversation if you didn't keep shutting me down. And we need to have it. If not for you, Stella would have come back to me."

Kelly gasped, her face pale. "That's not true."

"Of course it's true," spat Camille. "And you ended up being her worst option. You can't claim that she's happy. She's obviously been cutting herself for a while. When Greer called, she told me there were lots of razors in the playhouse. Stella never did anything like that when she lived with me."

Kelly swallowed. "I admit I had no idea. She covered it up well. She was always wearing long sleeves."

"Only a mother knows her daughter well enough to spot the signs that something's really wrong. You're so caught up in your job and your social life that you don't have time for a young girl. This is where it ends, Kelly. Maybe what's happened is all for the best. When she comes out of hospital, I'm bringing her home with me."

"Whatever, Camille. If you want to stand here and argue, that's your call. But I'm heading to the hospital." Kelly stared back at her.

Camille's eyes flashed with anger. "Don't you dare go there. If you turn up at Stella's room, I'll have you thrown out. You're not her parent."

"For the love of God, Camille," Rory pleaded, walking up to her. "Get in the car. We need to get to the hospital. What if Stella doesn't make it?"

Camille snapped around to him, her posture stiff. But then her eyes grew large and her shoulders sagged. "She *has* to make it. I couldn't bear it."

Rory glanced at Kelly then across at Greer and me, despair stamped on his face. Taking his wife's arm, he walked her back to the car.

Greer and I walked over to Kelly, who was staring helplessly after her sister.

"Kelly," said Greer. "Where do you want to go? Back to Aviemore or to the hospital? I know where you'd want to go, but I also know that Camille won't stop her nonsense. And you don't deserve that. You've done an incredible job with Stella."

Kelly shook her head, tears streaking freely down her face now. "No, I haven't. Camille's right. I haven't done a good job with Stella at all."

"No, Kelly. You did your best." Greer hugged her.

Kelly nestled her head into Greer's shoulder while Greer stroked her hair.

The scene suddenly seemed almost too intimate for me to be here, watching on. Greer and Kelly had a closer relationship than I'd realised. I moved away, to give them some space.

"Can we at least stop the war between us?" Kelly said softly.

Greer stepped back, holding Kelly's face between her hands. "There's no war. Never was."

"Then *why*?" Kelly cried. "You've never explained why. You just tell me we can't be together."

"This isn't the time, Kelly. We—"

"I'm going crazy." Kelly said. "Really."

Greer stared at the wet, leaf-covered ground, her shoulders rising as she took a deep breath. "You deserve better. I haven't known what to tell you. It's not you—"

"Of course it's me. There's something wrong with me."

"What? No," Greer gasped, shaking her head. "That's not it. Not for a minute. Not for a second. How could you—"

"Then what? Tell me."

"Okay. Okay, I'll tell you. It's your age. It's my age. You're too young. I'm almost thirty-seven. And, it's…well, you're so good with Stella, and I'm just not ever going to be the kind of person who wants to have children. I'm just not. I love them but I don't want the responsibility. What if you want to have a baby? I don't want you stuck with me."

Kelly bit her lip, crying. "Why didn't you just tell me these things?"

"Because…I was afraid you'd just brush it all aside and tell me it was okay. And then I'd believe that it was okay. And then a year, two years, five years in the future, we'd know it was a mistake. And I didn't want that."

"Can we talk about it?" Kelly pleaded. "Not right now. But afterwards. After we know Stella is okay and we have time to figure things out."

Greer nodded, tears running down her face now, too. "Yes, we'll talk. I do love you, Kelly. Please, God, let Stella be okay. Let her get through this…."

I now understood all those tense, whispered conversations of Greer's over the phone.

Charlie Keenan's words came back to me about Stella fighting her own battle.

Everyone was fighting their own battles.

29

ISLA

I ROUSED from sleep in a clammy sweat. I'd been dreaming of the house with the long corridor again.

Dark rooms.

Piano chords crashing.

Scarecrow hanging by a rope.

Symbol of a cross with a rose in the middle.

In my dream, I tried another room.

Trent, sitting on a chair in a hospital gown, staring back at me.

I tried the door that was always shut. But it was still locked tight.

Pivoting, I walked to another room.

Stella, on the floor, covered in blood.

As I woke from the dream, it took me a second to register that parts of the dream had been real.

Was I going to spend the rest of my life dreaming that dream, collecting every bad thing that happened and keeping it in a room there?

I liked it better when I was *Alice-on-the-outside*, unable to enter the strange world I was peering into. But yet again, I'd been compelled to walk inside the house. Instead of fading away, the dream was becoming stronger, more real.

An image of Stella being taken away in the ambulance inserted itself into my mind. I shivered.

It had been so hard to see behind the screen that she put up. A pang of guilt twisted in my chest. Had I pushed her past her coping point by asking her questions about Elodie and the past? If she'd died, I never would have forgiven myself.

I sat up in bed, bracing the chilled air. Stella might have died during the night for all I knew. The last I'd heard, Stella's condition was critical but stable. But things might have changed while I slept.

My heart in my mouth, I called Rory. He told me that Stella had improved and her doctors thought she'd make a full recovery. Hamish was okay and would be coming out of hospital later today.

Breathing slowly and deeply, I dressed myself. My leg felt stiff and sore as I pulled my track pants on. My head felt a bit faint from the anaesthetic I'd had yesterday.

Stella was going to be okay. I cursed myself for not thinking of the playhouse sooner.

The merest and most random of events could mean that things carried on as normal or that everything changed.

My memories were suddenly swept back all the way to my childhood, when Jake and I had stood in front of the shed at the bottom of our garden, peering through the cobwebbed window and seeing the pair of legs dangling mid-air. Could something small have stopped our dad from taking his life that day? A special dinner with his family? A phone call from a friend? The thought of that had haunted me all these years. But now I knew that the people closest to the suicidal person could only too easily miss that they were about to tip over the edge. Because the person had often been standing on an edge for a long time and showed few signs that they were about to fall from it.

Maybe it was you, Dad, who led me to Stella. You found a place where you wouldn't be disturbed to end your life—a small, familiar place—that's what Stella did, too. Maybe that's why I connected the pieces.

It occurred to me now that maybe Stella wanted to be found. She must have been there in the playhouse since she'd run off from the Keenan's place. I'd just taken too long to work it out. *Almost.*

I was at a loss to know what to do with myself today. I could stay here in the cottage and edit photos, but my mind was restless. Too much had happened in the past few days and I could barely grasp any of it. I wanted to be out, roaming somewhere outside. Only, because of my leg, I couldn't go far or risk doing anything too active. I decided to rug up and just go for a walk.

Winding a thick scarf around my neck and lower face, I set out.

There'd been snowfall again, overnight.

I had my camera in my backpack, not expecting to use it. I wasn't in the right head space. My legs were safely encased in the rain boots I'd found in the bicycle shed, so that I wouldn't chance getting my bandages wet.

Alban's Volvo was gone—it was just Jessica's car sitting in the driveway, beneath a frosting of snow. I glanced up at the house to see if the shy Rhiannon was peeking down at me. I'd gotten used to seeing her up there. But she wasn't.

I trudged up the snowy hills, taking it slow.

My back started to ache. I was placing most of my weight on my good leg and throwing myself out of kilter. Maybe I should just head back to the cottage. This walk might be considered too strenuous for fresh stitches. Stopping, I rested my leg for a moment, debating what to do. I hated the thought of going back and sitting inside. I decided to keep going.

The air temperature seemed to drop as I climbed the hills, the wind picking up and stinging my eyes.

I headed for the entrance of the old stone house. It'd be a refuge from the wind.

I squinted in the sharp light that bounced from the white-blanketed hills. A figure moved up at the point where the largest hill crested, next to the ruins. Who would be roaming around on the McGregors' property?

The thought came to me that it could be Trent. What if he was stalking me, like Mum had said he could be? But if so, why would he be up there poking around in the ruins? Wouldn't he be watching the cottage instead?

It hadn't been Trent who'd followed me that day in the forest. That had to be someone else—someone who hadn't wanted to be seen. So far, Trent hadn't made an effort to hide himself from me, and anyway, he'd been in hospital that day.

I could turn back. But it was daylight and out in the open. I was safe, wasn't I?

I tugged my scarf down from my face as I headed towards the stone house. It was instinctual—if I had to scream, I didn't want a woollen scarf covering my mouth.

The figure had stepped inside the ruins. They hadn't seen me. At least, I didn't think so.

Keeping my distance, I trudged through the snow until I had a view of the interior.

Alban—it was Alban.

I walked inside behind him.

He stood inside, his hand against the stonework, staring up at the sky through the missing ceiling. He wore a long jacket that had seen better days and faded jeans.

There was nothing left inside the ruins—no signs of domestic life. There was just a crude wooden shelf that had been hammered into the only protected part of the crumbled house—a part that still held a roof over it. The shelf contained a couple of lamps. I wondered if Alban sometimes came up here at night and lit those lamps.

He turned, noticing me.

"I thought you were out." I pushed my hands down deep in my pockets, unable to think of anything more sensible to say.

He shrugged. "Jess took Rhiannon out shopping in my car. Mine is safer in conditions like this. Hers needs new tyres."

"Oh. Well, I'm sorry to disturb you. I was just taking a bit of a walk."

He raised an eyebrow. "Didn't think you'd be out and about so soon after the accident."

"I just needed to get out for a while. Probably shouldn't. I should be resting my leg, I guess."

"I heard you got stitches. Lucky it wasn't worse. Hamish always was a bit of a reckless driver."

I gave a dry laugh. "Wish I'd known that before I got into a car with him."

"It's been quite an introduction to Scotland for you, hasn't it Isla?

Not a good one, I'm afraid. Hard to believe that all of this has happened. We're normally a quiet little hamlet."

A hint of pain entered his eyes and I wondered if he were thinking of the last time before this week that the peace was disturbed—the night a stranger came to Braithnoch and hurt Elodie.

I felt guilty as I thought of all the things I'd been speculating about Alban over the past few days. *The line painting on his office wall. The strange words that Elodie was supposed to have told Stella.* When I was alone, it seemed that Alban being his daughter's abductor could all add up and be true. But standing here, in front of Alban, I didn't know whether I could believe it.

"If I didn't know better," he said. "I'd say that you coming here has shaken Greenmire up. I'm not saying you caused any of it, understand."

"I'd hate to think that I was like an ill wind blowing through this town."

He laughed unexpectedly. "Bringing both bad and good, eh? Well, I can guess that you're anxious to get home. And I haven't exactly been helpful, I know. But I'll help you get on your way. You need portraits of me, right? It's as good a time as any."

I eyed him in surprise. "Now? Here?"

"Why not? Whatever you come up with will be fine with me. This is me, as I am. No pretenses."

I gazed at him with a photographer's eye. He looked windblown and a bit ragged—in a masculine sort of way that I guessed could work. But it certainly wouldn't make for the usual kind of portrait.

"I'll just let you know that you won't look exactly…professional," I said hesitantly. "Are you sure you don't want to prepare first, or something?"

"No one needs to see me sitting at my desk, looking like a numpty."

"Like a numpty?"

"Och, you know, like a big idiot sitting up straight and looking all pleased with myself, like the cat that ate the cream."

I grinned. "Okay then, it's settled. The portrait shoot happens now." I unpacked my camera.

"Right. Tell me where you want me."

Stepping about for a bit, I looked for the best spots for backgrounds and light. I decided to start with a crumbling archway that looked out to the distant mountains.

"Could you stand just inside the archway? I think it could look kind of epic with that scenery behind you." I frowned as Alban moved into place. "Just…relax and open up your expression."

"Are you saying I'm scowling?"

"I can't say that you're *not* scowling."

"I think I've got a permanent scowl on my face these days. I'm probably even scaring Rhiannon. I don't know if I can change it."

I exhaled. "I think I'll take it, at this stage. I don't know if there's going to be another time that you'll be this agreeable."

That elicited another short laugh from him. "You're a blunt woman, aren't you?" His eyes lingered on me.

My skin heated under the thick scarf I had around my neck. He wasn't flirting, exactly. Maybe it was *me* who was flirting with *him*. I realised in that moment just how attracted I was.

I shouldn't be.

As I took a few photographs of Alban, the small, narrow world inside the camera lens seemed almost too intimate. Everything else disappeared. A rushing sensation pulsed through my body. The look in his eyes—that intense, searching gaze—seemed to be for me rather than the camera.

No, his expression isn't for me. I asked him to open up and he's just trying to do that.

"How about we take some photos outdoors now?" Inhaling deeply and silently, I stepped out into the biting air.

I had to focus on getting the job done. He had such an easy charm that he'd jammed every one of my senses. No wonder Jessica loved him. And Greer and Rhiannon, too. Being with him felt safe and I somehow felt *alive*. He seemed larger than life and part of the surrounding landscape.

He went to stand in front of his centuries-old family home—the walls moss green in the crevices between the stones, snow white on the tops of the walls and distant mountains. The wintry light was sharp and clear. Despite his messy locks and old jacket, he seemed regal. Through the lens, the photos looked perfect. Alban McGregor, in his element, in his own little kingdom.

Hints of a weary sadness began to show in some shots. I kept taking photos, wondering if Alban was aware of that.

"How about some with the mountains in the background?" I suggested.

"Okay, but you're going to have to do a wee bit of climbing."

We headed around the back of the ruins and climbed the hills. Sharp, high boulders stuck up out of the ground, bare of snow cover.

The mountains were beautiful, mystical.

I stepped around a bit on my new vantage point, taking photos of the mountain range.

"Hang on there." Alban grabbed my arm. "Did you not see the steep drop off there?"

Taking the camera away from my face, I looked down—*straight down*. He wasn't joking about the drop off. It was dangerous. *Broken-bones-and-death* kind of dangerous. The drop off led into a valley and moors.

"That's the Flanagans' land," Alban told me. "Don't go wandering up here alone. You need to keep your wits about you, Isla, and not blunder about like that." He grinned then, still holding my arm.

I nodded, exhaling, my head buzzing from the sight of that steep drop and the fact that Alban was so close to me right now. He seemed reluctant when he released his hold.

Or was it me who was reluctant to move away?

I could no longer tell.

30

ELODIE

Greenmire, Scottish Highlands, December 2015

VOICES CROWDED into Elodie's head.

She could hear Stella. Stella was telling her to never be alone with someone. Who didn't Stella want her to be alone with? Why was her head so fuzzy?

Don't be alone with him. Don't go to the playhouse with him, Stella had said.

Who was *he*?

She couldn't picture his face or who he was. She knew he was close to her and that he'd always been in her life. She remembered snatches of the things that he'd said to her: *Love comes from respect. You will respect me. And you will love me, Elodie. Come here now and give me a kiss.*

Someone else's voice jumped into her head now.

Mia Dunning.

Mia was her best friend at school. At least, she had been. Elodie had told Mia some of the things she'd been told. About love. About respect. Days later, Mia told her that her mother said she wasn't allowed to play with her anymore. Her mother said that everyone who lived at Braithnoch Square was strange. Elodie knew that Braithnoch Square included four properties—belonging to her family, the Keenans, the Chandlishes and the Flanagans. Mia even said that Stella Keenan was a bad influence and that Elodie's parents shouldn't allow her to come around and babysit.

Elodie had pushed Mia after she'd said that. Then she'd gotten in trouble from Mr Kavanagh.

But Mia shouldn't have said what she did. She was wrong.

Elodie remembered running through the forest. She'd been trying to get away from someone. But who had been chasing her?

She could feel wet branches scratching her face as she ran through the forest. She wanted to ask Mr Kavanagh if he'd seen her footprints and if he could tell how fast she had run. He'd once told her you can tell a lot by footprints. He said that you can tell that someone is running for their lives, by how far apart and deep their footprints are, and how jagged their route. And you can tell by the sharp way the prints twist in certain spots that the person kept checking behind.

He looked funny—Mr Kavanagh. A bit like a King Charles Cavalier dog—the kind that are tri-colour. *Cavvy Kavanagh.* His hair was the same kind of brown and it was shaggy, his eyebrows thick and black, and his beard and moustache kind of blond. Tri-colour. She knew that Hamish called him the mad professor. Stella called him the weirdo.

Sometimes, Mr Kavanagh call her to stay after class and he'd talk about her paintings. He always told her how good they were, what a good artist she was. She felt proud in those moments. But then he'd ask other stuff—stuff that made her feel strange, stuff that she didn't want to answer.

She tried to push herself away from those thoughts. She wanted to escape this hospital bed and run away. But she couldn't.

She saw herself now, standing in the hallway outside Daddy's office. She could see all the photographs of herself and Mum and Dad. She saw the pictures of herself that she hated, because she could see the things in her eyes that she wasn't telling. She saw those pictures every day. She wanted to slap them down from the wall and smash them to pieces.

Come in, she heard Dad saying. He was asking her into his office.

Dad worked hard in his office and she wasn't usually allowed in there.

I heard that you pushed another girl at school, he said. *Mr Kavanagh called me. Why did you push Mia?*

She said bad things about us, Elodie told Daddy.

Dad asked her to sit on his lap. He stroked her hair and told her that Mia was just jealous. He told Elodie to remember all the things that were special about her. He told her that he loved her and asked her if she loved him.

She asked him if he loved Mum the way he loved her, because she wasn't sure. His eyes grew distant when he answered, even though he said he did. He never looked at Mum the way that she looked at him. She never saw him hug Mum anymore. She didn't even remember the last time she'd seen the two of them cuddle each other. When he kissed Mum, it was just a quick kiss on the cheek, like a chicken pecking at the ground.

But when he held Elodie, sometimes he held on too long and too tightly, bending his head to her shoulder—as if he would never let go.

Dad never seemed excited about the baby. Elodie would prattle on and on about who the baby would be and what he or she would do. Dad would listen for a while, but he always seemed distracted.

Her mind flipped back to the woods. She recalled being inside the playhouse, on the cold floor. Wind baying and snapping outside.

She remembered the person who chased her in there telling her that she had to be grown up now, that Mum was in the hospital having the baby, and Elodie was here all alone. She'd been confused. Mum had gone to get potatoes, not to have the baby.

She felt his hand on her shoulder, the man who'd told her that— the man with her *inside* the playhouse.

31

ISLA

AFTER UPLOADING the photos I'd taken of Alban, I heated myself up a can of soup. Relaxing my sore leg on a stool, I ate the soup with a thick piece of bread.

I almost had all the photos I needed. The landscapes, Alban's architecture, his house and child. And now Alban himself. The only thing left were the family shots. Alban, Jessica and Rhiannon together. I didn't know how to jump that last hurdle. But I'd do it, and then I could go home.

I opened my laptop, checking the photo shoot. I sighed in relief. They were as good as I'd thought they were. It had been a happy coincidence running into Alban up there in the hills. The portfolio brief had asked for the man behind the public image, and the photos I had couldn't have come closer. I couldn't take all the credit. It was Alban himself who made the photos come alive, his old clothing giving him a timeless look.

Outside, the wind had increased in strength, bending the branches of the trees.

An ill wind.

Alban didn't know yet that I'd known Trent from before. It was *me* who'd brought the trouble here. Trent had outright refused to admit that he'd rigged up the scarecrow. But if not him, who else? His bitterness over our past relationship was obvious. I wished I knew what he'd done to me. The *not knowing* was surely worse than knowing.

I grabbed my laptop and went to sit on the sofa, right next to the heater. I brought the stool with me, too, propping my leg up.

What had the web address of his website been? It was just his name, wasn't it?

Trent Jay Dor—something.

Dory? No.

Dorian? No.

Dorring? That was it. Trent Jay *Dorrington*.

I browsed the internet and found his website.

His artwork was very creative—it caught my attention first. Lots of fantastical drawings of animals and people merged together. Next, I swiped through some of his photographs. He'd been to a stack of different countries. Thailand, Bali, Canada, New Zealand, Japan, USA and Europe.

I didn't know where to find the picture he'd shown me of myself. Every picture on his website was neatly labelled in detail. Would he have photos of *me* neatly labelled as well?

My finger paused on the search button of his website. Then I tapped in the letters of my first name.

Two photos sprang up.

The photo of me at the nightclub and another one.

God. It was me, again. With the same shoulder-length red hair and the fringe. This photo wasn't as closeup as the one in the nightclub, but it certainly looked like me. I zoomed in. Yes, it was definitely me. Why didn't I remember wearing my hair that way? I'd never known my hair to be anything other than long and brown. The photo was taken outdoors, in the country. A road ran along in the foreground. The background lush and green, but not tropical. Cows with thick fur stood behind a wooden fence. Maybe the photo was taken down in the southernmost part of Australia. Tasmania even.

I looked happy in the photo, my cheeks bright pink from the cold. Sitting back, I stared at the image, trying to make myself remember. The more I stared, the more familiar Trent began to seem. Or was I just tricking myself? I could almost hear him laughing,

I squinted, trying to make out the lettering on the sign that was located around the bend of the road.

A-R-D-N-A-G-R-A-S-K.

I'd never heard of it. I tried looking it up, but there was no Ardnagrask in Australia. I frowned at the suggestion that Google had come up with. *Ardnagrask, Inverness.*

Chills swept through my body.

There had to be another explanation.

Browsing to a Google map, I looked up Ardnagrask. It was a tiny place in the country. Full of country roads, wooden fences and cows.

Unmistakeable.

He had to have edited the photo and pasted me there in the scene. I'd never been to Scotland. This photo was a lie.

Why would he do that?

Copying the photograph, I ran it through some apps that would show me how the photo had been altered. The software examined photographs at a forensic level, checking for areas where the light and edges and textures didn't quite match.

The photograph tested as original. Straight off the camera and unaltered.

Stunned, I sat rigidly, watching a flock of birds fly across the pale sky outside the window.

No. The photo wasn't real. Because if it was, it meant that I'd been here before. In Scotland.

A carnival ride of thoughts spun in my head, making me dizzy and nauseous.

I don't remember dating Trent. Could I have forgotten coming to Scotland, too?

I picked up my phone from the kitchen table. I felt as if air was exploding like firecrackers in my chest as I called home.

Jake answered.

"Where's Mum?" I asked breathlessly.

"*Hello, Jake,*" he said in a mock annoyed tone. "Well, hello there, Isla. Nice to hear from you."

"Sorry. I...need to know something in a hurry."

"Mum's asleep. Call back in a few hours maybe?"

"Look, you can answer it. I just need you to tell me the truth okay?"

"Is this going to be some kind of trick question?"

"No, no tricks. This is serious. Okay? I just want to know one thing. I've never been to the UK before, right? This is the first time."

"Er, wouldn't that be something *you* would know?"

"Just…tell me. Is it true that I've never been here—to the UK and Scotland before? Please. I know this sounds strange, but there's a big chunk of time that's missing from my life, and I—"

"You should talk to Mum, 'sis," he cut in. His voice sounded different—careful and serious. He should be telling me I was nuts and trying to make a joke of it. But he wasn't.

"Jake," I whispered. "You know what I'm talking about, don't you?"

He blew out a heavy breath. "Yeah, okay. I don't know much. I was still at school back then. Mum had to fly over to the UK and get you. All I know is that you came back sick. Like, really sick. Mum told me we're never going to talk about your trip. You'd forgotten it and she said it was for the best."

I gasped silently, reeling from what Jake had just told me.

It was true. Trent's photos were real. I'd just assumed that when I used to date Trent, it'd been in Sydney. He was Australian, too, after all.

But had I dated him here, in Scotland?

"Thank you," I breathed. "Can you tell me one more thing? What was I like…when I came back?"

"You were nuts," he said without hesitation. "Like a zombie. But a zombie that hardly moved. You just sat in a chair in your room, mostly. You didn't even care what you wore."

"God. Why don't I remember any of this?"

"Why would you want to? There's funner things to remember than sitting in a chair all day, sis'. Mum's not going to be happy with me when she knows I told you."

"You didn't tell me, exactly. So you're off the hook. I figured it out myself. Hey, what time is it there?"

"Two in the morning. I'm uploading videos of our band."

"Oh God, sorry. I didn't realise it was *that* time of night."

"S'ok," he said, yawning. "Take care, sis'."

After saying goodbye to my brother, I sat on the sofa with my arms tightening around my knees.

How was I even supposed to process this? It felt as if my own mind had betrayed me, deleting memories at will.

There was no record of my previous trips on my passport. It'd been blank. I'd had to get a replacement just before I'd come here, paying extra to get it quickly. I thought I'd lost my original passport —the one I'd gotten when I was eighteen for my trip to Bali.

Had Mum thrown my old passport away?

I had so many questions. I was desperate to talk to my mother.

Why had I been in Scotland? What did I do while I was here? How did I meet Trent?

I tried looking through his website for more clues. I found nothing. In frustration, I closed the web browser.

My photography portfolio was still up on my computer screen.

The picture of the church caught my attention—the one that I had photographed on the way back from Inverness. For a moment, the church merged with a different image. It merged with the image of the house from my dream.

I could no longer picture the hazy vision of the house without seeing the exterior of the church.

In my mind, the door of the church opened. Inside, a long corridor stretched into darkness.

The house is the church.

The church is the house.

How was that possible? The church had a spire and cross on its roof, but I'd never seen that in my dream.

Feverishly, I flipped through all the pictures I'd taken of the church. From a standing position immediately in front of the church, the spire and cross couldn't be seen. And at night, they probably couldn't be seen at all. In my dream, it was always night.

My breaths came in shallow gasps. *It's not a coincidence that I picked the church out when driving along the road with Greer. The church is a memory.*

What was special about the church? Why had I dreamed about it for years? It was small and very ordinary. Greer must have been bemused by the fact that I'd even noticed it or wanted to photograph it.

I couldn't answer any of these questions.

But maybe Trent could.

If I contacted Trent and met up with him to talk, it could well be the worst decision ever. This man had hurt me in some way—physically and mentally. He was almost certainly the person who'd hung a scarecrow outside my door. He wasn't someone I should be wrangling with while I was alone in this country.

He might be willing to talk with me over the phone. Any kind of contact with him could be dangerous. But I was desperate for answers. So desperate that I was prepared to do this. I hoped that he was somewhere far away by now—back in Australia even.

There'd been a contact phone number on Trent's website. If I didn't call now, I might lose my nerve.

My heart raced as I tapped in the numbers.

I waited, swallowing, preparing myself.

"Hello? Trent Dorrington speaking," came his voice.

"Hi, Trent…."

"Isla."

"You knew my voice," I said in astonishment.

"Of course I know your voice."

"I'm…I'm calling to apologise. I still don't remember anything, but I spoke to my mother, and she remembers your name. So, I know now that you were telling the truth."

A silence stretched and pulled tight.

"How can you not remember me?" he said finally.

"Two years ago, I had a severe illness. I don't even remember being in Scotland. I honestly thought this was the first time I'd been here. But I saw a picture of me—and you—on your website, and it was taken in Ardnagrask. Scotland."

"I'm finding this extremely hard to believe."

"Did you know I have epilepsy?"

"No. You never told me that."

"Well, I do. I had a series of seizures and it affected my memory. I was ill for months, apparently. My mother had to fly to Scotland and bring me home."

"I had no idea. This is insane."

"You didn't know about that? About my mother coming to get me?"

"Nope. Not a clue. You were fine the last time I saw you, so this must have been sometime after."

I don't believe you. Did you take the breakup badly? Is that why you hurt me? I knew I couldn't ask those kinds of questions. I had to remain calm and find out what I could about the church.

"What were we doing, that day in Ardnagrask?" I asked.

"We were with another couple that I knew," he replied. "My friend Stefan and his girlfriend, Heidi. His father had a farm out that way and we went and had lunch there. Stefan was the one who took the photos of us."

"I remember none of it. What other kinds of things did we do?"

"Just the usual. Movies. Sightseeing. Lazy Sunday mornings in bed."

A hot blush travelled from my chest up to my cheeks. I was glad he couldn't see that. "Oh, okay. Nice."

"We had fun together, Isla."

He could tell me anything right now and I'd have no way of judging whether it was true or not.

"How did I meet you?"

"This is so surreal, Isla. You were here to study photography. In Edinburgh. I was studying art. I'm a trust fund baby. I do a bit for my father's mining company, but I was studying when I met you. Still am."

I studied photography in Edinburgh, I mouthed to myself silently. I braced myself for my next question.

"Thank you," I said. "There's just one more thing—"

"Is this about the scarecrow? Because I'm telling you, that wasn't me."

"Okay, I believe you," I lied. "This is about something else. It's about an old church that I spotted the other day on a trip to Inverness. For some reason, I thought I'd seen it before. Did we happen to stop at a little church when we were dating?"

"A church? We did look at one in Edinburgh. It wasn't little though. It was a cathedral. You thought it was beautiful."

"No, this isn't a cathedral. It's tiny. Isolated. At the side of a highway."

"Well, I have no idea. I don't remember a church like that."

"It's probably not important. Maybe it just seems important because it's the first thing that I remembered."

"Seriously?" he said. "The first thing you remember about Scotland is an old church and not *me*?"

"It's a start." I tried to inject a light tone into my voice.

"Maybe we could try a reboot," he said casually. "Go out for dinner. Might help jog your memory."

I hesitated before answering. "I would, but I—"

"Please don't come up with an excuse. Yeah, I fucked up when I tried to kiss you at Aubrey's house and then I fucked up more when I overdosed. It's not who I am and it's not who I was when you knew me before."

"Trent, I'm feeling way out my depth here. I still don't know you."

"I could make you feel better. You won't know unless you give it a try."

"I'm sorry. I can't."

"Yeah." He sighed. "Look, if you change your mind, I'm here in Edinburgh. Not too far away."

"Okay. Thank you. I appreciate that."

He ended the call.

A tremor passed through my chest.

I'd done it. I'd called him.

But I had more questions than answers.

I hadn't sensed danger during the conversation and he hadn't sounded like someone who'd been stalking me.

But then, maybe I wasn't a good judge of that.

32

ISLA

I GLANCED OUT THE WINDOW. This day was growing progressively dimmer and it was only midday. Every part of me ached for the deep warmth of the Sydney sun. I was shaken to the core. My mind had betrayed me, stripping months away from my memory.

Trying to stay warm, I moved about the cottage, making myself a cup of tea. I switched on the heater and watched the fake flames spring to life.

The image of the church sprang up before my eyes. I'd never seen it so clearly outside of a dream. It shocked me to be fully awake and picturing it like this.

The door inside the church that had always been locked was suddenly wide open. I could see candles flickering inside. Thick, stubby white candles. Their light glowing in otherwise inky darkness.

I gasped as more details of the room came into view.

Cracked window.

Coats hanging on the wall.

Rosary beads hanging on a chain, slightly swaying.

I felt cold. So cold.

The piano chords that I always heard in my dream crashed into my mind. So clearly this time. *Uneven, jarring chords that made no sense.* And not just the piano but another sound.

Screams. Tortured screams.

I felt pain twisting inside my stomach.

I jerked to my feet, standing up straight.

The screams I'd just remembered were my own.

The bad thing that happened to me—it happened in that church.

I paced the room, hearing my screams echo again and again in my mind. I could see the symbol of the religious cross that I'd always seen—the one with the rose in the middle.

I tried to force myself to remember more.

I remembered an agonising sensation of pain in my stomach.

Had someone repeatedly punched me?

Had I been raped?

I could almost remember a bed—springs sticking into my back and hip bones.

Oh God.

Terror swirled inside me.

The wheels of a car crunched the gravel outside.

The sounds and visions vanished.

I couldn't see who was out there from here. For a second, I thought of Trent. But there was no way he could have driven from Edinburgh to Greenmire in that space of time.

It was most probably Jessica returning from her trip with Rhiannon. But the car didn't continue up the driveway, instead stopping outside my door.

Could it be Greer? Anxiously, I smoothed my hair. I didn't feel like seeing anyone right now—not in this state. I felt half-crazed, like a tiger locked in a tiny cage.

A knock came at the door.

That wasn't like Greer. She was more likely to call me on the phone and tell me she was arriving.

Stepping to the door, I cracked it open.

Rory Kavanagh stood there, dishevelled, his eyes reddened.

"Isla, I shouldn't have come here. I just...there's no one else in this town I can talk to."

"Come in," I said automatically.

Scents of sweat and whisky travelled inside with him.

I closed the door as he dropped himself into the armchair.

246

STRANGER IN THE WOODS

"Can I get you a tea or coffee?" I asked.

He exhaled, shaking his head and combing his fingers through his shaggy hair repeatedly. "It's too hard, this life. Too hard. Things hit you out of nowhere, and then what are you supposed to do? Just start again in the new direction that life has set you in? How many times can you do that?"

I tensed. "Rory, is it Stella? Is she okay? She didn't—?"

"She's okay. She's doing all right, considering."

I stared at him in relief. My legs weakened and I sat on the sofa, opposite Rory. "Thank goodness."

"Yeah. A big relief for all of us." He blinked, his eyes suddenly wet. He didn't look like someone who was feeling any kind of relief.

"Something happened, didn't it?" I said.

"Yeah, something happened." He leaned his head back on the armchair. "I discovered something this morning. My dear wife has been cheating on me."

"Hell. I'm sorry." I didn't know what I'd been expecting him to say, but it wasn't that.

He sighed, eyeing the ceiling. "I don't know what to do."

"You so didn't need this right now. What a kick in the guts."

"Yeah. I know Camille didn't mean to tell me. She blurted it out in a fit of rage. She was angry that I didn't support her when she had that altercation with Kelly. She thought I should have blasted Kelly. She even said it was half my fault that Stella ran away. Because no kid wants to live with a boring old schoolteacher. Ha, maybe she's right. Maybe I'm the most boring person on the planet. Anyway, that's when she told me that she didn't love me. She never loved me. She'd been seeing someone else for four years. *Four. Fucking. Years.* Practically the whole time we'd been together."

I stretched across to squeeze his arm. "That's brutal. Wish I had a stiff drink or something to offer you. But I've got nothing."

"I've already had enough to drink. I've been drinking since last night. Not a wink of sleep." He fixed a weary gaze on me. "Camille isn't the woman I thought she was. I mean, what are you supposed to do when you find out something like this?"

"I don't know, Rory," I said softly. "I just don't know."

"This is going to be the talk of Greenmire if it gets out. At the very least, they'll know that Camille and I have split up. That kind of thing always provides a hotbed of juicy gossip. Things were already bad. I mean, I'm the teacher whose stepdaughter ran away. Now I'm the teacher whose step-daughter tried to commit suicide. I know what people will be thinking. They'll be wondering if I'm the right kind of person to be teaching their kids."

"Oh Rory, none of it is your fault."

Tears ran in streaks from his bloodshot eyes now. "I loved Stella like she was my own. I don't know why I couldn't reach her. I don't know why she does any of the things that she does."

"Maybe this will prove to be the turning point," I said, trying to project a note of hopefulness in my voice.

"Well, I hope so for her sake. Maybe if I was the one she had a problem with, then she will come back and live with her mother. Because I won't be there in the home anymore." He gave a sad shrug. "Anyway, you were probably in the middle of some work when I barged in here. I should leave you in peace." He looked at me curiously then, as if seeing me for the first time since he walked in. "Actually, hate to say this, but you're looking a bit rough yourself."

"A lot has been happening. I'm still in shock about Stella. And there's…other stuff."

"The car accident?"

"No. I mean, that's added to it. But it's something else."

He sat straighter, his brow wrinkling. "Okay, what are we talking about? I've just offloaded on you. Now it's only fair that you offload on me."

I dropped my head down into my hands. "I'm still processing it all."

"Sounds bad. Sometimes it takes a while for everything to go through the wash. I can see something has gone pretty wrong for you. I'll hang here until you're ready to talk. It's the least I can do."

"No…I…the last thing I want to do is burden you with my woes right now. You have more than enough woes of your own. And really, I just need to be alone for a while to sort it out."

Rory set his eyebrows in a way that reminded me of a teacher trying to encourage an underconfident student. "I'm not going to abandon you."

"You won't be abandoning me, I swear. Look, I'll call you a cab and get you home…I mean, wherever you want to go. You're not in any condition to be driving."

"Yeah, I shouldn't have driven over here. That was a damned stupid decision. But you're going to tell me what's been bothering you, whether you like it or not. Hey, I will have that cup of tea, if that's all right."

"Of course it is." Rising, I went to boil the kettle. I wasn't ready to talk, but the man sitting on the sofa was a half-drunk, sleep-deprived guy who'd just had his life burn to ash. I wasn't going to succeed in making him understand me properly.

With the tea made, I handed him a cup and then sat back on the sofa.

Rory sipped his tea with an intent expression on his face, as if he were deep in thought. "Isla, just say it. You'll feel better for it."

"It's kind of strange. Well, it's very strange."

"Say it."

I breathed deeply. "Okay. You know the man who was found in the forest a week ago? The one who'd overdosed?"

"Yup."

"Apparently, I used to date him."

"Say what?"

"It's a bit of a crazy story. I'm not sure you're in any state of mind to hear it."

"Actually, if it involves a bit of misery, lay it on me. I need to know I'm not the only one in turmoil."

I hesitated, not knowing where to start—because I didn't know the start of the story. I didn't remember dating Trent. I decided to start with the afternoon at the hospital. "You know the afternoon that I met you at the café and then Aubrey showed up? Well, Aubrey told me that this guy—Trent—wanted to talk to me. He was still in the hospital then. I thought he wanted to apologise for stringing up the scarecrow outside the cottage."

"That's right—he's the Australian who hauled the scarecrow up into a tree."

"Well, supposedly. There's no proof. And he denied it."

"Aye, right," he said sceptically. "Then what?"

"The reason why he wanted to see me was to ask why I was pretending not to know him. But I was sure I'd never met him before arriving in Scotland. Then he showed me a photograph of the two of us together."

"Wow, that's a wee bit creepy."

"Totally. I had no idea what was going on. So, later, I called my mother and I asked her if she'd ever heard me mention a guy named Trent. She had. She told me that, yes, I used to date him. Just before the episode in which I lost a chunk of my memory."

"What kind of episode? What happened?"

"I'm an epileptic. I get seizures sometimes. This was a big one that I don't remember. I was sick for months." I eyed his incredulous face. "It gets worse."

"I'm all ears."

"When I used to date Trent, it was *here*, in Scotland."

He gulped a mouthful of tea, staring at me. "But you said this was your first trip here?"

"Yes. That's what I thought. I don't remember coming here before. But I did."

"Mind blown."

"I warned you that it was a crazy story. I was very ill. My mother flew over to Scotland to fetch me. She said I was in a very bad way. Barely speaking. Bruises all over me. Something awful happened to me, but I don't know what."

"Oh wow. Really? So, are you thinking that it was that Trent guy who gave you the bruises?"

"It seems that way. But I just don't know. My memory isn't clear."

He inclined his head, as if an idea had occurred to him. "Isla, how did you come to accept doing a portfolio for Alban McGregor? Who invited you? I mean, is it possible that someone got you back here to Scotland on purpose?"

I shook my head. "I found the proposal in the ad section of a photography website. I don't even know why I found the idea of it so enticing. I barely ever left Sydney for jobs, let alone heading overseas."

"Hmmm." He thumbed the fluff on his chin that passed for a goatee. "Maybe it was *you*."

"What do you mean?"

"Well, maybe you needed to come back for unfinished business. Your subconscious knows what happened here, and that's what really spurred you to return." He gave a nonchalant shrug. The kind of shrug people give when they think they've said something huge but they're unsure of your reaction.

I stared back at him. As soon as he'd spoken the words, I realised I already knew it was true. This whole trip had simply been unfinished business. Scotland was meant to be my new start—a place to find out what I wanted out of life. But in reality, there'd been pieces of my life missing and I'd returned to claim those pieces.

"Rory, you're right. My subconscious memories must have had a lot to do with me coming here."

"And now you've got to find out what happened." He nodded.

"I have no idea how I'm going to do that. The only memories I have are so fuzzy."

"We need to investigate this Trent guy. Find out who knows him. Find out who his girlfriends from the past were and talk to them."

"We?"

"Aye. I want to help."

"I could be stirring up a lot of trouble."

"Sometimes, trouble needs to be stirred."

"It feels like I've already stirred things up, just by being here."

"Might as well keep it going, eh? Do you have any memory of Trent at all?"

"No. Except, maybe his face is starting to seem familiar to me. It's hard to explain."

"Do you remember anything at all about your last trip to Scotland?"

"It's all just blank. Except one thing—a place. It's just a tiny old building. I've been dreaming about it for the past two years."

"What kind of building?"

"A church. It's just off the main road on the way to Inverness."

He raised his eyebrows. "A church? Okay, well…that's something."

"It's not much, but it's all I've got."

"So, what are your dreams about?"

"I feel like I'm in psychoanalysis." A nervous giggle shot into my throat.

"As a teacher," he said, "I've had to do a fair amount of that. Shoot."

"Okay. It's dark. Night. I'm standing in the doorway and I can see inside to a long corridor. There are rooms to either side of the corridor. In my dreams, one of the rooms always used to be locked. But now, today, it's wide open. I can see inside of it. There are candles. I can hear a piano. But it's like a crazy person is banging away at it. There are rosary beads hanging down somewhere overhead. And there's a cross with a rose."

His forehead creased. "A cross with a rose?"

"Yeah. I can't explain more than that. Probably a religious picture or something. And, I'm in pain. Someone is hurting me."

"*Jesus*. That's not sounding good."

I shuddered, the sense of pain and terror floating before me.

Downing the rest of his tea, Rory eyed me over the edge of the cup. "Isla, have you talked about this with anyone else?"

"No. I mentioned the church to Trent, but he didn't remember it. No one else."

"Ah, it's a shame you mentioned it to Trent. He's the one most likely to have hurt you, right? I think it's a good idea not to tell anyone else. Until we know what we're dealing with. Someone out there knows what happened to you. For now, it might be better that you keep your cards close to your chest."

"Rory, the thing is, I'll be going back to Sydney in a few days. I won't have time to look into this. I just…want to go home."

"You're going home so soon?" He fell silent for a moment, as if mulling over what I'd told him. "Maybe that's a good thing for you. But if your memory is starting to return, it might just drive you crazy. Seems to me you came here for a reason."

I nodded. It seemed odd but reassuring that Rory wanted to help me. Like we were a team and I didn't have to do this alone.

"Hey," he said, "first thing you need to do is to take a look at this church you mentioned."

"I couldn't ask Greer to take me there again. She's so busy. I'll take a peek when it's time to leave—I'll get the taxi driver to stop, and I'll run down and look through the windows."

Leaning, he set his teacup down on the coffee table, then turned to me with serious eyes. "I'll take you."

"I couldn't. You've got much bigger things to worry about. With Stella. And now the thing with your wife."

"Stella is being looked after by a team of professionals. And she doesn't want to see me. My wife doesn't want to see me either." He gave a hollow laugh. "And it's Sunday tomorrow. My class of kids especially doesn't want to see me."

I smiled at his wry joke. The last person I would have wanted to see on the weekend was one of my teachers.

"It's a long way to where the church is," I told him.

"I've got time. How about I swing by here tomorrow morning?"

"Rory—"

"It's all booked in." He pulled out a pretend notebook and pencil from his pocket and wrote a pretend note. "Pick Isla up at nine thirty. Go to odd little church at the side of the road. Look for suspicious candles, crosses and pianos." He half put the pretend notebook back in his pocket, then retrieved it and wrote another message. "Isla to buy Rory a coffee for his trouble."

I laughed.

All the while, threads of anxiety shot through my veins. Should I really do this? Rory seemed sure. Me coming to Scotland had been no coincidence—that much I was now certain of.

33

ISLA

COLD TREMORS SHOT through me as I waited by the spruce tree out on the roadside.

It was a pretty spot, with the blue shades of the spruce contrasting against the snow. But this place was tinged with such sadness that I could almost reach out and touch it.

It had been Rory's idea to meet near the spruce, away from the prying eyes of anyone at the McGregor house. He'd told me he didn't want any more rumours being spread around about him than there already were. I didn't know if I'd ever felt sorrier for a human being than Rory. His wife and step-daughter had turned against him and he was also haunted by the death of a young girl who'd been his student.

I'd called my mother last night, in a last-ditch attempt to find out about the church and put off going there today—but she hadn't known anything about it. There had been a lot of tears and apologies from her for not telling me about Scotland. But I understood. She'd just been trying to protect me.

Rory was right on time, practically to the second.

The road was clear of any other traffic as I ran to the passenger door and slipped inside. We greeted each other with nods, neither of us willing to talk for the first couple of minutes. The whole thing seemed almost cloak-and-dagger—a secret rendezvous in which we were going to investigate a mysterious old church. I suppressed a tense laugh and almost wanted to tell Rory to forget it. Yesterday, I'd felt like I'd fallen through the rabbit hole with Rory as he'd poured out his anguish. Somehow, I'd then been comfortable enough to share my own stuff. Actually, he'd practically forced it out of me. But maybe I didn't know him well enough to be sharing my murky dreams with him.

I took a breath. I told myself I wasn't nervous because of Rory. I was nervous due to the thought of seeing inside the church. This was an opportunity I wouldn't have gotten but for Rory, and I just had to find a way of keeping calm.

He glanced my way. "Today's the day, huh?"

"Yeah. I'm sure it's just going to be a wild goose chase, but at least I'll know for sure. I can't thank you enough for suggesting this."

"Och, it's no bother. I'm actually looking forward to it. Get out on the open road and clear my head a bit. And I'll admit I'm a wee bit curious to know if the church is going to match those images in your head."

I shot him a weak but grateful smile. "How are you doing today?"

"Feeling like I've had a weight dropped on my head from a great height. But apart from that, I'm fine." He gave me a sad wink.

"I felt so bad for you yesterday. Are you sure you're all right? We don't have to go today. Really."

"Yes, we do. Quit worrying."

"Have you heard how Stella is?"

"She was a bit better last night. I'll call the hospital later and try to find out. It's a bit early yet."

The morning swiftly turned darker, snowfall sweeping across the sky.

"That looks set in," he remarked.

"I'm so not used to this. Snow and icy roads."

"Well, I am. And I'm not Hamish Keenan." He exhaled. "It's going to take you a good while to get past the accident. But I'm a good driver and this car's got good tyres on her."

"I'll try to stop panicking. But no promises."

"Good girl."

Rory began telling me tales about the school at which he worked,

255

to take my mind off the road. After a while, I could tell that the stories were as much for him, too, to take his mind off Camille.

"Have you had any breakfast?" he asked, half an hour into the trip.

"No, not yet."

"There's a small village up a bit further. I'll pull off and we'll get a bite to eat. How's that sound?"

I told him that sounded good, but in truth, my stomach was in knots and I didn't feel like eating. But I wanted the chance to buy him something as a token for his time and trouble, and this might be my only chance.

Small barely described the size of the village. The main strip consisted of five buildings—a tiny café, a post office, a grocery store, a butcher and a pub. And only two of those were open—the café and the pub.

The atmosphere inside the café was gloomy despite the quaint red-and-white decor. Shouting down Rory's protests, I bought him sausages and eggs and a coffee. I had scrambled eggs on toast, which I picked at more than ate.

I gazed out the large window, trying to quieten the noise in my head. This was a crazy mission. We might even be trespassing by trying to enter the old church. But Rory hadn't hesitated for a minute. He hadn't even questioned what anyone else might think was just a dream of mine.

Rory's phone buzzed. He moved to the end of the bench seat, turning his head away as he answered. "It's none of your business where I am. No, I'm not. Of course I care about her. I tried to be there for you. But you threw it all back in my face."

I watched pain and regret stitch lines and furrows into his face. I knew he was talking with Camille. He ended the conversation quickly and shoved the phone back into his pocket.

"Want to go?" I said quietly.

He nodded.

As dim and depressing as the café had been, at least it had offered protection from the elements. I ran with Rory through the blustery wind and into the car. I felt even less safe in the car as we started out again. I tried to hang onto the words that Rory had said earlier. He was a safe driver. His car had safe tyres. He was used to this weather.

Rory didn't launch back into tales about the school. He drove on, withdrawing into himself. I preferred the cheerier Rory, and I cursed Camille for having called him when she did. I had nothing between me and the road now.

With a start, I realised that the snowfall was going to make it harder to spot the church. Rory wouldn't know where it was. It was up to me to find it, otherwise this trip would have all been for nothing. I didn't exactly know where it was. There were very few landmarks along the A9. The landscape was mostly just countryside.

Taking out my phone, I tried looking up the area on Google Earth. But the internet was so sluggish it was impossible.

Rory glanced over. "It's the weather—making the internet slow."

I pressed my lips together. "I don't remember the spot where Greer pulled off the road. It was a last-second decision on her part. And I didn't think I'd be coming here again."

"It's okay. I took a quick look first thing this morning. I think I found the one you mean."

"You did? I should have been the one doing that. I don't know why I didn't think of it."

"I'm a teacher. Preparation is mostly what I do. We should be coming up to the church soon. Keep your eyes peeled."

About fifteen minutes later, I spotted the top part of a church.

"There!"

Rory nodded, slowing the car.

The side street that made a ramp off the main road was obscured with snow.

"Okay, here we go," he said, guiding the car carefully down the side road.

"A field trip like no other," I quipped, trying hard to push down the butterflies that were surging from my stomach into my throat.

Most of the church was obscured with brambles, just as before. Today, snow was steeped against the exterior and piled on top of the cross that graced the roof. I imagined that the church would get half buried in a snowstorm—the land dipped down so low here.

Emotions rushed at me as I stepped from the car. Was I really going to find any resolution here?

Pulling my knitted cap over my ears to shut out the wind, I started down the incline.

Rory grasped my shoulder. "Not so fast, Isla. There can be pits and hollows in the snow. You could fall into an old well, a frozen creek, anything."

"I don't remember seeing any creeks or old wells."

"They can be well-concealed. Doesn't look like anyone's doing any caretaking on this place." Letting go of me, he returned to the car and fetched a shovel. "Let me go first. I'll poke the ground."

"You brought a shovel along?"

"Always in weather like this," he said. He stepped ahead, prodding at the snow here and there. Until we stood at the front step.

Snow flaked off the handle as he turned it. "I don't think it's locked. I think it's just swollen shut." He twisted his head around to face me.

I took a deep breath of chilled air and moved beside Rory.

Together we pushed at the door with our shoulders. The old wood protested for a few seconds, then gave way.

Leaf litter and snow blew down a long corridor. Rooms led off the corridor on either side.

This is it.

My dream.

My memory.

My dream had never been about a house. It had always been *this* —a church on the road to Inverness.

My legs felt frozen rigid as I entered, the boards creaking underfoot.

I jumped and spun around as the door closed behind me.

Rory was holding two pen lights. "Too windy to leave it open. Here, take one of these."

Gratefully, I accepted the pen light. "You weren't kidding when you said you come prepared."

He shrugged, grinning, then eyed me curiously. "Remember anything?"

Biting into my cold lower lip, I nodded.

"Really?"

"Yes. This is the place."

"*Hell.* This is insane."

"Yeah." Anxious thoughts tumbled through my mind, my chest wall growing so tight I could hardly breathe.

We walked through the corridor to a large space filled with broken wooden chairs. The altar was simply a heavy desk. I turned to a dim corner of the room, already guessing what would be there. A piano. It was missing a few of its keys—the keyboard resembling a grimace with missing teeth.

"I'm sure there would have been a holy cross up on the wall here at some point." Rory studied my face as I stared at the piano. "Wow, you mentioned piano chords, too, didn't you? Anything else coming back to you?"

"Nothing specific. It's frustrating. But I feel...panicked. I mean, just being here makes me feel panic."

"Try to relax. You're safe."

"I know. I'll try."

"Hey, maybe I should go look around outside and leave you alone for a while. You might have better luck without me here crowding you. I'll see if I can find anything interesting out there that might jog your memory."

Nodding, I exhaled a stream of white air. "Thank you."

Rory shuffled back down the hallway, collecting the shovel that he'd left by the door before he went out.

I crossed the room to the piano. It looked even worse close up. Dirt caked the spaces between the keys. Animal droppings had smeared and dried everywhere, forming a disgusting crust.

This was the horrible thing that I'd heard playing in the background when I was here last. Who'd even want to touch this, let alone play it? Or had this church looked very different two years ago?

Backing away from the piano, I scanned the room. There was nothing else here of note. Anything of value must have been either looted or taken away a long time ago.

The only thing left to check was the rooms. I headed back into the corridor. I needed to look for the candles. And the cross and the rosary beads.

There were four rooms, each door hanging open except for one.

I stuck my head inside the first room on the right. Its walls were lined with shelves, most of which were broken and crooked. A metal filing cabinet stood against a wall. I opened the cabinet. It was empty, aside from a few folders. A picture of Jesus hung on the wall, unblemished apart from a hairline crack in the glass.

The next room on the right held nothing but more broken chairs and an armchair—the stuffing and springs exposed. Animal droppings told me that rats had torn the filling out of the chair. I imagined they would get starving hungry in the winter.

I tried the room opposite. In this room, the walls were decorated with cartoonish illustrations of children holding baby lambs and rabbits. I remembered a friend of mine telling me that her church had a crying room in which the faithful could take a fussing baby or child so that they didn't interrupt the church service. Maybe that's what this room had been.

I tried the last door on the left. This was the one I could never open in my dreams—until recently. It was always firmly locked.

The handle twisted in my hand and I cracked the door open.

The air smelled especially bad in here. A rusted odour combined with smells I couldn't identify. This room must have been shut up for a long time.

Covering the lower half of my face with the crook of my elbow, I entered.

There was not much more in here than the other rooms.

Deflated, I shone my light around.

A homeless person must have once lived here. Empty tins of food were piled up in a corner.

The beam of my pen light was too narrow to see the whole room at once. This was the darkest spot of the church and I could only see small pieces of it at a time.

I began putting the pieces together, my heart rate jumping with each discovery.

Candles on the shelves.

Jackets on hooks on the wall.

Bare mattress on the floor.

This was the room I'd remembered.

But surely I'd never lain on that filthy mattress in this filthy room?

There weren't rat droppings in here, at least. If the heavy door to this room had been kept shut, maybe that had kept out the rats.

A dark stain had spread across the centre of the mattress. I crouched to the floor, examining the stain with the pen light.

It's blood.

So much blood.

With shuddering breaths, I directed my light upwards.

Bare timbers spanned the ceiling, just as they did in every other room.

An empty bottle of medication sat beside the candles on a high shelf, gathering dust.

Wind blew in from a small crack in the window, making a wooden chain shuffle and clatter—a set of rosary beads.

It's all here.

The last thing I needed to find was the religious cross with the heart in the middle. I searched the room, examining every patch of wall and floor that I could. It wasn't there, else, I couldn't find it.

I stopped still, allowing myself to breathe. Why had I been in this room?

As I watched, the dim day changed to darkest night, flames sprang to life on the candles, chaotic piano chords smashed the quiet.

I could see it all as it was. When I was last here.

I knew, without any doubt, that I'd been here on this foul old mattress.

And I knew the blood was mine.

34

ISLA

I WANTED to run from this room and this church and go home. I didn't even want to return to Greenmire. I'd just beg Rory to take me straight to the airport and have my things sent to me afterwards.

But I couldn't do that.

I needed to find out more.

Panting, I leaned my back against the wall.

A memory of searing pain twisted through me.

Like someone pummelling my body, over and over. Like hard, vicious, angry punches. Until my ribs were sore, and my insides were jelly and the taste of blood was liquid copper in my mouth.

Wrapping my arms around myself, I protected myself from a battering that had happened a long time ago.

A hazy image formed in my mind of a person who'd stood over me, silently watching me scream.

There had been someone there, standing by the bed. But I couldn't see them properly. I could hear their voice. The voice said: *Stay quiet. You're not helping yourself.* Then I could hear them say, *I don't think she's breathing.*

Why did this person think I'd stopped breathing?

Bile shot to the back of my throat.

What could I do about any of this? What could be proven after years had passed? Even if a DNA test proved this was my blood, what then? If there were no witnesses—apart from the person who stood by the bed—how would the police be able to find out anything?

Numbly, I stumbled from the room.

I'd found out what I'd come here for, but I still didn't know anything. Not anything concrete.

Rory still hadn't returned.

Pulling open the front door, I called to him. "Rory?" The wind had an added force to it now, snatching my voice away.

I stepped outside, letting the door bang behind me.

For a moment, I worried that I'd been left here alone. I checked the top of the incline. Rory's car was still there, the wind blowing a dusting of snow from the roof.

"Rory?" I blundered through ankle-deep snow. Someone had been digging. A hole had been carved out, the shovel leaning against the wall of the house.

"Rory, are you there?"

A figure came from behind me—Rory.

"We'd better get out of here," he told me. "They're predicting a bit of nasty weather. Best hit the road."

"What were you digging?"

"I just dug here and there to see if I could find anything useful." He shrugged. "I didn't. How about you? Did you remember anything more?"

I nodded. "I'll tell you later. Sounds like we need to head off."

He turned up the collar of his jacket against the wind. "Aye."

We drove off into a blurred world of white and charcoal. My stomach clenched. I kept hearing the squeal of the wheels back when Hamish lost control of his car.

Rory shot two quick glances at me. "You look half scared to death, Isla."

"I haven't been in a snowstorm before. People really just keep driving through these?"

"Yes. Unless it gets really bad."

"I'd hate to see really bad."

"I didn't realise it was going to get this extreme. Hope I didn't rush you, but I could see the clouds were looking heavy out there."

"You made the right call. I'd hate to be stuck there in a blizzard or something." I felt sick at the thought of it. Being trapped in that church.

"Don't get alarmed," he said tentatively. "But the wind is really picking up speed. If it happens to get worse, we might need to stop off somewhere."

"Oh hell, do you mean we're heading into a blizzard right now?"

"It could be the start of one. Hard to tell."

"You do what you need to do. I'd rather stop than get blown off the road."

Rory gave a short laugh. "We're nowhere near that happening."

After a brief silence, Rory turned to me. "So...if it's not too soon to ask, what was it that you remembered from the church?"

I jammed my eyes shut. "It's all still so clouded. Maybe I was drugged at the time. There's a mattress in one of those rooms. An old, dirty, horrible mattress. With a big patch of blood on it." Pulling my mouth in as I recalled the fetid odour and horror of that room, I met his eyes. "Mine."

"Whoa." His jaw dropped. "Blood? Yours? You know that for certain?"

I nodded. "I remember...terrible pain. Like being kicked or punched. Or even cut."

"That's a complete shocker, Isla. You've got to go to the police. I'll take you there right now."

"No...I've still got nothing. They're not going to be able to do anything with the information that I've got. I mean, it's not really even information. Just some hazy bits and pieces."

"I know what you mean. I do. But you can't let the bastard get away with this."

"Thanks, Rory. You've helped me so much in bringing me out here today."

"If you could see your face right now," he replied. "You wouldn't think I'd helped you. You're looking like you've seen a ghost."

"I didn't see a ghost...but I did see someone. I remember. Someone was standing right there, near the bed."

"Bloody hell. Did you see his face?"

"No...all I see is a figure."

"Are you sure you can't see any of their facial features?"

"I'm trying, but I can't. It just won't come to me. I can hear them telling me to be quiet." I attempted to picture the scene in that room. Lying on that mattress, watching the draft make the beads sway on their chain, watching the candles flicker, watching the figure standing above me. The figure was pacing the room. Up and down. While the chords of the piano reverberated in my ears.

"Okay, what was their voice like?" he asked.

"It's strange. I can hear the words, but not the voice. It's like, I know what they said, but I can't pinpoint the voice."

I tried to hear Trent's voice in my mind. Was the voice his? It was useless—I couldn't tell.

Rory shook his head. "By the looks of it, it's all going to come back to you bit by bit. Let me know if you remember anything else."

We drove along in silence for the next few minutes. I sensed that Rory was giving me space.

The car was starting to feel like a moving tomb, with the dark day and the howling, snow-laden wind all around us.

I remembered something else.

Someone carried me out of the church. I could see a glimpse of their shirt. I'd grabbed onto the person's collar, confused and afraid. When I pulled on their collar, I caught sight of a dark tattoo on their skin. *A tattoo of a cross with a rose in the middle of it.*

That's it. The cross and rose had been a tattoo. Not a picture on the wall. A tattoo.

I was certain. I could see it clearly.

When I turned my head to tell Rory, I saw that he was looking distressed.

"Isla," Rory said gently, "I'm afraid we've reached that point."

I barely heard him above the noise outside. "Excuse me. I didn't—?"

"The storm. It's at the point where we can't continue."

"Of course. What do we do?"

"The town we stopped at before is coming up. We'll pull in there and wait for this to blow over."

I nodded, my heart racing in tune with my thoughts. Would we make it there in time? I hadn't noticed the storm growing in force. I'd been deep within my own mind. I'd tell him about the tattoo later, when I had the chance.

"If it keeps up, we might be stuck there, is all. I mean, like overnight. I didn't expect this. I'm sorry." He exhaled.

"You've got nothing to be sorry about. You can't help the weather."

"Just a shame it had to get this bad today. It was a rough enough day on you without this."

"It's okay. Really." I tried looking up a weather report on my phone, but the internet reception was completely down.

Rory eyed my dead phone, looking edgy, which made me worry even more.

After seven tense minutes, I spotted the low, greyish buildings of the town.

Rory, who'd been quiet for those minutes, muttered something I didn't catch under his breath.

The café was closed and shuttered now, but the pub was thankfully open. Rory parked outside. We ran for it, heads down against the battering wind and snow.

The interior of the pub was baking hot. A complete contrast to the world outside. A scattering of people sat at the bars and tables, looking at us with interest. I tidied my hair and clothing. Rory took my coat from me and hung it on a hook. The people here probably thought we were a couple. For the first time today, I considered the fact that I'd spent the day with someone else's husband. Camille probably wouldn't be happy about that, despite the fact that she'd apparently cheated on Rory.

"Are you hungry?" Rory asked. "Think I might grab a pie."

I shook my head. "No, I don't feel like anything." The church had taken away any appetite I might have had.

Following Rory over to the bar, I sat on a stool, elbows on the bench top. Rory spoke to the woman at the counter, ordering his pie and asking about a room.

He sighed as he looked back at me. "There's just one room. She says it's ours if we want it. I don't think it'll come to that, but if it does, I'll take the couch."

STRANGER IN THE WOODS

I couldn't help but grin at his awkward expression. "We'll figure it out."

The pub smelled of woodfire and stale beer. A large fireplace close to us radiated the heat we'd felt as soon as we'd walked in. The pub felt solid and safe after being in a car out in the storm. Still, I hated the sound as the windows rattled with the wind. I wondered how they didn't shatter.

An elderly man at the bar noticed my unease and winked at me. "It's a fair dreich out there, I'll give ye that. But don't you worry, hen. It's not near as shite as it gits. I used ta drive aboot in much worse dreich an' that. You know, it's a green yule what makes a fat churchyard."

I glanced quizzically at Rory, hoping for a translation.

Rory looked up from a text he'd received on his phone, seeming a bit distracted. "Dreich means foul weather. As for the rest of it, he's talking about an old myth that says a Christmas without snow brings death. Basically, he's telling you we're all going to be all right."

I smiled at the old man. "Thank you. I'm not used to this kind of weather."

Rory ordered us a couple of drinks—both beers. I wasn't a fan of beer, but Rory insisted I needed to try a good Scottish beer while in Scotland. I sipped at it. He'd chosen a heavy, malty beer that had a touch of coffee. It was good. Maybe exactly what I needed right now.

His phone rang then, and he turned aside to answer it.

The old man on the other side of me began chatting to me enthusiastically now that he'd learned I wasn't Scottish. But with his strong accent and turn-of-phrase, I only picked up half of what he said.

I caught snatches of Rory's conversation, even though his back was to me. *I'm doing exactly what I said I'd do. It's not what I would have wanted. But I've got no choice. You've given me no choice. You—*

He stopped talking suddenly. I guessed his phone reception had dropped out.

His movements growing agitated, Rory unwrapped his scarf and tugged at the collar of his shirt.

A woman served his pie at the counter. Rory twisted around to take it, nodding at her and putting his phone away. I caught a quick glimpse of the bare skin on his lower neck before he adjusted his scarf.

I saw something that made my breath stop.

He had a tattoo. Of a cross. With a rose in the middle.

My blood iced.

It was the same cross I'd seen on the man in my dream. The exact same. In the exact same place.

I glanced away quickly.

Lots of people had tattoos of crosses. It was common.

But was it common right there above the left collarbone? And like the one that I remembered?

Breath slowed in my lungs.

It can't be Rory who hurt me. It can't be.

If it was Rory, why would he insist on taking me to the place where it happened? Why would he risk bringing my memory back?

Or did he just want to test me, to find out if I'd remember or not? *Think.*

Rory had advised me not to tell anyone about my trip to the church. Was that because he didn't want anyone to know where I was?

Was the storm even that bad that we couldn't keep travelling? The old man didn't seem to think so. Had Rory stopped here for another reason?

I'd trusted Rory without giving it much thought. He was a local teacher. He'd seemed so earnest, so determined to find out what happened to Elodie. But even with that, his behaviour had seemed quite unusual, the way he'd gone through Elodie's things in her bedroom. Even the way he'd attached himself to me and made us a team—maybe that had been odd, too.

There's no way out, now. How can I get away?

My legs trembled. My head was a scattered mess.

"Just going to find a bathroom." I managed a smile at Rory.

"You okay?" he said.

I nodded.

The bathroom was across the room. The entire room felt as if it had tilted as I walked through the tables and chairs.

Stay calm. You're safe. There are people here.

When I reached the bathroom, I barely made it to the sink before I vomited.

I wiped my mouth, cleaned out the sink and stepped over to the window. The window looked out on a paddock. There was really nothing else around here, in every direction. The pub was the only place open.

What if the handful of people who were here all went home soon? The pub might shut up at a certain time. There might be no one else staying in the small motel section. This wasn't the touristy time of year. And this town wasn't in a particularly touristy spot.

If I stayed, I could end up alone with Rory.

This was a crazy situation.

Angling my head, I eyed the road. Two vehicles passed. People were still driving out in the storm.

A truck stopped outside and the driver brought a large box into the pub.

I took my phone out of my pocket. There was no reception. Maybe the pub would let me borrow their landline phone. But who would I call? No one could come and get me. Not Greer and not a taxi. No one was going to come out in this.

The driver jumped back into his truck. I stared out the window. Could I get a ride with him? A big truck should be good enough to withstand the storm.

But as I watched, he pulled the truck back onto the road and drove away.

My chance was gone.

35

ISLA

I HAD TO MAKE A DECISION, one way or another. Doing nothing was a decision as much as any other.

Touching my fingertips to the icy panes of glass, I watched another car pass by on the road. There was sporadic traffic out there.

It might be possible to flag someone down. The thought of that chilled me. I'd never hitchhiked in my life. Hitchhiking had always struck me as dangerous, even without my mother's dire warnings.

It was freezing in this bathroom. It was going to be many times colder out there. And I no longer had my coat. Unless I walked back through the pub and got it. But I could hardly walk across the floor in front of Rory, grab the coat and just run out of here.

I was aware of blood pumping through my veins. I made my decision. I was going to head out to the road and flag someone down.

My knuckles were cold and stiff as I unlocked the window and shoved at the aged timber.

Snow blustered in through the opening. I wound my scarf up high, over my nose. I knew nothing about walking out into this kind of temperature. I hoped someone would come along soon—a family in some big, stable SUV maybe. Someone safe.

The wind seemed to blow straight through my flesh and into my bones. The storm was so loud, I could barely think.

I trudged through the snow drifts, walking away from the pub and towards Greenmire. My leg hurt. I hoped I wouldn't get the stitches wet—if snow got in through the tops of my boots, it could happen.

Stinging tears wet my eyes. I kept walking, but I knew I wasn't going to be able to do this for long. Any minute, the cold was going to force me back to the pub. And Rory was going to know I'd been out here. I was certain my face was already stung red.

Twin lights shone yellow through the swirls of snow in the air.

The piercing sound of a horn made me jump. I turned to see a small truck. It passed me and then pulled over.

I ran to catch up with it.

The man that leaned across to open the door for me was middle-aged, his black eyebrows bushier than his hair. "What's up, love?"

"My car broke down," I shouted above the wind. "I need to get to Greenmire."

"Greenmire? Might be a while before you can get back to get your car. Tomorrow-like. Storm's not going to let up."

"That's okay."

Is it okay? Is this man really okay? He looked okay. So had Rory. But this driver might be my only option right now.

"You'd better get in, then. Greenmire's on my route."

"Thank you." My heart raced as I climbed up into the seat. With difficulty, I pulled my sore leg in and closed the door behind me.

"What's up with your foot?" he said.

"I was in a car accident a few days ago." At least I was telling the truth now.

"A car accident? You're not having much luck, are you? What's your name, sweetheart?"

"Isla."

"I'm Ted. Big Ted." He laughed. "Are you here for a holiday?"

"I wish. I'm here working. Photography assignment."

"Well, I hope you didn't just get here. We've had a good stretch for the past couple of weeks. Not a huge amount of rain."

"I've been here about that amount of time. It's been lovely." In Sydney, even in winter, the weather of the past fortnight would have been seen as dismal. But it wasn't dismal, not when the landscape was beautiful and not when you dressed warmly. The only dismal spots were the things that had happened that I couldn't explain.

God. *Rory*. Why had I even agreed to him driving me to the church?

Snow and wind pummelled the windscreen. I didn't know how the driver could even see well enough to drive in this, but he seemed confident.

Half an hour along the highway, the storm either began to ease or it hadn't been as severe closer to Greenmire.

We neared the main street of the town. I noticed the small police station that stood beside an aged willow tree. I'd passed by it a few times now.

"Actually, could you stop here?" I asked.

"Here? It'll be a bit of a hike into town." He looked out through the passenger side window. "Oh, it's the police station you're wanting?" He eyed me keenly as he parked the truck. "You're in a wee spot of trouble, are you?"

I nodded. "Yes. Thanks so much for helping me. I didn't know what I was going to do."

"Ach, that's why you were out there on the side of the road? You should have said something. I would have radioed the police."

"I couldn't get my head together. But I do now."

"Well, good luck."

I thanked him profusely and told him I was fine when he offered to help me out. He pulled the truck away as I made my way through the wind and into the police station.

The interior was tiny—a small counter with a single office behind it. A young man with short, white-blonde hair looked up at me expectantly.

"Is it possible for me to see Officer Bradley? Tash Bradley?" She was the officer who'd been there when we found Stella. At least she seemed a bit familiar.

"'Fraid not," he said. "She's out at the moment. I'm Officer Flanagan. Can I help you?"

"Kirk Flanagan, by any chance?" I remembered Greer saying that the people who owned the property directly behind the McGregors—the Flanagans—had a police officer son named Kirk.

"Guilty as charged." He smiled at his own joke. "Now, what can I do for you?"

I exhaled, gathering strength. "I think I might have something to report."

"Right." He surveyed me. "You *think* you might?"

"No, I—I do."

"Okay, what's your name?"

"Isla Wilson."

Taking out a notepad, he wrote my name down. "Hey, weren't you the one who informed police about the location of Stella Keenan recently? You're staying there at Braithnoch at the moment?"

"Yes, that's me."

"Is this related to Stella?"

"No."

"Okay. Go ahead, then."

"This is difficult. I was in Scotland years ago. I suffered an incident that I don't fully remember. I kept remembering…a place. I found that place today. It's about an hour up the highway, towards Inverness. It's a small church—a church that hasn't been used in a long time. Like I said, I can't completely remember, but I suspect that I was drugged and taken there. I remember being hurt by someone."

He raised his eyebrows. "That's…quite a thing that you're telling me."

"I know."

"When did you say this happened?"

"I'm not sure of the exact day, or exact week. It was two years ago."

"You don't have an exact month?"

"I can get that for you." My mother should be able to tell me that. It had to be just before she came to Scotland to get me.

"Okay," he said. "Do you have the exact location of the church?"

"Yes. I could point it out on a map."

"Good. I'll get that from you in a minute. You say you went there today?"

"Yes, this morning. I went with a school teacher from Greenmire. Rory Kavanagh."

"Rory? Okay."

273

"You know him?"

"Very well. Small town and all."

I immediately felt uncomfortable.

"So, you went to this church today?" he asked. "Can you tell me the purpose of your visit?"

"Yes. I went there to try to jog my memory. To see if it really *was* the place that I'd been remembering."

"You entered the church?"

"Yeah. It wasn't locked."

He frowned, scribbling on the notepad. "Go on."

I closed my eyes. "It was the same place that I remembered. And it had a piano, just like the one I'd heard before. And in one of the rooms…there was an old mattress. It's got blood all over it. It's *my* blood."

He blew out a long, surprised breath. "Well, that's not good. You said someone hurt you at this church. What happened?"

"I can't tell you precisely what happened. I remember…a lot of pain."

"What else do you remember?"

"Just one thing. The man who carried me out of the church had a tattoo. Just below his neck."

"Can you describe the tattoo? Better still, can you draw it?" He pushed the notepad and pen towards me.

I made a quick sketch of the cross tattoo.

The officer glanced from me to the sketch and back again. "Are you certain that was the tattoo?"

"Yes. I'm sure."

"Hmmm. There are a few people around town with this design."

"There are?" The possibility of more people here with the same tattoo hadn't entered my mind.

"So," he said, "you think someone who has this tattoo hurt you?"

"I have a memory of it."

"What do you remember them doing to you?"

"I don't know. I just…know this person was there at the time."

"Where's Rory now?" he asked.

"At a pub somewhere between Inverness and Greenmire. I left him behind."

"Wait, was it Rory you were worried about?"

I couldn't be at all sure of that now. If the cross tattoo was a common tattoo around here, then I could no longer say that it was Rory who'd hurt me.

"Look, I…I need some time. Can I get back to you?"

He studied my face for a moment, his pale blue eyes fixed on me. "Okay, well, sounds like a good plan. I'll need an approximate date that the alleged incident occurred. And some more details, when you have them. Otherwise, I'm going to have difficulty making a start with this."

I nodded. "Thank you."

He glanced past me, to the snowstorm outside. "How are you getting back to Braithnoch?"

"I'm not sure. A cab or something."

"Won't be able to get a cab, I'm afraid. Seems like you've had a rough day. I'll drop you there."

There was something odd in his manner. Ever since I'd drawn the tattoo for him, his tone had changed and become more focused. But he was a police officer—I could trust him, couldn't I?

36

ELODIE

Greenmire, Scottish Highlands, December 2015

ELODIE TRIED to push the dark, confusing thoughts away and think about good things. But it was a struggle. It was exhausting her just to think.

She tried thinking about Christmas.

But immediately, she felt anxious. Because she was supposed to be spending Christmas with the new baby and she couldn't do that if she was stuck here in the hospital. The larch cones she'd started painting were all still in the cottage. She'd been doing them with Stella. Did Mum know to put them up around the lounge room as decorations? They were supposed to be for the baby, to celebrate her first Christmas. And they were for Mum, too, to make her feel happier. Elodie hadn't had a chance to paint all of them yet, but she would when she got out of here.

How long would she be here in this hospital bed? No one was telling her that. She wanted to go home. She wanted to play soccer again and paint and play pretend house in the ruins up on the hill.

Part of her seemed like it had stayed behind, in the forest. She could see the forest the way it often looked first thing in the morning, a fog-enveloped ship drifting along. She was the captain of the ship.

Below, she could see the tattie bogles on the hill, their arms stretched out at their crazy angles, shadows long on the grass.

She could see craggy rock formations and forests between Braithnoch and the properties of the Keenans and the Chandlishes and the Flanagans.

Something was wrong. A bad feeling.

She tried to push it away, but it pushed against her.

The fog cleared, and she found herself standing in the forest. Right in front of the playhouse. Her ship gone.

Her throat clamped, and she tried to turn. But no matter which way she went, she somehow still ended up facing the playhouse.

Through the trees, the colour of the sunrise deepened. *No, that's wrong.* The sky should be growing lighter in the morning. She couldn't tell now whether the sun was dropping or rising. But she desperately wanted it to be morning.

Her heart thudded. All thoughts pulled away from her mind into a black vacuum.

Everything was racing.

"What's happening to her?" Daddy's voice rang out clearly.

Elodie heard the words, *cardiac arrest*, then, "You need to leave the room, Alban." It was Nurse Lucy speaking.

Next time she woke, it was still dark. It was always dark now. She was trapped tight, in her little world.

She felt terrible—worse than before.

Did they know she could hear them? Sometimes, she didn't think they could. Because they spoke about her like she wasn't even there.

Her father was there again—maybe he'd never left. He sounded almost angry now. "Tell me what I can expect. I need to know."

A man spoke. "I'm sorry, Alban, I can't answer that."

"Doc, is there anyone, anywhere who can bring her out of it?" Dad said. "I'll pay anything. Do you understand? I'll pay any amount. I'll find the money."

"I understand," the doctor replied. "Of course you would. But there's no medical facility in the world that could do anything more. I'm so sorry."

Sorry. That was a word Elodie was hearing a lot.
Everyone was sorry.
So sorry.
No one had answers.
And she was drifting again.

37

ISLA

FALLING SNOW MADE BRAITHNOCH A BLUR.

Things felt awkward as Officer Kirk Flanagan parked in the driveway of Alban's house. When he said goodbye and told me to take care, I was certain that he thought I was unhinged. My report at the police station hadn't made sense.

My heart battered at my ribs.

Dried blood spread across a mattress.

The old piano that looked like a toothless grimace.

How could I explain what happened to me when I didn't know myself?

I'd stay here until the storm eased. Then I'd go stay in Inverness and decide from there what my next move was—whether I should go home or stay and pursue this to the end.

I sent a one-line text message to Rory: *Sorry. I had to go. Isla.*

If he was innocent, I didn't want to leave him wondering where I was. He could be out in the snow searching for me.

I packed in a rush, taking all the clothes out of the drawers and wardrobe that I'd put there less than two weeks ago.

After double-checking that my medicines and passport were in my handbag, I ran across to the McGregors' house. I'd left a coat there and it was the only thick one I had left—I'd left my other one behind at the pub. I'd grab the coat from the house, return to the cottage and then wait for better weather. Maybe I couldn't get a cab until tomorrow. But maybe I'd get lucky and the storm would die down quickly.

Neither of the McGregors' cars was parked outside. The house was probably locked up.

But when I tried the front door, it was unlocked. Pushing it open, I walked inside the house. I slipped out of my boots and crossed to the mud-room.

My hand froze as I reached to take my coat from the peg.

Someone else was in the house. I heard footsteps coming down the hallway.

God, who could it be?

The steps were coming closer. If I stayed here, I'd be trapped. If I ventured out, I'd be seen, but at least I'd have a shot of getting away. And whoever it was, my best guess was that they already knew I'd walked into the house.

I stepped out, ready to flee.

Alban, in a long jacket and blue jeans, stared back at me.

"I didn't think anyone was—" I started.

"Jess's car needs new tyres and a few repairs. It's being fixed. She went out in my car with Rhiannon to her mother's house. She's coming back soon, before the storm gets any worse."

I took a deep, silent breath, trying to appear normal. "Oh. I remember now, about Jessica's car."

He frowned. "I was upstairs a few minutes ago. I saw Kirk Flanagan drop you off. Is something wrong?" He switched on the hall lamp. Yellow light flooded into the dark hall.

"No. He just gave me a lift home because of the storm."

"He did?"

I nodded, deciding not to try to explain further. Anything I said would just be a lie. The thought charged through me that I wasn't going to be seeing Alban again. That made me feel even more desolate. But it was even more reason for me to leave. Falling for him was wrong of me.

"Alban," I said, "I'm going to go stay in Inverness. I'm... not certain if I'll be returning. I'm sorry that I didn't get to do the family portraits."

"Is there a problem? Something wrong with the cottage? It's not... it's not a problem with Jess, is it?"

"No, the cottage is lovely. And so is Jessica. It's just personal reasons."

"Okay. Well, I'm sorry to hear that," he said, but his eyes still held a question.

I folded my coat across my arm. "I want to thank you for your hospitality while I've been here."

"And I've enjoyed our conversations. Listen, I can take you to Inverness when you're ready to go. After Jess comes back."

"Oh, thanks. But I'll get a cab."

"All the way to Inverness? That's a long ride." His eyes sharpened. "So, Greer doesn't know you're going?"

"No, I haven't had a chance to talk with her yet. The phone coverage was out, and I couldn't call anyone."

"The phones have been fine, here. A little bit of interference, but that's all. Where have you been?"

"Far enough to lose reception, I guess." I gave a playful laugh to cover up the fact that I was being evasive.

My gaze came to rest upon a black and white photograph on the wall. I hadn't ever noticed it before. It was situated in a dark recess, and I'd never seen it under the bright light that Alban had just switched on. This photo was of a young group of men. Five of them. They were standing in front of the scarecrows on the hill. It was summer. Their bodies were proud with the swagger and defiance of youth—shirtless, with sunlight hazed across their faces.

Although the sun was casting deep shadows, I could recognise them—a much younger Alban, Diarmid, Rory, Hamish and another boy who I could tell was Kirk, the police officer.

Every one of them bore an identical tattoo, just above their left breast bone. *The rose-and-cross tattoo.*

Kirk had told me there a few people who bore the tattoo, but he hadn't mentioned that it was *this* particular group. And he certainly hadn't told me that *he* himself had it.

The discordant notes of the piano broke through my mind.

Dark room.

Smell of rust and decay.

Someone pacing backwards and forwards.

One of the people in this photograph had been at the church with me. One of them had hurt me.

I could still hear the piano playing in my head.

A sudden thought occurred to me. *The piano*—if someone had been standing in the room while the piano played, there had to have been more than one person at the church.

I clamped a gasp tightly in my throat. There could have been a whole group of people there for all I knew. Maybe *all* of these men— some kind of cultish group in which people got drugged and tortured.

If that were true, I was already in deep trouble.

"Are you all right?" Alban asked.

"I—Everything's fine." I straightened the coat that was folded over my arm, fiddling with the lapels. "I have to thank you and Jessica for all you've done for me. It's been a wonderful experience."

A frown rippled across his forehead. "Isla? Your voice is shaking. It's obvious that something's up. I don't want you to go like this. Whatever it is, I'd like to know."

"You're right…there *is* something. My mother's ill. We're very close and I'm not dealing with it very well."

He tilted his head slightly, as if he didn't believe me. I was sure I didn't sound believable. My mind was racing.

He reached for my arm. "Isla, please. Let me help."

I pulled my hand away. "It's okay. Really."

"Don't run away from me again." His words rushed out, the tone deep.

"Again?" I questioned.

His expression grew strange. He squeezed his eyes shut, shaking his head. "I didn't mean to say that."

I took a step back.

Yes, you did mean to say that. You just admitted that there has been another time in which I've run away from you.

You know me from before.

38

ISLA

THE SHRILL SOUND of the kitchen phone pierced the air.

Alban sighed heavily, his gaze fixed on me. "Would you give me a moment? It might be Jess. Come through with me. We need to talk."

I nodded. Walking after him, I tried and failed to keep my breathing even. Did he know I was afraid of him?

Where could I go from here? Snow was piling up in fast layers outside. Night was almost here. Greer was in Aviemore with Kelly. It was the middle of a snowstorm. She couldn't come and get me. I could run to either the Keenan's or the Chandlishes houses. But both Hamish and Diarmid had the rose-and-cross tattoo. Even Kirk—the only police officer on duty right now—had the tattoo.

There was nowhere safe to run. I had to find somewhere to hide until I could figure out how to get away from this place.

Where was Jessica? Alban said she'd be coming back soon. Once she was here, Alban would have to put his mask back on and pretend to be the devoted husband and father.

Behind Alban's back, I pulled my coat on, buttoning it up.

Alban answered the phone. "Rory? What's going on?" He swung to me, his eyes guarded, then turned his back again. "Yeah, she's here. What—?"

Alban snapped his words off suddenly. He stared off into the

283

distance, past the living room and through the soaring plate glass walls.

A bright orange spot glowed up in the hills.

It was as if the hill were on fire.

Even from here, I could tell which hill that was. *Scarecrow hill.* Someone had set the scarecrows on fire. Five columns of flames shooting skyward from the wide blanket of white.

An urgent knock resounded through the house. A knock at the front door.

"Rory, got to go," Alban spoke into the phone. He flicked his gaze my way, his mouth agape. "Stay here."

As Alban jogged through the house to the door, I followed but stayed far behind, stalling in the corridor.

I heard a male voice. It was Kirk, the police officer. "Alban, we've got an emergency situation. Stella Keenan is missing from the hospital. The girl's on suicide watch. She hasn't been here, has she?"

"No. *Hell*," Alban responded. "Do they have any idea where she went?"

"No one has any clue. She was reported missing about half an hour ago, but she could have been gone longer. Hey, what's with the fire up on the hill?"

"Wish I could answer that. I only just spotted it myself," said Alban.

The fire—it was Stella. I was suddenly certain of that. She'd said she'd make the scarecrows burn one day. That meant she was out there. Alone and scared.

I had to find her. That was the only thing that was clear right now. It might have been me who pushed her over the edge. I couldn't leave her out in the storm.

Alban was still talking with Kirk. I grabbed my shoes from outside the mudroom, then headed down the hallway to the laundry. I remembered seeing a door that led outside in there. Wind thrust through the door as I unlatched it and pulled it open. I closed it behind me and headed straight across to the forest, pulling my coat's hood snugly over my head.

The forest would hide me.

I could see the moon now, storm clouds moving furiously across the sky. The snowfall had stopped.

The night air was lighter than I imagined it would be. I remembered Gus Chandlish mentioning the glow on a snowy, moonlit night. It was true—once my eyes had adjusted, I could see my way forward enough not to blunder into trees.

Behind me, someone called out Stella's name, the beam of a torch flashing. Officer Kirk. He must have decided to look for her out here, too.

I crouched to the ground.

There were others. I heard distant shouts above the wind.

Fleetingly, the thought crossed my mind that Kirk could have been pretending about Stella being missing, knowing that I could hear him. This could be some brutal game played between Alban, Rory and Kirk.

I glanced back around at the fire glowing through the trees.

Whatever else was true, I was sure that it was Stella who set the scarecrows on fire. She was here.

I kept running, ploughing my way through the snow drifts and staying silent. If I called out to Stella, then Kirk would hear me.

The air grew brighter as I neared the columns of flames. A man ran past in the open—Kirk.

Kirk paced up and down near the fire, inspecting it and retrieving his phone. "Haven't located her yet. There's a fire happening up here on the hill at Alban's place. I came to check it out. Found an empty can of kerosene at the scene. I'll guess that the kero was poured over the scarecrows before setting them on fire. Yeah. Yep. Okay, I'll—"

Another man, silhouetted in the orange glow, stepped out from the trees. He punched Kirk twice in the head.

Kirk stumbled back.

A third punch sent Kirk flopping to the ground, unconscious.

Who was that? Why did they hit Kirk? Blood spurted through my veins, making my heart thud out of time.

Pulling myself to my feet, I fled deeper into the forest.

Someone was following.

I twisted around. My foot caught on a rock, pitching me forward. I landed hard on my hands and knees. Pain exploded through my body.

Scrambling to my feet again, I inhaled quick, deep mouthfuls of chilled air.

Hands caught me and dragged me to my feet.

I whirled around. "Hamish!"

He was drunk, smelling of whisky, cigarettes and sweat. "Are you okay?"

I sensed that he wasn't going to hurt me. But I still couldn't trust him. "It was you who hit the police officer, wasn't it?"

"I fucking hate him. Hate all the police dogs. He's gonna make Stella keep running. I told mum and Camille not to call the police. They didn't fucking listen."

"Where's Camille? Is she here somewhere?"

"She's on her way. They didn't watch Stella properly at that damned hospital."

"How do you know she's here?"

"Someone got into our shed and stole a can of kero. The only people who know where the key is hidden is me and mum and dad— and Stella. So, it had to be her."

"How long ago did she leave the hospital?"

Hamish stared at me drunkenly, as if I hadn't spoken. "She lit the bogles, I know she did. I know her. I know Stella. No one else knows her like I do. No one. No one knows...."

Alban ran past, at a distance, calling out my name and then Stella's. He didn't see us.

Hamish turned to watch him, his grip on me slackening.

I shoved Hamish back and tore away from him.

I raced across the wide-open section between the forest that belonged to the McGregors and the forest that belonged to the Chandlishes. Storm clouds covered the moon now and the night had darkened.

I thought about the day Stella had taken me to the bridge that spanned the creek. Could she be there? The creek wasn't far from here.

I couldn't go the same way she'd taken me last time—through the peat marsh. But I could go the way that I'd walked with Rory, just in reverse. I'd follow the path through the forest that led from scarecrow hill to the fence line, then turn left and follow the path straight up.

My face froze as I blundered along the path. I stuck within the cover of trees, trying to stay out of view. I yanked my scarf up over my mouth and nose.

Stella, where are you? Did you go this way?

I listened for a gurgle of water but heard nothing. I almost thought I'd gone past the bridge when I spotted it. The water in the creek had frozen over, a dull luminescence on its surface.

The moon shone out from the clouds again.

A girl sat on the bridge, long legs dangling.

Stella.

She wore boots—boots that were too large for her. She clutched an overcoat over a doctors' hospital gown. I guessed she'd stolen the boots and overcoat from the hospital. She must be freezing.

I crept closer, scared that if I rushed her, she'd run off. And I wouldn't be able to catch her.

Stepping onto the bridge, I walked close enough for her to hear me without me having to call out and alert the others that were in the woods. Hooking a finger into my scarf, I manoeuvred it down over my face so that she could see who I was.

She tilted her head as I approached, then scrambled to her feet.

"Stella, please, I just want to help."

She clutched the railing of the bridge. "Everyone wants to help. I don't want their help."

"Tell me what you want?"

She didn't answer. She didn't want to talk to me. Maybe she didn't want to answer questions—maybe she couldn't.

Boldly, I took another step. "You made the scarecrows burn. You said you would. And you did."

Swallowing, I kept walking, all the way up to her. "You did it, Stella. It's a beautiful fire."

I held my breath in the needle-fine stretch of silence that followed.

"I want them to know," she said finally. "I want them all to know."

"You lit the fire because you wanted to tell everyone something, didn't you?"

She nodded hesitantly.

"They can all see it now." I desperately wanted to ask her what it was that she wanted to tell everyone. But I sensed she wasn't ready to do that.

She wrapped her arms around herself. "I got the kero from my grandparents' shed. I didn't want to steal from them, but I had to."

"They won't mind."

She stared up at the sky. "Is it still burning?"

"See the smoke? It's still burning."

"Good." She eyed me suspiciously. "They pumped me full of drugs at the hospital. I don't feel right. It's like one half of my brain is dead and the other half won't stop. *It won't stop.* I can't stop the thoughts. I want them to stop."

"When I was a teenager," I told her, "they put me on all kinds of drugs. I thought I was going crazy."

"Why did they put you on drugs?"

"I have epilepsy. Even now, sometimes, they get the drug wrong. Or sometimes it's the dose that's wrong. And sometimes, it's hard to know if it's the drugs or an on oncoming seizure, or both. It's scary."

She hung her head. "I'm scared. I feel...*wrong.*"

"All I know is that you'll get through it. You will. You'll get to the other side."

"What does it matter? There's nothing on the other side. Nothing good."

"Listen, Stella, I had really bad depression as a teenager. An effect of the epilepsy. It doesn't affect everyone that way, but it did do that to me. And I'm still here."

"How did you get better?"

"I learned ways of coping. I can teach you." I turned my head, checking to see if anyone was coming.

"Who are you looking out for? You're waiting for someone. Did you call someone and tell them I was here?"

"No. I didn't. I don't have a phone with me."

"Something's going on. Why do you look so scared?"

"I don't like being out here at night. Are your grandparents at home? Can we go there?"

She shook her head vehemently, taking a step back from me.

"You're going to get too cold out here," I said. "Look at you. You haven't got enough warm clothes on."

The night darkened again as she continued to back away, her posture stiff.

"Stella, please."

"Get away from me!" In a flash, she spun around and fled.

I tried to follow, but she merged with the dark forest too soon.

"Stella!" I called in desperation. I'd had her, practically in my hands, and I'd let her get away.

She'd run in the direction of the peat marshes. If she fell into the snow-covered bog and suffocated there in the mud, I'd never forgive myself.

"Stella! Stella!" I was screaming now, running. Giving away my location to anyone within range. But I couldn't make myself stay quiet.

A tall figure ran up to me, breathing out white mist. I didn't recognise him in the dark before he spoke. "Isla, what a night. Between the bogles and Stella missing, I don't know what's going on."

"Peyton!"

"Aye, it's me. I've got Aubrey and Diarmid out looking, too."

My heart fell when I heard Diarmid's name. He was one of the men with the tattoo. But at least Aubrey was with him.

"I found Stella."

"You did? Where—?"

"She ran off. It's my fault."

"Hey, don't blame yourself. That kid tends to run away a lot." He swept a lock of hair back from his eyes. "Where did she go?"

"She was on the bridge but now she's gone—that way." I pointed desperately.

"Poor kid. I'll get a proper search party organised. I'll get the whole of Greenmire down here if I have to. Don't worry. We'll find her."

He took his phone from his jacket pocket. "Aubrey! Stella was just sighted near the bridge. She's headed for the marshes. Where are you? Well, get yourself over this way, dammit. Let Diarmid know, too. Hey, Isla's here. Yeah, I'll tell her."

Finishing the call, he pushed the phone back into his pocket. "She said we should all catch up for a round of hot chocolate once we find Stella."

"That would be nice. Peyton, I'm worried about those marshes. She knows how to find her way through it in the daytime. But it's night. And there's a covering of snow. I'm too slow with this sore leg of mine."

"Right. Look. I'll head there now and make sure she's not in trouble. If you spot my brother and sister, tell them to hurry. Aubrey will be better at talking to her than me."

I nodded, my breath cold in my throat and my lungs tight with fear for Stella.

39

ISLA

I STUMBLED FORWARD, watching Peyton's long figure speeding away. I hoped he'd find her quickly.

Retracing my steps, I headed back to the path and then along the wide-open strip of land that led back to Braithnoch and scarecrow hill.

The roaring fire had collapsed, still sending bright sparks into the inky sky.

I could no longer hear anyone out on the moor or in the forest.

Had the others really gone?

Or were they still there, with their torches switched off, just standing in the moor and waiting.

The thought made me shiver. I didn't know what was really going on here. Everything felt uncertain and hidden from me.

A faint cry carried on the blustering wind. A girl's cry.

Stella was out there on the moor somewhere.

My right leg hurt with every pounding jolt as I ran out into the open. The lonely wind screeching on distant hills and the thick darkness sparked danger along my spine.

I heard her again. Straight ahead.

I could just make out the craggy hills of Braithnoch, with its crumbling, original stone house. I'd taken portraits of Alban there just yesterday. That already seemed like an age ago.

Another cry came. Further away.

Why was Stella crying out like that? She'd been so silent before, not wanting anyone to know where she was. Was someone making her scream on purpose?

A terrible thought occurred to me. If a group of people were out there, playing a game with me, they could be using Stella to draw me out. If so, I was running straight into a trap.

Something was wrong. *Really wrong.*

I was heading directly into danger.

Everything inside of me screamed *run. Turn around and run.*

But I couldn't leave Stella.

My heart in my throat, I struggled across the snowy moor, approaching the archway of the old building. The weakest reflection of light from the snow splashed across the stonework. But the light didn't reach inside the archway.

It was so, so dark in there. Cold sweat bathed my body under my clothing, shivers racing up and down my back, my leg feeling almost useless.

Just walk inside, see if she's there, and walk straight out. Maybe she's just hurt. Maybe she fell and twisted her ankle.

I knew none of that was true.

Her cry hadn't been the cry of someone who'd twisted their ankle.

It had been the helpless cry of someone who was terrified.

Mustering up courage, I took a step.

Every inch of me didn't want to go in there.

Images, sounds and smells from the room in the church reeled in my mind.

Mattress of blood.

Candles in the dark.

Rosary beads swinging.

Brutal pain tearing through my body.

Agonising waves shooting in my head.

Maddening, tormenting, manic chords of the piano.

A crucifying sense of loss, a hollowness worse than the pain.

I forced myself forward.

The arch was overhead now. I moved inside. "Stella," I whispered. "Are you here? Are you hurt?"

I was keenly aware of my heart beat.

Then I heard a whisper close by me. "Shhh."

Stella's voice.

Why was she asking me to be quiet?

I kept my voice so low I could barely hear it myself. "Come with me. Please."

The reply came swiftly this time. "He'll see us."

"Who?"

I heard boots shuffling around. And I heard someone's loud breaths—someone who wasn't Stella. He swore under his breath. I couldn't tell who it was. But whoever he was, this wasn't a game to him. He wasn't enjoying the pursuit. It was the sound of someone who was desperate. The footsteps tramped away, to the side of the building that faced the mountains.

"He caught me," she whispered. "But I got away."

Stella's hand slipped into mine, clutching it, holding on tight. We inched slowly towards the archway, keeping our footsteps silent, each of us holding our breath.

40

ISLA

A CRACKLING sound preceded the sudden flare of a match. A man was hunched over, his back to me, lighting the match. He flicked the match into one of the glass lamps on the shelf, then swivelled around.

"Peyton," I gasped.

Whoever had been in here was gone and Peyton had found us.

But by the way Stella began backing away—pulling me with her —I knew the truth.

No. *No, no, no.*

Peyton is the one Stella's afraid of.

The glow from the lamp flickered against the aged walls behind him. He took a cigarette out of his pocket and lit it. His eyes were a strange mix of determined and anxious.

"Peyton," I said quickly, battening down my nerves. "Thank God you're here. We've found Stella. I'm taking her back to her grandparents now."

"Should have stayed in Aviemore, Stella," he said, ignoring me. "It was okay before you came back."

"I'll go back. Tonight." Her voice trembled.

"Ah, I don't even know how things got to this point," he said, a hint of confusion in his voice.

"You *know*," Stella cried at him.

He blew out a nervous stream of cigarette smoke. "I haven't done anything wrong."

"You told me it wasn't wrong. You told me my mum said it was okay," Stella said. "But it was wrong. You shouldn't have done what you did."

I listened with growing horror.

Peyton gave a shake of his head. "It was all fine by her. She wanted you to grow up a bit."

"You're telling lies," Stella raged at him. "When I told Mum, she said it was a bad thing. She said I must have made it up because I didn't like you."

He inhaled deeply on his cigarette. "You *did* like me. *You loved me.*"

"No," she insisted.

"Peyton," I broke in. "I'm going to walk out of here now with Stella." Being bold and direct was the only thing I could think of. I nodded tensely at Stella.

He stared as if noticing me for the first time. Angrily, he puffed on the stub of his cigarette and threw it against the wall. The next moment, he reached inside his jacket and pulled out a long-bladed knife. Seizing Stella by the hand, he yanked her away from me and brought the knife up under her chin.

Every nerve in my body jumped and fired. "Don't! Don't you dare hurt her."

"I'm just setting things right," he said, his voice filled with a strange, controlled rage. "You two won't understand. Everything has to be...right. You have to keep things straight. All in order."

Tears tracked down Stella's face, glistening wetly in the dark light. "You're a fucking molester."

"You liked hanging out with me," Peyton told her. "You loved me. Admit it."

"I didn't love you," she said. "You made me say it. You made me believe it. I thought *I* was the one who'd done something wrong when Mum caught you kissing me."

He made a derisive sound between his teeth. "Why didn't you just bleed out in the playhouse, Stella? It's what you wanted."

295

"Every cut was because of you," she cried. "For the last two years, every cut was *you.*"

"You can't pin that on me." He shook his head. "That's not right. I'm not to blame."

Stella's voice rose. "I was a twelve-year-old kid, Peyton. It took me two years to realise that."

His expression deadened. Dropping his arms from Stella, he began pacing the room, knife still in hand. He paced in a regimented way. Two steps one way, three steps in another.

My mind filled with a black despair. I had a single thought: *survive.*

I edged towards Stella, putting a finger to my lips to make sure she stayed silent. Peyton wasn't noticing either of us in this moment.

Keeping my gaze fixed on Peyton, I took her hand. Holding onto her, I began inching towards the arch.

He angled his head around. "Stop moving. For fuck's sake. Don't make this hard on me."

"Peyton," I said. "Here's what's going to happen. Stella and I are walking out. You are going to go back to your own house."

"You know that's not what's going to happen," he told me.

I believed him.

"It's the best thing for you." My voice shook. Talking to him wasn't helping. I was speaking out of wild desperation.

A hollow laugh emitted from his chest. "I'm not two years old, Isla. I'm in trouble. Very big trouble."

"No, you're not. Not yet." I shot Stella a quick glance, hoping she knew that I didn't mean that.

Peyton's face twisted darkly. "I'm not going to jail. Not even for a minute. It's not right to lock someone like me away. This is all a grand injustice."

"Then let us walk out of here," I said. "That's the only way to fix this."

"I *am* going to fix this," he hissed. "I'm going to make it better. Everyone else is gone. I told Kirk I saw Stella hitching a ride out on the road. Aubrey and Diarmid aren't even here, but you guessed that, right? It's just us." He closed his eyes and then sprung them open wide like umbrellas. "You, Stella, are going to stab your good friend

Isla. People will believe you did it. Because you're a crazy loon who just escaped from the nut house. And because Isla is the goody two shoes who tried to stop you from killing yourself in the playhouse. Then you're going to cut your wrists and jump off the edge of the drop-off. You'll do a better job this time—the cuts will be so deep you'll bleed out in a minute. If the fall doesn't kill you first." He trembled, his face showing a manic fear. "It's perfect. I've got it figured out. Everything goes back to normal after that."

Stella shook her head, retreating into the wall. "I won't do it."

He dragged her towards him, turning her and grasping her in a bear hug from behind. Shoving the handle of the knife into her fingers, he closed his hand tightly around hers. "Of course you will." He forced her arm outwards, making jabbing motions with the knife. "Look. Look at you, Stella. You're a crazy little girl."

We can't get out.

He's going to kill her.

It's my fault. I sent him straight to her.

Stella's face was milky-white in the dim glow. Her eyes huge and terrified.

The glow of the lamp was fading. The fire was almost out of fuel.

Not seeing Peyton and his knife would be even more terrifying than seeing him there in front of me.

He charged at me using Stella as his puppet, slashing at me with the knife.

I screamed, trying to protect myself.

Breath sucked from my lungs as the knife swept across my abdomen.

The knife sliced in through my clothes, into my skin, into my flesh.

My body dropped to the ground.

"Fuck you've got a loud scream," he taunted. "But that's okay. If anyone should happen to hear you, you screamed because Stella stabbed you. You're dead now, Isla. Your guts are cut open." He stared down at the thick blood on the knife's bade, transfixed, looking queasy at the sight.

"I didn't want to do any of this," he said with distaste. "This isn't *me*. I wasn't the one who left you in that revolting old church,

Isla. But no, good old Peyton gets sent to do someone else's dirty work."

I stared up at him, his words instantly clearing everything else out of my mind. "That was *you* who carried me out of that church?"

"Yeah," he said.

"That man had a tattoo…" I whispered.

"You mean this?" He blinked at me, yanking his shirt and jacket across to expose the flesh on his left collarbone.

He had the tattoo of the cross and rose.

"You remember seeing that?" He scowled. "And I was assured you'd lost your marbles and your memory wasn't ever coming back. Oh well, it's all come to another ending now. Some might find that poetic."

"Who sent you there?" I rasped. "Who?"

He gave a thin, brittle laugh. "You actually remember *me* but not *them*? That's insane. I get blamed for everything, don't I?" He gazed down at the bloodied knife again, his eyes growing blank. "Ah, Stella, I wish I didn't have to do this. I loved you. But it's gone too far. I don't have a fucking choice."

"Peyton," I cried. "You do have a choice. You haven't killed anyone. You can—"

As I spoke, he gripped Stella's arms. "Just in case the knife didn't go deep enough, you're going to stab Isla again. Then it's your turn."

With a guttural shout, Stella bucked her head backwards, smashing him in the chin. She ripped herself loose from his clutch.

The last tiny pocket of light extinguished inside the lamp.

An angry, cheated roar burst from Peyton's lungs.

I knew that Stella had gone.

I closed my eyes. *Go, Stella. Run hard. Don't stop. Please don't let him catch you. Please don't let him….*

He raced after her.

She was fast, but he'd caught up to her before with ease.

Stella, run….

Twisting myself around, I half-sat, clutching my stomach. How bad was the wound?

Your guts are cut open. His words rang in my head, shrill and loud.

If he caught Stella and did what he said he'd do, he'd be back to make sure I was dead.

I refused to allow Peyton to come back and take my last breath. I was an easy target here. I struggled to my feet and then blundered out into the night.

The moor stretched out, impossibly wide and long.

Each breath came shivery and shallow through my throat.

"Where are you?" Peyton's voice thundered through the dark air. He wasn't far away—somewhere between me and the long stretch of land that ended at the McGregors' house.

I crouched to the frozen ground. He wasn't looking for me. But I didn't want him to see me.

Peyton ran a short distance, then stopped and headed in the other direction.

He didn't know where Stella was. If he knew, he wouldn't be running backwards and forwards. Somehow, she'd managed to evade him.

Where could I go?

The only answer was *away*.

My arms tight across my stomach, I ran through the snow.

The ground grew sticky, thick.

My legs sunk in.

In an instant I knew where I was. The peat marshes.

I tried to walk my way out, but in the darkness, I just waded in further.

Terrified, I attempted to wrench myself around. Get out of here.

I fell onto my hands and knees. Mud and snow enveloped me.

The strong beam of a torch swept from side to side.

Peyton hadn't had a torch. It wasn't him.

"Isla!" called the voice.

Alban.

Terror flashed white in my brain.

Are you the one who sent Peyton to the church, Alban?

You knew me from before. You said I'd run from you.

How do you know me? What was I running from?

What did you do to me?

41

ISLA

THE TORCH'S beam came to a stop on me.

Alban gave a shout, charging up the hill and across the stretch of moor.

"Isla!" He ran straight in, arms closing around my body. Hauling me out.

He tore off his overcoat and set me down on it. Then ran the torch's light over me, a dark smear of mud across his forehead. "Isla, what happened?"

I'd gone numb. Crawling deep inside myself. I shrank back, wanting to tell him to stop touching me. To leave me. I couldn't form words.

"Please tell me," he urged, shrugging off his jacket and placing it over me. "How did you end up in here? Did someone do this to you?"

The glow of Alban's torch arced across the night as he drew back, illuminating two figures. Peyton was standing dead still, Stella in his grasp, holding a gloved hand tight across her lower face.

"Stella," I breathed, involuntarily.

"You saw Stella?" Alban's face creased in a deep frown.

He rotated his light, shining it where I was looking. But the moor was empty in that direction, now.

Alban made a hasty call. "Kirk, you okay now? Good. I think

Stella has been sighted up here, after all. Yeah. And I found Isla. She's hurt. I'm not sure, she's not telling me anything. I need urgent help up here. We're on the Braithnoch moor, near the peat marsh. Yeah, next to the old house."

Could I trust his phone call? Believe that he was bringing help? Kirk had been unconscious on the ground the last I'd seen him, so was Alban really even calling him? Peyton had made a fake phone call when he'd pretended to call Aubrey and Diarmid. I'd suspected nothing. And could I trust Kirk, anyway? I didn't know any of these people. Why had Peyton thought it so amusing that I didn't know who'd sent him to the church? Who had it been?

Fingers trembling, I grabbed Alban's torch and shone it around in a circle, jerking the beam from place to place, searching for Peyton.

Alban shoved his phone back into his pocket. "What the hell's going on tonight? I found poor Kirk out cold on the ground earlier. Hamish punched him. The world's gone mad."

My torch light illuminated two figures.

Peyton was right there.

A short distance behind Alban.

He still had his hand over Stella's mouth, preventing her from crying out.

"No," I breathed.

Alban whirled around, springing to his feet. "Peyton? What—?"

Peyton dropped his grip on Stella. For a moment, I thought he was going to let her go. But when I focused on his face, I saw it was the last thing on his mind.

"He's going to kill you," Stella cried, her voice thin against the storm, pitched high with terror.

Peyton punched Stella hard to the side of her head and shoved her to the ground. She collapsed instantly.

"What the fuck?" Alban advanced towards Peyton, stopping dead as Peyton brought up a knife in his fist.

"It's *her*." Peyton told Alban, glancing in disgust at the crumpled girl lying on the snow. "All because of her. I didn't want to do any of this. We were friends once, Alban. But I can't let her destroy everything."

With a yell, Alban ran at Peyton.

301

The two of them went down onto the ground, locked in a struggle. Gasping, I trained my torch's beam from the men to Stella. Stella hadn't moved, a spatter of dark red liquid on her white doctors' coat —my blood from when Peyton made her stab me.

People could die from a single punch to the head. And she was just a young, fragile girl. *Please don't die, Stella.*

I wanted to get to her and move her off the ice. All she wore was that thin coat and an even thinner hospital gown underneath.

Snow began falling again. I could see the moon.

With the moon reflecting on the falling snow, the night lightened by degrees. I had a clear view now of the two men wrestling with each other.

I knew what Peyton's intent was. He was sticking with his plan. Stella had to die last. He needed me dead first and then Stella. Alban would die, too, because Alban had gotten in the way. Then Peyton would cut Stella's wrists and force her to jump off the hill's steep edge. He'd make her take the knife with her—to make her look like a killer. And then Peyton would go home to his parents' house, with no one the wiser. He'd clean himself up, dispose of his blood-soaked clothing, hide any bruises.

A single thought pierced my mind.

Get the knife.

I crawled onto the ice. My limbs frozen and locked up. My head still faint. The wind was whipping the snow with a furious rage.

Keep going.

Alban punched Peyton's face, making blood spurt from his mouth and ear. But Peyton still gripped the knife.

It was a fight to the death.

I inched closer.

Almost there.

Peyton rolled Alban onto his side, landing a sharp punch to his temple. He lifted the knife up high.

Breath sucked dry from my lungs.

He's going to kill Alban.

I needed a weapon. But there was nothing here.

There's snow.

Gathering up an armful of ice, I threw it hard at Peyton's face.

It was enough. Just enough. Alban forced Peyton's arm down.

The knife skidded away. I grabbed it.

Moonlight glistened in the sheen of sweat on Alban's forehead as he punched Peyton again, his eyes grown wild.

Two figures ran up the hill towards us.

Kirk first, then Hamish barrelling up behind.

Kirk heaved Alban off Peyton and dragged him to his feet.

Hamish helped Peyton up. "What the hell's Alban doing to you?"

Alban spat blood on the snow. "That animal just hit Stella. He had a knife."

Kirk released Alban, shining his torch over the ground, finding me holding the knife and finding Stella lying still.

"Hold him!" Kirk instructed Hamish.

Hamish's mouth dropped open as he obeyed, grabbing Peyton. Peyton struggled, but Hamish was stronger.

Kirk handcuffed Peyton's wrists behind his back.

Hamish's expression swapped from confused to incensed as he caught sight of Stella, a string of swear words exploding from his mouth.

"Get on your knees." Kirk shoved Peyton forward, making him fall to all fours. Kirk stripped off his own coat, throwing it to Hamish so that he could cover Stella.

I'd had everything wrong. Peyton was the only bad one here. There was still confusion, still questions unspooling in my head. But the rest of them weren't like Peyton. There was no evil brotherhood that tied them together.

I must have misunderstood what Alban said to me before, in the house.

"Someone better talk." Hamish stared from Kirk to Alban, wrapping Stella in the coat and gathering her up in his arms.

Alban helped me to my feet. "I think Isla might be able to tell you, when she's able to."

The knife dropped from my frozen hand. I held both arms across my middle. "Peyton tried to kill us both. Please check Stella. Is she breathing?"

"She's breathing," Hamish told me. "I better get an ambulance here for her."

"No services can get through right now," Kirk told him. "The roads are closed. I spoke with Tash just a short while ago."

"Well that's a pile of shite." Hamish's eyes narrowed as he turned to Alban. "How'd you know Stella was up here? I heard Kirk on the phone to you and I heard him mention Stella. So, I followed him."

"I came looking for Isla," Alban told him, wiping sweat-soaked hair back from his face. "I thought I heard a scream. I found her. Then Peyton landed a king hit on Stella and pulled a knife on me. That's all I know."

"Fuck." Hamish exhaled a long stream of white air. He lifted his chin around to face Kirk. "Kirk, sorry man. I shouldn't have decked you before. You were just doing your job."

Kirk stared back, unwilling to accept his apology. "Get your niece out of the storm. Pronto."

Hamish nodded contritely, backing up a step and then rushing away with Stella.

"Okay," Kirk breathed. "You look hurt, Isla. Did Peyton hit you in the stomach or something?"

Peyton turned his head to stare at me, fear in his eyes. He attempted to get to his feet.

Kirk kicked him hard in the centre of his back. "I told you not to move."

"Peyton stabbed me," I told Kirk.

"Stabbed?" Alban bent to lift my ripped jacket, scraping the mud away. "Hell. *Hell.* Why didn't you tell me?"

Trails of bright blood streamed out where the peat mud had been scooped away.

Kirk eyed the cut. "That's bad. I think maybe the mud was packing the wound and stopping the bleed. I'm afraid you'll have to stay up here until an ambulance can get through, Isla."

"But we're in a damned storm," Alban exclaimed.

"She could bleed out if you move her," Kirk said. "I've seen it happen. Take her to the shelter over there. Keep the cut sealed any way you can."

"If there's no other choice," Alban said. "Jess has a medical kit at home. She keeps it in the laundry." He pulled his phone out of his jacket pocket. The screen was smashed. It must have happened during the fight. Alban tried making a call, then shook his head. "It's broken. Could you get someone to get the kit up here?"

"Okay. Maybe Hamish could run it back." Swinging his head around, Kirk watched as Peyton tried to struggle to his feet again. Kirk seized Peyton's arms. "I have to take this one down to the house and restrain him there."

"Kirk," I called. "I just want you to know something. It was Peyton—at the church. He was the one with the tattoo. He admitted it to me. But there were two of them. I don't know who the other one was."

If I died tonight, I wanted it known who'd been there at the church —at least the one person that I knew of.

Kirk considered my words. "Okay. We'll get that sorted later." He marched Peyton away.

"What's that about a church?" Alban gathered up his coat and jacket from the ground. "No, tell me later. I've got to get you to the old house." He attempted to lift me.

"I can walk."

"Maybe, but you shouldn't. So, you're not."

Alban took me in his arms to the ruins.

He placed a torch on the shelf and then laid his jacket down on the floor. He placed me gently on top, then put his jacket over my frozen body. I drew shallow breaths, afraid that deep breaths would make blood flow faster from the knife wound.

Alban then ran out and returned with a load of spongy-looking moss and snow. He tried to clean the cut with the snow, then laid the moss gingerly over the cut and held his hand firmly on top. "I don't know if this is the right thing to do or not. But it's all I can think of."

I gave a brief smile. "Your neighbour…Charlie Keenan…told a story about Griogair and the peat on the battlefields. He said it saved his life."

"Ach. I know that story. Don't worry, I didn't get this idea from a Griogair myth. Peat moss was used on thousands of men during the First World War. It's good stuff, apparently." He sounded confident but he looked worried. "I hope it works, Isla."

The wind blew in with a fury from over the mountains, screeching over the moor like hungry ravens, finding its way into the ruins everywhere. My head felt lighter than it had before. Every part of me felt weak.

"Are you okay? Isla, please, open your eyes."

I hadn't realised I'd shut them. "I'm awake. I'm okay."

He watched snow spiralling in through the crumbling archway for a moment, then shook his head. "I'm sorry as hell that all this happened. I can't explain what happened with Peyton. He's always kept out of trouble. Unlike Diarmid. He must have had some kind of psychotic snap."

"He's been bad...for a long time."

A look of confusion crossed Alban's face and he stared at me. "I had no idea." Alban wrinkled his brow. "Isla, what was it you were telling Kirk about Peyton's tattoo?"

How did I explain? "I remembered the tattoo...from before," I started. "Bad people locked me away...hurt me. At an old church. I know now that Peyton was one of them."

"Christ. He locked you away and hurt you? When? I don't understand. Did this happen this morning?"

"No, not today. First, please, tell me—what does the tattoo mean?"

"It means nothing. It was a stupid spur of the moment decision, one drunken weekend when we were lads. We all have it." He stared downward, repositioning his hand on the moss. "Me, Rory, Kirk, Hamish, Peyton, and Diarmid."

"Peyton wasn't in the photo...."

"Photo?"

"The one on the wall in your house."

"Ah, okay. He was away with his father the day that was taken. That was when you got scared, wasn't it? When you saw that photo. I swear to you that the tattoo doesn't mean anything bad. Look, the cross part of the tattoo simply represents the divider between the four properties. If you were looking at them from the sky, you'd see a cross. Hundreds of years ago, as Griogair's family grew, he divided the properties into four equal lots. The legend goes that a rose bush was planted in the spot where the four properties intersect. So, that's the rose part of the tattoo. Rory is distantly related to the original Braithnoch family, so he got a tattoo as well."

STRANGER IN THE WOODS

"That's all it is?"

"I swear to you on my life, Isla. That's all it is. Now, you must tell me what Peyton did to you. I need to know. *Now*."

"I don't know what he did. My memory…is fuzzy. It happened… years ago."

"Years? But you—"

"Just listen. Please. I travelled to Scotland once before. Two years ago. Something happened to me back then. Something very bad. My mother flew over and brought me back to Sydney and it took me a long time to recover. I completely lost my memory of my time here. But I'm starting to remember small things."

"My God." He exhaled then, staring up at the patch of sky through the open part of the roof. "Now I know for certain that it was you."

"Alban? What do you mean? Are you saying that you knew me from before? You did, didn't you?"

I waited breathlessly.

"It was brief," came the answer. "It was in a nightclub. We met and had a dance together. I was pretty drunk. And so were you. We went outside and talked for a bit. It was summer. I asked for your number, but you ran away from me. And that's the end of the story."

"Why didn't you tell me?"

"You said you'd never been to Scotland before. I even questioned you about that, and you assured me it was your first visit. You reminded me of that girl, but I thought my memory was wrong. Like I said, it was a brief meeting, and I was drunk. And you looked different. Your hair, for one thing. Your hair was red last time and you had a different hairstyle, or something." He sighed in confusion. "I thought there was the tiniest chance that it *was* you, but you didn't want me to know. I couldn't work it out."

A question formed in my mind that embarrassed me. But it was ridiculous to be embarrassed while my insides were slowly bleeding out.

"Did we…spend the night together?" I asked.

"You mean, did we sleep together?"

"Yes. *That*."

"No." His reply was swift. "We didn't go anywhere together. It was just a dance and a chat. Like an idiot, I poured my heart out. I'd had way too much to drink. I'm sure I scared you away."

"Was that what you meant when you said to me, *don't run away from me again*?"

Dropping his head, he nodded. "I didn't mean to say that. It just came out. I think, subconsciously, I must have known you were the same girl. But I kept telling myself that you couldn't be. Because if it was you, then it made no sense at all that you were here and pretending to be someone else."

"But...why were you in a nightclub dancing with girls back then anyway? You were married. To Jessica," I breathed. "Forget it. It's not my business. I—"

He closed his eyes. "Jessica and I had been separated. The marriage wasn't working."

"Oh...."

I wanted to keep asking him questions, to find out the answers to everything buzzing in my head, but I felt myself sliding into a thick mire. As if I was still in the peat marsh, with the mud enveloping me.

I heard Alban calling my name, but I couldn't answer.

42

ELODIE

EVERY TIME ELODIE tried to run away from the playhouse, it loomed before her. One minute she thought she was in a dream but the next minute she wasn't sure. The minute after that, she felt as if she were a tree—a larch—in the forest, unable to move and unable to run.

The playhouse never used to be a bad thing. It had been there as long as she could remember. Ever since she was small, her father would take her for a walk through the woods and he'd tell her about the playhouse. He'd tell her stories about back when he was a kid, like her. She loved hearing those stories.

But the playhouse had become a bad place, now.

The dark shadows inside seemed like they could jump out and eat her alive.

Someone was inside the playhouse, roaming about.

A tall man.

And then suddenly, she was inside the playhouse, too.

She saw the man's face.

Peyton.

Her mind whirled. Like leaves in a windy forest.

Peyton was the one who chased her through the forest.

He was the one who made her go inside the playhouse.

He reached out to her.

A bunch of pills sat in the palm of his gloved hand. "Have these, kid. They're safe, don't worry. They'll just make you feel sleepy."

She didn't want them. She didn't want to be here with Peyton.

But he stood there with his hand out, with the pills.

She was only sure of one thing—he wasn't going to let her go.

43

ISLA

VOICES SURROUNDED ME, drifting on slow currents.

A deep warmth penetrated me, balmy on my face. Fire crackled, smoky scents in the air.

The storm raged outside but it no longer felt like it could tear me into the sky and carry me away.

I felt a tugging sensation on my stomach.

My eyes cracked open.

I was in the McGregors' living room, somehow lying in the middle of it. Every chair and sofa seemed occupied with people, with yet more standing. But my vision was fuzzed, like looking through a glass pane covered in ice.

I guessed then that I had been put on top of the long, plush ottoman that I'd seen in here. From my memory, it was big enough to fit two people lying side by side and end to end. I touched the fabric to the side of me, running it between my fingers and then turned to look. White sheets had been placed beneath me. I tried to look and see what was happening to me, but I was too weak to sit.

I noticed Jessica kneeling beside me, then, scissors in her hand.

I cried out in alarm, my voice so hoarse I could barely hear myself.

"Isla," she said soothingly, "we're getting your wound clean. I had to cut away some of your clothing so that we could clean away the mud."

Aubrey and Nora appeared—Aubrey handing Jessica a jug of water. Jessica poured the warm water at an angle over my stomach. Nora mopped up the water spill with white towels. Jessica then spread a cream on my skin. Working quickly, she began taping up my skin. I felt my flesh being pulled together. Jessica then pressed bandages over the tape, fixing them with more tape.

"This is the best I can do, I'm afraid," Jessica told me. "The cut is as clean and as sterile as I can get it. You've lost a lot of blood, but your blood pressure is better now. We can't get an ambulance here yet, but you'll be taken to hospital as soon as one can get through the roads."

I nodded, trying to process what she'd just told me.

"How long has it been since your last tetanus needle?" she asked me.

Tetanus? I couldn't think. "When I was still at school. I'm not sure."

"Sounds like you'll be okay," she said reassuringly. There was a strain in her eyes that belied her calm expression. Perhaps it was because Jessica's home was her place of sanctuary from the world, and tonight, the world had invaded it.

"God, you scared us." Aubrey squeezed my arm. Her eyes were red, her face drained. Her fingers trembled on my arm.

"Aubrey...." I didn't know what to say to her.

She shook her head, stopping me. "Kirk's got my brother out in the kitchen." A bright tear slid down her cheek. "I never want to see him again. Ever."

"I'm so sorry," I whispered.

"I hate him. I didn't have a clue." Each word seemed to catch fire and burn as she spoke it. She bent her head, sobbing.

I eyed the room, searching for Stella. I found her sitting with her legs up on a sofa—wrapped in a blanket, one eye swollen and bruised. She stared back and a silent message passed between us. *We made it.* No one but Stella and I knew what it had been like in the stone ruins, trapped in Peyton's hands. And no one but Stella knew what it had been like over the months that Peyton had been abusing her, when she was just twelve.

Rory and Camille sat on either side of Stella. Rory nodded at me, his expression looking half numbed, half in shock. I returned a tight smile of apology.

Around the rest of the room, I could see Hamish and Charlie Keenan. And Alban. Alban sat in an armchair, draped in a blanket, his eyes closed. He must have half-frozen to death up there on the moor without his jacket and overcoat. He'd given both of those to me.

Diarmid was standing and looking out at the forest through the glass wall, his posture rigid, hands in fists by his sides. Wind battered snow against the glass panels.

Beyond the half-wall that housed the kitchen, Kirk must be guarding Peyton. Aubrey had said they were both there.

Rhiannon wasn't in the room anywhere that I could see. I guessed she was upstairs, asleep.

"Could you fold some towels and elevate Isla's legs a little?" Jessica instructed Nora.

Nora set about doing what Jessica had told her, then stood and addressed the room. "Anyone want a tea or coffee?"

When no one answered, Nora said, "Okay, I'll go make some and bring in a tray, and you can all sort yourselves out. I think poor Kirk might need a hot drink, too." Nora bustled from the room.

Rory rose and walked across to me, sighing loudly and shaking his head. "Isla, can't tell you how glad I am you're okay. At least, I hope you'll be okay. I had no idea what happened to you until I got a call through to Alban."

"Today was so confusing," I admitted to him. "You did good, Rory."

"Ach, tonight was a terrible way to get your resolution," he said.

I knew that he meant Peyton.

A deep frown drew Camille's dark eyebrows together, her lipsticked mouth warping into a grimace as she glared at her husband. "Just what—*exactly*—is going on here? You went somewhere today with Isla? Just the two of you?"

Rory's hands twitched as he held up his palms. "Camille, this isn't the time or place."

"Don't try to silence me, Rory," Camille said. "It's a simple question. Did you go somewhere with Isla today or not?"

He sighed. "We went to see an old church, if you must know. Isla needed to get to the church, but she had no transport. I offered to take her. It was—"

Camille made a scoffing sound. "An old church that she needed to get to? Aye, right. Not so pure yourself, are you, Rory?"

Jessica's head jerked up, eyes widening in alarm. "Would everyone mind keeping the arguments to a bare minimum? We have two patients here."

"I'm sorry," Camille said. "Forgive me, Jess. Rory was getting me a wee bit riled." Taking a breath, she turned to him. "Let's fix this. As soon as the storm dies a bit, we'll all walk across to my parents' house —you, me, Hamish, my parents and Stella. We'll stay there overnight, and tomorrow, we'll take Stella home with us. Where she belongs."

Rory twisted his head from side to side, keeping his voice respectfully low. "We can't take her home. She's a patient at the hospital. She needs medical care—for her cuts and bruises now as well."

"She's *my* daughter," Camille fumed. "I'm not having her sent back to the unit. They didn't do a very good job of keeping her safe, now did they? Look what happened."

Rory swallowed, lowering his head. "What happened was that Stella decided it was time to speak up." He turned to Stella, giving her a warm smile. "And we're glad that you did."

A small, exhausted smile flittered on Stella's lips.

Camille put her arm around Stella, pulling her close and kissing her temple. "Yes, good for you, honey. You've told the police and it's all over now. That disgusting man will be going to jail, and you've got nothing more to worry about."

Stella recoiled, her expression going stone cold. "You didn't think he was disgusting when he was touching *you*."

Camille moved back, blinking. "That's enough—"

Hamish eyed Camille, his mouth agape.

Rory's expression swiftly changed, his eyes widening. "*Peyton Chandlish* is the guy you've been seeing, Camille? *That's* who you've been cheating on me with?"

Camille's entire body stiffened. "Of course not. For God's sake,

Rory, this isn't something for public discussion. Jess asked for quiet—"

Jessica nodded. "Yes, please. We're all trapped here together. This isn't the time to air your dirty laundry."

Camille's mouth flapped open and shut and open again, as if it had become a useless contraption attached to her face. Her nostrils flared as she gaped at Jessica. "Dirty laundry? *Dirty laundry?* How dare you? All this pretense you go on with. Jessica McGregor, the perfect wife and mother. Well, you don't get to be innocent in all this. Why don't you tell Alban what his good little wife has been up to?"

Alban was awake now, staring at his wife. "Tell me what, Jess?"

"Leave it alone, Camille. Please," Jessica begged helplessly, pulling herself to her feet. "Rhi is asleep upstairs and—"

"Oh, shut up about your precious child," Camille snapped. "Rhiannon this. Rhiannon that. You treat her like a China doll. Like everyone has to tiptoe around you just because you've got a baby. Well, guess what, Jess, people spit out babies every damned day. You're not special."

"Okay, you've had your say." A warning tone entered Jessica's voice. "Leave it there. I'm going to go check if you've woken her."

"Oh no, you don't." Camille crossed her arms. "I just got outed publicly. Now it's your turn. We were *both* seduced by Peyton Chandlish. We had crushes on him when we were teenagers. And when he came after each of us during the last few years...we were like putty in his hands. He played us."

Letting the blanket fall away, Alban stood. "Jess? You...and Peyton? Is that true?"

Jessica's lower lip trembled. "Nothing ever happened. He just used to come around sometimes. As friends. We were all friends, once."

Alban was locked in a direct gaze with his wife. "I don't believe this. *Peyton.*"

Jessica's skin was chalky. "It was mostly just when we were separated, Alban. I needed a friend. I didn't know that he was—" Jessica glanced across at Stella, stricken, before facing Alban again. "I didn't know. And you can't say you weren't going to clubs with your friends during that time. How do I know what you got up to? I was at home with Elodie. I couldn't exactly go out partying."

"I didn't sleep with anyone," Alban retorted.

Jessica's eyes were huge, innocent. "Neither did I. I promise you, I didn't sleep with Peyton. He wanted to...but *I* didn't."

Camille made a short, spluttering laugh. "Is that a twist of the knife in my back, Jessica? He wanted you, but you didn't want him? You were always the pretty one, weren't you, Jess? The pretty, pretty tease. The one who got Alban. Now you're the one who turned down Peyton."

The muscles in Jessica's jaw twitched and grew tight. "Well, I was right to turn him down, as it's turned out."

"How was I supposed to know?" Camille exploded. "I didn't have a clue what he was doing to my daughter."

No one spoke.

It was easy to tell that everything that was being said now had been simmering for a long time. The mood in the air was feverish, boiling. Rory, Camille, Alban and Jessica stood locked into position —their sudden silence heavy as the blanket of snow outside.

It was Stella who broke the quiet, her voice small but with a power in it I hadn't heard before. "You knew, Mum. Because I told you—"

Camille drew her arms in protectively, her expression crumbling as she turned to her daughter. "I thought you were just saying things because you didn't want Peyton coming around. I never thought that Peyton could be capable of—"

"You didn't *want* to know!" Stella accused her. "Whenever I tried to tell you, you shut me down. You told me I was making things up."

Camille cried freely now. "Please. This is like a knife in my back, Stella. I understand that you're upset. You've been through a night-mare tonight, but I'm hurting, too. Look at me. I'm in so much pain, sweetie."

Jessica inhaled a deep breath, seeming relieved that the accusa-tions had bounced away from herself. "Look, we're all in a terrible situation here. Stuck together in this blasted storm. I'm going to have to request that everyone calm down. Yes, we've all got things we wish didn't happen. But I'll remind you we have a very ill person in the room. And, Stella, you need rest. This isn't good for you right now. Maybe we should all just stay quiet now. We're not helping things."

The last thing Jessica had spoken repeated itself in my mind: *Maybe we should all just stay quiet now. We're not helping things.*

Then another voice rang out inside me, saying: *Stay quiet. You're not helping yourself.*

Why did I just think of that?

My mind spun with memories.

Cold, dark room.

Candles.

Rosary beads.

Cross and rose.

Piano.

44

ISLA

AND THEN I SAW HER—THE person standing over me in that dirty room in the old church.

I saw her face in the flickering candlelight.

I heard her voice.

Jessica.

I stared as she knelt next to me, packing away the things from her medical kit.

It was Jessica who'd been with me in that room.

I could see an image of Jessica pacing up and down in the room at the church. Bending down over me while pain wracked my body. Speaking the words: *Stay quiet. You're not helping yourself.* And then saying: *I don't think she's breathing.*

My gaze switched to her medical kit. It was the same bag she had with her at the church. I remembered it.

What did you do to me, Jessica?

She noticed my eyes on her, a crease forming on her pale forehead. "Isla, are you all right?"

My words came out in a whisper. "It was *you*...."

"Hmmm?" she murmured.

"It was you, in the church."

"What church?" She didn't look at me now, carefully fitting everything back into the kit.

"The old church that Rory was speaking about. Peyton was there…and *you*. Two years ago."

Her fingers froze as she picked up a roll of bandages. "I'm not sure what you're talking about. You weren't here years ago."

"Yes, I was." I watched her carefully.

Alban seemed to catch onto the quiet conversation between Jessica and myself. He stepped across to us. "Isla? You're not saying that Jess was at that church, too? Surely not?"

Before I could answer, Jessica tilted her head up to her husband, a smile brightening her face. "Don't get upset with her. It's common to be a bit delirious after something this awful. All the trauma and blood loss."

Jessica probed her medical kit and pulled out a bottle of pills.

"Silly me. I forgot to give you a couple of these, Isla."

"What are they?" Alban asked.

"Oh, just something to help her relax." Jessica nodded. "They'll help with the pain."

I glanced from Alban to Jessica. "I don't want the pills."

"Perhaps we should take Isla upstairs and let her get some decent rest, then," said Jessica, no longer talking to me directly.

"I'll take her," Alban offered.

"No, you've done enough already," said Jessica quickly. "You already carried her all the way here across the moor, and you need rest, yourself. Hamish can do it. He's caused enough trouble tonight and needs to redeem himself."

Stella slowly crept across to the ottoman on which I was lying. She picked up the bottle of pills that Jessica had just put down.

"These are like the pills that Peyton used to give me." Stella gazed at the label, a look of disgust forming on her bruised face.

Snatching them away, Jessica dropped the bottle into her pocket. "All bottles of pills look similar." A smile stretched thinly on her face.

"They're *exactly* the same," Stella insisted.

Jessica sucked her lips in. "They're a very common medication."

Stella's voice quivered. "Peyton told me you gave them to him. He said you were a nurse and you'd told him that sometimes, girls going through puberty need some extra sleep. He'd give me the pills and do things to me that I don't remember properly. Bad things."

"Jess?" Alban eyed his wife. "*Answer me this.* Did you give Peyton the drugs?"

Jessica's hands retreated into her pockets. "It slipped my mind. I did, a few times. It was a long time ago. He'd been having trouble sleeping. He was a friend of ours, Alban. Why wouldn't I help him out? I'd no idea he was giving them to poor wee Stella. I swear I never told him to give them to *her.*"

An odd look came over Alban's face. He reached to take the bottle of pills from Jessica's pocket. He inspected the label closely, his breaths becoming ragged. "Jess. These are the same kind of pills that our Elodie was forced to take."

Jessica mouthed the name, *Peyton.* Her arms reached around her stomach as if she were physically ill. A sharp cry wrung from deep in her throat.

Alban's voice sounded like stone being crushed to dust. "It can't have been Peyton who killed our daughter, can it? *Can it?* It's impossible, right? He was in Inverness at the time. His alibi was rock solid."

My breath caught. The way that Peyton had paced about in the ruined house shot into my mind. In straight lines. Like an aimless soldier. Like the path that Elodie's abductor had taken out of the forest. But I'd read the alibis of the neighbours here at Braithnoch Square. Peyton had been in the clear.

"He was here in Greenmire at the time," Jessica whispered, her eyes huge and suddenly dazed. "He went to Inverness later."

Alban shook his head. "You didn't tell the police that, Jess—"

"I didn't tell because I never thought in a million years that—" she began, but her words tore away from her.

A horrified realisation rose in Alban's eyes. "It *was* Peyton. And *this* house is where those pills came from. The drug that killed our daughter."

Aubrey cried out, turning to stare at Diarmid.

Rory walked up behind Stella protectively. "Are you okay?"

Tears streamed down Stella's face. "No one would listen. Elodie told me the same bad stuff that Peyton told me. I told her to stay away from Peyton. I tried to tell Mum, but she said I was just being silly. I came back to Greenmire to tell, but I didn't know how. I thought everyone would blame me."

A roar burst from Alban's chest. "I should have killed him up on the moor." He charged forward.

Rory and Hamish raced to hold Alban.

"Don't destroy your life." Rory battled to keep Alban back. "You've got Rhiannon. Don't do it."

Jessica's eyes went dead. She packed away the rest of the kit, methodically, piece by piece. Everything except for the scissors. I watched her drop the scissors into her jacket pocket, her expression absent.

She took stiff steps out of the room while everyone's eyes were on the raging Alban.

I watched her walk towards the kitchen, her hand inside the pocket in which she dropped the scissors. There was something very wrong about her movements. Almost robotic.

I knew what she was planning to do.

I called Alban's name, but he didn't hear me. In his blind rage, he wasn't capable of hearing me.

My breath stilled in my chest.

Jessica's scream shattered the air, clean and sharp.

Something—a chair maybe—skidded and crashed across the kitchen floor. Kirk's yell was drowned by her frenzied cascade of shrieks.

Diarmid rushed into the kitchen.

Seconds later, he staggered into the living room to face everyone, his eyes wide and dazed. "She's stabbed him. She stabbed Peyton."

People ran past me, into the kitchen.

Camille restrained Stella, keeping her from going, too.

Five minutes later, everyone knew that Jessica had stabbed Peyton in his carotid artery using a pair of scissors and that Peyton was dead.

One by one, everyone returned to the living room, dropping into seats, faces numb, heads limp, voices as sober as mourners at a funeral.

Aubrey clung to Diarmid as he made a phone call.

Kirk entered the living room, dropping into an armchair. He looked lost as to what action to take. He ended up allowing Jessica to go upstairs as long as someone accompanied her. She could remove her blood-spattered clothing, but it had to be kept in a plastic bag. Nora Keenan volunteered to go with her.

The house plunged into silence again.

Alban, his face set in a stony shock, stood staring into the flames of the fire for a moment before walking off to his office. He didn't want anyone with him, saying he needed to be alone. I pictured him sitting in his office and staring at that photograph of the forest on his wall, finally knowing who abducted Elodie. Picturing Alban like that crushed me.

Rory and Hamish helped me from the ottoman to the sofa, pushing a footrest under the leg with the stitches. My head and body began to feel fiery hot, my flesh prickling under the blanket.

A slow terror pulsed in my mind. Had an infection whipped up inside me? There were no antibiotics here, no help.

As minutes went past, the storm eased, the baying wind sounding distant now and no longer trying to knock down the house.

A loud motor hammered up the driveway outside, then stopped abruptly.

Police? Ambulance? No, it didn't sound like either of those.

Kirk went to the door. The people entered and spoke with Kirk out in the kitchen.

When the people entered the living room, I saw that they were Gus and Deirdre Chandlish. They must have come from their house in some kind of all-terrain vehicle. I guessed that the call Diarmid had made was to his parents, to tell them that Peyton was dead.

There'd been no screaming or crying at the sight of their son dead out on the kitchen floor. Gus stood resolutely, as straight as a soldier waiting for war, every muscle in his jaw taut. Deirdre—her face blanched of colour—silently held her arms out to her children, Diarmid and Aubrey.

Aubrey fled to her mother's arms.

Diarmid walked up to them, but he stopped a short distance away. His mother kissed the top of Aubrey's head, extending an arm. "Diarmid...?"

Diarmid shook his head slowly, his blue eyes hard as flint. "This could have ended a long time ago."

Deirdre smoothed Aubrey's hair, her lips pressing together as she frowned. "This is a time for family to stick together. We've come to take you two home, so that neither of you have to stay in this house with the…with your brother."

Diarmid's expression remained unchanged. "But everyone else in this house has to stay locked in here with him. Every single person here has been hurt by what he's done. And you both just let it happen. That's why you didn't come the first time I called you, isn't it? You always knew he'd get arrested one day. And you wanted nothing to do with it."

Aubrey's eyes were huge as she extracted herself from her mother's arms, staring from Diarmid to her parents in confusion.

Deirdre shrank into herself, her shoulders shaking. Her hand clapped over her mouth as if she had vomited. She exchanged a long glance with her husband. She collapsed to her knees. "We should have done something about him years ago. Why didn't we…?"

A vague look of disgust crossed Gus Chandlish's face. "Get up off the floor. As if we're not dealing with enough already."

Deirdre sat back on her heels, unable or unwilling to rise to her feet again. It was as if everything that had once been Deirdre Chandlish had flatlined, and this was all that was left. When she spoke again, her voice strained from deep within her lungs, breathy and abject. "You knew something was wrong with him, Gus. *You knew that.* Always covering up for him. The photos of young girls he hid away. The mementoes he kept in that damned box. The way he bullied Aubrey and Diarmid. The way he marched about like a damned soldier every time he was upset or angry. Even stringing that damned bogle up in the tree a week ago. He was wrong in the head. But you just wouldn't have it."

I eyed her in shock. She and Gus had known about Peyton for a long time. A vision of the hanged scarecrow stole into my mind. Why did Peyton do that?

Aubrey stared at her parents with red, wet eyes, her face grown white. "You both knew all that and you covered it up? Why? *Why?*"

"I can tell you why," said Diarmid, barely controlling himself, a rage underlining every word he spoke. "Because the company and the Chandlish name were more important. They let him get away with

323

everything, Aubrey. You never believed me when I told you it was Peyton who put straw under your pillow during the night and made those stupid damned noises on the stairs. He got a sick thrill out of scaring a little girl out of her skin, making her believe that the bogles were coming to eat her. You believed Peyton because he was always able to put on a good show. He fooled everyone. And now look what he's done."

Gus's response to all of it was to stand even straighter. "It's over now. Peyton's gone. Nothing can be done about any of it now."

Deirdre's chin quivered. "Is that all you can bloody well say? That's it?"

Seconds ticked and decayed in the silence that followed.

I watched the surreal scene play out, my mind crowding with questions while my body steadily grew hotter and hotter. I felt myself separating from the room, my thoughts fuzzing and my head weighing heavily on my shoulders. My temperature felt as if it was still rising.

Gus turned his head away from his wife, gazing through the plate glass wall. "It's a good snow out there. We need the blizzards to come through every now and again. Wipe the slate clean. Make everything right again."

Deirdre stared up at him open mouthed.

A clattering of feet sounded on the wooden stairs in the hallway.

Nora Keenan came rushing into the room. "Did Jessica come down here?"

Officer Kirk jumped to his feet. "No, she didn't."

Alban sprinted from the office. "You don't know where Jess is? Isn't she with Rhiannon?"

Nora shook her head. "She insisted on me fetching a toy that the little one had left in the blanket box in your bedroom, Alban. But I went through the box and couldn't find it. And when I came back to tell her, she was gone."

Alban grasped her arms. "Where's Rhiannon?"

A look of fear entered Nora's eyes. "She must have taken her."

Outside the house came the roar of a car engine.

Alban and Kirk sprinted from the room together.

45

ISLA

The next year. March.

THEY FOUND Jessica in her SUV a short distance up the road. The snow drifts had prevented her from getting very far. She'd had Rhiannon wrapped in a blanket and strapped into the same seat belt as herself. From what I'd heard, Jessica had been dazed and uncommunicative.

Sometime after that, emergency crews had begun clearing the roads around Greenmire. Ambulances and police had finally been able to get through. After a forensics team had come and gone, Peyton's body had been taken away—wrapped in a sheet and zipped into a body bag.

I hadn't seen any of that. Greer told me the details much later—she'd driven straight to Greenmire as soon as the roads were clear.

Stella and I had arrived in hospital by ambulance. Deirdre Chandlish had been taken to hospital, too, suffering from shock.

I'd undergone immediate surgery on my stab wound and had the stitches on my leg redone—which had opened up again—with treatment given for the infection that had begun to rage through my body.

The doctors told me I came close to dying. Alban's peat moss and Jessica's wound cleaning had been lifesavers.

Later, Stella had been sent away to a special retreat, to rest and recover. Her mental health had been severely impacted and she wasn't doing well. She wasn't having contact with anyone from Greenmire.

I'd returned to Sydney for the months of recovery that followed. There were court cases yet to come, but for now, it was a kind of purgatory for everyone. There were still so many unanswered questions and so many judgments yet to happen.

———

POTTED PALM TREE leaves ruffled in a gentle breeze as I sat in my mother's sunroom in Sydney, curled in a macramé hanging chair that had been here ever since I could remember.

I knew that Alban would take a dim view of this room, with its potted plants and palm tree wallpaper. But it was home to me. And I needed *home*. My trip to Scotland had swept me into dark places I hadn't known existed.

My brother sat on a chair nearby, strumming his guitar. He and I had stayed up until the early hours last night, playing cards and talking. Yesterday was our Dad's birthday. It was an unspoken rule between Jake and I that on Dad's birthday each year, we would play cards in the sunroom and drink his favourite Royal Salute Scotch whisky. I'd only had a tiny glass of the Scotch, but I could almost still taste the smoky notes of marmalade, hazelnut and vanilla on my tongue.

Our dad used to sit in this room every Sunday and read the newspapers, a glass of Scotch next to him. Then he'd play cards with Jake and me.

I'm feeling lost, Dad. Wish you were still here.

"Gotta go, sis'." Jake pulled himself to his feet, his hair falling across his face as he set the guitar against a wall. "You okay?"

"Yeah," I lied.

"You look like shit. But not as bad as you did when you first came back." He grinned to show that he didn't mean it.

326

I pulled a mock offended face at him. "Thanks, brother. Where are you going?"

A sudden shy look embedded itself into his face and he shoved his hands into the pockets of his jeans. "Out."

"Out to see Charlotte again? I'm happy for you, Jake. It's going well, huh?"

"Settle. We're just friends."

"Friends who spend every free minute of the day together."

He shook his head dismissively as he left the room, but I could tell he was smiling.

In the stillness that followed his absence, I felt a sudden rush of anxiety shooting from my stomach into my throat. I wanted to ask him to stay and keep playing his guitar. It was soothing. But he had places to go and I had to sort out my own stuff.

Images began looping in my head. *The church. Peyton. Jessica. Trent. Elodie.*

Attacks of anxiety like this came and went constantly, making my skin burn and adrenalin chug through my veins.

The mental fatigue of not knowing exactly what happened to me in the old church constantly ground me down. So far, Jessica had refused to talk.

I could see her so clearly, standing over me in that room. And I could hear her voice, above the din of that damned piano.

She was being held in custody. I knew that Jessica was up on at least two charges. The first was manslaughter, for stabbing Peyton to death. Her lawyer was going for a plea of temporary insanity, due to the extraordinary circumstances and the state that Jessica was found in after she tried to drive away with Rhiannon. The second set of charges concerned the illegal supply of sleeping medication to children and me for the purpose of abuse. As far as I understood, that court case was to determine three things: whether Jessica supplied the drugs to Peyton knowing that he was going to use it on Elodie, Stella and me, whether she took part in any of the abuse, and whether she directly gave any of the medication to us.

I could understand what Jessica did in relation to killing Peyton, but the thought of the second charge being true was sickening. Had she really been involved in any of that? It wasn't looking good for her that she'd withheld information about Peyton's whereabouts on the night Elodie was abducted. And I knew for certain that she'd been at the church and stood over me while my body was twisting in pain.

I was deeply conflicted. She'd seemed genuinely shocked when she was told what Peyton had been doing with the medication she'd given him. And she'd cleaned and bandaged the wound that Peyton had inflicted on me and taken care of me. But was all of that just because she knew that would be expected of her? I didn't know.

The only bright spot—if it could be called that—was the discovery of who had abducted Elodie. And the knowledge that this person was never going to harm another child. Now, Greenmire knew for certain that it wasn't a passing stranger who'd chased an eight-year-old child through the wood that night. It had been one of their own. I could sense the town in mourning—a fresh mourning for Elodie but also mourning for their lost innocence. The predator had been among them all that time.

It had been Peyton who'd taken the photographs of young girls in the changing rooms at dance practice a decade or so ago. It was Peyton who'd assaulted Stella when she was twelve and caused her to run away from home. It was Peyton who'd been grooming Elodie.

People speculated that he hadn't meant to give Elodie a lethal dose of sleeping medication. He'd probably given Elodie the same dosage he'd given Stella, but Stella at age twelve had already been the height of a short adult woman.

I'd had two weepy conversations with Aubrey over the phone. She'd kept apologising for Peyton, but what he'd done wasn't her fault. She told me she'd been certain it was Diarmid who'd tried to frighten her with the tattie bogles when she was a child. It had been Diarmid who'd first told her the myth about the tattie bogles—but then, lots of children in Greenmire scared each other with those stories. The old myth was confined to Greenmire, apparently.

I learned a lot about Aubrey and her past from those conversations. From the time she was five, she'd begun finding straw on the stairs and under her pillow in the morning, and she'd be terrified. Peyton had been fifteen then. She'd developed a phobia of the scarecrows. When she was a teenager, she'd carved faces in wood for the scarecrows and hammered them into the stakes. She'd done that to try to gain some control back over the scarecrows. All the time, it was Peyton who'd been playing a sick game with her.

My mother poked her head around the doorframe. "Isla, you've got visitors. Are you up to seeing anyone?"

No, I wasn't up to seeing anyone. I was back in my cocoon. Retreating from the world.

"Who is it?" I asked tentatively.

"It's Greer Crowley and a friend of hers, Kelly."

"Really?" I said, shocked. "Here?"

Mum nodded. "Will I—?"

I inhaled. "Yes, of course."

She vanished back into the hallway.

Unfolding my legs, I tried to look as if I hadn't been sitting in the one spot since I'd woken this morning, which in actual fact, I had. I hadn't showered since yesterday and my hair was in a messy knot. I wasn't looking like the image of a professional photographer. *Rational me* knew that didn't matter anymore. The whole thing about Greer hiring me to do the portfolio was in tatters. The magazine feature was no longer going to happen. But still, it was hard to let people see the real me.

Greer and Kelly walked in.

With smiles on their faces and dressed in light summer clothes, the two of them could have been any carefree couple, in any summery place in the world. The last time I'd seen them both, I'd been rushing with them through a Scottish wood in a desperate race to find a young, suicidal girl—in a greyish drizzle close to twilight. All wrapped up in bulky winter gear. And afterwards, there'd been tears and misunderstandings between Greer and Kelly.

The way they looked now, I barely recognised them.

Greer squealed. "Isla! Hope this isn't too big of a surprise. But… you did invite me at one point. So here we are."

"Can't believe it!" Standing, I hugged them both. "So good to see you two."

"We just met your brother out there," Kelly told me. "He's a wee bit cute, isn't he?"

I laughed. "He's always been cute. When he finally realises it, he'll be dangerous."

Mum brought in glasses of fresh orange juice, and we all sat at the glass-topped wicker table—small-talking about the weather and Scottish food and Sydney landmarks. Everyone was steadfastly avoiding talking about the things that had happened the night Peyton Chandlish died.

"So," said Greer, smiling brightly, "Kelly and I can't wait to see this city of yours, Isla. I'm going to hold you to your promise of showing me around."

My mother gasped in delight. "Oh, there's so much to see. We could all go together."

"I was hoping you'd say that," said Greer. "I've seen you and Isla in your Instagram pictures together. You two look like you have so much fun."

"It's a plan." Mum glanced at me. "If you're up to it, Isla."

I nodded, a grin slipping into my face as I turned to Greer. "I have to put myself back out there at some point or other. And you went out of your way to make me feel at home in Scotland. Mum and I would like to do the same for you and Kelly, here."

"Poor Kelly desperately needed some time away from everything's that been going on," said Greer. "The whole thing with Stella has been a big shock. And I couldn't think of a better place to take her than here."

"Well, I'm glad you came. How is Stella?" I asked. "Is she…back with her mother?"

Kelly shook her head. "No. She didn't want to. And besides, the child protection unit wouldn't have allowed it. So, we gave Stella the choice of staying with me or going to live with her grandparents. But she chose someone we didn't expect. *Rory*. He was as surprised as anyone."

"I wouldn't have expected that either," I mused.

"Yep. She was always so negative about poor old Ror'." Kelly gave a wry smile. "But as we've found out since, that was just because it seemed to Stella that he was supporting Camille. Stella's realised now that Camille kept Rory totally in the dark about Peyton. Oh, it's terrible. Something that I didn't understand is why a paedophile like Peyton was hanging around my sister after Stella left town. But we know why now. Camille was giving piano lessons to three young girls in her home each week. And that's why the bastard was going there so much. Seems that he'd zeroed in on one poor lass named Amy, and he'd been busily grooming her, even taking over the piano lessons at times."

I gasped. "This must all be so hard on you and your family."

"Yes," Kelly replied. "My mother is beside herself. Hamish has been drinking heavily and not helping anyone. Rory is divorcing Camille. And Camille might be up on criminal charges yet, about her knowledge of what Peyton was doing to Stella, and maybe to Amy as well. I don't know how much she knew. My sister is trying hard with the victim angle, but she's not a victim. Why didn't I know what had been going on over there? I should have—" Kelly broke off, tears springing into her eyes.

Greer's arms came around her. "Camille chose wrong. But you didn't. You didn't know. And you kept Stella safe for two years." Greer's eyes were wet, too, as she glanced from my mother to me. "It was a hard choice for Stella to leave Kelly. She loves Kelly dearly. But she wanted to return to Greenmire and reconnect with her old schoolfriends."

Mum exhaled, her eyes wide at all she'd been hearing. "That poor girl. Isla told me all about her. I imagine she'll have a long road ahead of her."

"A very long road," agreed Kelly, sighing. She dabbed at her eyes with a tissue. "Would you mind if I use your bathroom?"

Mum rose. "I'll show you the way. This old house is a bit of a rabbit warren."

As Mum and Kelly left the room, Greer touched my arm. "How are you?"

I sucked my lips in tight. "I'm getting there."

"I just can't believe that all these things were happening under my nose. And Jessica…Goodness, I mean, she always seemed strung-out and over-anxious, but I never thought—" As she snipped her sentence short, her eyes squeezed shut. "Oh, listen to me, Miss talk-too-much. It's not up to me to speculate. It's up to the courts."

A slow wave of nervous exhaustion hit me. "The first court case is just a week away."

"Yes, it is. Which brings me to the other reason I came to Sydney.

I know you've been called as a witness for the prosecution in Jessica's trial. I wanted to come and give you some support in person. I mean, listen to you, so worried about how everyone is doing, while you've been to hell and back yourself. You need some TLC." She shivered, stroking her bare arms. "I've got goose bumps just thinking about that church. So eerie how you wanted to stop and photograph it that day."

"If not for that trip to Inverness, I wouldn't have seen the church. And I might never have remembered it."

"Life is strange," said Greer. "All these wee coincidences that sometimes lead to things we couldn't have imagined. I've had trouble turning my mind off at night. I keep thinking…if you hadn't realised that Stella was in the playhouse, she would have died. And Peyton would have kept on doing the awful things he'd been doing. And we might never have found out what really happened to Elodie." She rubbed eyes that suddenly seemed tired. "I shouldn't keep on and on with these thoughts. My mind is just like my mouth—never stops. But you know, the McGregors and the Keenans are like family to me. And you too, now. You're one of us, whether you like it or not." She smiled warmly.

I smiled back. "A part of me will always remain in Scotland. I'm sure of that." A question rose in my mind. I didn't want to ask it, but I had to know the answer. "Greer…why did you choose me—for the photography assignment? Did you have any clue I'd been in Scotland before?"

"Not the barest inkling. Don't sell yourself short. Your portfolio was simply the best. Your landscapes—they were the most stunning I'd seen. Not just among those photographers who applied for the job, but *anywhere*. You'd been shortlisted for a major award for goodness' sakes. You just seemed the right choice."

"Thank you. I shouldn't have asked. I just—"

"Don't apologise. It's been a confusing time for you, you poor thing. It seems that part of you knew what happened here and you needed a resolution."

"That's true. I didn't even know what was driving me at the time. As soon as I saw your ad, I began pushing myself so hard to get to Scotland. Now I know why."

———

THE FOUR OF us spent the next few days visiting the parks, museums and restaurants around the city. Mum was in her element—she loved Sydney with a passion.

When it was time for me to head back to Scotland for the court case, I had not only Mum on the plane with me, but Greer and Kelly.

Whatever was coming up next, I wasn't alone.

46

ISLA

THE BLEAK SCOTTISH sunrise had sputtered and dissolved into a dull, grey morning.

I ran through the drizzle with my mother and Greer to the Inverness courthouse. It was a high court where serious crimes were heard —solemn trials—with a Lord Justice General presiding. I watched the lawyers walk in with their wigs and robes and it suddenly all felt terrifying. I knew the way that I was feeling must be magnified many times for Jessica.

Immediately, I was whisked away to wait in a special room for witnesses for the prosecution.

The court case was about to start, but witnesses weren't allowed in the court room until they'd been questioned by the prosecutor. I already knew that Alban wouldn't be in the witness room. He was neither testifying for or against his wife. I didn't know most of the people in the witness room, except for Camille. Camille being there was a surprise to me, seeing as she was a good friend of Jessica's.

I'd been told that first up, all the prosecutor's evidence would be given to the jury—bottle of pills, blood test results, DNA and other items. After that, the expert witnesses who would explain the evidence would be called. I wouldn't be allowed to sit in the public gallery until after I'd had my turn at the stand.

Stella's testimony had already been given, in a police interview, and part of that testimony would be shown today, via a video. She wouldn't be present in the courtroom, due to her age.

The judge had closed the courtroom to the public and the media. We'd had to make special applications for support persons and family to be able to attend.

Before the court case was due to start, Jessica would be called to plead guilty or not guilty. If she pleaded guilty, the trial wouldn't proceed, and she'd face sentencing. Within minutes she'd pleaded innocent and I was informed that the trial would go ahead.

The next thing to happen was the assembling of the fifteen members of the jury. Jessica, with the advice of her defence lawyer, would attempt to reject any of the jurors that she thought might take a negative view of her.

It was two hours later that I was called to the stand.

People watched as I made my way across the floor. The room went pin-drop quiet, except for a shuffle of papers. The court room looked as if it had been furbished in the 1950s and left that way—the judge and lawyers in their wigs adding to the look of age and formality. The air smelled of wet shoes and clothing.

Jessica glanced my way and then turned her head sharply. She looked much the same as she had the day I'd first met her at Braithnoch. Carefully styled blonde hair. Elegant but nervous, with a tense bearing in her shoulders.

I knew now that she'd been hiding secrets.

I wondered if she was suffering as much as any mother ever had who'd made a terrible mistake. No matter what happened during the trial, she'd never get the chance to right the wrong she'd made. Elodie was gone and nothing could bring her back.

After I was sworn in, the prosecutor explained to the jury that I had suffered an acute illness two years ago. He asked that the jury refer to the notes of my illness given by my doctors and psychologist. He explained to them that I had a case of amnesia and that I'd almost completely forgotten my previous trip. He also informed them that they had my blood and DNA test results—evidence that showed I'd been present in the old church two years earlier.

The prosecutor then had me tell my story about travelling to the church with Rory and what I'd seen and remembered there. And I had to tell my account of being trapped in the house ruins at Braithnoch, including what Peyton said about me, the church and the person who'd sent him there.

The defence lawyer rose to her feet then. She was a small, pert woman, with thick black glasses perched on her nose, and she reminded me of a librarian. But she didn't speak like a librarian. She was intense, drilling me on every point that I'd spoken, trying to make my account sound as unreliable as she possibly could. My memory loss made that job easy for her. She also cast a great deal of doubt upon my blood sample—saying that it wasn't clear whether it was menstrual blood or not. She painted a picture for the jury of a student who didn't have much money and who might have needed to squat at an abandoned building for a few weeks—the old church. She speculated that the empty cans of food and rubbish had been mine.

The questions being fired from the defence lawyer were awful and humiliating and I couldn't wait to escape from the stand.

After the defence was done, the prosecutor re-examined me on some points, trying to affirm to the jury that I wasn't the crazy loon that the defence had made me out to be. But I wasn't feeling hopeful. Even *I* was starting to doubt myself. After all, if I couldn't remember that time of my life, anything could be true.

I went to sit in between my mother and Greer in the public gallery, my heart thudding.

Mum closed her hand around mine. "You did well, honey," she whispered.

I hadn't done well. I'd stumbled over my words. I'd had to relive that horrific night on the moor in front of all those people as well as try to explain events from the past that were fuzzy.

I was glad that Stella didn't have to take the stand in the courtroom.

The next witness for the prosecution was called to the stand— Camille Keenan.

Camille glanced about nervously, avoiding looking in Jessica's direction, her dark hair slicked into a neat bun and her lips glossed with red lipstick.

"Ms Keenan," began the prosecutor, "how long have you been friends with Jessica McGregor?"

"Ever since the first year of school," came the reply.

"How would you describe your friendship in recent years? Close or distant?"

"It was...close."

"How often did you see each other and what was the nature of the meetings?"

"At least once or twice a fortnight. Just to catch up over coffee at a café, or at each other's house."

"Ms Keenan, did you and Jessica ever discuss Peyton Chandlish?"

She fixed her eyes down at her hands, rubbing her knuckles together. "Yes."

"What did you discuss about him?"

"We both thought he was...attractive. We'd both crushed on him when we were teenagers, and so I guess when he started dropping around to see us, it seemed a bit of a thrill."

"Could you tell us specifically what Jessica said about Peyton?"

"She said...uh...well, you see, her marriage to Alban had been rocky for quite a while. And she said that if Alban didn't shape up then she might have a better option. She said...she said that Elodie wasn't an obstacle." Camille rushed her last words, then fell silent, sucking in a deep breath.

The prosecutor frowned—in a way that seemed practised, for the benefit of the jury. "Can you please give us Jessica's exact words about Elodie not being an obstacle?"

"She...Jess...said that Elodie wouldn't get in the way of her being with Peyton," Camille whispered. "Because Peyton was fond of Elodie."

"Could you please speak that louder, for the record?" the prosecutor instructed her.

Camille repeated her words, stammering.

"Ms Keenan," said the prosecutor, "we have a statement from you that concerns an unusual conversation you heard between Jessica and Peyton Chandlish. Can you tell us how you came to overhear it?"

"Yes," she responded. "This was the first time that I met Isla Wilson. She was walking away from my parents' house. I was walking along the same path. I'd heard that my daughter, Stella, was there and I wanted to see her. I also planned to…I planned to meet with Peyton. But when I talked to him on the phone, he told me he was too busy. Stella ran off when she heard that I was coming and so I decided to keep walking and go to see Peyton, anyway. The Chandlishes' house is just a bit further up that path. But when I got close, I heard him talking with someone. It was Jess. She seemed upset. I was curious, and I ducked behind a tree and crept closer in order to listen."

The prosecutor nodded. "Okay, now what did you hear?"

"Jess asked Peyton what he was going to do. Peyton said he was going to string *one of them* up because *her* father had died by a suicide hanging and he thought it would have more impact. He was laughing about it. Jess told him it might be going too far and that she'd find another way to get rid of *her*. Peyton grabbed Jess roughly, saying he was in too deep. Jessica said he wasn't the one who needed to worry—that *she* hadn't even seen his face last time."

"At the time, did you know who the person was that they were talking about?" asked the prosecutor.

"No."

"Did you realise at a later point who the person was?"

"Yes, I did," Camille answered. "Days later, when I heard about the scarecrow being strung up in the tree, I wondered if Isla was the woman they'd been talking about."

"Objection, my Lord," called the defence lawyer. "The witness is speculating on the meaning of words that she claims two others spoke."

"I'll allow it," said the judge. "The witness is answering Counsel's question without making any claims. Objection is overruled."

The prosecutor faced the jury. "You will see in your notes that a scarecrow was hoisted up in a tree directly outside the cabin in which Isla Wilson was staying. It had a noose around its neck and the appearance could be perceived as threatening." He gave the date and approximate time of the discovery. "We do in fact know that it was Peyton who put the scarecrow in the tree, because we have statements from his mother to say that she knew about this. A few days after her return from an overseas trip, Deirdre Chandlish found some instant photos in her son's home office, in their basement." The prosecutor instructed the jury to refer to copies of the photos they'd been given. "The photos were of the scarecrow when it had been cut with an axe from its original place on a hill and after it had been strung up in the tree. When she confronted her son, Peyton, he claimed it had been a harmless prank. Also, among the instant photographs, were pictures of Isla walking through the forest, including a day in which Isla visited the children's playhouse where Elodie McGregor was taken after she was abducted."

I listened, horrified, thoughts ricocheting in my head. Jessica knew about the scarecrow. It sounded as if it had been Jessica's plan to do something to scare me and make me leave. But Peyton had taken the prank too far. Maybe she'd simply wanted him to stomp around outside the cabin or something a lot more ordinary than the scarecrow idea. It had been Peyton stalking me the day I'd visited the playhouse. I guessed that he'd meant for me to see glimpses of him, to scare me. I wondered how long he'd been stalking me. He knew about my father dying by suicide. That meant he'd looked deep into my past. Maybe he had been watching me ever since that night in the church, to check if I'd started remembering anything.

I knew now where those bruises on Jessica had come from. Camille said that Peyton had grabbed Jessica.

The prosecutor flipped through his notes, looking through his tabs. "I have a statement from you, Ms Keenan, in which you say that you became intrigued with what was going on between Jessica and Peyton after that. Can you explain?"

"Yes," Camille answered. "It seemed that it could be a secret romance. Jess didn't react when Peyton got a bit rough with her. And the stuff they talked about in the conversation I overheard seemed to me like two people who were doing things in secret—"

The defence lawyer objected, but again, the judge allowed Camille's words to stand.

"I'll make the point here," said the prosecutor, "that we have an earlier statement from Isla Wilson, in which she gave an account of an entire bag of medication going missing from her cottage. This medication was her round of epilepsy drugs, which were vital to prevent seizures. It could be surmised that a campaign of terror was being mounted in order to force Miss Wilson to leave. First the stolen medication and then the very threatening scarecrow hung from a noose outside the cottage. To that end, it appears that Mrs McGregor and Peyton Chandlish were worried about Isla Wilson staying at Braithnoch, lest she start remembering—"

The defence lawyer objected again. The judge overruled the objection.

"As I was saying," said the prosecutor, after thanking the judge, "Mrs McGregor and Peyton Chandlish appeared to be worried that Isla would remember events from the previous time she spent in Scotland—events that had been wiped from her memory by her illness. Camille Keenan overheard Mrs McGregor saying to Mr Chandlish that he didn't need to worry because Isla hadn't seen his face last time. This suggests that Isla was either drugged, unconscious or sleeping at the time that Peyton had contact with her."

The prosecutor referred to his notes. "Ms Keenan, earlier we heard the testimony of a parent of one of the children who used to come to your house for piano lessons. Ms Lee Dunning. She stated that her child, Mia Dunning, then aged nine, had felt uncomfortable on a number of occasions when you had left the room and Peyton Chandlish had taken over the lessons. Ms Dunning stated that she spoke to you on one occasion about her misgivings concerning Peyton. Is this correct?"

"Yes," Camille said.

"What did she say?"

"She said Mia felt that Peyton had sat too close to her and touched her arms and hands and face more than was necessary."

"Ms Dunning said that you brushed her misgivings off. Is that correct?" the prosecutor asked Camille.

"No, I wouldn't say that. I listened, and I said that I wouldn't allow Peyton to take over her lessons again. I'd only done it in the past when I'd had to take a phone call or something like that. Peyton was often at my house during the afternoons I held piano lessons. I thought he was there to spend time with me. Obviously not."

Camille looked more miffed than horrified.

The prosecutor nodded encouragingly. "Did Peyton ever give Mia a piano lesson after Ms Dunning had the talk with you?"

"No," said Camille firmly. "He did not. I didn't allow it."

"We've heard the testimony from your daughter, Stella, via video," continued the prosecutor. "She tells that Peyton gave her sleeping pills on a number of occasions."

The prosecutor read out a list of things that Stella said Peyton had done to her. Tears sprung into Camille's eyes.

I hadn't heard the details before. My stomach twisted.

"Did you have knowledge that Peyton was giving Stella sleeping medication?" asked the prosecutor.

"No," Camille stated. "I saw the bottle a couple of times. He just said that they were for himself. He said that Jess had given them to him."

"Did you have knowledge that Peyton was doing the things to Stella that I just read out?"

She shook her head. "I never saw any of that."

"So, you didn't know that Peyton was molesting Stella?"

"No, I did not."

"Lastly, Ms Keenan," said the prosecutor, "what was your relationship with Peyton during the past few years up until the time of his death?"

She wiped tears away from her face with her palms, sniffing. "It's...complicated. I was happy in my marriage to Rory. I honestly loved Rory. But I'd always had a silly infatuation with Peyton. When he started paying me a lot of attention—coming around and chatting with me, I guess I felt flattered. We kissed a few times. We...slept together six times in the past four years. That was all. I shouldn't have. I regret it."

"Thank you, Ms Keenan," said the prosecutor, "that's all."

The defence then cross-examined Camille, trying to tear down her statements, asking if she was just making things up about Jessica in order to gain a plea deal for herself because she was up on child endangerment charges. Camille denied this vehemently. The defence also questioned Camille relentlessly about her affair with Peyton and her failure to report him when Stella had said he'd molested her.

The session in court was done for the day. All of the witnesses for the prosecution had been called.

Everyone filed out.

Mum hugged me as we walked out into the rain-soaked street.

"Are you all right? My heart was in my mouth the whole time you were up there on the stand."

"I feel like I want to vomit," I answered truthfully.

"Let's get you away from here," she said. "I wonder if anywhere here does peppermint tea?"

Alban—standing with Kirk Flanagan in the street—glanced my way. I couldn't help but wonder what he was thinking. I'd just testified against his wife. He looked troubled, angry.

Greer joined Mum and me at a small café. Mum ordered me a light lunch that I barely ate.

We headed back to Greer's after that to avoid the press, who were out in force on the streets. They hadn't been allowed in the courtroom and now they were looking for any morsel they could find.

Mum took over the kitchen that night, making us all a curry. We sat with big bowls of korma watching a comedy. But I couldn't focus on the movie. I dreamed of the church that night, over and over again, waking up in a sweat each time.

The three of us headed back into court at ten in the morning. At least this time, I wouldn't have to testify.

The defence was meant to begin their case with their own set of witnesses that the prosecutor already knew about, but a surprise witness took the stand first. Jessica.

A buzz of shocked voices spread around the courtroom, growing so loud that the judge had to call for quiet. No one had expected Jessica to testify.

Greer whispered to me that the prosecutor's case against Jessica must be strong for Jessica and her defence lawyer to have decided to do this.

I watched Jessica take uncertain steps to the stand, her back and head bent forward as if blown by a cold wind.

After she was sworn in, she straightened herself rigidly, hands folded over each other, spots of high colour in her cheeks.

The defence lawyer began by giving the date that Peyton abducted Elodie and asked Jessica why she left the house.

Jessica gave a deep nod, seeming to gather herself. "I was at home with Elodie, as usual. I realised I didn't have the ingredients I needed to make a cottage pie. Alban was on his way back from Edinburgh and would be with Elodie soon. And so, I told Elodie I'd run out and grab what I needed to make the pie."

"Understandable. It's a common experience of mothers to realise that they need to run down to the shops for ingredients to make dinner. What time did you go out?" asked the defence.

"I'm not certain. It was well before dark."

"What time would you normally start dinner?"

"Depending on the dinner, anytime between four and six. But on this day, I realised early that I needed more things to make dinner with."

"Okay. And where did you go immediately after you left the house?"

"I drove towards the Greenmire shops."

"What happened next?"

"I...didn't get there. I had a phone call. From a friend. This friend sounded panicked and afraid. I...felt that I needed to go and help them. As you do when a friend is in trouble."

"Of course," said the defence lawyer. "Who was this friend, Mrs McGregor?"

She cast her eyes downward. "Peyton."

"Peyton Chandlish?"

"Yes."

"Can you explain the entire incident to the court?"

"Peyton was in a tremendous panic, as I mentioned. He said he'd hit an icy patch somewhere on the A9 and caused an oncoming car to veer off the road. There was a young woman in the car. She was hurt. I told him to call an ambulance. But he was in shock and not responding rationally. He couldn't even tell me exactly where he was. As a nurse, all I could think was that there was a woman perhaps seriously hurt and she had no one to help her. I knew that Alban would be home for Elodie soon, and so I decided that the only thing I could do was to go and find them and help the woman. I drove along the road towards Inverness, looking out for headlights at the side of the road."

I listened intently.

"So, your training as a nurse took over," said the defence, "and you wanted to give medical attention to this woman. You were worried that she could even die if you didn't find her. Is that correct?"

"Yes."

"And did you find them?"

"Yes, I did. I found the two cars, parked near each other."

"What happened after that?"

"Peyton was dazed and wandering about," said Jessica. "And the woman was in her car. I examined her in the car. She had a minor head injury and some bruising. She seemed to be in pain. There was an old church at the scene. The woman entered the church and found a horrible old mattress and laid herself down on it. It seemed that she knew her way in there in the dark. I—I wondered if she was living there. There were foods cans and clothing nearby. She looked dirty and unkempt, which makes sense if she was squatting at there and—""

"Objection," called the prosecutor. "There is no evidence to say that Ms Wilson was living at the church."

The judge overruled the objection.

"Thank you, my Lord," said the defence. "Please continue, Mrs McGregor."

"Peyton seemed to snap out of his shock," said Jessica. "And I asked him to call an ambulance, which I thought he did. I couldn't do any more at the scene, and I had to get home to Elodie and so I left."

"Okay, so you assessed the woman for injuries as best as you could. How serious did you consider that her injuries were?"

"They appeared minor. But I still thought she needed to go to hospital for a proper check."

"Did you give the woman sleeping medication?"

"No. I brought out my medical kit from my car, which contained the medication. I must have dropped it at the scene. It was very dark in the church and hard to see."

"Did you observe the woman screaming?"

"At one point. I...asked her what was wrong, and she simply said she was scared. It seemed like a simple panic attack. I told her that help was on the way."

I shook my head silently. How could the intense pain I remembered feeling have come from a panic attack?

The defence lawyer continued. "We've heard the woman concerned—Isla Wilson—on record as saying that you said, '*Be quiet.*

You're not helping yourself and '*I don't think she's breathing*'. Is that correct?"

"I might have said something close to the first thing. I was starting to get labour pains at this point and I guess my bedside manner wasn't as gentle as it normally would be. But I didn't say the second. She was most certainly breathing."

No, Jessica, you did say that second thing.

But I was starting to doubt myself. Her version sounded so believable.

Was I wrong? Was it possible that as well as forgetting things, my mind had invented things that didn't even happen?

"So," said the defence to Jessica, "your labour started when you were in the church?"

"Yes."

"We've heard that Miss Wilson remembers Peyton carrying her and she also remembers seeing a tattoo on his lower neck. Do you know how these two things might have occurred?"

"Possibly, yes," said Jessica. "I asked Peyton to carry her out of the church and put her back in her car. I heard rats in the church and didn't want her left there. She might have seen his tattoo when he lifted her back into her car."

"Okay," said the defence. "And then what happened?"

"I drove back to Greenmire. The pains became so severe that I had to stop and pull over. I…I gave birth to my daughter Rhiannon on the side of the road."

"And I understand that you were approximately eight months pregnant at the time?"

"Yes."

"That must have been extremely painful and terrifying," said the defence lawyer.

"Objection, my Lord," called the prosecution. "Irrelevant."

"Overruled," said the judge. "We'll wait to see where the defence is taking this line of argument."

"Thank you, my Lord," said the defence, straightening her glasses. "My point is that Mrs McGregor was not in a state to be able to do anything at this time other than focus on the experience of a preterm birth. The labour came on rapidly, without pain relief of any kind, and then Mrs McGregor was forced to give birth alone, at the side of the dark A9."

The prosecution remained silent.

"Is that a correct summary, Mrs McGregor?" asked the defence lawyer.

Jessica nodded. "Yes. Very painful and very scary. I was worried the baby would die."

From the soft murmurs I heard around me, I could tell that many people in the gallery had swung to Jessica's side. Things hadn't sounded good for her during the prosecutor's questioning of his witnesses. But things had now taken a sharp turn.

Was this the true account and had Jessica just given the answers to all of my questions? Had the pain I'd felt come from a car accident and from the sheer panic I'd experienced afterwards? The panic could have been a seizure. Had I really been so short of money I'd been squatting at the church?

I understood now why Jessica had taken the stand. She wouldn't have been able to explain any of that story had she not testified. The prosecutor wouldn't have allowed her to.

"Mrs McGregor," continued the defence lawyer, "on this night, did you find out Isla Wilson's name?"

"No. She didn't tell me her name."

"Miss Wilson returned to your property two years later, to undertake a photography portfolio for your husband's architectural business. Is that correct?"

She nodded. "That's all correct."

"Did you recognise her as being the same woman from the night of the car accident?"

"Yes, I did."

"What was going through your mind at the time?"

"I thought she'd come to do harm to my family. I thought she might be mentally unstable. I was terrified of her."

I gasped. I'd had no idea that she was scared of me. I tried to see things from her point of view. A strange woman Jessica had tried to help two years earlier had suddenly reappeared in her life, insisting she'd never been to Scotland before when Jessica knew that she had.

It explained so much.

The defence considered Jessica's words. "And did you ask her to leave or do anything to make her leave?"

"I spoke to Peyton," said Jessica. "And he had a few ideas. But I told him not to do anything. I was too frightened of her to ask her to leave. I thought I'd let her to do the photography portfolio and then maybe she'd leave and not bother us again."

The prosecutor raised an objection, but the judge overruled it.

The defence thanked the judge and turned back to Jessica. "You were at the mercy of this woman—Isla Wilson—who was staying at your property, wondering what she planned to do."

Jessica nodded again. "Yes."

I felt people's eyes on me. I wondered what my mother was thinking of me right now. Everyone would be believing I'd made it up about not remembering Jessica and that I'd returned to Scotland deliberately to taunt Jessica. I cast a sideways glance at Greer. She looked stricken.

I trembled. Was that really why I'd returned? What was wrong with me?

I wanted to run from the courtroom. But I stayed, feeling too numb and burned inside to move.

"Returning to the night of the car accident," said the defence, "did Peyton Chandlish know that your daughter, Elodie, was alone that night?"

Jessica froze, seeming to take several breaths before taking a gulp of water. "Yes. He knew."

"How did he know?"

"I—I told him. I said I had to get back to Elodie because she was home alone."

"When did you tell Peyton this?"

"Soon after arriving at the scene."

"At the time that you left the scene, did Peyton know you were having labour pains?"

"Yes. It was obvious. Also, I told him that labour pains had started coming on fast and I had to get to hospital."

"Did you mention that your husband, Alban, was on his way home?"

"No. I didn't think to say that. I didn't have a clue that Peyton..."

was the monster that he was. *I didn't know.*" Tears glistened wetly on her face.

"Thank you," said the defence lawyer gently. "That's the end of my questions."

I didn't know what I should feel. Relief? A sense of closure? I could return to my life in Sydney now and close this chapter of my life.

Peyton could no longer hurt any children. No one had to worry about him getting off on any technicalities or going to jail only to get out again in a few years' time. He was dead.

When I glanced at Mum, I saw hope rising in her eyes.

The only thing left now was for Jessica's lawyer to bring out her witnesses for the defence.

But first, the prosecutor would have to cross-examine Jessica. From the way his brow was furrowing as he ruffled through his notes, I could tell that he'd realised his case had dissolved. Still, when he began his questioning, his voice was swift and confident. "Mrs McGregor, why didn't you simply call the police when Peyton called you for help? There was no need for you to go. You could have sent the police to find Peyton and help the woman, correct?"

"Peyton didn't want the police involved. He was upset and panicking."

"Please just answer yes or no."

"Yes."

"So, we've established that you could have and should have sent the police."

"Objection, my Lord," said the defence lawyer as she stood. "Prosecution has only established that Mrs McGregor could have sent the police. To say that she should have is just an opinion."

"Sustained," ruled the judge. "Please strike the words *and should have* from the record."

"Thank you, my Lord," said the prosecutor politely. "Mrs McGregor, would you agree that taking a two hour round trip towards Inverness and back—while your eight-year-old daughter was alone in the house—was an extreme course of action? Yes or no?"

"Objection, my Lord, prosecution is leading the witness," said the defence. "Mrs McGregor didn't realise the site of the accident would be so far along the road when she set out."

"Sustained," replied the judge. "Counsel, can you please rephrase that?"

"Yes, my Lord. Mrs McGregor, would you agree that leaving your eight-year-old daughter alone in the house to go and search for the scene of an accident would have been better handled by the police?"

"Objection, my Lord," said the defence. "Counsel has already asked that question."

The judge sustained the objection.

The prosecutor appeared slightly ruffled when he nodded in the judge's direction. "Mrs McGregor, do you agree that you left your eight-year-old child alone without making sure an adult would be there to watch her?"

"I thought Alban would be—" Jessica spluttered.

"Please just answer yes or no," insisted the prosecutor.

"Yes."

"At any time between deciding to leave your house and leaving the church, did you call your husband to ascertain how far he was away? Yes or no?"

"No."

"In other words, you were being secretive about the fact that you were leaving the house and leaving Elodie alone?"

"My Lord," objected the defence lawyer. "Prosecution is making assumptions."

"Sustained. Yes, Counsel," cautioned the judge. "If you wish to ask a leading question, please show us what led you there."

"Yes, my Lord. Mrs McGregor, it's not making sense to me why you'd go to help a friend and a strange woman, while leaving your young child alone on an isolated property. And not even attempt to ascertain when your husband would be arriving. I put it to you, that instead of the story you're telling us, Peyton called you for a romantic tryst and you met with him at this church. And this romantic tryst involved a third person—an unwilling young woman that—"

"I object, My Lord." The defence lawyer jumped to her feet. "Prosecution is making up wild stories that have no basis in the facts at hand."

Jessica's face had turned white. She shook her head, gasping between quick sips of water.

"Overruled," said the judge, after a moment's consideration. "Counsel, I'll allow this line of questioning. But please approach each part of your scenario separately, so that we can all follow how you arrived at your conclusions and so that the defendant knows exactly what she is being asked."

"Thank you, My Lord." The prosecutor bowed his head. "Mrs McGregor, we've heard from your good friend, Camille Keenan, that you had romantic feelings towards Peyton. In fact, we have the testimonies of several witnesses who agreed that you had a crush on Peyton from the time you were a teenager. Do you agree that you had romantic feelings towards Peyton Chandlish in the year before your daughter Elodie died? Yes or no?"

"Yes. But I didn't know—"

"Please keep your answers to yes or no."

She breathed deeply, dropping her head. "Yes."

"I'd like to talk about the church now," said the prosecutor. "The church is full of rats and very dirty. Yet you allowed someone who— by your words had a head injury—to lie down in a filthy, rat-infested, abandoned building."

"Objection, my Lord," called the defence lawyer. "A heavily pregnant woman could hardly stop a healthy young woman from entering the church."

"Sustained," said the judge. "Please strike the Counsel's last sentence from the record."

"Mrs McGregor, we've heard the testimonies of both Isla Wilson and Stella Keenan. Both witnesses heard Peyton say his only part in these events was to come to the church under someone else's instruction and take Isla away. I put it to you that you that under your instruction, Peyton brought an unwilling Isla Wilson to the church, whereupon you drugged her and enacted a form of torture on her. All part of some game you and Peyton had been taking part in, involving female adults and female children—"

The defence lawyer jumped to her feet. "Objection! My Lord, prosecution is making up wild stories again."

"No...." Jessica's voice shook. "That didn't happen."

The judge sustained the objection and directed that the prosecutor's words be struck from the record.

I wanted this to be over. I wanted to escape into myself and shut out the prosecutor's terrible words. He'd warned me that he'd have to be tough to bring out the truth. But as far as I was concerned, the truth had already come out. There had been a car accident. My mind had somehow manufactured vague memories of terrible things that didn't happen.

"Mrs McGregor," said the prosecutor in a calmer voice, "your DNA and fingerprints were found at a number of places around the room in the church. You touched the shelving and the window panes. Strands of your hair were found embedded in the dried blood on the mattress and floor. Your fingerprints were found on the bottle of sleeping medication that was left on the shelf. This evidence is consistent with you being inside that room for a much longer period of time than what you have told us. You stated that you were in the room for no longer than a minute. However, that isn't true. Do you agree that you were in that room for longer than a minute?"

"It could have been longer," Jessica said. "It's hard to remember. It was two years ago."

"It's not a hard thing to remember," replied the prosecutor. "Either you walked in and out, or you stayed long enough to touch different places in the room and drop strands of hair. Do you agree you were in the room for longer than a minute?"

"I don't remember."

"You stated earlier that you must have accidentally dropped the bottle of sleeping pills from your medical kit. Yet, they were found on a shelf in the room. How do you suppose the bottle got onto the shelf?"

"Someone must have picked it up and put it there."

"Hmmm," said the prosecutor. "We heard from an expert witness earlier who stated that only your fingerprints were found on the bottle."

"Perhaps someone with gloves?" Jessica suggested.

"Why would someone with gloves go to the trouble of carefully picking the bottle up and placing it on a shelf? Can you think of a reason for that, Mrs McGregor?"

"No. I have no idea. Perhaps Isla did it. Maybe even when she went back to the church with Rory." Her words were rushed, grasping.

Was she hiding something, after all? I leaned forward, watching her closely.

The prosecutor paused, referring to his notes. "We have a forensic report here that states that the bottle had been in place on the shelf for two years, which was evident from the accumulation of dust around and on top of it. And the condition that you say Isla was in—a head injury and in the middle of a panic attack on a dirty mattress—it doesn't sound like someone who was taking care to put a random bottle of pills up on a shelf for safekeeping, does it? In fact, we know now that Isla was most probably in the middle of a major seizure. We also know that Isla arrived back at her apartment in Inverness early that night. We have a statement from the landlady to say she sighted a man carrying Isla up the stairs. The landlady—Donna Gordon—has identified that man as Peyton Chandlish. Donna gave us a statement to say that Isla looked as if she was passed out. Now, this doesn't sound at all like someone who took care to put a random bottle of pills on a shelf in that church room—so much care that she left all your fingerprints intact—wouldn't you say, Mrs McGregor?"

"I don't know," Jessica stammered.

"Mrs McGregor, the fact that Peyton was seen carrying Isla back to her apartment fits exactly with what Isla and Stella heard him say. He said that he was instructed to return Isla to her apartment. I'm going to ask you straight out. Did you put that bottle of pills on the shelf in that room in the church?"

"I don't remember."

"What were you doing at the time that had you so distracted you don't remember what you did with a bottle of sleeping pills?"

Jessica's eyes were huge. "I probably just had to put them some-where. I was distracted by more important things. I had to wrap up the baby and rush her off to hospital."

Loud whispers of confusion charged around the courtroom.

Even the prosecutor looked confused, but he quickly hid it, steeling his expression once again. "Mrs McGregor, you just stated that you wrapped the baby up—inside the church. That doesn't fit with your earlier testimony in any way, shape or form. So, you're now saying that you had the baby *at the church*?"

Jessica's gaze skated between the prosecutor and her defence barrister, her lips parting helplessly.

"Objection, my Lord," called the defence lawyer. "Counsel is putting words in the defendant's mouth."

"Overruled," said the judge. "Mrs McGregor, you will answer Counsel's question."

"I misspoke." Jessica's voice had hoarsened.

"That's an odd point to get confused about," said the prosecutor. "A very odd point." He stopped speaking to look through his stack of papers. "The evidence presented to the jury, as I noted earlier, does show two distinct blood types were present on that mattress. Is it true that you had the baby there at the church rather than on the roadside?"

Jessica nodded limply. A sob broke from her throat. Her breaths seemed to be coming rapidly and she was clutching the stand as if she were trapped there.

Confused whispers again rushed around the gallery. The members of the jury were staring intently at Jessica, waiting for clarification.

The prosecutor hesitated, his shoulders rising in a deep inhalation, as if he wasn't sure what to ask Jessica next.

Jessica's defence lawyer attempted to stop proceedings, due to her client being under extreme duress. But the judge disallowed this and said that the trial would continue after Jessica had composed herself. She was given a fresh glass of water and a clean handkerchief to dry her face. But the handkerchief couldn't stop her cascading tears.

The prosecutor resumed his questioning of Jessica. "Mrs McGregor, I will remind you that you swore to tell the truth and nothing but the truth. Is that correct?"

"Yes."

"Mrs McGregor," said the prosecutor, "I'll ask you again. Why did you tell us that you'd taken your baby from the church?"

Jessica's face was stricken. "Because…it wasn't me who gave birth to a baby there. It was *Isla*."

47

ISLA

I COULD NOT HAVE HEARD Jessica correctly. Those words were wrong. The words of a desperate woman. She was lying again.

All heads turned my way. Even those of the judge and lawyers.

I turned and met eyes with Alban. He looked as confused as everyone else, except that his eyes still carried that slow burning anger that I'd seen earlier.

The courtroom was in uproar and Jessica's defence lawyer again asked for a recess. Jessica stated that she wanted to continue. The prosecution and defence lawyers approached the judge, and the three of them spoke together quietly. It was obvious that defence lawyer wanted to stop proceedings—she kept shaking her head and putting forth arguments.

The lawyers then returned to their seats.

"This is most irregular," said the judge, speaking openly now. "But based on the extraordinary circumstances and the issues at hand, especially due to the fact that this matter concerns a child, we will continue as we were. Being that this is potentially new information being offered by the defendant, Mrs McGregor, she will give a full explanation of her last answer, according to the last question that was asked by the counsel for the prosecution. And, Counsel, you may not ask additional questions. At the end of Mrs McGregor's account, we will decide what action is appropriate. Counsel, could you repeat the last question you asked?"

The prosecutor nodded, his expression tense. "Yes, my Lord."

My mother's hand on mine was the only thing anchoring me to the court room. I didn't know what was coming next or what Jessica would say.

"Mrs McGregor," said the prosecutor to Jessica, taking care to say each word slowly, "why did you tell us that you'd taken your baby from the church?"

Jessica's eyes glazed as she began. "I can't do this anymore. All the accusations about hurting children and drugging people. I didn't do any of that. I didn't know what Peyton was doing. I swear."

"Please, Mrs McGregor," said the judge, "you will stay with the facts."

"Yes, my Lord," replied Jessica.

She inhaled deeply. "There was no phone call from Peyton. What I did have was a phone message. From Isla." Jessica paused.

What lies are you about to tell, now Jessica? Are you trying to save yourself?

"Isla was about to do something that would destroy my marriage. She was going to ruin everything," came the words from Jessica's mouth. "I...wanted to stop her. I'd just found out that she was driving from Inverness that night. I told Elodie I was going to buy potatoes and then I left. I...didn't know what else to do."

Jessica almost whispered the last words, as if they were too painful to speak.

My breath stopped hard in my chest. *Me ruin Jessica's marriage?* What was she talking about? Alban told me that he and I had only spent a couple of hours at a bar together. There'd been no romance, no affair. Wouldn't I have remembered Alban if there had been?

The thought that I hadn't remembered Trent came crashing into my mind. And then something else. I had a glimpse of myself driving along a dark road—the A9 road from Inverness.

I told myself to breathe. It meant nothing. I used to live in Scotland. Of course I'd driven about. The rest of it was just more of Jessica's lies. But pinpricking waves of fear ran up and down the backs of my legs as I waited for Jessica to speak again.

Jessica took a drink, staring downward. "All I wanted to do was to get her to pull over so that I could talk to her. But she had her phone turned off. When I spotted her car driving towards me, I flashed my car's headlights. She veered off the road. She was startled, I guess. Maybe my headlights got in her eyes. Maybe she hit a wee patch of oil—I don't know. She skidded off the road and down an embankment. I pulled straight off the road after her, to check that she was okay. Her car wasn't damaged. And she wasn't hurt either. Not seriously. Just shaken up, mostly. She'd hit her head and she was a wee bit confused. But she didn't seem badly hurt. She jumped out of the car. We had words. We decided to talk inside an old church that was nearby, just to get out of the howling wind. It was dead dark in there. I used my phone's light and found some candles and matches. I lit the candles. There were...big rats running about. I guessed we disturbed them. They were going crazy. It was near winter and the rats were probably hungry. They were running over the piano, making a terrible din. I think they might have even had a nest of babies inside the piano, because I saw some very young rats running out of there."

Rats. Rats had made that noise on the piano. It made sense. Those chaotic, frenzied chords.

Did that mean she was telling the truth? I had to admit that her voice sounded different. Since I'd met her, she'd always sounded so restrained and uptight. And in the courtroom earlier, she'd sounded stiff and rehearsed. But now, her words spilled from her, as if unchecked.

Jessica's eyes sealed shut and she bent her head. "Isla...went into a seizure. I immediately understood that she was going into a seizure. I thought it was from the car accident. I didn't know that she had epilepsy. She needed to lie down, and there was nowhere else for her to lie down except on the mattress in that room."

Jessica paused again. Did she know that everyone in the courtroom was hanging on every word that she said right now? Was she stringing us all along? If so, she had to be putting on the performance of her life.

"Then she...began crying out in pain," Jessica said. "I checked her. And I knew that she'd gone into labour. The labour had come on quick and fast. There was no time. Isla had gone into a state in which she didn't seem to know who she was or what was happening. She was screaming. A fast labour—especially a first labour—can produce extreme pain. I went to get clean blankets and my medical kit from the car. I put one blanket on the bed for Isla to lie on and kept the other for the baby. I assisted Isla with the delivery, putting a hand on her stomach and telling her when to push."

Jessica stopped, sipping her water anxiously. My mind whirled.

No. There was no baby. I didn't have a baby. I was screaming because she hurt me.

"I asked her to be quiet," Jessica continued, "because she had stopped pushing. She was terrified, and her terror was stopping the labour from progressing. I told her to be quiet because she wasn't helping herself. The head crowned, and I caught the baby. I started to panic, as the baby didn't seem to be breathing at first. I might have said that out loud—I'm not sure. I checked her again, and she was okay. Then I cut the cord with the scissors from the kit and wrapped the baby. Then I disposed of the placenta in the well outside."

I don't think she's breathing. Those words had been about a newborn baby, not me.

If there was a baby, what happened to it? Did she dispose of it, too? Down the well, buried together with the placenta? God, what am I thinking? This didn't happen. None of this happened.

Mum squeezed my hand. I realised my breaths were so shallow that my head was growing faint.

Jessica sobbed, dabbed at her eyes and continued. "I...I gave Isla some sleeping pills to calm her. Then I called Peyton and...well, I asked him to do a favour for me. He was at home, in the basement when I called. I told him there was a girl asleep in an old church near Inverness and told him exactly where to find it. I asked him to take her back to her apartment in Inverness and I gave him the address. I told him she was a friend who was in trouble, but I didn't explain. He said he would do what I asked."

Jessica stared out at the courtroom. "He was a friend. I'd no reason to think he would go to my house and hurt my daughter. I'd even asked him to come to dinner that night, with Alban and Elodie and myself. Like I said, we were good friends. That's why I didn't tell the police about him being at home earlier in the night. I honestly believed he went straight to Inverness to get Isla. Because he did take Isla home to Inverness, so I had every reason to believe that he went straight there." The hurt and anger in her voice sounded real.

"Mrs McGregor, if you would return to the church and tell us more of what you claim happened there," instructed the judge, "that would be helpful."

"Yes, my Lord," Jessica whispered. She took a sip of water, then coughed and spluttered.

It felt as if my entire life—my sanity—hinged upon what she would say next.

Jessica's eyes were firmly shut as she spoke. "I left the church. I put Rhiannon against my chest and I drove towards Greenmire hospital."

Her words fired at me like bullets.

The baby was *Rhiannon?*

My mother was crying. I knew she'd already figured out what Jessica was leading up to.

Why would Jessica tell such a crazy lie—about her own daughter? I shook my head at Mum helplessly.

Jessica's wails filled the courtroom. "Rhiannon is all I have now. She's mine. She's been mine since she was born. Do you understand?"

Wordlessly, Jessica signalled to the judge—telling him that she was either done with her story or wasn't capable of continuing.

I could no longer hear the muffled noises and whispers of the court room.

Images assembled themselves in my mind. I could see Jessica kneeling beside me in that room in the church.

I had a memory of an enormous pressure and pain bearing down on my groin. I heard the word, *push.* I felt the release—a sudden and overwhelming release from the agony.

And I heard Jessica saying, *I don't know if she's breathing.*

48

ISLA

I STEPPED out of the courtroom, the sound of Jessica's mournful sobs following me. Arms came around me from either side. Mum and Greer. Else I would have fallen.

The corridor turned dark. I was back in the church, walking inside of it.

Night.

Smell of rats and decay.

Filthy mattress on the floor.

Piano chords echoing and banging around the walls. An insane musician sitting at the seat, orchestrating the pain inside me.

Screams in my ears. My own.

Wind blowing in through the cracks.

Something I lost.

Something torn from me.

Pieces of me.

Pieces of her.

A baby.

Where did I go from here?

How could I have forgotten an entire pregnancy and birth?

If it was true—why did Jessica take Rhiannon and pretend she was her own?

And what happened to Jessica's baby?

My mother said something. I couldn't hear her. My body was stone—while my mind sped away. A runaway train on the tracks. Rumbling, sparking, roaring louder than the wind, no longer attached to anything that could reign it in. Everything outside the train was blurred streaks.

People turned their heads as I passed—their curious eyes looking me over—as if Jessica's revelations would have made physical cuts all over my body. I felt as if I *had* sustained those cuts. Every part of me bleeding through wide open wounds.

I needed to get away. Away somewhere where all those eyes weren't on me.

Alban marched past me, his eyes dazed and his hands on his head, as if his whole world had collapsed.

"Excuse me," said Greer, "I'd better go to him."

"Go," Mum told her gently. "Before he ends up walking out into the traffic or something. I'll stay with Isla."

My mother guided me out into the cold, brisk morning air and along the street. We stopped at a small park and sat shielding ourselves from the blustering wind.

Over and over, my mind kept replaying scenes from the church. Like a movie I'd seen a long time ago and was beginning to remember, now that I'd started watching it again.

I felt a fullness and stretch in my belly—a memory. Walking along a hall somewhere full of young people with backpacks—a university—trying to pull a large jacket around myself, around my middle. Trying to hide myself. And running to the bathroom and vomiting.

God, I've been through a pregnancy. An entire pregnancy that I'd blocked out of my mind.

Rhiannon wasn't Jessica's biological child.

What else had I done? Had I been a home-wrecker? Was Alban the father? Or someone else?

But if Alban was the father, then Alban was telling lies.

Without warning, bile rose up into my throat. I was going to be sick. I raced to find a bathroom, Mum running behind me.

In the small public bathroom, Mum held back my hair while I

vomited into the sink. Just the way she'd done when I was sixteen and had come home drunk from a party. She'd never been quick to judge me, and I was grateful for that, now. I was in a world of pain and confusion.

The hour passed, and it was time to head back to the courtroom. To hear the rest of what Jessica had to say.

Mum walked me back to a seat in the gallery. I met Alban's gaze and looked away quickly. His eyes were intense, searching—and strange. Greer had stayed by his side and was sitting with him now. I caught her sympathetic glance before I turned to sit.

Jessica walked in, her hair smoothed and neatened, the red blotches gone from her face. She still appeared drained, but she was much more composed now.

The judge opened the session. "We are here to listen to the rest of the claims of Mrs Jessica McGregor. I will remind the jury and all who are present that these claims are at this time unsubstantiated. Mrs McGregor's claims are extraordinary, and the jury will keep that in mind. I will also remind the jury that Mrs McGregor's story is in answer to the last question asked by the prosecutor, which was *why did you tell us that you'd taken your baby from the church?* This account from Mrs McGregor is simply an answer to that. So far, the story has raised many questions, but those questions are for another time. The case at hand is the one outlined by the counsel for the prosecution in his opening statement and is the one that Mrs McGregor will be judged on today." He turned to Jessica. "Now, are you ready to continue?"

Jessica gave a nervous nod.

"Very well, you may proceed," said the judge.

"Yes, my Lord," said Jessica. Her gaze dropped to her lap as she began. "I met Isla Wilson a little less than three years ago. We never met in person. I communicated with her via notes and phone only. I saw her, but she never saw me."

What did she mean? Had she been watching me?

Jessica seemed to be gathering herself. I still tasted bile in my mouth from earlier. *What had I done?* Whatever it was, everybody in this courtroom was about to hear it at the same time as me.

"Isla was studying at university in Edinburgh when I met her,"

ANNI TAYLOR

Jessica said. "She was studying photography. She was in a desperate spot. She needed money and was worried she'd have to return home. I didn't know why. It wasn't important to me to ask. We...had an arrangement. She respected my desire for privacy and I respected hers. At the time, I was separated from my husband and I very much wished to repair my marriage. I know now that it was wrong of me, but I believed that a baby would help. I believed that Alban wouldn't divorce me if we had a new baby in our lives."

I listened with growing horror. What part had I played in this and what part had Alban played?

Jessica swigged the water as if it were wine—or as if she wished it were. "I had a seven-year-old child, Elodie, and I'd been trying to have another baby for at least five years, without success. It wasn't going to happen. Alban didn't want to go through IVF or anything like that. As far as he was concerned, the marriage was over. The marriage hadn't been solid from the start, but I didn't want it to be over. One morning...I went to the university and placed a note on the notice board, about wanting a surrogate."

I heard an audible gasp and realised it was my own. Around me, I heard shocked whispers. Somewhere behind me, I heard Alban curse.

"Four girls contacted me," said Jessica. "Isla was one of those. She seemed...perfect. She was intelligent, well spoken, pretty. And she would be heading back to Australia when she finished her course. And so, we made an agreement."

Staring at Jessica, I shook my head silently. What kind of trouble could I possibly have been in that I needed money so desperately? *I'd signed up to be a surrogate?* She couldn't be telling the truth. She'd had time to think in the break from court. Surely she'd concocted this story?

"I made it clear," said Jessica, "that we'd never meet. I wanted complete secrecy. Isla agreed to this. She said that when she headed back home, she was happy to put the whole thing out of her mind and never contact me again. Which is exactly what I wanted."

She dipped her head, sighing. "I—I told Alban I wanted us to have a couple of weeks away. For us to have a last-ditch try to reconnect as a married couple. He didn't agree, at first. But I called his mother, crying, telling her I wanted to save my marriage. I guess she

362

put a wee bit of pressure on Alban. Anyway, she minded Elodie for the two weeks and Alban and I went to stay at a hotel in Edinburgh. At the same time, I paid for Isla to stay at a hotel nearby. I'd had her use an ovulation predictor kit, and this was at her fertile time of the month. Essentially, what I did every second night was to take a collection of sperm from my husband. I'd bought the type of condoms that don't have spermicide—I told Alban that I had an allergy to the other kind. I put the collection into an insemination syringe and rushed it away in my handbag, down the street to the hotel room where Isla was staying. If you keep sperm moist, sterile and at room temperature, it can remain fertile for up to half an hour—even as long as an hour. I kept the time to within fifteen minutes, where possible. I'd put the syringe into a paper bag outside her door, then call her. I'd watch, secretly, to ensure she opened her door and took it. This went on for two weeks."

Mum threaded her fingers tightly in and around mine.

Jessica held her head in her hands for a moment, her eyes huge and frightened, as if she couldn't believe she was telling everyone this. "Weeks after the Edinburgh trip, Isla sent me a text message to say that she was pregnant. She'd used one of the pregnancy test kits that I'd given her. I hadn't expected it to work, to be honest. But it did. I guess I shouldn't have been surprised. I was just in shock at this point, thinking about the wheels I'd put in motion. There was no turning back now. I...used a urine sample that she supplied to me to confirm the pregnancy with a doctor. I pretended it was my own. From there, I got weekly reports from Isla on how she was doing. I hired a doula to give her monthly wellness checks. For myself, I...I used prosthetic bellies. I took one from the hospital that was used for training staff in the maternity ward. The rest I obtained online. Everyone believed I was pregnant."

She stared out at the jury, then at the gallery. "I began to believe it myself. Isla was just the carrier who supplied half of the biological material, but I was the mother. That's how it works with a surrogate. That's how it's supposed to work. And the baby was biologically my husband's. I didn't think I was doing anything wrong. Isla needed money. I needed a baby."

Tears began streaming down Jessica's face again. Her carefully smoothed hair in disarray again. Her face blotchy again. I sat frozen in my chair. There was too much information coming at me all at once. I couldn't process it, let alone make sense of it. How did this even connect with the night at the church?

"Do you need to take a moment, Mrs McGregor?" asked the judge.

"No, my Lord," she said, wiping away the wetness on her cheeks with a fresh handkerchief. "I'll continue."

"Very well," he said.

Pushing the handkerchief down deep into a jacket pocket, Jessica bent her head to the microphone. "Alban moved back into the family home and we were a family again. Elodie was excited that she was going to have a new brother or sister. Everything was going well. But when Isla was six months pregnant, things started to go wrong. She sent me a text to say that she wanted to meet in person. She said that she didn't know whether she could go through with it. I talked her around. Things went back and forwards like this for the next two months. Until…finally…Isla told me that she was returning to Sydney and she was going to keep the baby. I was devastated. Completely devastated. She had moved to Inverness by this time. We'd agreed early in the pregnancy that she wouldn't stay in Edinburgh, so that none of her friends would know about her pregnancy. On this night, Isla said she was driving from her flat in Inverness, back to Edinburgh, to pick up some belongings she'd left with a friend. And then she'd be flying out."

Stopping, Jessica twisted her hands together. "To me, it was if she was tearing my child away from me. Because that's exactly what she was doing. I…I decided I needed to talk with her in person. I thought that if she saw me, and saw how much I already loved the baby, she'd change her mind. But her phone was switched off and I couldn't contact her. If I let her get to Edinburgh, it would be too late. I'd lose my baby. I'd no time to think. I told Elodie I was going out to get things for dinner. And then I drove out to the A9, towards Inverness, keeping a sharp eye out for Isla's car. When I sighted her car, I flashed my car's headlights. And…I've already told the rest of what happened at the church…."

"Isla, honey," Mum whispered, "are you okay?"

I nodded. But I wasn't okay. Jessica was talking about me, but I didn't recognise the person as being *me*. I struggled against the images that were appearing before me, trying hard to push them away. These things couldn't be real.

"I called Elodie three times on my way to hospital," Jessica continued. "When she didn't answer, I thought she was just caught up in the console game she'd been playing. I couldn't wait to tell her that she had a new sister."

She hesitated before speaking again. "The moment I arrived at hospital, I knew I was in trouble. They'd find out I hadn't given birth to Rhiannon. I hadn't been able to prepare properly. But the baby needed medical care. I knew almost all the doctors and nurses who were on duty that night. I had to think quickly. I was able to delay a check-up on myself because, naturally, everyone understood that my priority was seeing that the baby was okay. And then I falsified a record of my own examination. After that, I…I tried to call Elodie one more time. And again, there was no answer…."

Jessica bowed her head. "I was worried about Isla, too. I'm not a monster. I didn't call her for three days—I was in shock about Elodie you must understand. But I did call her. To my surprise, she didn't remember me. It was obvious that she didn't remember having a baby, either. And I didn't see a reason to tell her. I ended up calling the doula and telling her that Isla had lost her baby. I…I also told her that Isla was a drug addict who was recovering from an overdose. I asked her to go and care for Isla over the next week. And I asked her not to mention the baby because it would…traumatise Isla too much. Yes, the overdose was a lie. But I didn't want to leave Isla alone in that state."

Jessica didn't speak again.

Every piece had slotted into place. Jessica had told it all. I sensed a relief in her. Her stiff, straight posture had given way.

I stopped struggling against the things she'd told.

Small, sharp pieces of memory pierced my mind, summoned by Jessica's story. Pieces of everything and everyone.

The texts. The notes. The paper bags at my door. The stretchy, growing stomach. The woman who came to see me each month—the doula. I had vague memories of all of it.

The story that Jessica had just told was the one that was true.

49

ISLA

April 2018

My MOTHER and I had been staying in Inverness since Jessica's court case, at Greer's house. Greer came and went between her house and Kelly's house at Aviemore. Mum and I walked a lot along the River Ness—me trying to get my head straight and Mum trying to support me. I understood now how much she'd tried to protect me when I'd returned from Scotland two years ago. If I was this much of a mess now, I couldn't imagine how bad I'd been back then.

Jessica had been found not guilty of the charges involving the supply of sleeping medication to Peyton for the purpose of abusing children and any involvement in the sexual abuse of children.

She still had the manslaughter court case pending. And now there would be two new court cases for her to attend. One to determine her guilt in illegally procuring a surrogate and her actions the night I gave birth to Rhiannon. The other was to be a court case to determine custody of Rhiannon.

I was in a state of deep confusion. I didn't know yet what I wanted in terms of custody. In the interim, full custody had been awarded to Alban.

I hadn't seen Rhiannon at all since my return to Scotland. Things were too muddled, too confused and strange. All I knew was that the last thing I should do was to rush in and further add to the pain of a little girl who was already missing the only mother she'd ever known.

A set of blood tests had been ordered to determine for certain who Rhiannon's biological parents were—and it had been determined that Alban was the father and I was the mother.

Two dark-eyed, dark-haired people had produced a blue-eyed blonde child. It was biologically possible, we'd been told. Recessive genes for fair colouring had come together, from Alban and myself. One chance in four. Not that unusual we'd been informed.

Only now, when I looked at photos of Rhiannon could I see what I couldn't see before. She didn't look like Jessica at all. She was pieces of Alban, pieces of me, pieces of herself.

The weight of it pressed on me from all sides. Whatever happened, she was forever my child. I was her biological mother.

Mother. The word was foreign on my tongue, clunky in my mind.

I didn't feel like Rhiannon's mother. Or like a mother at all.

I saw Jessica as Rhiannon's mother—at least, I couldn't yet unhook my image of the two of them as a unit yet.

My own mother saw no such obstacles. She'd recognised me in Rhiannon's features as soon as she'd set eyes on her. Rhiannon was mine as far as she was concerned.

Mum hadn't seen Jessica and Rhiannon together the way in which I had. Hadn't seen them in their matching outfits. Hadn't seen how obsessively protective Jessica was of her.

Jessica's behaviour towards Rhiannon made terrible sense now. She was using Rhiannon as a shield as much as she was protecting her. The outfits were a foil—a thing to fool the eye. I hadn't seen past it. Matching mother-daughter outfits hadn't been an unusual thing in my world.

I didn't know how to feel about Jessica. She'd taken from me what she believed was rightly hers—the baby. She could have killed me there and then in the church. She could have had Peyton dump my body somewhere. I might never have come home to Mum and Jake, might never have been seen or heard from again. I'd have been one of those sad and tragic pictures of missing persons in the news.

I'd ended up coming to Braithnoch and staying there right under her nose, unknowingly tormenting her. It had been Jessica who'd asked Peyton to do something to scare me away. It had been Jessica who'd stolen my medication. It had been Jessica who'd rummaged through my handbag, checking my passport to make sure I hadn't regained my memory and was lying about never having been to Scotland before.

She'd been trying to make me leave. But she wasn't evil, or a killer.

But I hadn't forgiven her yet. The image of the room in the church kept closing around me, like a dirty, aged coat.

She left me there.

With the rats and the dirt and the dark. And Peyton.

Mum and Greer had done some sleuthing about the previous year I'd spent in Scotland. What they'd discovered had tipped my world upside-down yet again. Mum knew which university in Edinburgh I'd studied at and which course I'd taken. Together, Mum and Greer tracked down a girl I used to share a small flat with. Mum had remembered the first name of the girl, which I'd told her years ago. Her full name was Emily Seidel. She'd been studying art back then, and now worked teaching art at a wellness retreat in Germany, which was her home country. She hadn't heard about the case—she wasn't someone who kept current with the news.

Mum paid for Emily's flight to Scotland. I had a vague memory of her face—bright blue eyes peeking out from beneath a black fringe. Her German accent and the way she laughed also seemed familiar. But I was unable to recall the months we'd spent together in Edinburgh.

Emily told us that we'd rented the flat for three months, the last month of which I'd begun dating a man named Trent Dorrington. She said Trent had quickly become possessive, almost immediately putting pressure on me to come and live with him. One night, he'd invited some friends of his to a small party that Emily and I were throwing at our flat. Trent's friends had trashed the flat, causing a large amount of damage. Trent had assured us that he'd pay for the damage. But he became angered when I turned down his offer to stay with him at his place. He left Emily and I to pay the bill—twenty thousand in Australian dollars.

Emily said we'd both had no choice but to return home to our own countries. We were broke, in debt and unable to rent anything else due to the damage caused in our names. We'd had to find temporary accommodation at a backpacker hostel. But Emily said that I'd suddenly come up with the money, without any explanation. And I'd told her I'd changed universities and was going to finish the rest of my studies in Inverness. She said she tried to stay friends, but I distanced myself. She finished her course and returned to Germany and didn't hear from me again.

It wasn't hard to guess where I'd gotten the money from. Jessica had said she'd paid me thirty thousand in Australian dollars.

Emily and I had hugged at the end of our meeting and promised we'd keep in touch.

It was the last piece of the puzzle. I now knew why I'd been so desperate for money that I'd agreed to become a surrogate for Jessica. Also, I now knew that although Trent hadn't done anything that caused me to lose my memory, he hadn't been the innocent he'd painted himself as.

I knew everything now, but I was still lost. I'd seen a psychologist twice over the past fortnight. She'd told me it was possible that I would never fully regain my memory. It was as if a hole had been burned through a year of memories in my brain, just like the burned pages of a diary. Burned to smoke and ashes.

There was one question I was desperate to know the answer to, but knew I never would. *Why did I change my mind about the baby?* Why did I want to keep her after I was a few months into the pregnancy? I'd been a young university student with no desire to start a family.

The kettle boiled, shaking me from my thoughts.

In Greer's sunny kitchen, I poured some tea for Mum and myself.

Mum walked in as I was stirring the sugar and milk into the hot cups of water. She had her hand cupped over the phone receiver.

"Isla," she said, "It's Alban." Her eyes were wide open. She'd looked like that almost constantly since she'd been in Scotland, bewildered by the truth of what had really happened to me last time I was here.

I gulped a quick breath. Was I ready to talk with Alban? We'd barely spoken since the night he'd pulled me from the marshes on the moor. Things had been too raw. We'd each been dealing with our own demons.

Taking the phone, I tried to calm the sudden squeezing sensation in my chest. Thoughts of Alban mixed with images of Peyton and Jessica and Rhiannon in my mind. I could see him with his wife and daughter, the family that had seemed perfect when I'd first seen them together. And I was transported back to that night with Peyton on the moor. I could almost feel the blade of Peyton's knife plunging into my flesh, feel myself sinking into the ice-cold marsh, feel the terror as Peyton had Alban pinned to the ground.

I managed a half-whispered hello, suppressing a desire to put the phone down and walk away.

"Isla…," he began, then stopped.

"How are you?" I said.

"Holding on. Well, trying to. You?"

"Same."

"I know. Right now, I don't even know how to pick up the pieces."

"How is…Rhiannon?"

"She's doing her usual things. Playing with her wee giraffe. Avoiding vegetables like the plague. Trying her best escape routines every time she's put down for a sleep."

His words pulled a smile from me. "I hope she's been okay."

A slow exhale came through the line. "She knows something's wrong. She knows Jessica's not around. But my mother's been staying here. And Greer comes to see her. Maybe it's enough for now. I don't know. I…."

He didn't finish his words. And I didn't step in to rescue him. I knew why. The newness and awkwardness of the two of us talking together about Rhiannon—*our child*—had made both of us tumble into silence. I felt like an imposter, a delusional woman pretending a stranger's child was her own. Surely someone would come and tell me that this was wrong—the blood tests were wrong; Jessica's story was a lie and Rhiannon didn't really have my facial features.

The psychologist I'd seen had told me it was normal for me to feel this way. I'd go through stages and I shouldn't try to rush myself through them.

The media had been waiting and hoping to grab a photo of Rhiannon and me together: *The real mother reunites with her child.* That was the part of the story that everyone was waiting for. But so far, they'd been disappointed.

"Isla," Alban said, breaking the deep stretch of quiet. "We've got some things to talk about. Would you come to Braithnoch?"

My stomach wrenched. "Come *there?*"

"I understand if you can't do it. It can be somewhere else. Anywhere you choose."

"No…it's fine. But the press? They'll be waiting for something like this."

"I thought of that. The local police—Kirk and Tash—said they'd scout the area first. Greer could take your mother and mine and Rhiannon out somewhere. I mean, I can't have Rhiannon here while we talk."

I flicked my gaze towards Mum. "My mother would be overjoyed. She can't wait to meet your little girl."

Mum held a hand over her mouth as she nodded, excitement rising in her eyes. She was anxious to meet her first grandchild and she hadn't been doing a good job of hiding that fact.

"Rhiannon's also *yours*," Alban pointed out, then sighed heavily. "Listen…just come. It'll all work out. I'll do whatever I have to do to make things work. For Rhiannon's sake. Whatever you choose to do, it's okay. No one should expect anything from you."

I inhaled the scents of tea and fresh flowers in Greer's kitchen. "When?"

"Today. This morning. If that works. My mother would like to meet you as well." He made a low, wry sound. "No pressure."

I made a tentative agreement to arrive there at ten in the morning. An hour later, Greer, Mum and I were on our way to Braithnoch.

My mouth dried as we neared, an anxious beat tapping in my chest. This place had been Jessica's domain—the place she'd tried to keep me away from. I kept my gaze away from the distant hills and the moor. My blood had seeped into that moor and I didn't want a visual reminder.

Immediately outside the house, the heather was in bloom, looking to me like huge, fantastical powder puffs.

Alban was waiting there, holding Rhiannon. A blonde woman of medium height stood beside him. She hadn't been at the courtroom—she'd been minding Rhiannon that day and she'd also told Alban that she couldn't bear to hear any details of what had happened to Elodie.

I said a brief hello to Rhiannon, trying to remember to smile naturally and not to stare at her too long.

I met with Alban's mother while my mother and Greer took Rhiannon for a short walk. I knew that Mum was itching to hold Rhiannon, but she held herself back, letting Greer take Rhiannon's hand.

Alban's mother might have been a blue-eyed blonde, but she had the same intense way of regarding me that Alban did, and the exact same way of tilting her head to the side when considering my words. A warmth exuded from her when she hugged me. "I see you in Rhiannon," she said to me quietly.

Alban's mother, my mother and Greer left with Rhiannon in Greer's car.

Alban approached me. "Come inside. I'm sorry—it's a bit cold in here. I should have gotten the fire started. Summer didn't last nearly long enough."

"It's fine. Really." I gave him a smile that felt tight on my face.

I walked inside with him, where, despite my protests, he began stacking wood in the fireplace. He wore a checked shirt—the same shirt he'd been wearing the time I'd watched him chopping firewood in the fog.

He soon had a fire crackling and then offered me a hot drink. We sat in front of the fire on two armchairs with our cups of tea. I was grateful for the fire then because it gave us somewhere to focus other than each other. I didn't even yet know what I was going to say.

"Isla," Alban began. "It's an insane situation. I want you to know you can ask me anything—anything that's confusing you. If I can answer it, I will. I haven't had a chance to say how sorry I am that my wife put you through what she did. I don't even have words."

I bowed my head, watching steam rise from my cup of tea. "You're not responsible for what she did."

"I know. But I keep tossing it around and around in my head. If I'd been a better husband somehow, if she hadn't been scared of losing me—"

"Then she wouldn't have gone down the surrogate path? I mean, she wouldn't have tried so hard to have a second baby?"

"Yes. That's exactly what I mean."

I hadn't expected that kind of honesty from Alban. He could have painted Jessica as evil and himself as a saint if he'd wanted to.

"*Could* you have been a better husband?" I asked.

He sighed. "Everyone could do better than they're doing when it comes to relationships. Maybe I worked too much or didn't appreciate her enough. I don't know. My mother won't hear a word of that. I'm her perfect boy. She won't even speak Jessica's name at the moment." His face crumpled as he glanced away. "All of the terrible things that happened because of this, because of how insecure Jess felt...."

"Alban, the psychologist I've been seeing told me we tend to want to go back in time and work out what we could have done to fix things. But if we did the best that we could do at the time, with the knowledge that we had, then we need to stop blaming ourselves."

I thought of my mother, who still blamed herself for Dad's suicide, as if she might have stopped it if she'd done something differently. But she couldn't have guessed what was happening deep inside my father's mind. Because he never told her and never let it show.

Alban nodded slowly. "Your psychologist is right. I want to go back and change everything. So that I can bring Elodie back."

The sight of the jumping flames blurred as my eyes grew wet. "It's been a set of dominoes falling, one after the other. One thing causing another. If I had never dated Trent. Or if I'd moved out with him when he wanted and let him pay for the damage to the flat. If I'd never contacted Jessica when I saw her message on the uni notice board...."

His voice hoarsened. "But if not *you*, then it would have been another girl. Jessica would have still gone ahead with her plan."

"But another girl might have seen the whole thing through to the end. Unlike me. I went back on the deal."

His gaze flicked to me and he studied my face. "That's one of the few things keeping me sane right now. The fact that you wanted to keep Rhiannon. Considering everything else that's happened, that's the one thing I'm hanging onto."

"Alban...I—"

"Ach, I wasn't saying that to put pressure on you. I know there's a lot of attention and pressure on you right now. Everyone wants to know what you're going to do. But I want you to know that I don't expect you to stay in Scotland. I don't expect you to have a relationship with Rhiannon. It's just...well, the fact that you wanted to keep her when you were pregnant just feels better to me somehow. Rhiannon wasn't just a transaction to you, she wasn't just about the money."

"Thanks, for not putting pressure on me. I don't know what's right or what I need to do. The most important thing is what's best for Rhiannon."

"What's best for her depends on what's best for *you*. It'd be worse for Rhiannon in the long run if you stayed because you think you should. Because it will all fall apart, sooner or later." He crushed his eyes shut. "None of us want that to happen. We'll be okay, just Rhiannon and me. I'll give her everything I have. And she's got people around her who love her. Her grandparents and Greer."

"I need some time. There's been so much focus on the court case that I haven't had the mental space to figure this out."

"And the court cases haven't ended, either. Ah, such a tangled mess this is." He gave a short, rueful laugh. "Looking at wee Rhiannon, I can't regret that she happened. Not for a second. She's a treasure. But the craziness of how it happened...what my wife did...."

I sipped at tea that was already growing lukewarm. "It must have been a strange couple of weeks for you at that Edinburgh hotel, with Jessica running off to my hotel room every night or so."

"She'd just say she needed some fresh air and she was going for a walk. I guess I didn't think much of it. I got myself pretty drunk every night during that time. I knew it wasn't what I wanted—I didn't want to get back with Jessica. But she'd laid a pretty heavy guilt trip on me, saying we needed to try to repair the marriage for Elodie's sake. And so I did. I tried my heart out."

"Did it work?"

He shook his head, staring at the tea he'd barely drunk. "You know what they say about wringing the neck of a dead horse? That described that fortnight we spent together. Of course, I'd no idea what that trip was really all about. In my wildest dreams, I couldn't have guessed that she had a surrogate waiting in one of the rooms of a hotel nearby."

"It's unbelievable that we actually met the night that fortnight started," I mused.

"Yes." His eyebrows lifted in a look of bewilderment. "If only we'd known." A smile flitted across his face then. "Since you don't remember, I'll set the scene for you. There was a group of very drunk Scotsmen carousing at the bar. One of them was drunker than the others and trying hard to convince himself he was having a good time. *Me.* Jessica planned to meet me there at the hotel the next morning. I wanted a divorce. But she was desperate to try to get back together one last time. I shouldn't have agreed, but I did. Anyway, the group started singing loudly—and I must apologise for hurting everyone's ears. I spotted a lovely girl, sitting alone and looking sad. I took your hand and started dancing with you. I thought you'd run away after-wards. But you didn't. You stayed and chatted for a while. Then you got a phone call and you fled."

"Jessica must have arrived at the hotel early," I said, "because she spotted me talking with a man and she called me on the phone, ordering me to return to my room. Now I know that man was *you.* Jessica told me I was to stay there in my room the whole time. That much I remember now. So, what was she like during that trip? She must have pulled out all stops to get the marriage on track again."

"You'd think so. But she was strange. One minute all over me and passionate—and the next minute dead cold. How can I describe this? Even when she was passionate, it was a desperate, disconnected kind of passionate. At first, I thought she was just anxious for us to work things out. But most of the time, she barely looked at me. She didn't love me. She just loved the idea of the marriage and the house. She liked everything perfect, everything her way. That's what she was going to miss, I think."

I placed my cup on a side table, then crisscrossed my arms over my shoulders, my thoughts spinning away again. "I didn't guess that about her. I just thought she was all about Rhiannon. Protecting her from the world. Which was understandable after what happened to Elodie."

"She wanted to be number one in Rhiannon's eyes, always. In a jealous sort of way. She even tried to stop Rhiannon and me from being close. She'd get upset if Rhiannon wanted Daddy to read her a story instead of Mummy. Things like that."

"I noticed Jessica was upset a lot."

"Aye. Upsetting herself was a talent of hers. Always jealous of me and Rhiannon. And jealous of the Chandlishes and what they had. She didn't want to stay here at Braithnoch. She wanted us to move away. She wanted me to take on bigger projects and stop locking myself away at home, so we could buy some big fancy house in Edinburgh."

"I thought..." Hesitating, I sucked in my lips. "I actually thought you might be abusing her. Hitting her. Because she seemed upset so much."

Alban shot me an odd look. "You thought that about me?"

"I'm sorry. Yes, I did. Besides Jessica being upset, she had bruises. We all know now that Peyton made those marks, but I didn't know that at the time. And, one morning I heard you shouting at her...."

"It kills me to know you thought I was hurting Jess. I think I know which morning you're talking about with the shouting. Jess had told me I needed to stop the photography profile and send you home. She said she couldn't bear having a stranger living at Braithnoch, and if I didn't tell you to get out, she was going to take Rhiannon and go somewhere where I couldn't find them. Very damned dramatic. I didn't understand it at all. The portfolio idea had been Jessica's in the first place—she was the one who wanted me to go further in my career and she was the one who urged Greer to start contacting magazines. I shouldn't have lost control and started yelling at her though—that was dead wrong of me."

"I knew Jessica didn't like me being here," I told him. "I know why, now. She played the victim well."

"Yeah. Yes, she did. I'm pretty certain that a doctor in town—Dr McKendrick—thought that Jess was a victim, too."

"Dr McKendrick?" I said in surprise.

"Do you happen to have met her?" he asked.

"Yes, I went to see her when my medication went missing."

"Okay, well, Jess and I went to see her after Jess had confirmation from another doctor that she was pregnant." He paused, shaking his head. "Of course, Jess wasn't really pregnant. Anyway, Jess had told me that she wanted to see Dr McKendrick because she wanted an abortion. I didn't know how I felt—Jess gave me no time to consider my feelings. But I accepted that it was her body and her decision. Adding to the confusion, I was suspicious at this point, thinking that Jess might have had an affair and that was how she'd gotten pregnant. I'd been so dead careful with my use of condoms. But I went along to support her in her decision. But once we were in there, Jess totally changed. She suddenly said she wanted to keep the baby. I made an off-hand remark about getting a paternity test. I shouldn't have said it, I know. It was wrong of me. But I couldn't understand any of what was going on. Jess started crying and said she thought I'd be happy about the baby. And, so, in the doctor's eyes, I looked like a great big belligerent monster."

I now had my answer as to why Dr McKendrick didn't have a high opinion of Alban.

I frowned. "But if you thought the baby wasn't yours, why did you decide to stay with Jessica?"

"It took me a while to accept it. I didn't think it was possible I'd caused her pregnancy. She'd been so hot and cold during our trip away that it made sense to me that she'd had a brief affair. But she talked me around. I ended up thinking I was being stupid to be suspicious of her."

The conversation lulled. I could sense Alban's despair over how much his wife had deceived him and much he hadn't known.

There were still so many questions clouding my mind.

Alban had said to ask him anything, but the questions were all so awkward.

"I'm sure this is none of my business to ask," I started. "Never mind, it doesn't matter...."

"Isla, we need to put everything out on the table. That's why I wanted to talk to you. So that neither of us is left wondering about things that only the other could answer."

"It's just, well, how did Jessica manage to fool you that she was pregnant for so long? I mean, I know about the fake bellies, but didn't you ever see her undress? Didn't you ever...uh...?"

"Have sex? That's a reasonable question. We did a couple of times in the first two months. But then she said she was tired and had a condition some women develop in pregnancy—sciatica. And so I understood and left her well alone. She complained that it was getting worse and she needed to sleep alone so that I didn't knock her and cause her pain during the night. She slept in another bedroom during the last months. In all truth, I was throwing myself into my work and trying hard to accept that this was going to be my life. With Jess. So, I probably blocked out anything that was a wee bit odd and didn't notice it. A new baby was coming, and I felt I had no choice but to see this through. Jess's stomach got bigger, and from my side, things just seemed much the same as when she was pregnant with Elodie. In my wildest dreams, I couldn't have guessed that the pregnancy belly was fake."

"You never wanted to touch her and feel the baby kicking?"

"Of course. I tried a few times. She'd say the baby was asleep and wasn't a very active baby anyway. Most of the time, she seemed to want to keep to herself and didn't want anyone touching her. She complained mightily about people thinking they had the right to put their hands on pregnant women. She wasn't like that during her pregnancy with Elodie. But I guessed that the whole marriage breakdown we'd been through had had a toll on her. She was irritable and weepy a lot and I thought it was my fault. She was even growing distant from Elodie—pushing her away at times."

"That's so sad for Elodie."

"Aye. I tried to explain to her that Mummy was just feeling bad because of the pregnancy."

I recalled the gold-painted larch cones. Had Elodie wanted to make those Christmas decorations to make her mother feel a bit brighter?

Thinking of the larch cones made me think of the forest. I was reminded of the aerial photograph of the forest on Alban's office wall, and of the painting that hung beside it.

"Alban, I have a question. You don't have to answer it."

"Okay? Lay it on me." But his voice sounded a little guarded. I was certain he'd picked up on the trepidation in my own voice.

"It's the pictures on your wall—in your office," I began. "I know what they are. Both of them are tracking the movements that Peyton took out of the forest that night. The night that he took Elodie."

The muscles in his face and neck tensed. "You guessed that?"

I nodded. "I didn't understand it at the time. I didn't get why you'd keep something like that on your wall, to look at every day."

"You must have thought I was pretty damned strange." He exhaled heavily. "I had those pictures there because I was obsessed with finding out who'd killed my daughter. I'd seen a similar pattern in other places in the woods, ever since I was a teenager. Not just at Braithnoch Square, but in other places around Greenmire. Tracks in muddy ground, that sort of thing. I couldn't get Kirk or the police to take me seriously. They thought I was grabbing at shadows."

"Oh, God. It was Peyton making those tracks, all that time."

He nodded. "Sometimes when I'd go for walks at night, I was certain I saw a pattern like that—in the way that someone had walked through the leaves or a faint set of footprints. But there was never anything concrete enough for the police. And I never caught the person doing it."

"That was why you walked the forest every night—to catch the killer?"

"Yes. I was certain it had to be someone local. Because of the patterns I'd seen all those years. I even mapped out the exact route and walked it myself all the time, because I wanted that path to remain. I wanted the evidence there, so that if I ever found the person who walked about in that kind of pattern, I could show the police and say, *look, it's a match.* I was driving myself mad, and I knew it, but I couldn't stop."

I eyed him sympathetically. "Rory suspected that it was someone local, too."

"I know. I guess I was a bit harsh on Rory. He told the police about some paintings Elodie had done. I thought he was trying to cast suspicion on us—on Jess and me. After all, I had arrived home in time to have been the one who hurt Elodie that night. There was a lot of suspicion thrown my way at the time."

"That must have been awful, to have people wonder if it could have been you."

He sighed. "Aye. Like a dagger to the heart."

A silence fell between us. I could sense the raw emotion wrapped up in what he'd just told me.

He fixed his gaze on me. "Isla, I haven't been entirely honest with you."

"What do you mean?"

"Earlier, when I said I didn't want to put pressure on you, about Rhiannon, I meant it. But, I actually do know why you wanted to keep her. I just haven't been sure whether it's fair for me to show you...."

"Show me what?" My chest suddenly felt tight. There had been too many shocks over these past months. I didn't know if I could take hearing anything else.

He exhaled slowly. "I can't keep this from you. When I went to see Jessica in recent weeks, she accidentally told me about a letter you gave her. When you first told her that you'd changed your mind about the baby, you put it in a letter. Jessica let it slip that she still had it, at our home. I went looking in the boxes where she keeps letters and old birthday cards. I found it there."

I sucked in a breath and then released it slowly, trying to process the thought of a letter in my mind. *A letter written in my own words.* A nervous excitement pitted itself against terror inside me. Once I'd seen the letter, I could never return to this point. I couldn't manufacture a picture in my mind of how I *might* have felt back then and use it to justify whatever actions I chose to take next. This letter would leave me in no doubt.

"Can I see it?" I said in a voice that was barely audible.

"Of course." He took out an envelope from his jacket pocket and handed it to me.

With fumbling fingers, I opened the letter. It was written in my handwriting—unmistakable:

DEAR JESSICA,

I've started this letter a dozen times and thrown it away.

But I need to tell you that I've had a change of heart.

I've tried so hard to change the way that I've been feeling. When we first started on this journey, I thought I could go through with it. And in the first months, I was okay.

At first, the baby was just this inconvenient blob of cells floating somewhere inside me, making me feel sick and bloated. Making my waistbands tight. I felt very disconnected from the whole experience. Most of the time, I could just about ignore that I was even pregnant. The baby was yours and that was that.

But a pregnancy is long. The further along I've gotten, the more the baby has seemed real. I'm six months pregnant now, and the baby is a person with its own personality.

I don't know if the baby is a boy or a girl, but it doesn't matter. I can feel it moving and turning. I can feel it settling to sleep. I can feel it bump me back when I touch it. It's started to feel like it's part of me. And letting go is going to be as painful as cutting off something I need in order to live.

I guess this all sounds pretty stupid. I know I agreed that I was just to be the baby's incubator and nothing more. I haven't even finished my studies.

But I can't let go.

I'll find a way to return your money to you. I won't cause you any trouble or ever let your husband know about this. I'll return to Sydney and you won't hear from me again.

I'm truly very deeply sorry,

Isla.

TEARS RAN DOWN MY FACE.

I'd written this.

This is me. My words.

I didn't recognise the girl who'd written the letter. But I felt for her.

"This must have hit Jessica so hard," I said finally. "I wasn't a very good surrogate, was I? Surrogates are supposed to know that the baby isn't theirs."

His voice was gentle. "You weren't a proper surrogate. By that I mean you hadn't decided one day that you wanted to be a surrogate and then you had all the psychological testing and such. You were just a young college student in a desperate situation. And a married woman who should have known better took advantage of you."

"And then, in turn," I said, wiping my tears away, "I made Jessica become desperate and willing to do desperate things."

"That's not your fault." His eyes glistened wetly. "The surrogate thing is not even the worst of what she did. The end part of her plan is the worst. The birth. She planned for you to have the baby in secret, with no one else in attendance but herself. She's a midwife and she knows what can go wrong. She used to say that most births are fairly uneventful. And I think that's what she was counting on happening with you. But at the same time, she knows how badly wrong that births can go. Sometimes she'd come home after the end of her shift with a story about a birth that went catastrophically wrong. She'd cry sometimes if the worst had happened and the baby was lost. A couple of times, it was the mother who died. The birth of Rhiannon happened unexpectedly, but she still stuck to her plan. Despite the terrible state you were in. And then she left you all alone in that place."

I didn't speak, watching the hurt building in his eyes. What he'd just said was all true. Jessica had played Russian roulette with both my life and Rhiannon's.

Alban shook his head. "And then she sent that monstrous bastard to get you. Peyton."

"She didn't know about Peyton," I pointed out.

He was no longer listening to me. "She alerted him to the fact that Elodie was home all alone. He knew Jessica wasn't coming back anytime soon. And the fucking bastard went straight to our house—to have his chance at Elodie while he could."

His face crumpled, shoulders trembling. "My poor wee Elodie had no chance. No chance at all."

I went to him, seating myself on the arm of his chair and encircling him with my arms.

He sobbed onto my shoulder. I cried with him.

Outside the glass wall, snow was falling.

50

ISLA

August 2018

IT WAS SUMMER IN SCOTLAND. *Blink and you'll miss it*, the locals had told me. But this year's summer had produced a lasting heatwave.

I wandered through the trees at the Ness Islands, snapping photographs. The day was rinsed with yellow sunlight, hot on my cheeks and bare shoulders.

I kept my face obscured under big sunglasses and a wide-brimmed hat. These days, I was very recognisable. My picture had constantly been in the news.

Jessica's face had been in the news even more than mine.

Her trial for the manslaughter of Peyton Chandlish had returned a verdict of temporary insanity. The jury was unanimous. At the time of finding out about the identity of Elodie's abductor, she'd been stuck in a house with him, her emotions at flashpoint. No one had tried to stop her from killing him because no one had noticed her—everyone's focus had been on stopping Alban from getting to Peyton. There'd been lots of witnesses to testify to her state of mind, including Officer Kirk Flanagan. Because it was a case of short-lived insanity, Jessica hadn't been sent to a secure mental health facility. She'd been allowed to go free.

The court case over what she'd done that night in the church was yet to come. But she'd lost custody of Rhiannon.

The court had determined that under Scottish law, it was illegal for Jessica to have advertised for a surrogate and also to have given me money above the amount reasonably needed. The baby was determined to have been legally mine throughout the pregnancy and after the birth. Jessica would have had to apply within six months of the birth for custody, and that time period was long gone. The court noted her care of Rhiannon as a mother during the past two years, but ultimately decided that she didn't have any custodial rights. Under an odd part of law—despite the DNA test proving that Alban was Rhiannon's father—Alban would have to adopt her to make himself her legal father, and I would have to allow this. If I had been married to another man at the time Rhiannon was born, my husband would have been Rhiannon's legal father, even though he wouldn't have been Rhiannon's biological parent.

Public opinion on the whole thing was divided. Many were on my side—I was the young university student who'd been used by a calculating woman, my baby stolen while I was left to die in a filthy old church in freezing weather.

But Jessica had gained a lot of sympathy from others—as the married woman who just wanted to complete her family with a second child, who was then pushed to desperate measures by a cruel surrogate. In the minds of Jessica's supporters, she was the woman who'd lost two daughters. I was painted as a wishy-washy student who'd played mind games with Jessica and flirted with her husband. My memory loss was largely disbelieved by those members of the public.

It was hurtful but there was nothing I could do about all the speculation. People only saw the snippets that were printed and posted in the media. They didn't know me and they didn't know Alban and they didn't know Jessica.

Breathing in the sultry air, I stepped out from the trees.

At the edge of the River Ness, a tot in a polka dot dress and wispy blonde hair in plaits tumbled on the grass. A man in dark glasses and a cap pulled down over his forehead was lying on a picnic rug, keeping a close eye on the little girl, grinning at her antics.

A girl of about fifteen walked up, her ear glued to her phone in typical teenage fashion. She slid the phone into her pocket, picked the toddler up and playfully swung her around. The toddler shrieked with laughter.

I snapped a few photographs, entranced by the scene. It was a happy moment, and there hadn't been many of those for many months.

Packing my camera away, I went and joined the man on the rug.

Alban turned to me, wordlessly—his smile for me, now.

He caught my fingers in his. My skin immediately heated. I felt like I was Stella's age again, holding hands with the first boy I'd ever had a crush on.

So far, we'd kept our feelings for each other secret. We simmered and waited and held back, never showing anything in public. Holding hands right now was the first public contact.

Stella, standing a short distance away with Rhiannon, noticed us holding hands and grinned. Her long blonde hair fluttered in the breeze—it had grown slightly darker over the past months. And she'd grown even taller. She'd been spending a lot of time with Rhiannon and me, as well as getting on with leading a normal life for a girl her age. She'd become like a big sister to Rhiannon, and I hoped that would continue. Her recovery was an ongoing process—she carried a lot of deep scars inside of her. She was doing well with Rory and was even catching up with her schoolwork. She was soon back on her phone, chatting away animatedly.

Rhiannon returned to rolling on the grass.

Alban laughed.

I loved hearing him laugh. *Did I love him?* Maybe. *Maybe more than I'm willing to admit to myself yet.*

My thoughts were confused by everything that had happened. Alban and I had been holding back because we both needed time. We'd also been careful not to show our feelings for each other in public so that we didn't give the media any additional fodder. And it was far, far too early to have Rhiannon dealing with seeing her father in a relationship with someone new.

Neither of us knew where we'd be in another six months, or a year.

For now, the focus was Rhiannon and what her future was going to look like.

I'd made the decision to stay in Scotland and make it my home. To raise a child I hadn't realised existed—*my child*. To become a mother.

I noticed Rhiannon staring off somewhere into the distance, back towards the stand of trees I'd just walked from. Turning, I glanced back over my shoulder. A woman stood there, facing in Rhiannon's direction, her long summer dress falling to her ankles, hat and sunglasses obscuring her face. I felt a chill creep under my skin. She reminded me of Jessica with her angular hipbones and height. There was also something familiar in the way she held herself, with her stiff posture and her hands clasped over her stomach.

As I watched, the woman seemed to notice my eyes on her. She retreated.

But it couldn't be Jessica. She was with her mother somewhere at the seaside in Brighton, England. Alban had spoken with her just yesterday.

The woman was perhaps a tourist who was travelling on her own, who'd stopped to watch the families having their picnics on the grass.

Rhiannon ran to me, rotating herself to sit on my lap. I put my arms around her. It felt natural. I was starting the journey of getting to know the child I'd only known as an unborn baby wrapped up tight and secure inside my belly.

EPILOGUE

ELODIE MCGREGOR

Greenmire, Scottish Highlands, December 2015

RUSHING and clattering noises swirled around her.

And voices. So many voices.

Shouting and crying out.

Elodie was in the middle of it all somewhere but it didn't seem that she was part of it. She was just listening in the dark.

Then it all stopped.

A man spoke. "I'm so sorry Alban...Jessica. There's nothing more we can do."

Elodie didn't know why the man was sorry. She thought he was a doctor, but there'd been so many doctors and nurses and so many different voices that she couldn't be sure.

Everyone sounded so far away today. Dad began saying her name over and over again, like he was trying to call her back from somewhere. Like that day he thought he'd lost her at the Ness Islands, when she was five. But he hadn't lost her. She'd just been on the other side of the trees.

Mum was crying almost too much for Elodie to understand her words. But she understood one word, and that word was *Rhiannon*.

And then she heard her—the baby. A wail, soft but clear as a bell.

Mum had the baby with her for the first time today. Rhiannon sounded so tiny.

Her sister.

Inside, somewhere deep, Elodie began crying, in tandem with her sister's cry.

It seemed that Rhiannon had made everyone start crying, because she heard Dad now, too. She didn't think that she'd ever heard him cry before. Not like this. She heard a choke in his voice and he couldn't finish his sentence. And now he was sobbing like he'd broken in two and everything inside of him was spilling out.

She wished she could walk out of the fog and tell him that she was okay. But she couldn't walk out of it.

It was too thick and she was too tired. *So tired.*

Dad sounded further and further away.

Rhiannon's cry was the last sound she heard.

AUTHOR'S NOTE

I hope you enjoyed **STRANGER IN THE WOODS.**

I've long wanted to write a story on these issues, including the difficulty for many children (like Stella) in being able to tell people what's happening to them.

This book was a bittersweet one for me to write. My lovely father passed away in the middle of me writing it, and I didn't return to it for months. He may not have understood the whole digital book phenomenon, but he was always a strong supporter of my writing.

ALSO BY ANNI TAYLOR

THE GAME YOU PLAYED
Emotional suspense. Cruel notes in rhyme taunt Phoebe about her missing two-year-old son, Tommy. The game has just begun.

THE SIX
Dark suspense. Young mother, Evie, is desperate to find a way to repay her secret gambling debt. But travelling to an island that runs a mysterious program for addicts is the worst mistake of her life.

POISON ORCHIDS
Dark suspense. Two backpackers arrive at a remote fruit farm, desperate for work. They find a strange cult and a charismatic owner who seems to be hiding his true intentions.

ONE LAST CHILD - Book 1 Tallman's Valley Detectives
Emotional suspense. Five nursery-school children vanish from a picnic. The kidnapper returns them years later. All except for one last child - the granddaughter of homicide detective Kate Wakeland. Speculation grows that the kidnappings were a revenge plot. Is the kidnapper someone Kate put behind bars years before?

THE LULLABY MAN - Book 2 Tallman's Valley Detectives
Emotional suspense. A decade ago, The Lullaby Man preyed upon young girls in Tallman's Valley. He stole into their lives, whispered in their ears, spoke of love. They think he died... but did he?

THE SILENT TOWN - Book 3 Tallman's Valley Detectives
Emotional suspense. Detective Kate Wakeland senses dark undercurrents swimming in the depths of her beloved town of Tallman's Valley. A sizzling end to the Kate Wakeland series.

EXCERPT: ONE LAST CHILD

STORY: Five toddlers vanish from a picnic. Three-and-a-half years later, the children are returned to their families by the abductor.

All except for one - Ivy - the granddaughter of homicide detective Kate Wakeland. The other four children say Ivy is dead.

Speculation grows that the mysterious abductor is enacting a cruel revenge plot due to a murderer that Kate put in jail years before.

PROLOGUE:

It was time to return the children.

Inside the van, the group of children—all blindfolded—sat obediently in their seats. Knees together, each clasping a toy in their hands. They had just been three when they were taken. Three-and-a-half years later, they were six, almost seven.

The driver gripped the wheel, keeping careful control on the steep descent. Stones skittered and rattled like bones in the van's undercarriage. Far below, the lights of Tallman's Valley were blinking on.

Twilight was coming in fast.

Sweat pricked the driver's hands inside woollen gloves. It was vital to stay hidden. Arrive in darkness and leave in darkness. Unseen by anyone but the children.

The returns would need to be swift and efficient. Each child back to his or her home.

All but for one child.

One child would not be returned tonight.

One child would never be returned.

CREDITS

Thank you to the many who helped with the research for this story. Thank you to my first readers (who either grew up in Scotland or travelled there extensively) for their suggestions - Carolyn Scott, Declan from Writerful Books, and Graham from FadingStreet. I'd also like to express my appreciation to the barrister and the professor teaching UK law who provided me with their insights. I'd also like to thank the group of people on Facebook who assisted with my questions, including Stephen McKenna, Cas Donnelly, Emma Bigwood, Nicole Salinas and Judith Bow.

Thank you also, and always, to my family. It has been a very sad and difficult twelve months of losing people dear to us. It has reminded me of what a close, wonderful and supportive family I have.

Printed by Amazon Italia Logistica S.r.l.
Torrazza Piemonte (TO), Italy

16476099R00233